Gavilán

Gavilán

A Novel

R. M. Lienau

SUNSTONE
PRESS

SANTA FE

Sunstone books may be purchased for educational, business, or sales promotional use.
For information please write: Special Markets Department, Sunstone Press,
P.O. Box 2321, Santa Fe, New Mexico 87504-2321.

Cover art by Jime Wimmer

Book and cover design › Vicki Ahl
Body typeface › Adobe Jenson Pro
Printed on acid-free paper
∞
eBook 978-1-61139-474-0

Library of Congress Cataloging-in-Publication Data

Names: Lienau, R. M. (Richard M.), author.
Title: Gavilán : a novel / by Richard Lienau.
Description: Santa Fe : Sunstone Press, [2016]
Identifiers: LCCN 2016017571 (print) | LCCN 2016022903 (ebook) | ISBN
    9781632931382 (softcover : acid-free paper) | ISBN 9781611394740
Subjects: LCSH: Federal government--United States--History--19th
    century--Fiction. | New Mexico--History--19th century--Fiction. |
    Texas--History--19th century--Fiction. | GSAFD: Historical fiction.
Classification: LCC PS3562.I4533 G39 2016 (print) | LCC PS3562.I4533 (ebook)
    | DDC 813/.54--dc23
LC record available at https://lccn.loc.gov/2016017571

SUNSTONE PRESS IS COMMITTED TO MINIMIZING OUR ENVIRONMENTAL IMPACT ON THE PLANET.
THE PAPER USED IN THIS BOOK IS FROM RESPONSIBLY MANAGED FORESTS. OUR PRINTER HAS RECEIVED CHAIN OF CUSTODY
(COC) CERTIFICATION FROM: THE FOREST STEWARDSHIP COUNCIL™ (FSC®), PROGRAMME FOR THE ENDORSEMENT OF FOREST CERTIFICATION™
(PEFC™), AND THE SUSTAINABLE FORESTRY INITIATIVE® (SFI®).
THE FSC® COUNCIL IS A NON-PROFIT ORGANIZATION, PROMOTING THE ENVIRONMENTALLY APPROPRIATE, SOCIALLY BENEFICIAL AND
ECONOMICALLY VIABLE MANAGEMENT OF THE WORLD'S FORESTS. FSC® CERTIFICATION IS RECOGNIZED INTERNATIONALLY
AS A RIGOROUS ENVIRONMENTAL AND SOCIAL STANDARD FOR RESPONSIBLE FOREST MANAGEMENT.

WWW.SUNSTONEPRESS.COM
SUNSTONE PRESS / POST OFFICE BOX 2321 / SANTA FE, NM 87504-2321 /USA
(505) 988-4418 / ORDERS ONLY (800) 243-5644 / FAX (505) 988-1025

For L. L., who slaved many hours over the ms.

Prologue

Although President Zachary Taylor, self-anointed hero of the Mexican War of 1846, wanted New Mexico and other Western territories to become states during his term, in no small part to keep them from allowing slavery, his wish was not fulfilled before his sudden death in July of 1850. Instead, New Mexico became a Territory in the Fall of that year, leaving it vulnerable to acquisition by the young Republic of Texas, which claimed the land west to the Rio Grande and north to its headwaters. The majority of Spanish-speaking and Indian citizens of New Mexico, having witnessed the treatment of their kind in what was then Mexico, and subsequently in the Republic, resisted the idea of becoming part of Texas. Nine years earlier, in June of 1841, a mixture of Texans, both civilian and military, with a nod from President Lamar, launched a "friendly," but armed, invasion of pre-territorial New Mexico, based upon a purported desire for better trade opportunities. The expedition, hailed as the "Santa Fé Pioneers" by the participants, became bogged-down, and failed. Remnants of the ill-fated party were arrested by New Mexico militiamen near present-day Tucumcari under Mexican Governor Armijo; others were killed by militiamen near San Miguel, before the rest were taken to Mexico City and imprisoned. Despite that defeat, Texas continued to push its claim in Congress, such that President Fillmore threatened military action should they attempt overt action against the Territory. To aid in preventing more incursions, Federal surveyors set most of the existing north-south line between New Mexico and Texas in 1859.

Texas claim activity moved underground, to the extent that agents were dispatched to Santa Fé, Albuquerque and other New Mexico centers to seek out sympathizers under the guise of looking for mineral deposits, which included salt.

1

A covey of pigeons created a flurry of sound and motion as they lifted off the rain-softened earth of the plaza. Airborne, they scattered, then gathered and fluttered to shelter under a nearby leafed-out mountain cottonwood, a single tree that struggled to survive in an otherwise barren landscape. They were disturbed from their afternoon inspection of the ground for insects and seeds by the cacophony of horses hooves clattering into the earthen canyon that delivered the end of the Santa Fé Trail into its namesake city. The hooves belonged to the mounts of a detachment of the 3rd U.S. Infantry, fifty-some strong, that rode point ahead of the wagon train out of Independence, Missouri, via Bent's Fort, Las Vegas, Bernal Springs, San Miguel and Pecos.

The soldiers were saddle-weary, dusty, hungry and thirsty. They had been away from the capitol garrison behind the Governor's Palace and the adjunct at Fort Marcy on the hill overlooking the town for nearly a week on routine guard-mount mission for the commerce train. They had assumed duty between Wagon Mound and Raton Pass from a blue-coat contingent out of Bent's Fort.

First Lieutenant Harold Beckner peeled his horse away from the column, brought his mount to a halt and motioned to a sergeant in the line as the troopers rode past. He said something to the NCO, who awarded him a cursory salute, then wheeled his horse around and loped off in the direction of the slow-moving caravan, which stretched almost a half mile along the final segment of the Santa Fé—Pecos Trail. As Beckner rode past the corner of a building a block south of the plaza, a few yards from the newly-constructed, narrow wooden bridge that spanned the Rio de Santa Fé, a sentry performed a precise snap-to with his carbine. The officer saluted in an off-hand way without a glance at the soldier, who immediately relaxed to a bored, loose parade-rest, his weapon, butt-down on the ground, supported by his right hand.

He rode forward in the saddle, an intent look on his unlined face, as though he were about to make the horse jump a hurdle. Several chickens protested his passing, while two small, barefoot boys made light of it with wild noise and gestures.

The hurdle was in the young officer's mind. Something seemed to be missing, or there was something added; where, he wasn't sure. Was it on the ride since, or was it before leaving the garrison? He decided to go back to the rear of the train where his friend Jesse Landry rode as a member of the civilian-staffed Santa Fé Militia. Perhaps the act would refresh his memory.

The militia, which included a sprinkling of Pueblo Indians, almost always duplicated the strength of the cavalry on these outings. There was good cause: the merchants had a large stake in the safety of the caravan and they were willing to pay fearless and adventuresome local youth to help protect it. The commerce train had to be protected from increasingly violent plains tribes, such as the Comanche, Apache, Kansa and Navajo, as well as free-booting "Anglo" bandits who roamed the virtually lawless west looking for whatever plunder they could find. They included gangs from newly-minted Texas, members of which had been known as "Texas Rangers," even before some of them were incorporated into the official organization formed in 1835.

Many New Mexicans took to using their name—which tended to include virtually anyone from that new republic—in vain. The expression *"Tejano"* was often used as an epithet. It was not unusual for serious injury or death to follow closely when directed at the wrong person.

These thoughts flitted through Lieutenant Beckner's mind as he passed the front of the train which trundled down the long sweep of the final mile of the trail into the scattered outskirts of the little adobe town named for the Holy Faith. It was composed principally of sail-cloth covered Conestoga wagons, or "prairie schooners," with the remainder several boxy Murphy freight wagons and two rough-riding, springless passenger stages. Ahead lay the *acequia madre*, the main south-side irrigation ditch that fed water to fields on that side of the town. That, in turn, was supplied by the little intermittent stream from the mountains to the east, the Rio de Santa Fé.

Beyond, he saw his friend Jesse astride his horse, his slight frame erect in the saddle, one hand on the pommel, his broad-brimmed felt hat pushed back on his head. Beckner recognized the man who rode alongside him, and with whom he held conversation, Jesse's fellow militiamen, Juan Ortiz.

Jesse spied Beckner, waved, and accompanied it with a broad, toothy grin. Beckner returned the greeting, but with restraint, since he was, after all, in uniform.

Harold Beckner had known Jesse Landry for nearly a year, since he had been assigned to the garrison at Santa Fé from his previous posting at the War Department in Washington. He had met Jesse a month after his arrival, when he had gone to the Landry General Mercantile for personal supplies. The young Landry was behind the counter, and they'd struck up a conversation and a friendship after Jesse kidded the lieutenant about an army officer's need for needles, thread, cloth, scissors, soap and candles.

Then there it was; the thing, the notion, that had been disturbing him. He moved along with the column on the opposite side, on horseback alongside the third Conestoga from the rear. A small man, Beckner reckoned him not much more than five and a half feet tall. He wore a black leather vest over a loose, button-free flowered shirt, black, wide-brimmed slouch hat and a vaguely imperious look that showed in his intense, insolent eyes and around his arrogant slit of a mouth. The army officer didn't remember seeing him when his cavalry detachment relieved the Bent's contingent or since. Yet here he was, as though he had simply materialized out of thin air. His mere presence was not enough to evoke these curious feelings. Any peaceful individual was welcome to join the train, especially someone with firearms, which were rare on the frontier in the hands of civilians; more so with benevolence toward the train and its purpose. Beckner felt he had seen the man before; if not in person, then in his mind's eye, but in a strained context, and that led to uncomfortable feelings about the traveler.

He turned away from his study of the rider in black. "Jesse!" he shouted. "What're you doing dawdling in this dust when we could be relaxing in a cool *cantina*!"

Beckner's horse snorted in frustration and tossed its head as he jerked the animal up short next to his friend. The column of militiamen behind them rode around and past the three-man group.

Jesse slowed his own impatient horse, Campeón, anxious to return to his corral, leaned toward the Union officer and in a mock whisper said, "I'm negotiating for Ortiz' fair sister!" Jesse's English was accented because of the Spanish influence, his native language.

"Fat chance, Amigo! What if I should appear?" Beckner laughed and pointed his gloved finger at Jesse.

"You stay away, gringo!" Jesse lowered his laughing eyes, pointed back, then turned to wink at Ortiz, who reacted with a grin.

The lieutenant sobered, waited two beats, then asked, "That man there.

Black vest." He jerked his head in the man's direction. "Know 'im?" Beckner had turned his horse around to walk alongside Jesse, with Ortiz on Jesse's opposite flank.

"Where?" Jesse pushed his hat down low over his forehead, raised his chin and frowned into the lowering western sun.

"He looks familiar," Beckner said.

Jesse shook his head in a short, jerking motion. "Which one?" He looked at the Union officer, then again toward the front of the train.

"To the right. Third wagon in line. Short in the saddle. Black vest, dark horse." He pointed with his gloved right hand.

Jesse looked in the direction Beckner indicated. "Right. I see 'im. Nope. Don't recognize 'im."

"Let it go. Probably looks like someone I knew." He hesitated, then said, "Dying of thirst. I'm buying."

"At this hour of the day? You must report, no?" Jesse squinted a pained expression at his friend. "Papa expects me at the mercantile with the cargo. Help unload." He pointed vaguely at the train, as though to indicate which wagons were his.

Beckner looked down at a boot. "Anything to keep me away from the sight of blue uniforms for a time." He looked up. " I do have to report, but after that..." He reined his horse back as the impatient animal smelled water and sensed home.

"Don't tell me you forgot the invitation to supper!" Jesse shot his arm out at Beckner.

The union officer rolled his eyes, shook his head, then slapped his right leg. "Damn! Slipped my mind." He looked up as he pulled his hat back and scratched his hairline. I'll be there!" He re-set his hat down lower, jutted his chin out and bugged his eyes out at Jesse.

"We sit at six, and you don't want to cross Francesca. Come early."

"I shall be present, sir!" Beckner gave a two-fingered salute to the bill of his campaign hat, nodded to Ortiz, spurred his mount and shot off at a gallop.

As Beckner trotted past the train and into the narrow road leading to the town, he slowed his horse to a walk for which the animal gratefully shook and snorted. He brushed the animal's neck up and down the left side, then played his eyes over the squat adobe houses on either side of the road, to the few scattered trees, then the intensely blue sky, whose single feature was sullied only by the buildup of ponderous afternoon thunder heads across the Rio Grande valley to the west. He noted again how the nearly black shadows contrasted with the intense sunlight, something that had amazed him from his first day..

He had been posted to the garrison in Santa Fé for almost a year and re-called the shock that accompanied his initial view of the high, semi-arid country. Precious little water, not enough trees to go around, flat-roofed earth houses that seemed to grow from the soil, dark and haughty people who spoke a "foreign tongue," wore odd, colorful clothes, and ate strange, spicy-hot food. Why would anyone fight for this? Let the Mexicans, Texicans and Indians fight it out. His hatred for the place and longing for the green of home was instantaneous. But even in summer, the air was cool at night, and more often than not, he had needed a blanket. The heat of the day could be offset dramatically by shade in the high, dry air.

The mornings began with brilliant sunrises over the Sangre de Cristo mountain range that dominated the town on its eastern verge, very different from what he had been used to on the damp, cloudy eastern seaboard.

On his first morning, after breakfast in the officer's mess that included something the locals called tortillas smothered with a tangy pork stew that assaulted his palate, he had donned his full-dress tunic, checked his boots and buttons, adjusted his saber, side-arm and hat, and marched nervously out the door and to the office of the Provost situated in the town garrison that lay to the rear of the rambling, block-long Governor's Palace.

"Lieutenant Beckner reporting, sir!" He had saluted smartly.

Major Middleton did not look up from the file he was reading, but fumbled a salute, mumbled a "welcome," then looked up after a pregnant pause. "Well, Beckner, you come with fine recommendations, although I see this is your first time on a mission of this nature."

"Yes, sir."

The major cleared his throat and looked him over. "Relax, Lieutenant. Sit." He extended his hand toward a wooden ladder-back chair in front of his desk.

"Thank you, sir." Beckner twisted on the seat to adjust the awkward cavalry sword fixed to his belt as the tip of the scabbard hit the floor with a resounding thud.

Middleton winced as he watched the young officer struggle with the archaic weapon. "Why—why did you wear that, Lieutenant?" He frowned and shook his head once in disbelief.

Beckner blanched. "I really don't know sir. Won't happen again."

"Right. I don't think you'll need it here. We generally fight—if we have to—with guns. Frontal attacks with sabers drawn are rare." He raised his eyebrows and looked down as he straightened a sheaf of papers against the surface of his desk.

"Yes, sir."

Middleton fingered a silver ink well, sat up straight and rolled his eyes toward the one, deep-set window that looked out onto the garrison parade ground. "Your papers—sealed, I must note—tell me you're here as an official agent of the War Department to gather information on certain activities in the Department of New Mexico. Their wording, mind you. And I'm the only one to know. What it says here." He stabbed the file in front of him with his index finger.

"Right, sir. You're the provost."

"I am aware of that fact, Lieutenant. And you can cut the 'sir,' Beckner. At least when we're alone." Middleton shoved the ink well aside, rocked back in his chair and locked both hands across the back of his head. "So, what is this about?" He frowned anew. "Why the secrecy? What do they expect to find? And once you find whatever it is you're looking for, what're you supposed to do?"

Beckner nodded, smiled and looked at the floor, then up. "Let me explain."

They spent more than two hours in the major's cramped office, going over Beckner's reasons for being in the Territory of New Mexico. They discussed the war with Mexico, now more than two years past, the ideas and loyalties of the old Spanish royalists, and finally, and most importantly, the enmity and tensions between New Mexico and Texas, and their disaffection after Bernardo Gutierrez de Lara and Stephen Austin's failure to cobble together a "tri-star republic."

Subsequently, there had been increasing Texan pressure to force the claim that all the land west to the Rio Grande, north to its head waters in Colorado and east along the Arkansas River, belonged to Texas. Washington had information leading to speculation that the Texans were planning more aggressive moves to back their claims, that there were sympathizers in the territory, even among native Hispanics, many of whom were unhappy with the Treaty of Guadalupe-Hidalgo, and that Texas had sent in agent provocateurs and spies. The War Department feared an underground movement, even rebellion, and they needed proof, or at least, someone to watch over the situation. Beckner was to be the first eyes and ears for the Union in its newly-acquired territory.

Middleton expressed his doubts, but could only agree to cooperate, since he was under orders. He moved to the seat created by the sill of the deep-set window behind his desk and placed both hands on his thighs. "Although you come with a certain amount of autonomy, your orders are to report to me." He sighed and looked briefly at the ceiling. "I'll have to find a place for you in the garrison here in town. Wouldn't be good to put you with the trooper contingent here or up on the hill. Could be dangerous."

"Dangerous?"

"Troopers talk. You understand. Don't have much else to do here. So far, we try to keep 'em from fraternizing, but that's not working well. As you may have noticed, fort's on the hill. Still a lot of suspicion amongst the Mexicans, and most of these young recruits don't appreciate the landscape, the dominant religion or the fact that if they want a drink, meal or a woman, there's a big language and cultural barrier. May surprise you, but these people are pretty damned protective of their women. Hot-headed they can be. There've already been some pretty mean dust-ups. And, your real reason for being here could leak out. 'Course, the officer class, well—"

"Yes, sir."

"Right." Middleton slapped his thighs and stood, moved to his desk chair, sat and squared himself, then tapped the document on his desk. "Also noted that if you deem it necessary, you're to be able to leave the garrison at any time and even work in mufti. That your understanding?" He raised his eyebrows.

"I hope it won't cause any problems, but it could be the case. Especially if I have to follow and observe someone. I'd be conspicuous in uniform."

The major sat back. "Right. And what are you—and I—supposed to do if you should uncover something? A dastardly plot, perhaps?" He pointed, first at Beckner, then himself.

Beckner shifted his weight. "Keep you informed, Major. And Washington, of course."

"Of course."

"And I suppose, if you agree it's necessary, to the commandant. Then squelch it. With force, if necessary. Meantime, though, we're to keep it to ourselves. The two of us."

Middleton stroked the day-old stubble on his chin and looked at the rough-hewn, open-beamed ceiling again, as though it inspired him. "Want me to assign someone to work with you?"

"Well, sir, it's the department's feeling that more than one—that's me—could draw unwelcome attention, and possibly affect security. The fewer who know, the better. That sort of thing. But that could change, of course. Shall we say, when needed, but until then—?"

"All right. Well, keep me posted. And good luck."

Beckner's reverie was broken as his mount reacted to being crowded past the first freighters to enter the town center at the southeast corner of the plaza, two doors away from the old Spanish Royalist *La Castrense*, or military chapel. He clicked at his horse to encourage him to make for the opposite corner. It was then that he spied a young woman with whom he was acquainted, who walked in the opposite direction under the porch to his right. She recognized him, but the most she could do was flash her eyes at him and give a faint smile accented with a tilt of her head, since her mother was at her side, black shawl shading her stern countenance behind which lured dark and fearful thoughts about these gringos in blue. Lieutenant Harold Beckner, 3rd Infantry, U.S. Army, understood—or tried to—and graciously doffed his dusty head-piece, smiled and nodded. He turned and looked as she passed, his imagination instinctively plying through the yards of somber cloth the girl wore. It was similar at home, but more so here, especially in terms of the strict guardians of propriety—or so he had heard—in places like New Orleans, Atlanta and Charleston.

He rode past the eastern corner of the palace, then swung his mount through the gate to the town garrison compound and trotted to the stable. A private in work attire which featured high, muddy, dung-spattered boots, approached and grabbed the reins of the happy horse as Beckner dismounted.

He pulled off his gloves and slapped the dust from his trouser legs and tunic as he strode across the yard to his room. He unbuckled his holstered Colt's revolver and swung it at his side until he reached the door. This he opened, then threw his gloves, the side-arm and his campaign hat across five feet onto his cot. Then he turned, pulled the door shut, and wheeled around in the direction of the gate and garrison headquarters.

He pulled a ring of brass keys on the end of a thin steel chain from his tunic pocket and unlocked the door to his office. It was a cramped cubicle whose natural light streamed from a newly-installed, single, narrow window that looked onto the fields to the north behind the military compound. His wooden roll-top desk was closed and locked, which served to give the impression to the uninitiated that the room was unused. A wooden file cabinet next to it held two thin volumes on its flat top; one, a string-tied folder of loose maps.

He closed the door and went to the file cabinet. With another of the keys, he unlocked the top drawer, then riffled through the contents carefully until he came to the file he wanted. He opened it on top of the cabinet, and turned the pages slowly. He stopped when he came to the fourth document, picked it up and peered at it intently. Thirty seconds later, he closed the file, returned it to the cabinet, and locked it.

He didn't wait for an answer after he knocked on Major Middleton's door, entered, closed it carefully, and stood silently two steps inside the major's office.

Middleton looked up.

"I think I spotted one of our targets. Came in with the train. Thought you should know."

"Finally, eh? Long wait. What now?" Middleton set the pen with which he had been writing down and concentrated on Beckner.

The lieutenant shrugged with his eyes. "I keep an eye on 'im."

Middleton cocked his head to one side and waited two beats as he drummed the desk with both sets of fingers. "Keep me posted, Lieutenant." Beckner had saluted, turned, and had opened the door when he continued, "And be careful."

Beckner hesitated, nodded without turning, then continued and closed the door quietly.

2

The Landry Mercantile fronted on the same street as the governor's residence and seat of government, Palace Avenue, roughly a half block east of that building, and on the same side of the dirt trace. The public part of the store consisted of one large room with a high, flat, open-beamed ceiling, typical for the area, and was integral with the generous Landry *hacienda*, stable, store rooms, smithy and *atrio*, or courtyard, which stretched out behind it in a giant, fifty *vara*, or approximately 2,500 foot square. A thirty inch thick, six-foot high outer wall, thirty feet in length, completed the compound rectangle, which protected the rear, north edge of the expansive property from the sometimes hostile outside world. Centered in that was a heavy, two-part gate, wide enough, when fully open, to admit a Murphy freight wagon, Conestoga or stage coach. The west and east rooms and walls of the Landry place were common with the Chávez residence on the west, and the Romero spread on the east, both equally as grand in scope. Behind these crowded manses was a road, the other side of which edged on corn, squash and chile fields interspersed with young fruit orchards, but wide enough for passage of the biggest wagons. All these structures were of thick adobe atop rubble granitic and sedimentary rock foundations. A six-foot wide *portal* fronted all the buildings along the main street. The portion that graced the mercantile featured new boardwalk for the convenience of ladies with long skirts and gentlemen with fine boots.

Only recently had a few tall, deep windows been installed regimentally along the public side in any of the buildings along the street, admitting southern light for the first time since their construction. These places had looked, as they still did, mainly inward, with crude windows, if at all, on the courtyard side, partly out of class attitude; partly as a bastian against physical attack. A third reason was the arrival of better glass set into multi-pane, mullioned window sashes from the east coast of the United States. But with the quieting presence of the United States Army, although not altogether welcome, fewer arrows, shot, shell and firebrands were of concern, and there was an increased interest in the comings and goings on the bustling streets of the town on the part of those behind the thick earthen walls.

After waving farewell to Ortiz, Jesse Landry rode through the plaza, which had rapidly become a happy, frenzied jumble of massed Conestogas, freight wagons, weary, sweaty mules and oxen teams still in harness, wagon masters and bull whackers who shouted commands, locals who converged to peer at goods, and merchants whose interests were focused on the newly-arrived cargo.

He wove his way through the turmoil, then turned onto east-west Palace Avenue, and wondered if he hadn't been hasty in turning down the suggestion of a drink. He was so thirsty he would have drunk anything cool and wet. His canteen had been emptied at midday with lunch when the train stopped in the depression called *Cañoncito*, just west of, but actually named for, the narrow defile *Cañon de Los Apaches*, to rest and water the animals. He turned in the saddle and squinted across the front of the Palace, past the parade of white cloth-covered transports and beyond, west toward *Doña* Tules' main saloon, and thought of its dark, velvet interior and the cool libations available there. He also realized it would be next to impossible to thread his way to the bar, since virtually every other man—along with some of the bolder of the distaff side—in town would have the same festive thoughts.

The sun was late-afternoon high over the flat, dirt-topped buildings of the town. Its intense light filtered through the leaves of the few scattered trees and dust clouds raised by the wagons, draft teams and people. To his right, three small children played noisily in the relatively quiet dirt street near a small, three-room adobe house across from the mercantile. Their mother issued from the house and scolded them loudly while an ancient man sat stone-like in a chair against one wall of the house, his bent figure propped up with a long walking stick in his gnarled hands. Jesse looked at the eroded, cracked mud plaster surface of the long wall of the Chávez house that constituted the corner, and became thirstier. He steeled himself to the idea of water, though, and shook his head in good-natured disgust as he guided his horse, Campeón, onto the road behind the compounds.

Two Murphy-type wagons were parked alongside the rear wall of the compound, overlapped onto the Chávez and Romero properties, their rear doors down. While the bull whackers un-yoked the oxen teams, the wagon master directed the off-loading of cargo to be moved inside the Landry compound. Jesse touched the brim of his hat when the wagoner looked up and nodded.

Both doors of the rear compound gate were open. Another wagon, a schooner, was backed into the yard. Incarnación Serna, his father's chief employee, stood with another man, as they discussed a bill of lading. Jesse guided Campeón up to the horse stalls, then reined him in.

"Any trouble up the trail, son?" Evan Landry stepped from the rear doorway of the store and approached his son as he dismounted. His father was two inches taller than Jesse's five feet, eight inches, and thicker in the torso, with a large, freckled Celtic face, reddish hair and full beard. His normal countenance seemed hard—almost steely—to those who didn't know him, but his bright green eyes beneath bushy eyebrows betrayed a basic kindness.

He had come down the Santa Fé trail a quarter century earlier, and survived its exactions and Governors Armijo's and Péréz' taxes in order to bring trade goods to sell. He had liked Santa Fé in general and a certain small, sweet, young *Hispana* in particular enough to stay, marry, and learn the language.

Jesse peered over Campeón's damp back as he loosened the saddle cinch. "Not this time, Papa. But there was a burned farm wagon and some Apache sign when we came through the pass. And a Murphy broke an axle before the canyon." He jerked his Hawken carbine from its scabbard, set it aside, then pulled the saddle and blanket away from the horse as the animal, grateful, started for the water trough, his stall and feed. After hanging the saddle, harness and blanket up, Jesse joined his father who now stood with Serna and the wagoner. He stopped, rested the Hawken carbine against his hip, removed his hat, and wiped his brow with a kerchief.

His father looked up with a question on his face.

Jesse pointed toward the house. "I need water. I'll stow the carbine. Be right back."

The thick inner walls of the *hacienda* were graced with covered *portales* from the back wall of the store to the kitchen, which occupied the rear-most part of the family quarters. Along one length was a row of four lilac bushes whose top branches reached nearly to the porch roof, and which complimented the single large, thick cottonwood that loomed more than twenty-five feet above much of the courtyard.

Jesse walked through the open door to the *cocina*, laid his Hawken against the wall, pulled the cover from a wooden barrel next to the wood stove and dipped a tin drinking ladle into the water. As he held the vessel to his mouth and gulped cool water, he noticed a strong aroma that wafted from a pot on the stove, and it triggered the hunger he had suppressed. He peered into the next room to see if Francesca were near, then cautiously lifted the lid off the pot and ladled some into his mouth with a wooden spoon that lay nearby. "Ah! Ah! Ah!" He wailed as he dropped the spoon to the floor, gasped, shook his hands and danced in a tight circle, squinting for something to wipe his burning mouth. He spied a cloth neatly laid out on the big, centered wooden work table, destined for preparing tortillas, grabbed it and wiped his stinging lips. For good measure, he dabbed at his forehead, then moved to the exterior doorway as he opened and closed his mouth, to suck in and release his breath deeply as he waited for the pain on his tongue to subside.

His father, Evan, stood next to Incarnación and the wagoner as all three concentrated on papers. He saw Incarnación say something to his father, then turn and enter the store while the older man and the wagoner watched him disappear inside. When the employee was out of sight, the wagoner reached into his buckskin jacket, removed what appeared to be an envelope, and handed it to the elder Landry.

Jesse backed up, dropped the cloth in a heap on the table, and returned to the courtyard. Behind him, Francesca, the housekeeper, entered, discovered the cloth, the spoon on the pine plank floor and the open pot, and muttered an epithet under her breath as she observed the Landry son stride across the open space.

As Jesse followed his father into the store, he was forced to walk around boxes, crates, barrels and swollen sacks to get to the door of the mercantile, then through a narrow aisle of confused goods in similar containers, depleted so long after the last train. He found him seated at his desk, turned toward the light from the door that looked onto the courtyard, reading. "Get some mail, papa?"

"Eh? Oh—ah, no. Bills of lading." Evan dropped the paper he was reading onto his lap, folded it, then tucked it carefully under the blotter that covered most of the desk surface. He stood, looked around as though searching for something, then reached up and straightened a line of hard-bound books on the shelves above the desk.

Jesse leaned on the counter across from the desk and faced his father. "Remember, Harold's due for supper."

Evan Landry turned and covered the short distance to the counter, grabbed a stack of papers and shuffled them idly. "Yes, I remember. Good. I enjoy his company." He looked up and smiled.

Jesse was reflective. "Sometimes he's curious about odd things."

"Who?"

"Harold."

"The lieutenant."

"Yes, of course. Lieutenant Beckner. Harold." The younger Landry furrowed his brow at his father's inattention.

Evan stopped and looked at his son. "Why? What did he say?"

"He was worried about a man who joined the train. Today."

"Oh, what would make him curious?"

Jesse shrugged, turned away to lean his back against the counter, and spoke to the rest of the store. "I don't know. Asked me if I knew him."

"Did you?"

"No."

"Well, it was nothing, then." Evan paused, then, "Does he ask questions about people often?"

"No." Jesse turned to look at his father again.

Evan stared at his son for a few seconds, manufactured a tortured smile, and turned back to his desk.

"Did any of the Colt's come in?"

Evan spoke with his back to his son. "No. Wagoner says they're all consigned to the Army. Won't be any on the market for some time." He brushed an insect away. "I've ordered 'em, but I reckon they can't turn 'em out fast enough."

"I guess I'll have to make do with that old '41 model fowling piece."

"You ready to help me inventory?"

It was at that moment that two customers, both women, entered the store.

As Lieutenant Beckner left the rude building known as Town Headquarters, 3rd Infantry, Department of New Mexico, he was torn between his thirst and the need for a bath. A logical sort, he figured that men had been dirty for long periods of time without suffering more than a snub on the part of their fellows, whereas they had been known to die from thirst. He also reasoned that there were few who would deign to complain. They, too, would likely reek of the road, their animals and themselves, and would thus be surrounded by a protective effluvia of their own making, thereby neutralizing his. He had never been what one would term fastidious. As a boy, his mother had insisted he bathe more often than he wished. It had been, as now, somewhat of a struggle. Heating water over an open flame, lugging it into the bathing room and pouring it into the tub, plus the entire ritual attendant to the laborious process. And the way soap made his skin itch. Worse in this dry climate, especially in winter. Liquid refreshment would come first and that would make the other far more palatable.

He liked to read, a trait acquired from his teacher-father, at home in upper New York state. He became tall—tall for the time, when the average man was under five feet, eight inches—with a shock of straight, brown hair; knowledgeable about more than most boys, young men and people in general. The West fascinated him, and he automatically liked "foreigners" and their languages. These characteristics, along with training in the law, his intelligence and ability to deal calmly with people, even in stressful situations, and a desire for adventure, led him to his present employment. This came after he was spotted by a well-placed senior officer friend in the War Department who knew of a need and divined its solution.

He made his decision, brushed his light brown hair back along his ears, straightened his hat, and strode through the gate. He and the sentry exchanged cursory military greeting, then he headed for the eastern corner of the Palace and the crowded plaza beyond. High to his left, the jade sky was puffed up with huge white clouds over the mountains. It was nearing four o'clock, and soon Santa Fé would experience its second afternoon shower. As he moved along the Palace *portal*, he was forced to wade through a herd of people which included local peddlers from the area, a mixture of both Hispanic and Pueblo Indian, hawking their wares. More than once he was forced to buy homemade soap and candles from just such an ad hoc merchant when the commercial variety from the East was in short supply. This time, it was more crowded, given the concentration of trail wagons lining the four streets that defined the plaza quadrangle.

To save steps, he left the long porch, and as he did, he spotted the man in the black vest he had seen with the train as he exited a café across the plaza. The man was alone, and picked his teeth as he moved. Beckner watched as the man stopped, looked around, then moved off toward La Tules' main *cantina* on Palace, west of the plaza, as he skillfully dodged the mass of animals and humanity. Beckner held back, then followed. Inside the crowded bawdy house saloon, the lieutenant observed the man stop and crane his head around as though looking for someone in particular. Then his quarry pushed his way through the crowd to the bar. There, he elbowed his way to the long, polished counter next to a man on his right who wore a fringed deer-skin jacket. Beckner excused his way closer, as he remained in visual contact. When he was not ten feet away, he saw the short man in the vest and the other man, who was half a head taller, nod to each other. The taller of the two then tossed his drink down, turned and forced his way to the exit and disappeared.

Lieutenant Beckner forgot his thirst and followed. When he reached the street, the man in the fringed jacket had vanished.

3

It was near dark when Lieutenant Beckner entered the somber, four-foot wide outer hallway that led from the street to the inner gate that led to the west side *portal* and courtyard of the Landry *hacienda*. He opened the high wooden closure, stepped inside and closed it. In front of him lay the wide porch which stretched along the west, or residence, side of the courtyard. At the formal entry one window along from the gate, he knocked on the crude, but massive door set deep into the thick adobe wall. A minute later he was greeted with a handshake by Jesse Landry, who led him deeper into the house and to the dining room. There, his host picked up two stemmed glasses of red wine and handed the army officer one of them.

Beckner tried the drink cautiously, then held the stem ware up to the taper light that radiated from a heavy wrought-iron candelabra suspended from the dark, open-beamed ceiling. "Not bad." He rotated his glass.

"From the *Rio Abajo*. Lower valley. South." Jesse jerked his head in that direction, as he sipped without taking his eyes off his guest. "Vines from Spain." Jesse looked at his glass and took another swallow. "I could offer you Pass brandy. Say the word."

"This is fine. I've tried the brandy. From El Paso?"

"Yes. The Pass."

Beckner found it curious and interesting that when his young friend spoke English he used expressions and contractions common with the drovers who came from Missouri and points east. He reckoned also on the elder Landry's influence. "The wine glasses? I don't see many in this town."

"My father prefers to drink from them. Says the wine tastes better." He flashed his guest a wry smile.

"I concur." Beckner grinned. "I haven't seen any in the store."

Jesse tapped his friend on the shoulder. "You haven't looked closely."

"Good evening, Lieutenant."

Both men swung around as Evan Landry entered the room from the somber hall.

Beckner set his glass down, took a step toward the elder Landry and held out his hand. "Evening, sir. Thank you for the invitation."

"Bah! You're almost family." Evan shook with one hand and waved his other in mock disgust. He backed away, looked first at his son, then around the room as he pulled a watch from his vest pocket. He inspected the time piece, put it away, and raised his eyes. "I see the young'un here has made sure to ply you with alcohol before we sup. First things first, correct?" Evan made a half turn in the direction of the open kitchen door. "Where's that woman? I see the table's been set."

"Francesca said she'd serve as soon as she heard your voice, Papa."

Evan Landry smiled at Beckner, strolled away, then turned to face him. "What my son is saying, Lieutenant Beckner, is that I am a loud man."

Beckner nodded his head in a good-natured fashion and raised his glass in a toast. "As you say, sir."

Evan turned again and picked up the remaining wine glass, also full. "I gather this is intended for me, *mi hijo?*" The elder Landry had absorbed much of the intimate Spanish of the Territory.

"*Si, Papá.*"

Beckner started to say something in regards to the Landry men's fall easily into Spanish, but was interrupted.

It was at that moment that Francesca hurried into the room carrying a large earthen-ware pot and set it down in the center of the long, heavy wooden table. She looked up at Beckner and smiled a greeting, which he returned in kind with a smile and half-bow. Francesca Lucía Anaya was in her early sixties, a few inches over five feet tall, with a pleasant, once girl-pretty face, and plump in a way not unattractive to many of the local men, Hispanic or not. Her long, greying tresses were controlled with a pair of braids she allowed to flow down her back. She and her husband had served the Abréu family since they were in their teens, then stayed on at Evan Landry's insistence after his wife's demise. With her always-smiling countenance, she seemed to bustle constantly, be everywhere at once and to all and sundry, constituted the warmth and ambiance of the house. The Landry men would have been bereft without her and her husband, Cipriano.

"Ah, here we are," Evan said. "Sit, gentlemen, and partake of Francesca's fabulous stew." He turned to Beckner and looked at him squarely. "This simple fare will suffice, I trust?"

"Indeed, Mr. Landry," Beckner answered. "I have become addicted to this food. Especially when the local spice is added."

The three men took their seats as Francesca doled out the stew in large bowls, after which she distributed plates of hot, thick flour tortillas folded neatly into cloth napkins for heat retention. She set out bowls of red, then green chile, along with a honey pot near the center.

"Francesca probably knows I burned my tongue on this same food earlier." Jesse looked at the woman ruefully as he tucked his napkin under his chin.

Francesca, busy serving, raised her head with a tiny, loving smile, but refused to look at Jesse, whom she regarded as a surrogate son.

They were finishing their desserts of *natías*, *biscochitos* and apple slices when Evan Landry studied his watch again. "I apologize, young gentlemen, but I have some accounts to see to before I retire. I hope you'll excuse me, Lieutenant." He swigged the last of his second glass of wine, took a swallow of water from a clear glass tumbler, then pushed back.

Beckner jumped up and pulled the napkin from his throat. "Not at all, Mr. Landry. Thank you, sir."

"My pleasure, Harold. The two of you relax." The elder Landry threw his own napkin onto his chair seat, headed for the door to the hall, then stopped and turned. "I expect you gentlemen have plans." He looked first at his son, then the army officer, who sat at the opposite end of the long board, nearest him.

Jesse looked up. "We're going to play some cards, then maybe to Velasquez's to listen to some music."

"You mean watch the fools fandango. Careful, now. All the drovers in town. Draws the local miscreants like flies, you understand."

Jesse looked down at his plate and blushed, then shot a glance at Beckner. "Don't worry, Papa."

Evan Landry nodded, took one last look at his son, turned and disappeared into the darkened hallway. He took down a shiny, tinned oil lamp from a wall peg near the door from the hallway to the outer patio porch, dug for a match in his pocket, and illuminated his surroundings in a flickering orange glow. With his eyes accustomed to the shaded, hand-held lamp light, he opened the outer door and moved onto the porch, closed the opening, then moved across the sandstone-paved porch and onto the packed soil of the large outside enclosure. He approached the outer double gate to the alley in a wavering cone of luminance that lighted his path, now free of the wagons that had occupied it earlier. A few yards into the open area, he turned his head briefly to see only suffused light from a narrow hall window near the dining room door. He looked up past the leaves of the cottonwood where pinpoints of light marked a myriad of stars in a sea of black.

He tapped three times on the thick, rough-hewn gate and waited, his ear close to the wood. Two seconds later, his query was answered in kind. He unlatched the personnel door set into the right gate and pulled it open slowly, careful to avoid squeaking hinges. Two figures stepped through the narrow opening and passed him without a word. They stopped while he closed the door, then followed three paces back as he led the way to the mercantile entrance, the lantern held high in his outstretched hand.

Inside the mercantile, Evan Landry scanned the house porch once more, closed and locked the door, set the lantern on the service counter, then leaned against his desk as the visitors watched silently. The burning oil wick cast long shadows, lost in the store section in piles of goods, most on the floor in rows, some in boxes, others in barrels, more on deep shelves, some as high as the ceiling.

With the light behind them, Landry found it difficult to see the two men who faced him. One was his height, clean shaven, and wore a fringed leather jacket under a grey, wide-brimmed hat. He was unable to see the man's face clearly, but it seemed to him to be long and narrow, with a sharp chin. His companion was shorter, and was dressed in a black vest and black hat with silver buttons that circled the crown. This man, his face mostly in shadow, wore a long-barreled revolver low on his right hip.

Evan Landry folded his arms across his chest. "This is dangerous." He spoke in a near whisper as he looked at both men, then settled on the taller of the two. "This is my house. I have family here." His mouth was compressed as he pointed, using an index finger without unfolding his arms.

The taller of the two men nodded. "We understand, Landry, but we had no choice—"

"No choice?!" Landry's voice became hoarse as he leaned forward stiffly, the muscles in his face tight. He paused and squinted at the man. "You're not *Gavilán!*" He looked at both men in turn, then returned to his study of the taller of the two.

"No. Rodman." He shook his head and gestured at the man at his side. "This is Blakely." He leaned back against the counter and folded his arms across his chest in imitation of Landry's posture as his anxiety rose.

Blakely nodded to Landry with steady, but cold, unsmiling eyes.

Landry glanced at the smaller man without moving his head, but made no move to acknowledge him. "So, you're 'G.R.?' Then why did you sign as *Gavilán*?"

"Only way I figured you'd see us."

"You met him?"

"Who?"

"*Gavilán*."

"No. I figured you'd lead me to 'im. Know his real name?"

Landry looked hard first at Rodman, then at Blakely, then back again. "Who are you?!"

"I told you. Name's Rodman. Maybe this'll help." He dug into a side pocket of his fringed jacket and produced a small metal object which he handed to Landry.

Evan Landry took the metal piece and peered at it closely as he turned it over several times. He looked up and handed the piece back. "How did you know to contact me?"

"Blakely here." He jerked his head in the small man's direction.

Landry looked at Blakely. "Yes?"

Blakely tilted his head. "I was give your name by a friend. He got it from someone who knows the head. Here." He pointed at the floor. "This *Gavilán* feller." He pronounced the Spanish word with flat "As."

"When you say here, you mean the territory?" Landry asked.

"That's right. Territory." Blakely ran his hand below his nostrils and sniffed.

Landry stroked his chin reflectively. "I see."

"You must have made contact somehow, Landry," Rodman offered.

"A meeting I attended."

"So—" Rodman shifted his weight.

"So, I believe you. But why no choice, Rodman?"

The visitors saw the consternation in Landry's eyes and glanced at each other.

"You read the message? We—You still have it, I trust?" Rodman asked.

Landry hesitated as his eyes moved rapidly in cogitation. He shifted his weight. "No. Of course not. I burned it." He stared at Rodman.

"Of course." Rodman searched Landry's eyes, then looked past his host at the mess of papers on the desk behind. "If it were to fall into the wrong hands—although—"

"Listen!" Landry cut Rodman off abruptly. "I'm well known here! If we were caught—if any of these people—if the army found out—I'd hang, along with the two of you!"

A pregnant silence ensued, then Rodman spoke quietly. "We know, Landry. We know. We wouldn't be here, but there's a problem." He extended both hands in a gesture of compliance.

Landry, his agitation affecting his composure, paced two steps away, then back. He held out both palms. "Why didn't you explain it in the note? Why come here?!"

Rodman pushed away from the counter. "Too dangerous. I didn't know who'd see the note. No time to establish a code. Anyway, better to talk in person."

Landry pulled a flowered kerchief from his pants pocket and wiped his forehead. "What is it, then? Tell me, then please leave." He folded the kerchief and returned it.

"There's a—" Rodman began.

Landry interrupted, pointing wildly. "Goddamnit! There's an army officer no more than fifty feet from here!"

Both visitors whipped their heads around and stared momentarily at the shelf-lined wall in the direction Landry had pointed. Blakely stepped away from the counter and turned his body to face the same way as he unconsciously fingered the pistol at his side. He looked up at Rodman, alarm on his face, then at Landry.

"What?!" Rodman exclaimed as he pushed away from the counter. "Here! Why?!"

"For supper. He's my son's friend. What do you expect? We live here. I can't stop him from having friends. But that's my point! These people are everywhere!" Landry shot his arm out, turned away, shook his head, then faced around.

"Any danger their coming in here?!" Rodman asked.

"Not likely. They plan to leave soon. You know young men." Landry sighed and jerked his head. "Door's locked. They'd have to knock." He wiped his forehead again.

Rodman rubbed his cheek. "We'll be gone soon. But listen to me first." He lowered his voice.

Landry looked hard at Rodman, but had calmed. "Say what you have to say."

"The arms shipment. It didn't make it through." His eyes bored in on Landry.

Landry waited several beats, then exclaimed, "What?! What arms shipment?!" His back bowed forward under the weight of Rodman's statement, his face stark and tortured.

Rodman looked at Blakely, then Landry. He shook his head. "What do you mean?"

"I mean to say," Landry said, "What arms shipment?!" He spoke in a hoarse whisper.

Rodman was silent for five seconds while he digested Landry's question as he stared at his host. "Landry, are you with us or not?!"

"Don't be a fool, Rodman, of course I'm with you, but what is this arms matter?!" His voice dropped to a deeper whisper as he shook his head rapidly in disbelief. "What the devil are you talking about?!"

"Arms—guns, ammunition. We may need them. How else are we—"

Landry raised his hands in protest as he stared at Rodman in wide-eyed incredulity. "Need?! What the hell are you talking about Rodman?!" He looked hard at Blakely, then back at Rodman. The tension he felt was showing up as his face flushed and his fists clenched.

Rodman's face tightened. "Listen, Landry, what are *you* talking about?!" He had lowered his voice to a hoarse, menacing whisper. He stretched his arm out and pointed at nothing with his index finger. "We got the U.S. Army right under our noses! They probably know something's going on! Austin's made no bones about our claim—Texas' claim to the river. And north. To the Arkansas. You think they aren't taking precautions? You think they don't have their own agents planted here?" He paced away in a tight circle, then faced Landry again. He calmed while he rubbed his hands together. "You fight fire with fire. In this case, that fire might be force. No, not might be. We have to be ready!"

"Well, Mr. Rodman, that's just my point! Here we stand, in my office, in my home, in the center of the capital, talking about insurrection! In the middle of the goddamn night!" He stared at Rodman. "It isn't safe to talk about it at all, and now you're talking guns!" He paused. He leaned forward in his intensity, almost in Rodman's face. "Who you going to give the guns to? The Mexicans? The Indians? They hate your guts! How many gringos are there here who sympathize with you? Most of them here are Union Army! The rest are people like me who just want to sell trade goods from Independence and Chihuahua. It's one thing to negotiate—even sue—for a peaceable transition, but a war?! We've already been through that. No. It won't work. And I won't go along. Who the devil are you going to get to use them?! You'd need ten thousand men!" He turned away, then continued, as he talked to the shadows, his voice moderated. "I have been—I am—in favor of Austin and the creation of a larger state. An expansion of the republic. The politicians and business people back east don't understand this country and the people. The politicians and businessmen in Austin—and here—can do a better job. I'm in favor of that. But I'm not in for violence. I'm not in for another shooting war. If Texas has a legitimate claim, we do it peaceably or not at all." He glanced at Blakely who was riveted on him, then turned again, his back to them, to lean the fingers of both outspread hands on his desk, his head lowered in frustration.

Rodman and Blakely looked at each other.

Landry turned around. "Where's the shipment? The arms?"

Rodman lowered his head and looked at Evan Landry from under his eyebrows and shook his head slowly.

Landry's eyes widened and his mouth dropped open slowly. "Goddamnit! You were going to bring them here! Damn you! What right—?!"

Blakely pointed his finger at Landry and snarled, "If you ain't with us, you're agin' us, Landry!"

"Take it easy, Blakely." Rodman's voice and hands were pacifying. He paced away into the darkness of the store, hand to chin, then faced around. "You're making this difficult, Landry. Serious breach of confidence."

Evan Landry straightened and looked hard at Rodman. "I ask you again, who told you to bring the weapons here?"

Rodman shook his head and looked at Blakely.

Blakely straightened. "I was tole to bring 'em here."

"Who told you?!" Landry was furious.

"Message I got on the trail. That's all I know."

"Jesus!" Landry paced away.

Rodman stepped back into the subdued, orange light. "You're safe, Landry. The weapons won't come here."

Landry turned to face the taller man. "Look, I stand behind the idea; the concept. Politics. Negotiation. Not warfare."

Rodman faced Landry and forced a tight smile. "Good. We'll be off now. No need to see us out. Better there be no light." He jerked his head at Blakely.

"Where is the shipment? What happened?"

Rodman looked at his diminutive partner.

Blakely tilted his head, paced away and turned. He looked squarely at

Landry. "We broke an axle. In the canyon. 'Bout a mile east o' the 'Pache Cut. Near the part they call Glorieta."

"Damn!" Landry exclaimed. "Is anyone with it? What did the troopers do? Did they inspect it?" He looked intensely at each man.

Blakely closed his eyes momentarily and held up his hand. "There's two bull whackers with it. Unhitched the mules. It's safe. They're with us."

"But what if someone—the army, freebooters, Indians—"

Both Landry and Rodman listened intently to Blakely, who shook his head. "They won't find nothin'. Top 'o the wagons got commercial goods. Arms 'er hidden in a false bottom." He looked at each of the others in turn.

Landry shook his head and stared into the distance. He said, "God," under his breath as he crossed himself.

"We need someone we can trust to go out there to help those men and repair the wagon," Rodman said. "Real quick."

"Damn it all, Rodman, I don't have anybody to do that." Landry paused, his breathing heavier than before. "Damn it, what a muddle! Even if I did find someone, they'd want an escort, and you know what that means! Bluecoats! And if the guns are found, it traces back to me!" He moved into the shadows, hesitated, then turned back. "Take some pack animals out there, remove the guns—at night— and haul them off in the other direction. Abandon the wagon. Let the Apaches have it, or whoever gets there first. Tear it apart for firewood. Take the guns back to Texas. How many and what type?"

Blakely, stiff with fury, stared at his angry, frustrated host.

Rodman looked at the floor for several silent moments, then looked up at Landry from under his eyebrows. "Okay, Landry. You can't help with this. I understand your predicament. Perhaps your idea is best. Yes. Best." He glanced at Blakely. "Can you tell us where we can obtain some drafts? Mules are best. Ours wandered off."

"I'll give you a name. What kinds of armament?"

"Carbines. Pistols. Ammunition." Rodman paused. "You planning on giving us up, are you, Landry?"

"No! Blast it, no! Hell, what's wrong with you?! If I went to the government, they'd hang me along with you!" Landry gesticulated wildly, then calmed and lowered his voice. "I told you, I'm with you. It's just a bad idea to bring guns into this. Let's do it the right way. That's my firm conviction."

Rodman nodded emphatically and generated another false smile. He looked at Blakely and nodded toward the door.

Landry scribbled on a piece of note paper and handed it to Rodman. "Tell this man, Guzmán, that you need the mules to pull a wagon out of a ditch or something. Not where. If he wants to send along one or more of his men, tell him you have your own. I suggest you buy the animals. He also has grain."

"All right," Rodman said. He took the paper, then extended his hand to shake Landry's.

An unsmiling Evan Landry hesitated, then relented and shook Rodman's hand reluctantly while Blakely walked around both men and waited at the door to the *atrio*.

Landry blew out the lantern flame and followed the pair to the outer door in the dark. "What are you going to do?"

Rodman stopped in the open doorway, but didn't turn around. He took two beats, then said, "A better question, Landry, is what are *you* going to do? I suggest you think this over. Carefully. You're in this with us, like it or not. The die has been cast." He shot Landry a backward glance, a move Landry did not see in the dark, then continued, "You need me, I'm at the *fonda*." He then followed the man in the black vest across the yard, through the gate personnel door and into the night.

The senior Landry stared after them, motionless, but saw nothing but blackness.

Rodman and Blakely were past the northeast corner of the Romero property, walking south, when the taller of the two leaned into his shorter companion in the faint light. "I'm not sure Landry was straight with us about the note. I feel strongly we should check his veracity in some manner."

"Veracity?"

"I don't believe he burned the note paper, Blakely."

"Yeah. I'll check into his whatchamacallit."

"Good man." Rodman reached into his inner jacket pocket for a cheroot, licked it, then proceeded to roll it around between his pursed lips.

"Fact is, I don't trust a man who'd marry up with a 'Meskin." The sneer on Blakely's face was not seen by his companion.

"Mm," Rodman commented. "Texas is full of 'em." He rolled the cigar in his mouth.

4

After Francesca cleared the table and wiped it clean with no small amount of fanfare, Beckner moved closer to Jesse at one end of the table as his host shuffled a deck of cards. He pulled a burning taper closer.

"Did I hear the outer door close after your father left?" The lieutenant asked.

"Yes. He had some papers to go over in the office." He dealt the cards. "Four hands, then we go. Whoever loses buys."

"You're on."

The Velasquez café was situated two blocks south of the plaza along another of the town's narrow dirt streets. It consisted of one large room that usually had a sea of rectilinear trestle tables and benches spread evenly throughout, but which had been pushed against the walls, creating an instant dance floor of freshly cut pine decking. Two glowing, top-shaded oil lamps hung from the low ceiling beams roughly centered, adding to the film of blue tobacco smoke and the moving shadows. A small, crude, locally-produced, L-shaped wooden bar and separate serving area at the rear opened onto the kitchen, which extended outside where haunches of meat were spit-roasted, weather permitting, along with tortillas and breads, in a beehive-shaped adobe and rock *horno,* or oven. The air reeked of corn *masa,* chile-laced pork, whole chickens and lamb shanks, mixed with the odors from pipes, cigars, cigarettes, and burning tallow.

The patronage was roughly divided between men and women, and most danced wildly as they twirled, shouted, laughed and waved their arms in rough unison to the fast beat of the music. The latter came from a group composed of four men and a woman in one corner of the room near the rear, who worked furiously at two guitars, a violin, a concertina and castanets. In the opposite corner was a monte table attended between it and the wall by the dealer and two patrons across from him. More people, mostly men, stood or sat along the periphery of the dance area. They grasped bottles and tumblers, smoked, shouted, joked, laughed, ate, and from time to time, expectorated, and missed the targeted spittoons a high percentage of the time, as they flicked ashes from cigarettes and cigars at random.

Jesse and Beckner edged into the room along the line of revelers, then moved to the rear where they were noticed long enough to order *aguardiente* for each. Beckner, having lost at cards, coughed up enough coins to pay for the room-temperature drinks. The two of them moved away from the bar, where other patrons, a few beyond drunk, pushed and shoved to get even more inebriated, and nearly knocked them over in the process.

Beckner leaned in close to Jesse's ear. "This never ceases to amaze me."

"What's that?" Jesse asked loudly as his smiling eyes danced about the wild crowd.

"These people."

"How?"

"Look, there. That woman. I've seen her before at the officer's ball. And a priest! Dancing!"

Jesse quaffed, then wiped his mouth on his sleeve. "Well, they're all having a good time." He smiled broadly.

"Yes, but—"

"Yes?" Jesse continued to scan the room, hardly cognizant of the lieutenant's remarks.

Beckner looked at Jesse with a mildly disdainful expression, hesitated, then returned his smile, amplified to a grin. "Right. They are. And well they should!" He began to bounce to the music as he realized he had probably come close to insulting his friend.

Jesse's head swivelled as he looked for faces he knew. He spoke again. "You gonna dance?"

Beckner shook his head slowly with a grimace. "Ah, I don't think so. I'd look awkward."

"Well, I am. See that lady over there?" He pointed with his chin.

"Which?"

"Red dress with gold trim."

"Yes. I think so."

"Hold the fort. Please?" Before Beckner could answer, Jesse turned and put his half-empty cup on the nearest table, then crossed the gyrating room as he dodged dancing couples at every step.

Beckner, nudged and brushed by the merrymakers around him, stepped back to the nearest table against the wall and watched as Jesse first talked to, then took the girl he had seen by both hands, and pulled her into the mêlée. Bemused, he took a long tipple from his drink, then winced as it seared his throat. He understood little of what was said around him, since it was principally in Spanish. When the music stopped, Jesse made a half bow to the girl, who blushed and moved back to her former position among a group of other women. He panted joyfully as he approached Beckner.

"You're good at that, Jess!" Beckner slapped him on the back.

"Thanks, but I can't dance, really." He puffed madly as he picked up his glass and drank.

"Looked like it to me."

"Ah, I just whirl around and stomp my feet to the music. It's fun." He grinned, his head still in motion. "Damn!"

"What?!" Beckner followed his friend's eyes.

He was a man of medium build, with a head of thick, long, black hair under a broad-brimmed black felt hat, and who wore a semblance of a uniform. A pistol hung from a second, cartridge-bearing belt around his waist, and a bright round badge was pinned to his dark blue shirt. He stopped a few feet inside the door and took in the raucous scene, then threaded his way through the throng toward the back. As he moved, Beckner detected a bit of a swagger to his walk. Some of the men in the crowd acknowledged him. They either hailed him as he passed, or shook his hand as he moved along, as though he were a celebrity. When he spotted Jesse, some ten feet away, he slowed and stared at the two, first at Jesse, then the army officer, then back again.

Beckner leaned into Jesse. "Who is he? What's going on?"

"Deputy sheriff. Dominguez. He doesn't like me." He shot Beckner a glance.

"What—"

"Tell you later."

Dominguez moved to within a few feet of the pair, then glared at Jesse, his face lowered.   Jesse looked away, then cocked his head sideways to look at the man. "Evening, Filemón." He sipped nonchalantly as he peered at the deputy from under his eyebrows.

Dominguez bobbed his head in an insinuating fashion, pointed his finger at Jesse, then sauntered past. He brushed Jesse as he did. "¡*Pendejo!*" He muttered.

"What the devil was that about? What did he say?!" Beckner's eyes were wide with incredulity.

Jesse waved his hand in a dismissive gesture as he swallowed the last of his libation, then used his sleeve as a napkin again. "Not a very nice word. He thinks I'm trying to take his wife."

"Why would he think that?"

Jesse winced, rolled his eyes and shook his head. "She's a pretty little wisp, and flirtatious as all get out. Hell, she trifles with everyone. He's wrong about me. I don't need that kind of trouble."

"So, why does he single you out? Have you—?"

"No! Blazes, no." Jesse arched his back in irritation and threw out his arm as though to stop someone. "She comes into the store, maybe once a week, spends money, leaves. Sometimes I attend to her, and we speak. But nothing. I'm not about to mess with her. Especially with him in his position. He's a hot head."

"Hot head?"

"He's jealous, and has a reputation. Violent. He thinks I have money. And be advised, that's incorrect." He looked hard at Beckner and pointed with his index finger. After a moment of reflection, he said, "He likes to rough people up. See the way he swaggers around with that damned badge and gun?"

Beckner swallowed the remains in his glass and raised his eyebrows. "Well. Guess I better watch my step, eh?"

Jesse adjusted his pants at the belt line. "You better, gringo!" He grinned broadly.

"Let's make ourselves scarce. I'm not comfortable being under the same roof with that fellow." He surveyed the noisy, smoke-filled room.

They made their way through the throng and onto the street, Jesse first as they brushed against two men who barged their way in as though he didn't exist. When Beckner was a few feet into the dark street, he turned at the angry shouts of three men who had exited the saloon to carry a knife-reinforced argument outside. He watched as three more men tumbled from the lighted building onto the street to join in the fray as they shouted epithets and gesticulated wildly.

He hesitated, then caught up to Jesse. "Did you see that?!"

Jesse looked back toward the saloon. "Glad we're not there." He moved on.

"So how old is the girl? The wife?" Beckner was breathless as he came alongside.

"Dominguez' wife? Maybe nineteen. Twenty at the outside. Why?"

They slowed to a stroll. The noise behind them reduced enough so that they could converse in a normal voice.

"Curious. And you're what, twenty?"

"Twenty-one next month."

They were silent until they reached the edge of the plaza.

"You told me your mother died when you were young. And the house—"

"I was eleven. She was an Abréu. All gone. Some cousins up in Taos, I think, and maybe somebody in Pecos."

"You speak Spanish."

"Learned it from her and *mis abuelitos*. Grandparents. Spoke it before I spoke English. The house was theirs. Just my father and me now. Francesca and Cipriano, of course. They're like family."

They angled across the central, open area of the plaza, still dominated by empty freight wagons as they dodged rowdy, drunken drovers here and there in the dim, shadowed light provided by lanterns placed in random doorways and a pair of torches in the plaza itself.

"And your father speaks it? Spanish?"

"Yep. Had to. If you want to do business, you better. He sometimes travels to Chihuahua." He looked at the army officer and smiled. "You—you're not much older."

"Twenty-six. An old man compared to you." Beckner smiled in return. "And Francesca?"

"Francesca's been with the family—she and her husband, Cipriano—since before I was born. She's been like a mother to me."

They turned the dark corner from the plaza onto Palace Avenue. Beckner slowed, and Jesse stopped to look at him.

"Gonna' turn in," Beckner said. "Patrol in the morning, and I have some reading to do. Thanks for dinner, and thank your father and Francesca for me, please." Beckner instinctively nodded his head in a formal gesture. He then turned to peer up the street that fronted the Landry mercantile and house. "Hey! What's that—?!" He pointed.

Jesse spun around to follow Beckner's sight line. As he did, they both saw the figure of a man as he left the mercantile under the faintly-lighted porch.

"What the—?!" Jesse uttered. "Hey!" He shouted as he took a step in that direction.

The man, who hurried, slowed, turned toward them for an instant, then ran across the street and disappeared behind a corner building.

Jesse looked at Beckner as they both stood still, immobilized by the shock of the sight.

"Wasn't that the man—?"

"Yeah, I think so! Damn!" Beckner looked at Jesse, eyes fierce, then raced off toward the Landry house.

Jesse was close behind him, then raced past and dashed through the open door to the mercantile. He slowed measurably, his breath coming in gasps as he entered the unlighted store. With his knowledge of the floor layout, he picked his way to the back, but nearly stumbled once.

Behind him, Beckner stopped in the doorway, then groped for the lantern he had seen hanging from a peg immediately inside the front door. He found it, pulled the chimney up, fumbled for a match, and lit it. He turned and held the lamp high. "Jesse! Hold on! Watch out!"

Jesse ignored him, encouraged by the meager light from the lantern. He slowed only when he came to the counter in the rear, where he stopped and looked around frantically. He then rounded the end of the long board and entered the area used as an office by his father.

Beckner was upon him, and held the lantern up. They stared at the floor where Evan Landry lay, his twisted body in a pool of blood that grew slowly as they watched.

"Jesus!" Jesse moved closer and knelt next to his father's lifeless body. He looked up at the union officer. "Jesus, Harold. He's dead! God!"

Lieutenant Beckner's face was screwed up the likes of which Jesse had never seen before. He stared, speechless, at the figure on the floor for several long seconds, then looked away, then at the ceiling, then the front door, as though attempting to penetrate and understand what had happened. "That man—!"

Jesse, still crouched next to his father, one hand on his dead arm, craned to look up at Beckner. "Who was he?! What's going on?!" Tears welled in his eyes above his pallid cheeks.

Beckner looked down at his friend and shook his head, his mouth slack.

At that moment, the door to the *atrio* opened and Cipriano Anaya stumbled in, his wife, Francesca, immediately behind him. She was wearing a nightgown, and her hair was disheveled from sleep. The belt was loose on Cipriano's pants, and a night shirt flowed over his waistline. They were both barefoot.

Francesca's mouth dropped open as she looked from Evan Landry, to his son, then the officer and back. "¡Ay! ¡Hijo! ¡¿Qué pasó?!"

Cipriano could only stare, his mouth agape.

Evan Landry's only offspring, his son, looked up at her, tears on his cheeks. He shook his head slowly.

Francesca slapped both her cheeks with her palms as her eyes opened wide. She began to wail, then slumped against the wall as her knees gave way.

Beckner set the lamp on the counter and went to her as Cipriano remained frozen in place, too shocked to budge. She reached out and fell against his chest as he put his arms around her and held her close. She stared past him at the shadowed figure on the floor.

Jesse stood up without taking his eyes off his father. "I don't know what went on here, but I intend to find out!" His words were choked, and his face had become a mask of rage.

Beckner turned to look at him. "Jesse! Calm down! Don't do anything! I'll go for the sheriff. You stay here with Francesca and Cipriano. Don't do anything!"

"No! I saw that bastard—whoever he is—and I'm going to find him!" He started for the open door to the house.

"Jesse! Stop! You don't know—" Francesca was like a rag doll in Beckner's arms.

Cipriano gathered his senses, turned toward the door and shouted, "Jesse!"

Jesse was out the door and shouted back. "I know where to find him! He was headed for the inn!"

Beckner guided a reluctant, hyperventilating and nearly collapsed Francesca out the door and into the darkened *atrio* as the frantic woman tried to look over her shoulder at her deceased employer, while Cipriano, still numb, but recovering, remained. Ahead of them, Jesse had disappeared into the house, where he left the door to the residence ajar. As Beckner guided Francesca inside, Jesse rushed out, his visage wild. He gripped a revolver in his right hand.

"Goddamnit, Jesse! Listen to me! Jesse! Don't do this! Let me help! I can—!"

Jesse ignored Beckner and was out the door and away as the lieutenant stood in the semi-dark hallway, helpless, the hysterical Francesca still draped across his arms.

Fueled by grief, rage and disbelief, Jesse panted hard as he ran the two blocks from the mercantile to the *fonda*. Several men and two women laughed, smoked and hoisted drinks as they milled about the entrance to the hotel. As Jesse approached at a run, they first watched him with bemusement, then scattered to let him pass as he seemed determined to barge through their midst without slowing. Most were aghast and silent, while two of the men shouted something at him he not only didn't understand, but to which he was oblivious. He rushed through the door and crashed into a man who stood with his back to the opening, which knocked a drink from his hand, and forced him to brace himself against a fall. The man tried to accost Jesse as he rushed by, but abandoned the idea quickly when he realized the intruder's mood was reinforced by a firearm.

Jesse was forced to slow as he pushed his way into the saloon area, blinded to everything and everyone in the sea of faces, some which turned from the gaming tables. One man approached, pool cue in hand, a frown on his face. Someone shouted his name, but he was beyond hearing anything save his inner seething of the moment. Then the mass of gay humanity parted for a moment such that he spotted his quarry. The short man in the black vest was standing against the bar, his back to the room, drink in hand, about to raise it to his mouth. Shark-like, Jesse sliced his way past the people in his way. His demeanor broadcast immediacy, and those nearest him backed away, as they sensed the alarm he carried. Silence spread through the room as he slowed and moved closer to the man who was blithely unaware he was being stalked. Then, as he realized something odd was taking place with the growing silence, Blakely turned to see what was happening and why the room was quieting.

He watched Jesse approach, his young frame tensed like a cat about to pounce, and knew something was wrong, but didn't relate it to himself, yet the youth with the pistol in his hand glared at him with reddened eyes and wet cheeks as he came closer. Blakely, aware now he was targeted, looked in disbelief from one man, then to another, as the people near him backed away, incredulous at the scene.

Jesse stopped three feet from Blakely. He was taller than his quarry by four inches. "You killed my father!" Both his hands shook, which caused the pistol in his right hand, still pointed at the floor, to quiver wildly.

Faces in the crowd reacted, stunned, as eyes moved from Blakely to Jesse and back. Blakely shook his head rapidly, but the frown he wore was taught and white.

"You killed my father!" Jesse shouted. Spittle flew from his mouth.

"What the goddamn hell y'all talkin' 'bout?! I ain't killed nobody, kid!" Blakely snarled, looked fearfully at those nearest him, then tried to regain his composure by turning half to his right and downing his drink in one swift motion.

A man in the crowd, pressed closer and called Jesse's name. Jesse ignored him and took a step closer to Blakely. The room rippled into silence, which started with the small circle around the two conflicted men. Soon, the only sounds were of disparate murmurs and feet that shuffled on the raw wooden floor.

Blakely turned to face Jesse with his back against the bar, the miniature tumbler still gripped in his hand. Then he executed a slow quarter turn to put his empty whiskey glass down. He spoke as he did. "Listen, kid, I don't know what the hell you're goin' on about, but you got the wrong man here! I been—" As he spoke, he pulled his hand back slowly, then dropped it to the butt of his revolver and drew it in one swift motion.

In the time it took Blakely to pull the long barrel from the holster, Jesse reacted to the move and raised his .40 caliber pistol. As Blakely's gun barrel came free of the holster on his right hip, the muzzle still pointed down, Jesse fired. The bullet hit Blakely two inches below the heart. Blakely's gun discharged, and the slug bored a hole into the floor half way between him and his assailant. He lurched back in shock, dropped the pistol, grabbed his chest with both hands, looked down at his wound in surprise, then slumped to the floor. He stared at nothing. Five seconds later, he was dead.

For another count of five, no one moved or spoke.

The man who had called Jesse's name pushed through the hushed, gawking crowd and came to his side. He was in his mid-thirties with a craggy face and a large mustache, and about Jesse's height. He put his hand on the youth's shoulder and looked first at the dead man on the floor then at Jesse. "Jesse. Give me the gun." His voice was mature, calm and controlled.

Jesse looked at him for a moment, his eyes immense, with no reaction, then returned his gaze to the man on the floor.

"Jesse. The gun."

Jesse held his pistol at his side. He shook his head slowly.

"Jesse, they've gone for the sheriff. You don't want that in your hand when he comes." He spoke in Spanish.

"No, Hilario. I'm going home. My father's dead." He turned, and the crowd parted silently.

"Jesse, they'll come for you," Hilario said.

"Let them. My father's dead, and that man killed him." He pointed with the gun. "He was about to kill me!" He looked at the faces that stared at him. "You saw it. You all saw that! He pulled his gun!" His head bobbed as though he were about to faint, then staggered sideways.

Hilario lent support by putting his arm around him. "Jesse, I'm your friend. I'm your father's friend. If what you say is true, it will be all right. I saw what happened here. Now, put your gun on the bar. Come on."

Jesse tore away and started for the exit. "No! I don't trust the sheriff. If he or that worm Dominguez want me, let them come and see what that little bastard did to my father!" With that, he pushed and shoved his way toward the door as Hilario and the others gaped after him. After he jostled several people aside, including a woman, he reached the outer door, then ran as fast as he could for home.

Lieutenant Beckner raced toward the hotel when Jesse passed him in the semi-darkness. "Jesse! Jesse! It's Harold! Wait!" Beckner stopped and looked toward the hotel. He saw a gaggle of people that had coalesced into a group, all of whom waved, shouted and moved his way. He turned and hurried after Jesse.

Cipriano Anaya, Francesca's husband, along with Incarnación Serna, his father's right-hand man, and one of the teen boys who helped around the store and house, were grouped around Evan Landry's corpse as they looked from one another and the body. Anaya had placed a blanket over him, which left only his feet exposed. They all looked up as Jesse approached. His breath came in gasps, and eyes were still wild. Anaya and Serna both surrounded him.

The older man put his arms around him and began to sob as Serna backed off. "¡Tu padre! ¡Ay, Diós, hijo! ¡Que triste, que triste! ¿¡Que vámos hacer?¡" "How sad! What are we going to do?!"

Jesse stood limply, his eyes filled with tears as he looked down at his father's body, the gun still held loosely in his hand. "I killed the son of a bitch. I killed him." His voice was a near whisper.

"¿Que? You killed? ¿Quien?"

"The man who killed him." His voice was flat. "El hombre que mató á mi padre."

Beckner rushed in from the street. His boots resounded on the wood floor. "Jesse! Jesse!" He stopped, breathless, as Jesse turned to face him. "You've got to get out of here! There's a mob coming!"

44

Jesse looked toward the street door as Serna and Anaya backed away. They heard shouts that came from the street.

"¡Hijo, véte!" Anaya hissed. He pointed toward the rear door.

"Don't worry, Jesse, I'll take care of the store! Go!" Serna pleaded, then started for the street door.

Jesse looked from man to man, then Beckner took him by the arm and guided him outside.

He pulled Jesse aside. "Jesse, Get out of here! Cipriano and I will bring your horse later."

"Where?!"

Beckner whirled around, his head back and forth, thinking. "Listen, go to the garrison corral. Other side. I'll be along soon."

"I haven't done anything wrong!"

"Blue blazes, Jesse, don't argue with a mob! Or me! We'll work it out later! Get!" He shoved Jesse toward the rear gate.

Jesse loped to the gate and opened the personnel door. Beckner was able to make out only a faint outline as he went through, then he turned toward the mercantile and the crowd that had filled it despite Serna's efforts to keep them out. Through the door he saw Serna wave his arms as he demanded that they leave.

5

Emiliano Baca, the High Sheriff, a tall, gruff man, wore a vested black suit, black Spanish riding boots, a black, wide-brimmed, high-crowned beaver hat, handlebar mustache, and a big belly. His face was ruddy and veined from drinking, smoking, and eating too well. He sauntered through the mercantile crowded with eager onlookers with an air of authority borne of position and a sense of God-ordained self-confidence. He was followed by a pleased, swaggering Dominguez and a second deputy who seemed tentative in the wake of the two self-possessed power brokers who preceded him.

Baca was no more than ten feet into the store when he turned to his underlings and ordered them to clear the building of salivating onlookers, a throng through which he was forced to plow.

Beckner, still in uniform, complete with blue tunic, but who appeared as though he had just returned from a violent military campaign, moved to the front of the troika which consisted of himself, lead employee Incarnación Serna and Francesca's husband, Cipriano Anaya.

When the sheriff arrived at the mercantile's open office area, he peered at the tiny delegation wordlessly, then looked down at Evan Landry's body. "Where's the boy?" He asked.

Beckner answered, "I assume you refer to Jesse Landry, sheriff. I don't know. He was very upset at his father's death."

"Who are you? Does the army represent the family?" Baca scowled at Beckner, then Serna and Anaya in turn.

"I'm a friend of the family, sheriff. As you can see, Mr. Landry was murdered." He waved his hand at the body.

"No, I don't see. At this time."

Behind Baca, Dominguez and the other deputy had successfully cleared the mercantile, although not without protests. Some of the herd absconded with a few useable souvenirs that would otherwise have cost them hard-earned coinage. While Dominguez joined the sheriff, his partner closed and bolted the street door, then followed.

The sheriff looked to Dominguez. "You say there were witnesses to the shooting?"

"Yes. I talked to several. Jesse Landry shot the man at the inn dead."

Beckner cut in. "Sheriff, Jesse Landry and I saw—"

Baca held up his hand. "In good time; in good time." He turned to Dominguez again. "Now, Dominguez, tell me what they saw."

The deputy reported that several witnesses claimed to have seen Jesse storm into the hotel, seek the unknown gringo out, raise his gun, shoot the man without provocation, and run out after threatening others.

Baca ordered his deputies to search the *hacienda*, which they accomplished within ten minutes, guns drawn. When they returned, Dominguez shrugged as he came through the patio door.

Baca jutted his chin officiously "Find him. Find him and bring him to me or to the *jusgado*. Get some men." Baca pointed by tilting his head, as he spoke with his thumbs hooked into the pockets of his vest.

Dominguez and the other man wheeled and started off toward the front of the store.

"Sheriff, I think you should know something about all this. We found—" Beckner's voice betrayed frustration.

"In good time, *hombre*! I have my job to do! Now let me do it." He waggled his finger. "This Landry boy is in trouble. He will be dealt with fairly, but we need to locate him." Baca calmed, peered at the shrouded body again, then turned to shout after his deputy. "Watch him, Dominguez. He's armed. If he gives you any trouble, you know what to do."

Beckner shook his head. His face was pinched as he spoke. "Sheriff, aren't you going to inspect the scene? Something happened here that—"

"What is your name, sir? And your rank?" Although Beckner stood an inch taller than Baca, he peered down his nose at the Army officer.

"Beckner. First Lieutenant Harold Beckner, sheriff."

"Ah, then, Lieutenant Beckner, you of the United States Army, you should respect authority, and I have that authority here! Sir."

"I most certainly do, sheriff, but this is different."

Baca rose up on his toes imperiously, then settled down on his heels. "Indeed it is, Lieutenant, it is different. This is not a war, insurrection, Indian attack, or any other matter for the army. It is a civil matter, and I am in charge. I know what I am doing, and I prefer to handle this thing myself. I prefer that you interfere no longer and remove yourself and these two gentlemen with you." With that, he swept his suit jacket back to reveal a sidearm at his belt line and looked from man to man, his mouth a thin line of suppressed anger mixed with pomposity. "I suggest you remove the body to the house."

Serna and Anaya both nodded and looked from the sheriff to the still body and back.

Beckner stared at Baca for a few seconds, incredulous, then with an imperceptible shake of his head, turned to the stunned Landry employees. "Let's go. *Vámos.* I'm sure the sheriff knows what he's doing here." He waggled his head toward the outer door.

A few feet outside, he huddled with Anaya and Serna. To Anaya, he asked that he gather personal things for Evan Landry's son, perhaps with Francesca's help, if able. He asked Serna if he was capable of overseeing the mercantile for a few days, to which the man answered in the affirmative. Serna then went with Anaya to the house to help, and to check on the prostrate Francesca, who had returned tearfully to her bed. Beckner remained behind and watched surreptitiously as the sheriff milled around for two minutes, as he stroked his chin and looked about, confused.

Anaya and Serna, both bearing small bundles, came up to Beckner in the dark as the lawman left the building.

"What are they doing?" Serna whispered.

"They've left." Beckner turned to look at the men in the shadows. "Evan Landry was murdered. You both know that." He saw their nods in the semi-darkness. "I don't know what happened at the inn, but I'm sure it wasn't as the deputy said. I don't think Jesse would shoot someone without provocation."

Both men were emphatic in their assent, although neither understood the long English word.

"Can you saddle his horse and put his belongings with it?"

Again, both men agreed eagerly.

"One more thing. We must keep this to ourselves. So far as you both know, Jesse has disappeared. I will try to get him in the hands of people who will iron this mess out and protect him as well. Understand? *¿Comprenden?*"

Anaya and Serna were once more forceful in their assent and belief.

"Good. While you're getting his horse ready, I'm going to have a look around Mr. Landry's office. Let's hurry. The sheriff may return."

Beckner entered Evan Landry's simple, but effective, inner sanctum warily, as he reckoned the sheriff might have posted a guard over the crime scene, which seemed to him only reasonable. That was not the case, a condition for which he was mystified, but grateful. His next thought was of the reason for the killing of the elder Landry. Why had the man he'd seen on the trail, and whose description showed up in an encrypted message transmitted in a secure pouch from Fort Leavenworth, come to the Landry Mercantile and shot and killed its proprietor? Was the short man in the vest, the killer, and if so, nothing more than an opportunistic thief? Or, on the other hand, was there something deeper, perhaps even a connection with Evan Landry? The idea was unthinkable, yet the disciplined military intelligence officer in him had to think in those terms, as distasteful as it was.

The lantern from the front of the store continued to burn on the counter, the result of which was to put the floor and much of the office area in flickering shadow. Careful not to touch the dead body which had yet to be removed to a household bier, he picked the lantern up, looked around, checked to ensure that the street door was shut, then placed the lamp up high, on the shelf where Landry kept a small library of bound books. Most were, oddly it seemed to him, fiction—novels—one or two in French and an equal number in Spanish, from the appearance of the titles. Once light was shed in a wider arc around the office area, he looked carefully at everything, as he recalled the six weeks of training he had received at the Army's special school outside Washington for such activities. The desk was difficult, with papers and bound ledgers spread scatter-shot. He didn't know where to begin, but because he had little time, hurried.

An ink-stained green blotter, its edges frayed and curled, lay under the mass of dispersed papers, most of which were bills of lading, personal accounts receivable or inventory lists. As he began to push the pieces of paper about, he caught sight of a white triangle that stuck out no more than half an inch from beneath the blotter on the front edge of the desk. Nervousness welled in him with the fear of discovery as he looked around the big, goods-filled room once more. Then he pulled what proved to be a scrap of paper from beneath the blotter. It was two inches by four, and had been folded in two at least once, then opened, such that the creases were deep. He looked at it briefly, noticed a short message printed in what he reckoned to be a male hand, folded it without reading it, and pushed it deep into a pocket in his tunic.

Beckner left the mercantile, then moved carefully through the rear gate personnel door with its high, step-over threshold, to check the area behind the Landry place from the north-south trace that paralleled the palace on the west to the east end of the three *haciendas*. He peered out over the fields across the road as well. In each case, he detected no one. Beside the stars, only the dim lights from the garrison to the rear of the palace and a few from the fort on the hill above the town showed from the north. He muttered to himself in his amazement that the sheriff had stationed no one to ensure that Jesse was not either escaping or returning by the route he now surveyed. He felt suddenly cold in the late, high-altitude air, but brushed the feeling away as quickly.

Inside the compound walls again, he helped Anaya and Serna bring the saddled and provisioned Campeón out of the compound through one side of the big gate, as they calmed the recalcitrant animal every careful step of the way. As they approached the corner of the Chávez place across from the palace, he sent Anaya and Serna back, with the admonition to avoid talking to anyone about what they had seen or heard, especially the sheriff or his agents. If he had been able, given the dark, he would have seen tears run down Cipriano Anaya's aged, dark, sunken cheeks.

Beckner guided Campeón slowly between the parade area behind the palace and the fields across the road. He kept his eyes trained on the plaza behind him, then turned left at the next corner and headed for the garrison horse barn and corrals. Once there, he soothed the horse to a silent halt and waited, close to the solid rear wall. He warbled a short whistle and listened. An answering whistle came from somewhere inside the open corral that began at the end of the wall. Campeón snorted and stomped. A few seconds later, a shadowy Jesse emerged from between the stripped-cedar corral rails.

"I'm glad to see you." He patted the horse's snout as he spoke in a voice barely above a whisper.

Beckner kept his voice low. "They're looking for you, Jesse. You've got clothes, food and water for a day or so. Your pistol and the Hawken. I'll try to calm things down, then you can come in and tell your story." He paused, and scoured the area as he did. "What happened? At the inn?"

Jesse crossed himself. "Jesus, Mary and Joseph, Harold, I found him and he pulled his pistol. He was going to shoot me. They saw it. The whole crowd!" He started to hyper-ventilate.

"Calm down, Jess. Dominguez told the sheriff you shot the man cold. So far, that's what he's buying."

"Damn! Baca is such a—!" He spat his words. "Who was he, Harold?! You asked me about him when we were coming in. Who the hell was he?!"

"Damned if I know, Jesse, but I aim to find out. I have to, that's for sure, if we're going to convince the sheriff or anybody else." Beckner did not see him shake his head violently in the dark. He continued, "Listen, you need to leave. For now. Oh—I found something on your father's desk that might—" He started for the piece of paper in his tunic pocket, then raised his head and took a half step backward as he sensed movement behind Jesse.

Jesse turned and crouched in reaction at the same time as he pulled his Colt's revolver from his waist band.

"If that's you, Jesse Landry, stand still in the name of the law." The voice came from the dark beyond the corner of the corral, and was in Spanish.

Both Jesse and the army officer recognized Dominguez' voice. Jesse understood the Spanish; Beckner by inference. Jesse had Campeón's reigns in his other hand, and when his body jerked at the surprise sound, the horse side-stepped and whinnied, which caused Jesse to lurch toward the animal. Beckner also moved, away from the horse's rump, which resulted in a confusion of sound and movement. A flash came from Dominguez' direction, accompanied by a loud report from his pistol. Jesse instinctively fired back. He and Beckner then heard a moan, then silence.

The lieutenant's mind needed only two seconds to realize what had happened. He ran around Jesse's mount and in the direction of the sound. When he returned a half minute later, he came up close to Jesse and grabbed his arm. "Goddamnit, Jesse, he's down! I couldn't determine, but think he's dead!"

Jesse doubled over. "¡Ay, Diós mío! Oh, no! God!" He looked up at Beckner. "What am I going to do?! I'm dead!" His voice cracked.

Beckner backed off and spun away, his hand to the back of his head in thought, then came back. "Where can you go? Who can you trust—not around here. There has to be—"

"I know a place."

"Away?"

"Yes. South."

"Yes. Go. Now! Get me a message somehow. Let me know where you are. Soon as you can. Now, go!"

Jesse leapt onto Campeón, spurred him, and was off into the night. As the sound of hooves died out, the union officer heard voices approaching from the direction of the plaza.

6

The sun rose out of the east with crystalline brilliance, causing the vast, rounded crest of the Sandia Mountains to cast a long, cool shadow over the Rio Grande Valley. Bernalillo's adobes lay quietly eclipsed, partially in shadow, partially in warm, early morning sunshine. Staccato with the soft thud of Campeón's hooves in the marshy sod above El Llanito, Jesse heard a rooster crow.

The drowsiness of the last hour or so was beginning to pass, and after licking his lips and trying to smack away the metallic taste in his thirsty mouth, he swung around in the saddle again for what seemed to him countless times, and stared intently north from where he had come. His eyes roved past the cottonwoods of the *bosque*, back and forth across the meandering river-flattened valley floor, up the undulating sides of the soft, rolling *piñon* and cedar-studded piedmont; then across to the steep escarpments of the black-sided mesas to the northwest. He saw nothing, bar several wisps of smoke coming from Santa Ana Pueblo chimneys. A light breeze, which varied between moist warm and cool dry, stirred the fresh leaves on the huge old cottonwoods through which he rode, and he heard a turtle dove in a tamarisk near the river coo to its mate. He thought about the differences between Santa Fé and the middle Rio Grande valley, how it was so much lower and how much warmer it could be, and glad the westerly spring winds had abated. Campeón trudged on patiently as he faced forward.

His thoughts turned to the long night gone by since exiting Santa Fé. Oddly, he had seen no followers. He wondered if Beckner had either justified his actions, sent them in the wrong direction, the decision was made not to pursue him, or they had merely been delayed. Whatever the reason, riding all night was his fate for fear of capture, or worse. He had dozed in the saddle a half dozen times, and often slipped into a dream state which became either rambling nothings or nightmares that awakened him with a start. He felt badly for Campeón, and realized the horse must have been sleep-walking at times. His sole, faithful companion would need feed and water soon. Twice, he nearly fell from the saddle, but the horse sensed the movement and prevented it with whinnying and prancing. Tears had run down his cheeks more than once when he thought of his father.

In the dreams that came and went, he variously thought about parts of his life, especially as a child, before his mother died. His memory of her was sweet, dainty and pretty; of a lavender aroma as she read to him, or taught him to write and cipher. The moments with her and her father, his grandfather, Antonio Jesús Abréu. For some odd reason, the memories were of sublime late afternoons or sunny mornings and involved long, indolent shafts of sunlight. Then the sequential deaths of his grandparents and its profound effect on her.

When he was older, hovering Francesca explained to him that his mother had experienced two miscarriages, and what that meant. Then the third and final child, a girl, had been still-born, but the complications were too severe for her tiny, frail body, and there was no medicine but prayers and desperate shrugs. His father had been inconsolable. He remembered how Francesca and Cipriano, without hesitation, surrounded him with love, comfort and parenting. How his father turned away the offer of marriage from a Taos cousin of his deceased wife, willing to take her place in all facets, a strong tradition amongst New Mexico families that suffered so many deaths in an unremittingly harsh country. How he learned, later, that despite his father's bachelorhood, of the discreet liaisons where he found solace in the arms of willing women. How he himself found girls—and mature women—increasingly attractive, and the mutuality of the condition which he was slow, even now, to recognize and appreciate.

He knew, although unspoken, that his father was secretly disappointed about something, but the fault of no one. Evan Landry was a big man. Taller than most of the Hispanics of the area, and bigger in girth; "larger boned," was the mantra. Oddly, the closest anyone among the native population came to resembling him was the nearly universally despised and feared Sheriff Baca. He, Jesse, more resembled his mother's people and their cousins, among them Roybal, Luna, Peralta and Chávez clans. Even his skin tone was swarthier. His father was ruddy, and after a snifter of Pass brandy or glass of wine, more so. Jesse was taller than most, but slight of build. His eyes had that round, clear, dark "Spanish" look. It wasn't until his later teens that he began to sense that he was in the cusp between two peoples. Some of this, some of that. He felt "new." But he also recognized beyond the shadow of a doubt that his father was proud of him and loved him.

When he entered his teen years, his father, with access to firearms, rare and expensive on the frontier, had taught him to load, aim and shoot; first the Hawken carbine, then the Colt's .40 caliber revolver now on his hip. Cipriano

Anaya, Francesca's husband, whom he regarded as an uncle, taught him horsemanship. Francesca revealed some of the age-old tricks and remedies of the local *brujas,* some of whose knowledge was traceable to the ancient Greeks. When he turned eighteen, he joined the militia, with his father's blessing, but who held deep concerns for his safety.

Now he, too, was gone.

Ahead, and to his right, a middle-aged woman appeared in the yard of a small, L-shaped house. She carried a wooden bucket to a yard well.

Campeón smelled the water in the nearby horse trough, turned his head, shook it and sneezed, then stomped to a halt and jerked at the reins. Jesse yanked on the leathers and patted the horse along the neck. The woman peered at him as she held her hand up to shade her eyes from the direct sunlight. He saw her eye the Hawken in its saddle scabbard and the Colt's on his hip. Three chickens ignored them in favor of tiny, invisible morsels on the ground.

"*Buenos días. El caballo nececita agua. ¿Está bien?*" Jesse called out.

There was no answer as she stared at the weapons, motionless, as the bucket dangled from her hand.

"*Ah. Está bien. No voy á robarse. Yo llego en paz.*" He smiled and touched the brim of his hat.

She relaxed and returned the smile. "*Bueno, señor. ¿Y tú?*"

Jesse dismounted, dropped the reins, and Campeón made his way, absent of urging, to the trough, while the woman offered Jesse a tin of water. He drained it without taking a breath. She looked him over, then offered him breakfast. She told him to lead his horse behind the house to the corral and get some hay for the animal while she prepared his food.

Her name was Consuela Tenorio, and her husband and son, even at that early hour, were already in the fields behind the house and the adjacent animal pens. As they sat in the kitchen, she watched him devour two fried eggs and pork chile stew over a flour tortilla. She sensed his discomfort, and asked him about his troubles. Why was he armed, given that guns were rare, and if present, indicated wealth, a military connection, or something more sinister?

Finished, he pushed back from the table and bowed his head as tears welled, then looked up at her and blurted his tale, an act that somehow brought the horror of the night before out of the nightmare state, made it more real and somehow soothing at the same time. Had she seen anyone answering the description of the man he had shot? No, but recently she, her husband and their son had noticed gringos riding through, both north- and southbound. What was unusual about them was that they had been in pairs, on horseback, and without an obvious connection to the trade caravans that came through on the Camino Real that ran between Santa Fé, El Paso del Norte and Chihuahua. In each case, they were armed, and remained aloof.

She told him they had also heard rumors that *Tejános* were in the area; that some had been heard bragging about "taking New Mexico," which was "rightly theirs," along with other alarming threats. Her husband had told of witnessing a knife fight between two men near the plaza in Albuquerque not a month before. Blood was let amid shouts of bluster and shrieks of pain, yet neither suffered death, but someone in the crowd rumored that the combat was over that very question.

When he was ready to leave, Consuela reached up and patted his cheek in a maternal gesture and offered him more food, which he refused, but for which he thanked her. He offered her money in return for the meal, which she politely refused, although he saw the forlorn shine in her eyes when she saw the coins he held out.

"Where will you go from here?" she asked.

"Do you know Los Maestas?"

"Not well, but my husband does. They live over there. Near the river." She motioned again. "He has sheep. Up on the west side." She gestured broadly. "He tans hides. My husband has traded with him. He is rich."

He looked away instinctively at the last word, embarrassed, for reasons he couldn't fathom at the moment. "My father trades—traded—with him. Can you direct me to his house?"

She got up, went to the open door and took two steps into the simple dirt yard which she had broomed clean before his arrival. She shaded her eyes against the sunlight, pointed south, then looked up at him when he followed. "Go along the road here. When you come to the road that goes to Jemez, look for two large cottonwoods. Go to your right, past the old house. No one lives there. His is the next one, beyond the corn field. I think. There are fruit trees."

"I thank you. For the delicious food and the hay and water for my horse." He touched his mid-section, smiled, took Campeón's reins and pulled himself up into the saddle.

When Consuela went inside to clear the dishes, she saw the coins he had left on the table. There were twice the number he had shown her.

Although somewhat languid with the remnants of fatigue, Jesse was feeling better as he guided his mount out onto the north-south Camino Real. He reckoned it had much to do with Consuela's sympathetic ear, accompanied by her assurance that she not only believed his story, but would offer no aid or comfort to any possible pursuer, including the high sheriff of Santa Fé or his agents. He looked first north, saw no one, then south with the same result. Campeón seemed chipper, and tried to speed up to a trot, which he dampened with soothing sounds and a restraining tug on the reins.

The Maestas house was larger than the Tenorio place. Shaped in the form of a large, open, letter "C," it featured a wide *portal* along the inside length between the two wings. This, and the front door, were arranged to face south, toward the winter sun. The house sat at the eastern end of nearly ten acres, and ran to the Rio Grande on the west. A small portion east of the house was composed of a sparse orchard, principally apples, with a smattering of peaches and an apricot, some twenty mature trees in all. Amongst the trees were patches of green to beige grasses, grazed by a pair of immature goats. The periphery of this area was cordoned off by a three-foot high fence of un-grouted basaltic rock which ran to the house and whose ends abutted it. On the west side, also integral with the house was an adobe, rock and stripped-cedar corral. Beyond was a clearing with corn, squash and chile, all in neat rows and in various states of maturity. Past that, to the river, was the *bosque* of shimmering green cottonwoods.

Jesse guided Campeón around the south line of the walled orchard to the front of the house, where he found a hitching rail. He dismounted and snapped the reins around the cross bar, then pushed his hat back an inch and looked the scene over. A continuation of the orchard wall ran across the front, parallel to the house, made a right angle and terminated against the west wing. A tiny gate of stripped-cedar on leather hinges sagged close to the center of the wall, which guarded a narrow opening. A dirt path ran more or less in a straight line to the porch. Halfway along was a small, stone shrine with a sad Madonna statue, head tilted, studying the weeds and native grass at her feet. Ahead, to the right of the house door, under the shade of the porch roof, was a brightly-painted *Guadalupana*, the patron saint of Guadalupe, with her expression mildly Mona Lisa-like in contrast to the statue of the virgin out in the yard. Her bare feet rested on a crescent moon, and glory rays spiked out from her open cartouche. There were two more doors, one in each of the wings, but none open as with the Tenorio house.

Still in the saddle, Jesse stooped to search past the trees in the orchard toward the main road, for what or whom he knew not, then patted his horse and dismounted. The animal expressed his gratitude to be free of his master's weight with a grunt and heavy breathing. He then passed through the gate to the house and rapped on the main door. It was answered not fifteen seconds later.

The woman who opened the door was no shorter than Consuela Tenorio, but looked so because of her ample bosom, stomach and hips. She had a surprised, worried look on her face as she wiped her hands nervously in her apron. *"¿Sí? ¿Quién es? ¿ Que quieres?"*

"Buenos días. Soy Jesse Landry."

After a moment to absorb the fact, her face lit up, and she blurted, "Oh? Oh! Ah! Jesse! Landry! *¡Páse! ¡Páse!* Come inside!" Her demeanor changed from frown to genuine broad smile, and her hands and arms spread to create a pair of welcoming wings.

"Thank you." He removed his hat as he stepped inside.

She moved aside and closed the door after him as she looked him over at the same time. "Oh, you look so well! How is your father?" She clasped her hands together in front of her bosom, and tilted her head to one side.

He looked at her briefly with a forced smile, his lips clamped to keep from speaking immediately, then looked around the big room to gain strength for what he was about to say. He reckoned the ceilings to be about seven feet high, with round, exposed beams supporting a decking of *latias*, stripped cedar branches, set in a herring-bone pattern. Across the room, centered, was a newly-installed, single, tall and deep, north-facing window. Sparse, but comfortable, hand-made furniture graced the rest of the room. The window provided one of the seats, with a pillow for the occasional visitor who wished to sit and look out at the distant Jemez range.

He looked down at her. "My father is dead."

Filomena Maestas took a moment to absorb the news, then she leaned forward, touched Jesse on the arm and said, "No!" Her face dropped and her hands fluttered as she tried to find a place for them to express her anguish.

"Yes."

Then she abruptly enfolded the young Landry in her arms and began to rock to and fro as she sobbed, and dampened his shirt in the process.

To their left, a shaft of muted morning light brightened the room, as a man entered through the outer door. He was no more than two inches taller than his wife, slight, with a full head of greying hair under a tattered, wide-brimmed straw hat. He wore a blue work shirt with leather suspenders that latched to beltless, dark pants.

He stopped, shocked at the sight of his wife hugging a young man, and shook his head silently in disbelief. "*¿Que pasa? ¿Que es este?*"

His wife looked over at him, lifted her head, rolled her eyes and spread her arms out in a gesture of futility. "*Ay, Sabino, este es el hijo del señor Landry. ¡Su padre está muerto!*"

Sabino Maestas, froze in place, dropped his mouth open, removed his hat, and shook his head in stark disbelief.

7

When Lieutenant Harold Beckner heard the rustle of feet and murmur of voices that approached the place near the northwestern extent of the town garrison buildings where he reckoned deputy Dominguez had fallen, he was torn between remaining in place and leaving as quickly as possible. He had only now come to consider that if he were to defend Jesse Landry's rash actions openly in any way, even promoting the novel idea of innocence until guilt was proven, that his role might be misconstrued, and his position as undercover envoy from the War Department seriously jeopardized. He decided to take the middle road for the moment. He would remain hidden in the dark along the long, north wall of the compound long enough to discern, if possible, who had come to investigate, along with their number, then effect a discrete exit.

As the rabble came nearer, he crept closer to the corner, his shoulders hard against the wall, head turned sharply left, and was able to pick out a familiar word or two, despite the fact that they were in Spanish, a language he had begun to respect and learn. As they approached, flickering orange light from a pair of lanterns illuminated the ground in front of them. When enough light was available, he saw Dominguez sprawled a yard beyond the corner, just north of the wall extension line. The voices from the group first rose, then fell to silence as they encountered the still form. Protected by the shadow of the wall, Beckner risked going closer, and, with his body plastered against the raw adobe, peered around. Five men stopped and stared at the figure sprawled at their feet. Baca, the High Sheriff, a prominent figure even in a crowd, was not among them. Their voices had dropped to near whispers, as though in their awe and reverence for the potentially dead, they might offend the victim were he to hear, even from oblivion. One man advanced, leaned over and poked at Dominguez' torso, then kneeled and touched, though tentatively, the man's chest and brow.

He looked up at his comrades and grinned, then muttered something about blood and breathing. The others began to raise their voices, which grew from hoarse whispers, with words such as "shot," "pistol" and "horse's hooves." One man said something about *la policía*, turned and sprinted off toward the plaza. Another shouted after him, and followed apace. Two of the others began to pry and prod at Dominguez preparatory to lifting him.

When Beckner realized the remaining man was looking around as though expecting the assailant to be lurking nearby, he sidled away, then moved mincingly for the other end of the compound wall, where he turned to look back. The last of the men, with lantern held high, had moved cautiously around the corner and treaded carefully toward him. He saw no weapon, but assumed the man wielded one. Beckner turned the corner and made for his office within the compound. There, he let himself in as quietly as possible, closed and latched the door carefully, then stood in the dark of the room. He waited to ensure that no one had seen him as he slowed his heavy breathing.

Eventually he became aware of the film of starlight bracketed by the black outline of the one north-facing window. He also heard voices that seemed to come from two speakers, one louder than the other. Reddish lantern light then overwhelmed the dim, blue nighttime cast that passed through the wavy glass of the opening. Human outlines passed by; first one, then a second, as he remained crouched behind his desk. A minute later, the figures passed the other way, back toward the shooting scene, their excited jabbering unabated.

He waited a full minute, then straightened slowly in the black of his small office, still struck by the events of the evening. He felt as though reason had left him. He was suddenly extremely tired, and wished he were in bed. He leaned against his desk and tousled his hair in frustration. Then he remembered the piece of paper he had taken from the senior Landry's desk. His energy returned with that notion, he pushed away and stepped to the window, looked and listened. Satisfied the searchers and curious had departed, he found a match and ignited the lantern on the top of his desk. As a precaution, he rolled the top up and set the lamp on the desk writing surface. He sat, reached into his tunic and removed the paper.

He spread the sheet out on the desk, then looked up at the window and cut the light from the lantern by turning the wick down to its lowest. He peered hard at the paper. The message was printed in cramped pencil, and apparently in haste, with several erasures, as though the writer was uncertain of his or her message. The characters were nearly illegible in places, and looking closely didn't help. He opened the wide top drawer immediately below the writing surface and removed a magnifying glass. With it, he was able to make out the tight letters. It read: "NEED TO MEET. REAR GATE. SUNDOWN PLUS TWO. G.R."

He leaned against the seat back, scratched the top of his head and pinched up his face. Then, as he recalled discussions during training about German, Italian and British secret ink formulae, he waved the paper back and forth over the lamp chimney. Within a few seconds, a second message appeared. He held the paper up to the light. It read, "URGENT. NEED HELP! PROJECT IN PERIL. GAVILAN." Beckner scowled at the note, motionless as he read the six words and the signatory name over several times as though doing so would make everything clear. As the paper cooled, the writing disappeared. He folded it into its original pattern, returned it to his tunic, extinguished the lamp, and sat back again, which caused the chair to squeak, dry wood against dry wood. He threw both hands behind his head, blew out a lung full of air, and shut his eyes.

The window panes in the north wall went blue-white, on and off, bright, dim, bright, then dark. Less than ten seconds later, the thunder rumbled through, followed by the pelting of heavy drops on the weed-decorated dirt roof and against the thick wooden outer door.

Among his peers, who knew little of his past outside the braggadocio he proffered, Gerald Thomas Rodman was a man of solid reputation and convictions, most of which were directed toward his self-aggrandizement, particularly when it meant the difference between wealth or impoverishment. He had moved from Tennessee to Texas nine years before, bringing with him two Negro slaves, a teenaged boy and girl, unrelated to each other, four horses, roughly one hundred dollars in gold bullion, some coins and a forged letter of recommendation purported to be from a national senator. He also bore a false story about daring-do on the frontier, whose exact location was always vague, which involved Indians and bears, something he himself came to believe over time. Rodman was on the move because, among other peccadilloes, he had created a stir among his peers when he caused the pregnancy of another black slave, herself a mere fifteen. This resulted in the elder Rodman, not unlike Viking fathers of old, ordered the prodigal to seek his fortune elsewhere, but provided him with seed capital in the form of the animals, the frightened black teenagers and the precious metal.

He wound up in Austin after selling the young Blacks and all but one horse, upon which he arrived, splendid in new clothes, attendant baggage and astride a fancy saddle. His fortune grew quickly, winning the equivalent of almost a thousand dollars at cards, where he met a member of the Republic of Texas ruling elite, who, in turn, saw in him something even the arrogant Rodman himself did not. Although his acquaintance with this man availed him a position that many would have killed to obtain, it was not until some weeks later when he learned that a large part of the man's assistance came at a price: he desired Rodman for reasons that were normally restricted to members of the opposite sex. The newly-minted Texican, fearful of losing precious ground should he rebuff the man's advances, managed to humor him at the same time he avoided real contact. He was relieved when shortly after, and before his bill for favoritism came due, he received his commission and traveled west and north on his surreptitious assignment.

He was guided to Santa Fé by two traders and a member of the Texas militia in mufti, accompanied by spare horses, food, water, trade goods for Indians, and a wagon load of commodities as cover. They headed west for El Paso, then up the Rio Grande, because the risk of crossing the Llano Estacado in the off chance of running into a band of Comanche warriors in a feisty mood was too great. In addition, traders plying the Chihuahua-Santa Fé Trail were a common site, and served as additional cover.

Once in the capitol of New Mexico, and after selling the trade goods, the wagon and the draft animals, Rodman settled into his routine, palming himself off as a currency broker handling exchanges between local tradesmen, U.S. and Mexican merchants. Ensconced in a good room at the *fonda*, or inn, he found himself in relative comfort, especially with the bullion-backed stipend he received each month from Austin, and considering the fact that he was, in effect, his own man with no one to oversee him directly. Further, he was instructed to avoid any contact with the legitimate representative of the Texas Republic, soon to be admitted as a state.

Until Blakely's appearance, he had had only two contacts with other "Texican" agents, both of whom reported to him that they were secretly scouting the mineral geology of the territory, with a mind for future mining prospects. They had also been admonished to avoid the legitimate representative, in part due to otherwise well-deserved suspicion on the part of the constituted government. Then, two days before the little man's appearance, a sealed, lavender-laced letter, purportedly from a woman in San Antonio, turned up, advising him to watch for the man in the black vest, and the reason for doing so. This alone served to raise his blood pressure and heart rate, but he did not expect the outcome that Blakely anxiously delivered upon his arrival.

Rodman was now faced with a dilemma. Blakely purportedly knew people who knew other people, and he was to lead Rodman away from his idyllic life and into the dangerous, but exciting part of his mission. But Blakely was dead. Part of the little man's message was that he and Rodman were to contact someone known only as *Gavilán*—"Hawk" in English. In turn, the mysterious *Gavilán* was to bring them into the secret circle of local pro-Texas conspirators. Immediately after learning of Blakely's untimely demise, his instinct was to become involved with Sheriff Baca's investigation, but realized within seconds that to do so would draw attention to himself, the last thing he or his masters needed. He was not so concerned that either the elder Landry or Blakely were dead, rather that he might find himself under suspicion and in personal jeopardy, something that could potentially lead him to the gallows steps.

As he moved through the milling crowd of enthralled gossipers in the hotel lobby, still reeling from the events of the last evening, he opened his pocket watch and reckoned it to be nine in the morning. He made his way onto the street and to the hotel stable where he retrieved his horse. From there, he followed Evan Landry's instructions, and made his way to the Guzmán place, where he purchased a *remuda* of three mules. He responded to the rumblings in his stomach with breakfast in an off-plaza café, and came away with a parcel containing a lunch of pork *burritos* wrapped in butcher paper. After asking directions to Cañoncito, as the three pack mules trailed behind him, he wended his way through the still crowded plaza and headed east along the Santa Fé-Pecos Trail.

Beckner slept deeply, a happenstance that served to amaze him, given the sudden stress with which he was faced, and he stirred to a bright, cloudless sky. His uniform partial, tunic with the collar open, two buttons fastened down the front, his boots a dull mess, he slurped a mug of hot coffee in the mess, and grabbed a chile-laced sausage wrapped in a flour tortilla. He strode off to Middleton's office as he wolfed the ad hoc breakfast down, vaulted over scattered puddles and dodged mud splashed by passing horses and wagons. His eyes watered due to the assault on his mouth from his mobile breakfast.

The major looked Beckner up and down silently after the lieutenant rapped on the door once and entered without invitation. He returned the junior officer's perfunctory salute, then raised his eyebrows questioningly.

"Sorry to burst in, sir, but something important."

Middleton sat back and began to tap out a rhythm with his fingernails on the arms of his wooden chair. "No time to dress properly, Lieutenant?"

"Sir—"

"I realize Santa Fé could be described as a frontier settlement, Lieutenant Beckner, but discipline remains an important part of the army even in this outpost of civilization, and the young and impressionable recruits stationed here—"

"Major, sir—"

"Please allow me to finish, Lieutenant." He paused. "Thank you. Yes, this is Santa Fé, and these people here are Mexicans, many of whom are little more than ignorant peons, but all the more reason for us to look and behave our best." Middleton stood and took two steps to the window, where he turned his back to Beckner and looked out, his hands clasped behind his back.

Beckner was reminded of a drawing he had seen of General George Washington.

"We have growing discipline problems, you see. Young, impressionable farm boys lured into liaisons with these girls here—wanton, some of them. Not all, certainly, but many—"

"Major Middleton—"

Middleton pivoted, angry. "Lieutenant!"

"Sir! There's been a murder."

Middleton stared at Beckner, silent, then moved back to his desk. "Yes, I know, Beckner, a man was killed last night. Two men, in fact. And a third wounded. That pompous ass of a sheriff—what's his name?—Baca, I believe, came here this morning to inform me of it. He also said that one of the officers from the garrison was present at the scene. Of the first killing." He continued to stand, but let his eyes rove around the room, awaiting Beckner's response.

"Yes, sir, it was I, sir." He paused and frowned as the wheels in his head spun. "Wounded, sir? You said a third was wounded?"

"Yes, I did, Lieutenant. Wounded."

"I see. Do you know who?"

"Apparently one of Baca's men. Unknown assailant. Why?"

"Curious. A rather grievous night. Sir."

Middleton waited a full five beats. "Indeed. And what were you doing there, Lieutenant? At a civilian murder scene?"

"Major, as you know—"

"I asked you a simple question, Lieutenant, as provost of this post, I am—"

"Major Middleton, the Landrys are friends of mine. I was there at their invitation. To sup. But there's more to it, sir. It was the senior Landry who was shot and killed."

"Jesus Christ, Beckner, what more could there be to it?!" His voice had lowered to a feral growl.

"Well, Major Middleton, sir, I believe the murder involved our friends from Austin." Beckner had stiffened at the grilling, and his voice carried the notion, something Middleton did not miss.

The major stared at Beckner and slowly raised his chin as his eyes widened. He resumed the chair behind his desk. "I see." He sat forward, back erect, then forced himself to relax while he released his breath loudly. "And what brings you to this surmise, Lieutenant Beckner?" He paused. "You may sit, Beckner. Take a load off. You look terrible." He waved his hand in an offhand, dismissive gesture and looked away.

"I prefer to stand, Major."

"Suit yourself." Middleton took on an air of aloofness and straightened a sheaf of papers on his desk as he contemplated what he had thrust upon him.

Beckner recounted the events of the prior evening, and as he did, Middleton's demeanor softened. Half way through his recitation, the major again indicated the spare chair to the lieutenant, to which Beckner responded positively.

"So, Beckner, who is this 'Gavilán?'" Middleton leaned forward intently, as he fidgeted again with a small article from his desk.

"I do not know sir. I don't even know what the word means, but I'll find out. I want to go back to the Landry place after our meeting to see what's going on."

"Sounds Spanish. Of course." Middleton opened a drawer below the desk surface, removed a small, worn book and riffled through it. He muttered as he flipped pages back and forth, then stopped and read. He looked up at Beckner. "Hawk."

"Hawk?" Beckner raised his eyebrows.

"Hawk. Yes; hawk. Bird of prey." The major closed the book, returned it to its hiding place, and closed the drawer.

"Could be a code of some sort. Could refer to an individual. It's what I suspect."

Major Middleton agreed it was time for the younger officer to get closer to the meat of the situation by "going undercover," as Beckner termed the venture. Middleton blanched at this reference, but said nothing more than to wish Beckner luck in his pursuit. If Beckner had known, the fact was that the major was jealous. This junior officer was free to move about, involved in an important adventure at the behest of the War Department while he, a battle-hardened veteran officer, was confined to a boring, thankless desk job.

Beckner returned to his barrack room, changed into mufti, donned a neutral-color felt hat he had purchased locally, and armed himself with a short-barreled, non-military revolver which he secreted in a special pocket inside his jacket. He left his quarters, checked his office, locked the door and walked along the dirt street alongside the military compound and the palace. At the south end of the street, near the southeast corner of the palace, as he started to angle across onto Palace Avenue, he saw the man in the fringed leather jacket. He was astride a horse, leading three mules as he crossed the plaza, headed for the trail terminus. Beckner stopped, pondered with wrinkled brow, then resumed his travel, but at a quickened pace.

When he entered the Landry Mercantile, Incarnación Serna was at the counter, engaged in a sale with two women. A man nearer the entrance inspected a barrel that bloomed with shovels, rakes and hoes. Beckner halted, then moved to the east wall and its floor-to-ceiling shelves replete with soft goods, lanterns, pots, pans, crockery and flatware. There, he turned his back so the customers would be less likely to see his face, pulled the brim of his hat down another inch over his forehead, and picked up a blue-enameled steel cup. He watched from the corner of his eye as Serna finished with the women, who then exited the store, their goods tucked happily under their arms. The clerk recognized Beckner and started to move from behind the counter. The officer looked at the male customer, then, without turning full face to Serna, shook his head in a short, jerky motion. Serna stopped, looked at the customer, and moved slowly back to his former position. Another three minutes passed as the man took a shovel to the counter, paid for it and left.

Beckner went to the back of the store, where Serna took his hand and shook it hard.

"I am very glad to see you, Lieutenant." Serna's countenance was a mask of anxiety, his back bent as he worked his hands together. He retreated nervously, alternately looking at the front door and the military officer.

"Glad to see you, Incarnación." Beckner put his hand on Serna's shoulder briefly in an attempt to calm him. He looked back briefly toward the street door. "I can't stay long, in fact, I'm in a rush. Tell me, has the sheriff or his man returned?"

"Oh, yes! He was here this morning. The sheriff, Baca, he and García. They searched. Again. The sheriff, he was very angry. They tried to make us afraid. We didn't. We didn't say nothing. And we won't!" He nodded his head, then shook it heavily from side to side, his eyes closed in sincerity.

"Listen, Incarnación, there may be a message from Jesse. I don't know who might bring it, but please, if it's on paper, hide it. If it's by word of mouth, please remember details. Tell the others. But no word to anyone outside this house. Understand? ¿Comprendes? And warn the messenger to be silent."

"¡Sí, señor!" Serna's eyes went wide.

"Another question. What does the word *Gavilán* mean to you?"

Serna frowned and looked at the ceiling, then began to wave his right hand around, lifting, then looping it down, then up again. "A bird. A terrible bird that falls to the ground and kills little animals." He brought his hand down and made a grabbing motion.

Beckner tilted his head questioningly. "Like—like a hawk?"

"¡Sí! A hawk!" Serna nodded emphatically accompanied by a forced, worried grin.

"Incarnación, have you heard of someone called that? *Gavilán?*"

Serna shook his head slowly, his mouth in a severe down-turn. "No...no. Never. *Nunca.*"

Beckner nodded. "All right. Thank you." He looked toward the bright street again. "I must go. Tell Francesca and Cipriano I was here, and not to worry. I will find Jesse. He'll be safe."

Beckner started away, stopped, and turned to look at Serna. "Incarnación, when is the funeral?"

"Oh, I don't know." He shook his head and looked down, then up. "*Diós*, it should be from the mouth of his son, Jesse." His eyes began to water.

"Incarnación, I hope to see Jesse soon. He may not be able to return soon. I will ask him what he wants to do. If he cannot return, can you, Cipriano and Francesca handle it?"

Serna pondered, then nodded sadly. "We will talk to the priest. He was here today. We will, yes."

"Good. I'm sorry, Incarnación. Truly. It may have to be that way."

Serna accompanied the lieutenant to immediately short of the street door, where they shook hands as the Landry employee nervously scanned the street for observers. The officer then returned to the military compound where he retrieved his horse. This time, he eschewed the Army saddle for a civilian type.

When he rode out of the compound at a trot, he left behind a somewhat bewildered stable monitor and gate sentry, puzzled at seeing Beckner for the first time in civilian attire. When he reached the road known locally as the Pecos Trail, which doubled as the western terminus of the Santa Fé Trail, he urged his mount into a gallop.

8

*F*ive people sat at the big, thick wooden table centered in the Maestas kitchen. The somber mood was enhanced by the shadows cast by the sharp sunlight that shafted through the single, east-facing window. Jesse sat slumped in a chair at that end, his back to the lighted rectangle, which prevented the host family, all of whom faced him, from discerning his features and expression, save his outlined head and the nimbus of hair caused by the bright, mid-morning sun.

Sabino Maestas sat opposite him at the other narrow end, in the place where Filomena, his wife of thirty-three years, usually sat during meals, her station chosen to enable her to be up and down between the meal board and the modern cast-iron wood-fired stove. She now sat to her husband's left, her seat out from the table, back straight, head and face Madonna-like, as she worked her hands slowly in her wide lap as though saying the rosary with her beads, which at this moment lay on a table next to her bed. Across from her was their youngest, their son, Javier, fifteen, who resembled her in face and ample stature.

Seated next to Filomena was their only daughter, Mercedes, a svelte, pretty and budding eighteen, who resembled neither of her parents to a great extent, but who, with her clear, dark eyes, found herself feeling something more and different than sorrow for the young man from Santa Fé who sat to her left.

It was explained to the young Landry in an almost apologetic manner, that their eldest, at twenty-three, Francisco, had gone to Albuquerque for supplies, but was expected to return that evening. The elder Maestas couple did not speak of the two children who had died many years earlier, prior to those now viable. If Jesse had experienced the death of a child as they had, he would have seen the remains of that simple, wracking fact that never completely left their eyes.

Filomena felt it her bounden duty to feed Jesse, but he was able to persuade her, with profuse thanks, that he had eaten his fill earlier.

After a silence which Jesse found wearing, Sabino ventured the notion that a bit of wine would be in order. Filomena huffed that it was far too early and that it would be an insult to Evan Landry's fine memory. No, she declared as she got up, apple cider, a product of their small orchard, would be more appropriate.

Sabino Maestas, still wiry in his early-sixties, and no taller than Jesse, had skin that was not only dark, but leathery and scarred here and there, the result of working outside for most of his life. The hair on his head remained full and mostly black, with tinges of grey around the ears. His eyes were kind and reproachful, but betrayed strength and intelligence. "I knew your father before you were born." He peered straight at Jesse, then moved his head and nodded as he took the glass proffered by his wife.

Jesse thanked Filomena for his drink, raised it to all present, sipped and set it on the table.

"He came here—to Bernalillo—with his partner. A Frenchman. Alarie, I think," Maestas continued. They were looking for sheepskins to sell in Missouri. Because of him, your father, I needed more sheep, and then I made money. He also took my wool." He smiled, then sobered, as though embarrassed by this admission of having profited.

Jesse returned his smile and nodded.

Maestas shook his head. "But why would anyone want to kill your father? Who was this man?"

Jesse studied the surface of the table. "I don't know. He went there, to the store, after dark. We saw him leave. We found nothing missing." He stared blankly at his cider cup.

Maestas glanced up at Filomena, who remained standing next to him, cup in hand. "So maybe he was not a thief. But—you followed him? Then—" He scratched his head in puzzlement.

"I followed him to the inn. I should not have, I know, but I did. He went for his gun. I shot him." He lowered his head and moved it slowly back and forth. "¡Ay, Diós mío!"

Filomena lowered and shook her head as she crossed herself. Mercedes, demure in her posture, head down, peered at Jesse out of the corner of her eye, the slightest of a smile of approval on her line-free face. Javier, his jaw slack, looked from Jesse, to his parents in turn, then back at the Santa Féan.

"And you were seen?" Sabino leaned forward with an intense frown.

"Yes." He looked up. "The place was crowded. Many." Jesse fidgeted with his cup. He bit his lip and shook his head.

"And no one tried to stop you?"

"Some wanted me to wait for the sheriff, but no one stopped me. They were afraid. I had the pistol. Soon after, a crowd came to the store where my father lay. I left before the sheriff arrived."

"So they look for you?"

"I don't know. I saw no one between here and Santa Fé." He shook his head. "I have a friend. Of course, there is Incarnación, Francesca and Cipriano. They helped me. But my friend, Harold Beckner—"

"Beckner?"

"Yes. He is an officer in the Army of the United States."

Sabino sat straight up. "What?! An army officer?!"

"Yes." Jesse raised his hand, palm out. "There is no problem. He is a good friend. He helped me escape the sheriff."

"Hm. I don't like this. I don't trust the gringos and their army." Maestas sat back and worked his hand across his tight mouth.

Jesse shook his head emphatically. "No. He is a good man. A good friend. My father liked him. And they have brought order. But listen, there is more."

Maestas looked at Jesse from under his eyebrows. "Yes?"

"When I was leaving. When Harold Beckner brought my horse. The miserable cur Dominguez, Baca's deputy, found us. Behind the army corrals. It was black as pitch. He shot at us—"

Maestas leaned forward again. "Yes. And—?"

Jesse took in, then released, a deep breath and swallowed hard. "I fired back. I think he is dead." He put his hand to his head and ran it through his hair, a look of anguish across his face.

A long pause ensued while Sabino Maestas stared at Jesse. As his wife, son and daughter looked at each other and Jesse, Sabino stood and walked slowly away toward the interior door, then back, his head bowed in thought.

Jesse stood and turned toward the window. "I told Harold I would get him a message. To tell him where I am."

Filomena Maestas leaned toward their young guest. "¡Pobrecito!"

Sabino spoke to the wall, his voice controlled, but low. "This is very dangerous. You must stay here. We will hide you. We have a place."

Javier stood. "I will go."

His father turned to face him. "You will go? You will go where?!" He frowned.

"To Santa Fé. To take the message." He looked up at his father, eyes wide with sincerity.

"No, Javier! Don't be a fool. You are too young." He paused, then went to the boy and put a hand on his son's shoulder. "You are brave, Javier, but no. They would trick you. Perhaps even arrest you."

"That's true, Javier. Thank you," Jesse said. "It would be dangerous." He shook his head.

Javier's eyes still wide, he searched the faces around the room. Mercedes nodded at him, smiling.

"I will go. Or Francisco will go." Maestas paced away again.

"Pienso que todos necesitamos ir a la iglesia para suplicar al Señor." Filomena whispered. "I think we should all go to church and pray to God."

Sabino shook his head vehemently. "No, Filomena. Others might see him with us and word would spread." He pointed with his chin. "No. You go. Take Mercedes and Javier. Jesse must not be seen. Pray for the soul of our dear friend Evan Landry."

Jesse stood and took Filomena's hand. "Thank you." He looked at Maestas. "I appreciate your invitation, but I must go. If I stay here, you all would be in danger as well."

Mercedes rose and moved next to her mother. She looked at Jesse and caught his eye.

"You will be safe, and so will we. My father and Francisco are very smart. Whoever seeks you will not find you here. We have a place away from prying eyes." She waved her hand vaguely in the direction of the rest of the house.

Jesse looked at her, a pained expression on his face. "I agree to stay for a day or two, then I must go."

"Where?" Maestas asked. "The sheriff, and probably the army, are looking for you. How will you prove your innocence?" He threw out his arm to point at nothing.

"I don't know. I can't think now." He ran his fingers through his hair.

"This army officer—how do you know him?"

"He rides with me. When we guard the train. I'm in the militia. He was at dinner with father and me. We went out, to dance, to have a drink, and when we returned, we saw the man running away. He saw him, too." Jesse paused. "Another friend saw what happened at the *fonda*. Hilario Varela. Boot maker. He was a friend of my father. He will stand by me." He smiled briefly, then sobered as fear returned to his eyes. "But there is Dominguez..."

"Jesse, who is to receive the message from you?"

"Beckner. Lieutenant Harold Beckner. But it can be given to anyone in the house."

"This lieutenant, will he come here?"

"Perhaps—"

"You must rest. Filomena, go to church now. Take Mercedes and Javier. If anyone asks why you are there today, say that you pray for a cousin."

"I want to stay here with you and Jesse, papa," Javier said.

"Yes, of course. Go out and continue your work as though nothing has happened." Maestas pointed at his son. "Wait! Put Jesse's horse in the far corral. Tell no one, Javier! Understand, *hijo?*"

"*Sí, papá.*"

"Sabino, a neighbor gave me food. This morning." He pointed.

"Where? Who?"

"Tenorio."

"Consuela," Filomena said.

"Did you tell her?" Sabino asked.

"Yes. She said she would watch for the sheriff or other strangers."

Filomena nodded strongly. "She will not tell."

"I agree," Maestas said.

Filomena stood, ready to leave for the church, when she looked at Jesse. "Your father. Where will he be buried? When?"

Jesse looked down and away. "I don't know. I need—I will send a message. He should be next to my mother." He nodded, then looked at each of the four others in the room.

Filomena guided Jesse to a small bedroom where she insisted he lie down. She closed the curtains on the sole window to darken the chamber, left and closed the door. She and Mercedes then exited the house, their heads covered with black *rebosos*. Javier led Campión to the corrals in the rear of the house where he removed the saddle and other gear. He fed, watered, and quartered Campeón out of sight, close to the *bosque*.

Jesse lay flat on his back. His eyes moved wildly beneath closed lids, visions of Campeón's wide face, eyes wildly fearful, then of his father running from the mercantile into the corn field north of the *hacienda*, then young Mercedes Maestas, an aura of subtle girl perfume about her, taking him to an unfamiliar, but warm and safe emotional place, when he groaned awake to find his mouth open and saliva wetting the corners. He blinked several times, ran his shirt sleeve over his mouth, smacked his cracking lips and winked foggily at the ceiling, as his heart thumped.

He heard muffled voices rise and fall beyond the simple Z door, then silence. When they came again, he forced himself to move despite his torpor, sat on the edge of the bed, collected his thoughts, tousled his unruly hair, stood and wobbled.

As he opened the door to the hall, he realized the day had passed to late afternoon, with the sun low in the west. Through the opening to the kitchen, he saw three figures seated at the table. When he stood in the doorframe, Sabino Maestas rose halfway from his chair and motioned for him to come in.

"You slept well, I hope, Jesse." Maestas smiled broadly.

Filomena looked up, her countenance warm, then left her chair and moved toward the work counter. "You must be hungry. It is time to eat."

Jesse scratched his head and winced. "I am. I am also thirsty."

Filomena turned from the chore she had begun and fetched him a tin of water.

A young man who resembled Sabino stood and watched Jesse as he walked toward the big table.

"Jesse, this is Francisco, my son." Maestas gestured.

Francisco held out his hand, which Jesse took. The younger Maestas was taller than his father, thicker through the body, but with well-developed muscles. His visage was calm but firm, with dark, honest eyes. Jesse would learn that he was a man of few words. "*Mucho gusto.* With pleasure," he said. His smile was muted as he looked steadily into the visitor's eyes.

"*Lo mismo.* The same," Jesse replied.

The three men sat as Filomena bustled about. Jesse drank and set the tin cup on the table.

"I told Francisco what happened," Sabino began. "He wants to help."

Francisco and Jesse nodded to Maestas, then to each other. Francisco was unsmiling, but to Jesse's mind, committed.

"You killed this man, this gringo, yes?" Francisco asked.

"I did. But not before he killed my father."

Francisco's mouth was firm as he nodded his approval.

Mercedes came into the room. Sabino and Jesse looked at her, but Francisco's eyes remained fixed forward, his mouth set in the suggestion of satisfaction.

She hesitated, then went to Jesse, stopped next to his chair and smiled down at him.

"Did you sleep well? You look much better." She batted her eyes and looked him over as she caressed her hair and angled her young head to one side.

While Jesse rose half-way out of his chair in honor of her arrival, Sabino and Francisco watched her and Jesse, then traded quick glances without moving their heads.

Without turning, Filomena spoke. "Mercedes. Help me. Get the dishes." Although Filomena had not seen the transaction, subtle as it was, between her daughter and the young male visitor, her mother's and woman's instincts operated at full force.

Mercedes tossed her braids, raised her head imperiously and swished away. "Sí, mamá." Filomena turned, shot a look at Jesse, then raised an eyebrow at her husband.

Sabino cleared his throat. "Francisco will leave in the morning for Santa Fé. You must tell him where to go and whom to contact. It is best you give him a letter to carry."

Francisco watched Jesse's reaction unemotionally. "I will find this Beckner and bring him with me."

9

Lieutenant Beckner pushed his mount hard the first half mile, then reined him in to a walk and stroked the horse's neck in appreciation for his hard work. He scanned the road ahead, and saw no one save a boy of ten leading a donkey toward town with a bundle of *piñon* and cedar kindling roped to an x-shaped wooden rick holder lashed to the docile animal's back. He hailed the youngster, and in his broken Spanish, asked if he had seen a man on horseback leading a *remuda* of mules toward Cañon de los Apaches.

The boy answered, as he pointed broadly, that he had indeed, and no more than a half hour before. The lieutenant tossed the grateful minor a coin, and spurred his horse to a gallop. At the top of the ridge that overlooked the sweep of valley before the Apache cut, he stopped behind a large bushy cedar tree and peered again. He roved his eyes eastward along the trail to the narrow opening. He saw neither human nor animal, but he also knew that didn't mean none were there. He moved cautiously as he guided his horse onto the rutted trail, took a look over his shoulder, then proceeded down into the bowl-like canyon that rose to the left, and opened and stretched far to the south.

He moved slowly at first, then as the terrain sloped off onto flatter, but undulating ground, he spurred the horse to a gallop. As he approached the short, rocky, narrow defile named for the Indians famous for attacking travelers there, he slowed to a trot, then a walk. He was nervous at the possibility of encountering a horse-spooking snake or a hole that might ensnare a hoof, break a leg and end his mission suddenly and without result, not to mention the unthinkable crisis for his mount. He also kept his eyes peeled for any hint of an observer, especially on the ramparts that overlooked the canyon and its approaches. It only made sense that if the man in the fringed jacket were up to no good he would also be cautious and on guard, perhaps with confederates. When he entered the narrow, rocky pass, he slowed even further, and stayed out of the intermittent stream bed, close to the sheer, north-side canyon wall. He stopped every few yards to reconnoiter, then, when he figured he would be more obvious in the saddle, dismounted and led the horse on foot. He craned his neck to look in every direction, especially the rock-bound heights.

As he continued to move slowly and cautiously, a quarter mile past the mouth of the canyon, he had yet to see anything but the evergreen-covered slopes, the high, sheer sedimentary rock outcrops and the trickle of water that meandered along the cottonwood and willow-lined bed of Glorieta Creek. He worried that he was wasting his time. He had no good idea where his quarry was headed with the three mules. It could be much farther along the trail, and here he was, possibly wasting the day in this dangerous gorge. Perhaps his quarry had headed south. Perhaps the man was lying in wait in one of the several narrow canyons that lay to the north. And why? What were the burden animals for? His stomach tingled with unanswered questions and nervous anticipation.

High to Beckner's left a rounded hill, oddly out of place in this very angular setting, rose prominently from the canyon floor. To his right was a high ridge, then flatter terrain, then high, evergreen-covered cliffs to the line where the plane of the mesa-like structure stretched tens of miles to the south. To the north, a series of softer, rounder hills marched to the base of the Sangre de Cristo mountains. He stopped to search above, behind and ahead. It was at that moment he heard the whinnying of a horse. It echoed briefly, then died out, but he sensed that the sound came from the direction he was traveling, east. He pulled a brass field glass from a saddle bag, raised it, and spent a full minute searching, alternately with his naked eye, then with the little magnified circle the instrument provided. Finally rewarded, he reckoned the motion he spied to be about a quarter mile in front of him, partially hidden behind heat-distorted, dancing foliage. He was uncertain, but thought he saw bobbing heads and the occasional glint of sun on metal. The image was wavy with heat that rose from the sun-baked ground.

He led his horse off the trail and up a mild slope to a coppice, where he tied the reins to the trunk of a small ponderosa. He gave the patient animal a sugar treat from his pocket, then made his way back on foot. A minute later, after he picked through underbrush and around ball-shaped cedars to avoid detection, he was close enough to see the activity he had spotted through the telescope. He settled on his stomach across a flat rock and raised the spyglass again and steadied it against a small boulder.

He spotted three men, all with their shirt sleeves rolled up, hats down low in front to shade their eyes from the sun. Beckner reckoned the tallest was the man he had been following. One of the men, to his surprise, had very dark skin. He reckoned him to be a Negro. But why here and now? He had seen no one of that race in the caravan. Between them, they were in the process of removing long, narrow wooden crates from an oddly canted wagon, then strap them to the mules he had seen earlier in the plaza. Fifteen minutes later, they were finished. The lieutenant watched as they conferred, then two of the men, including the black man, collected their jackets, strapped on side-arms, mounted their horses and led the heavily-laden mules onto the trail, east-bound. The third, Beckner's target, rolled his sleeves down, folded his leather jacket, packed it into a saddle bag, pulled himself up into the saddle, and rode away in the direction from which he had come, in Beckner's direction. Beckner rolled away behind a bush and waited until the man on horseback had passed. Once he was well out of sight, the army officer made his way cautiously to the site of the stricken wagon.

It was a Murphy type, its tongue pointed westward, toward Cañoncito and Santa Fé, its rear axle broken. One wheel had three broken spokes which impaled the ground. He looked inside. The floor of the vehicle was open, planks removed, revealing a chamber beneath. Spread away from the gaping hole on the remainder of the true bottom, and in random piles, were bales and boxes that appeared to contain dry goods, utensils and other innocent domestic items. The ground on either side of the wagon was strewn with more of the same.

Beckner checked his surroundings again carefully. He listened for any sound that might indicate the approach of an observer. Satisfied that he was alone, he walked around the rear of the wagon to the side nearest the steep slope that led down to Glorieta Creek. He looked underneath the carriage. A portion of the underside had broken away, something he reckoned had occurred when the axle struck a rock or log, that broke into the wood of the hidden compartment. He scoured the area, then looked downslope. Halfway to the creek, lodged against a tree and a rock, was a crate. He retrieved the field glass and focused in on the box. He saw no markings. With a length of rope from his saddle pack lashed to the front wagon wheel, he lowered himself down the rocky, inhospitable incline to the wayward crate. As he stood at a thirty-degree angle, he wrapped the end of the rope around his waist and tied it off in a square knot. He peered over the top of the crate to look at the backside. The face nearest the rock was splintered along its length such that half the wood jutted out and away from the box. He leaned over, stretched his safety line to its limit, and managed to roll the box over, with the broken side toward himself. He finished breaking the wood, then pulled it away to reveal part of the butt and breach of a carbine. More lay alongside and behind.

He made a quick decision, and half-clambered, half pulled himself back up the steep, rocky slope to the road, untied and re-wound the rope which he returned to his saddle bags, mounted his horse, and set out at a gallop toward the hamlet of Glorieta.

At the top of the rise above the canyon behind him, he reined in his horse, turned in the saddle and peered westward toward the Apache cut. No sign of followers. A jackrabbit raced across the dual trace and disappeared in a thicket. Ahead of him, the land swept down into the area known as Glorieta. To his right, the cliffs that rose to the mesa several hundred feet above were steep and inhospitable. To his left, the valley continued with variegated geology north into the Sangre de Cristo massif. Ahead, the trail followed the path of least resistance, which included a well-defined, lesser mesa-like out-cropping of rock to the left. Well-treed, it would be difficult to see any person or animal hidden alongside the trail.

He scoured the ground in front. It was amassed with hoof-marks, but that was to be expected; he was on the Santa Fé Trail. Many were deep, caused by heavily-burdened horses, mules and burros. He heard and saw nothing, so he clicked his mount forward at a walk.

He rode another ten minutes when he thought he heard sounds other than the occasional call of a bird, and signaled his mount to halt. Then he was sure. Men's voices ahead and to the left. He dismounted, led his horse off the trail and secured him to a tree. He pulled the brass field glass from the saddle bag, then moved on foot, off the road, as he avoided noise-producing twigs and branches.

The ground was damp, grassy, and thick with cedar, *piñon* and ponderosa trees, some of which reached more than fifty feet in height, but whose branches, especially those of the *piñon*, often reached to within a few feet of the ground. They all aided his efforts at stealth. Soon he saw a cabin with a pitched roof, its walls constructed of mud-chinked logs. It sat on the gentle slope which ran to the base of the rock outcrop on the northern edge of the trail. He raised the magnifying instrument to his eye. He reckoned the dwelling to be no more than ten feet by fifteen feet. The two men he had seen at the site of the broken wagon, the white and black, were moving the crates from the mules into the hovel.

He watched as they finished moving the crates. When they completed their task, the black man lead the mules off into a more heavily-wooded area near the rock cliff, while the white unpacked equipment obviously meant for setting up camp.

The army officer stood, moved behind secure cover, and pondered the situation for a minute, then returned to his horse.

Major Middleton sat at a table by himself in the officer's mess when Beckner, still in his civilian attire, walked in, a condition that caused stares and frowns from officers seated at tables and gathered about the bar. A captain rose hesitantly to challenge Beckner. He looked first at the new-comer, then at Middleton, where Beckner's eyes were focused. The major, still seated, waved the concerned captain down.

Middleton, his eyes wide, eyebrows up as he chewed a mouthful of food, looked Beckner over as the young officer approached. He sat back and touched his lips with his napkin as Beckner sat without asking permission. He cleared his mouth, took a sip from his water glass, then spoke. "Well, Lieutenant, to what do I owe this untoward honor?"

Beckner scanned the room, then leaned in as he faced the senior officer, his arms on the table. He maintained a low voice. "Sir, we can discuss it here, but I feel it better where we will not be overheard. Your decision."

"I take it this is important, otherwise you would not interrupt my supper." The major drank again.

"It is, sir. Quite."

"So. You appear a bit the worse for wear. Been clambering about in the wilderness, have you?" Middleton used his napkin with a minor flourish.

Beckner ignored Middleton's tone and remark. "Time to involve the troops, sir."

"I see." The major paused. "Have you supped?"

"No, sir. I thank you kindly. I will do so later. I fear this situation needs more immediate attention."

"Well, to my office, then, Lieutenant. Shall we?"

Beckner stood as Middleton drained his water. "After you, sir."

As the two Union Army officers exited the mess, Beckner in stride with

Middleton, the younger and slightly taller man looked at the major. "Sir, the help I need. It's beyond the normal."

Middleton glanced at Beckner. "Oh? Of what nature?"

"In addition to troopers, I require that someone be watched. Pretty sure I know who our man is, but I won't be able to accomplish the task for the next day or two. Personally, that is."

10

Francisco Maestas was up and dressed, his face and neck splashed with cold well water, shortly before dawn.

His mother, Filomena, her maternal instincts still attuned to her children as it had been since the birth of her first, despite the fact that her eldest had not made a sound, popped awake. She rolled out of bed, careful not to alert her husband, Sabino, a heaving lump next to her on their narrow pallet. She drew on her woolen poncho, stepped into a pair of soft, Pueblo-made deer skin slippers and headed for the kitchen.

Francisco, who knew his mother would be up and fussing over his breakfast and trail food, made for the corral in the rear of the house. He watered and fed his roan, then saddled the brute. He patted his belly as he did to prevent purposeful bloating on the part of the horse, while the animal whinnied, stomped and peered around at his master in protest. He led the horse out through the gate, closed it and mounted.

As first light crept over the Sandias to the east and overtook the last of the blinking western stars, he goaded the horse around the corn and chile fields toward the river. A smaller corral of adobe and cedar sat at the edge of the *bosque*. It was here that his brother, Javier, had sequestered their visitor's horse, Campeón, the night before. Francisco checked Jesse's animal, made sure he had food and water and was not visible from the main road, and returned to the house.

After a meal of beans and pork *carnitas* wrapped in a tortilla, Francisco, his saddle bags over his shoulder, kissed his mother on the forehead as she made the sign of the cross and looked up at him with something akin to reverence. The sun was not quite past the mountain crest, but daylight bright, as Filomena's son waved to her from the saddle. He pulled the brim of his hat down over his eyes and guided the roan away from the house, then northbound onto the Camino Reál.

The air, damp from the river-fed cottonwoods, remained chilly, a condition that evaporated quickly.

By the time man and horse angled up out of the wide, flat valley of Rio Grande, they had passed two farm wagons and three kindling-laden burros coming down from the piedmont and headed for the Pueblos of Santa Ana and Zia. Francisco was keen to spot any non-Indian men on horseback, especially in groups of two or more, and more especially with firearms; even more so those headed south with glints in their eyes. Ahead, as far as he could see, the grooved trail was devoid of humans or animals.

Lieutenant Beckner, in clean and pressed campaign blue, hat properly adjusted, mounted his horse, turned and looked at the detail of seven troopers behind him, raised his gloved hand, and made the sign to move out. Sunlight was only now shafting over the rounded humps and peaks of the Sangre de Cristo Mountains above Santa Fé, and the air was chillier by at least ten degrees than that which covered the Middle Rio Grande Valley to the south.

Under special orders from Major Middleton, 3rd U.S. Infantry Provost, they had eaten breakfast, filled their canteens, arranged for three days of provisions, and requisitioned ammunition for their saddle carbines.

A ruddy-faced sergeant, his mouth hidden by a thick, handlebar mustache, the front of his campaign hat bent rakishly upward in front as a sign of his veteran status, pulled alongside Beckner. As the mounted column left the town garrison and trotted onto the road on the east side of the Palace, he looked at the officer. "What do you think, Lieutenant? Sir."

Beckner turned and glanced at the non-commissioned officer. "About what, Sergeant.?"

"Well, sir, about what we're goin' after. Who and all that." The sergeant swallowed hard and frowned as he realized the inanity of his question.

"We'll have to wait and see, won't we, Tandy?"

"Yes, sir." Sergeant Tandy faced forward as he bounced to the stride of his horse, erect in the saddle.

Beckner reconsidered his answer. He decided he needed the sergeant's undivided attention and cooperation. "Looks like there might be some illegal arms, Tandy. In the canyon. Need to find the men responsible." He looked behind, then faced around.

Tandy grinned. "Yes, sir. We'll do our damnedest!"

"I have every confidence, Sergeant." Beckner grinned privately.

Tandy turned to look at the six troopers behind. He shouted, "Look sharp, men!"

As they passed the corner of the inn which occupied the southeast corner of the plaza, Beckner thought of the two junior officers assigned to lounge around the hotel in mufti to watch the man in the fringed jacket, and hoped they were doing their job crisply. When he had explained his suspicions and requirement to Middleton the night before, he had felt as though he were risking much more than revealing his true mission. To the contrary, and to his surprise and pleasure, Middleton had not only agreed to place the young, bored officers at Beckner's disposal, but had offered to be involved as well. The major had wanted to go directly to the hotel and demand to see the register so as to identify the man who had been seen with the gun transport. Beckner had to dampen his enthusiasm and insist that to do so would more than likely alert their man as well as any others yet unidentified, and thus possibly demolish the work done to date. Middleton, deflated, but convinced, had agreed to stay aloof and let Beckner run the show as he saw fit.

The newly-recruited, ad hoc spies were told, late at night and by lamp light, that the man they were to watch and follow was suspected of unnamed criminal acts, and that proof was needed, along with possible associates. They were to be discrete, and avoid detection at all costs, even if it meant abandoning their quest. Beckner found himself unsure of their abilities, but consoled himself with the knowledge that he was doing the best he could given the circumstances. Things were progressing, he told himself.

A little more than an hour later, after taking to a gallop on and off beyond the town limits, the military detail dropped single-file down into the canyon before the Apache cut as dust rose from the horse's hooves. There had been only local farm and ranch traffic to this point, and of no concern to the men in blue, although curiosity among those who watched members of the gringo army pass was higher than normal.

Beckner halted at the bottom of the trail as it joined the valley floor, and Tandy held his gloved hand up to stop the troopers behind. He came alongside Beckner as the lieutenant scoured the ramparts in front of them through his brass telescope.

He didn't look at the sergeant as Beckner said, his voice muted, "I don't expect trouble, sergeant, but please tell the men to keep a sharp eye out for any movement, especially up there." He pointed to the rocky ledges above and on either side of Apache Canyon.

"Yes, sir." Tandy pulled at his horse's reins, then stopped and cocked his head at Beckner.

"Sir, I don't mean to pry—that is—"

"Yes, Sergeant, I think I know what you're going to ask me."

"Yes, sir."

Beckner looked at Tandy, then toward the cut. "There's a wagon in that canyon. Beyond the cut. Yonder." He pointed. "Broken down. A cache of arms—carbines—was found nearby. False bottom in the wagon. So—"

Tandy frowned. "Yes, sir. We've got some renegades, then?"

"So it would seem, Tandy. Now, since we don't know who they are or their purpose, it's best we be on our guard." He paused as his horse stomped impatiently while he stroked his long neck. "When we get to the wagon, assign two of your men to scale down to the creek bed and look for more guns or crates of same. I will continue east with the other four. Is there a good tracker amongst them?" He jerked his thumb over his shoulder.

Tandy turned in his saddle and looked back at the line of young faces staring at the two leaders. "One, sir. Jorgensen. Says he's part Mohawk. New York." He raised an eyebrow in the manner of a shrug.

Beckner turned to look, then faced around. "Very well. Send him with me. When you're through with the wagon, direct the arms crate and any others found back to the garrison with the pair, then catch me up. We'll be on the trail, but if we leave it, we'll leave sign. And Tandy—"

"Sir?"

"Everyone check their weapons before we move out." He pulled his pistol from his belt holster. "Ready to fire. But not without my order. Clear?"

Tandy nodded deeply, saluted, then turned his mount and returned to the file of soldiers.

Francisco, his canteen to his lips, drank sparingly and in short sips as he moved his head from side to side, then front and rear, as he looked for rising dust, distant figures different from the *piñon*, sage and scrub cedar that dotted the landscape, or anything in motion. He was above and away from the main trail, on part of the Ortiz Mountain piedmont immediately south of the wide, meandering Rio Saládo whose intermittent trickle ran to the Rio Grande two miles to the west. Ahead of him, after dropping down onto the flat river plane carved by the meandering stream, he would have to climb the winding road up La Bajada, the descent from the rolling plain that led to the base of the Sangre de Cristos that rose on Santa Fé's eastern verge.

He hung the canteen from the saddle pommel, then wiped his mouth and raised his eyes to the task ahead as he tore a bite from the red, chile-laced jerky in his hand. He stopped and stared, motionless. He was sure he saw a puff of dust near the top of La Bajada, near the sharp escarpment formed by black lava rock, then something moved, Yes, there is was. Not only one; possibly two—no, three. He was sure now. Four riders headed his way as they dropped down off the miles long, mesa-like structure hundreds of feet above him.

His stomach gave a twist. He had a good idea of who they were and their mission.

At the top of the rise where Beckner had stopped to reconnoiter the day before, he halted his four-man detail. As he had then, he looked back down the trail. He saw Tandy as he directed two of the troopers who prepared to rappel down the slope to the creek bed. He faced around, then signaled the men with him to follow single-file and with hand gestures to stay on the lookout.

As they approached the place where he had hidden his horse before, he halted, dismounted, and bade the men do the same. He gathered them in a circle, then whispered his commands. "The cabin up there is our target." He pointed. "Spread out. You two, go that way. You, that way. I'll take the center. We'll circle. Drop down at ten yards and await my signal."

Trooper Jorgensen asked, "What're we a-lookin' fer?"

"Two men, possibly more. Armed. Watch for mules and any surprises left and right. You're not to shoot unless they fire first. If they're there, I'll negotiate. Understood?"

All nodded assent.

"All right, move out. Quietly!"

Two of the soldiers crept off to the right, while the other pair moved to the left, all with their carbines at the ready. Beckner started out as well, his pistol pointed forward at hip level. When they were all in place, and Beckner had signaled to wait, he moved forward cautiously, one careful step at a time.

The cabin proved to be empty, a condition which in no way surprised the lieutenant.

As he stood in the shade of the empty cabin, the men milled around, and in and out. One of them stared, agape at the dusty, debris-strewn interior.

"What'd we expect here, Lieutenant?"

"There was a report of some illegal arms." Beckner turned and walked out into the light.

Jorgensen came up to him. "Had a look that-away, sir."

Beckner peered hard at him. "Yes?"

"Looks like four or more animals. On the trail. Only they ain't all horses."

"No?"

"No, sir. Looks like mules, too."

Beckner nodded. "Good, Jorgensen." He turned to the other men. "Mount up, men. We're going to see what we can see from here on." He returned his attention to Jorgensen. "How long ago, Jorgensen? Can you tell?"

Jorgensen pulled his hat off, scratched his head and made a face. "Ground's damp from the rain last night. I reckon this mornin'. Maybe near sunup. Fire's been out about that long." He put his hat on and adjusted it.

Beckner nodded in satisfaction. "Means they're a couple of hours ahead. But moving slowly. We can overtake them."

As they made their way back to the horses, they raised their heads at the sound of another horse coming from the west.

Sergeant Tandy rode up to Beckner and halted. "Sir."

"Sergeant." He looked up at the ruddy-faced, mustachioed man who stared down at him from the saddle.

"Only the one crate, sir. Sent it back with Baxter and Cohen." He was breathless.

"I fervently hope that all carbines are accounted for when we return, Sergeant."

"Them two 'er reliable, sir." He jerked his thumb. "'Sides, I tole 'em if any were missing they'd be needin' new hide. Yessir."

Beckner nodded. "Good."

"What'd you find here, Lieutenant? Anything?"

"They've moved on, Tandy, but we're going to give chase." He paused, then looked in Jorgensen's direction. "Jorgensen!"

The trooper turned and came up to the officer. "Yes, sir?"

"Jorgensen, take to horse with dispatch and follow that mess on the ground. You can move faster by yourself. If you see the track leave the trace, fire a single shot. We'll be along. If you don't see us by the time the sun's noon high, head back. We'll rally then."

"Right, sir!" Jorgensen ran for his horse, mounted, and was off at a gallop.

Beckner stood with his hand to his chin. "Tandy."

"Yessir?"

"Tandy, take your most experienced man from this group and head back along the trail."

"Sir?" He frowned in obvious disappointment.

Beckner reacted to his expression with a smile. "No concern, Sergeant. You'll like this."

"Sir?"

"When you get to Apache cut, follow the creek southwest. Head for Tijeras Canyon east of Albuquerque as fast as you can. Go behind the mountain. Know the route?"

"Yes. Been over it twice."

"Good. You have food and water."

"The three days rations we left with."

"Of course. Uh, when you get to the canyon, set up—out of sight—and watch the road in."

Tandy's face lit up with a wide grin. "I understand, sir! You figure them renegades 'er headed 'round the mountain fer Albuquerque, right?"

"That's correct, Sergeant Tandy. And do us both a favor. Stop referring to me as sir all the time."

"Sir?"

"Please." He looked at the sergeant from under his eyebrows.

"Yes, si—Lieutenant."

"Thank you, Tandy." Beckner paused and studied the ground. "Now, if you spot them, and I think you will, I want you to follow them. Remember everything you see and hear. I'll need to debrief you later. But be damned careful. When you reach Albuquerque, whether they've settled or not, send your man back to tell me. All right. Be on your way."

"Right." Tandy saluted smartly and turned to look at the three remaining men.

"Tandy!" Beckner followed the sergeant.

"Lieutenant?"

"Your man. Make sure of this." He waggled a finger and lowered his voice as he came close and looked up. "Tell him that I, and *only* I, am to receive this message when you spot the gun runners. Is that clear? Under pain of courts martial."

"Absolutely." Tandy nodded, his lips compressed, eyes filled with excitement.

Beckner became reflective.

Tandy frowned. "Sir? Lieutenant?"

"You're going to need money." He reached for his belt pouch, opened it, fished around, then produced several pieces of paper and some coins. "Scrip. If this doesn't work, buy what you need with this."

"Gold?"

"Indeed it is Sergeant. For contingencies such as this." He smiled.

Tandy touched his cap. "Thank you, Lieutenant Beckner."

Beckner became contemplative again. He scrubbed his chin. He looked up at Tandy again. "Tandy."

"Yes, Lieutenant?"

"On second thought, Tandy, whether you spot our quarry or not, one or both of you go on to the encampment west of the town. Tell the officer in charge you are on orders from HQ in Santa Fé; that you've been looking for a man—let's see—absent without leave. That you've lost his trail and you're to await for an officer—me—to follow. Do not tell them your true purpose. Is that clear?"

"Yessir, Lieutenant Beckner."

"In other words, wait for me." Beckner started to turn away, then looked up again. "Tandy—who's going with you?"

Tandy looked behind, then down at the officer. "Private Milton, sir."

"Good choice. Luck to you both, Sergeant." Beckner threw the NCO a sloppy salute.

The sergeant turned away, new enthusiasm in his demeanor.

Francisco Maestas did not have to urge his horse down onto the wide, flat, meandering Rio Saládo which passed through the Pueblo of Santo Domingo on its way to the Rio Grande. The animal smelled the moisture that transpired from the thickets of ditch willow and Russian olives that lined the intermittent flow. His master walked the mount along the edge of the sparse stream until they found a puddle containing relatively clean water, and the horse was able to slake his thirst.

As man and horse rose from the river bed onto the plain which led to La Bajada, Maestas discerned not faces, but body size and horse shade of the four riders who approached. He also saw that they were armed, their saddle carbines and long-barreled pistols prominent. One of the men, on the lead mount, was large—almost too large for his horse. Their saddle bags bulged, and blanket rolls graced the horses' rumps behind each saddle, which signaled the intent to remain on the road for more than a day.

Five minutes passed before the group came alongside.

The big man in front reined his horse around so that it blocked Maestas' path. "Good day to you, young man." Sheriff Baca spoke in Spanish. His eyes were shaded by the wide brim of his expensive hat.

"*Buenos días,*" Francisco Maestas answered.

Baca leaned forward in the saddle, such that his arms rested on the pommel, reins held loosely in his left hand. He took another five seconds before he spoke, as he spent the time studying Francisco's face. "Come far?"

"Who asks, and why?" Maestas looked at Baca with unflinching eyes. His horse danced.

Baca turned to look at the other men, two of whom clicked their mounts forward a few feet. He looked at Maestas, again, one eyebrow up. "I ask, boy. And I ask because I want to know."

"First, I am not a boy. I am a man. And who might you be? Why do you make it your business to learn of my travels?" Maestas rocked his head from one side to the other in obvious annoyance. He sat up straight in the saddle and sucked in his breath as his tension rose.

Baca chuckled, looked at his right boot, then up. "I am the High Sheriff. Of Santa Fé."

Maestas shrugged. "That fact has no meaning for me. This, sir, is not Santa Fé." He swept his arm in a wide arc, looked at the sky, then back at Baca.

Baca nodded, smiled, looked at the ground, then up. "You are quite correct, sir. You are indeed a man, and you are under no obligation to answer my question."

He paused. "I will ask another question, and more politely. Perhaps, after reflection, you will answer." He had lowered and moderated his voice.

"Ask and I will consider your request."

"Mm, yes." Baca smiled ruefully at Maestas' fearlessness. "Have you, by chance, seen a young man, a *coyote*, on a grey horse? Travel this way?" Baca pointed vaguely in a southerly direction.

"*Coyote?*" Francisco peered at Baca with one eye closed.

"Half gringo. Headed south. Possibly through Bernalillo." Baca pulled his hat off his head and scratched it vigorously.

"I assume you seek him. Is he accused of some foul deed?"

"He is guilty of murder. And of wounding another."

"And if I should see this fellow, although that would be difficult, since I am traveling north, with whom should I speak? You?"

"Or any of these men, or my deputy in Santa Fé. Dominguez." Baca gestured broadly.

Two of the other men nodded as all three scowled at Maestas.

"I would be most happy to oblige you, should I, if ever, see this man." With that, Francisco reined his horse away and clicked him forward to circle the group that faced him.

He had gone two lengths when Baca called out to him. "May we know your name?"

Maestas halted, and without turning, hesitated, then said, "Maestas."

"I don't recognize you. Do you live in Santa Fé?"

Maestas looked over his left shoulder as his horse agitated. "No."

"Where, then?" Baca's voice had become insinuating.

"El Llanito. Why do you ask or care?"

Baca chuckled, then shouted, "No reason, my friend. Only curiosity." He waited a count of three. "But I will ask you to warn any of your neighbors who might wish to harbor this fugitive that they, too, will be considered guilty of his crime."

Maestas looked straight ahead, but did not stop. "Of course." He then spurred his horse.

11

Beckner had instructed Incarnación Serna that if he or another member of the Landry household were to receive a message or a visitor with information from or about Jesse Landry, the manner in which he, Beckner, was to be contacted. Serna, or a trusted associate, was to leave a sealed note for him with the town garrison duty officer saying that an order he had placed for a personal item had arrived at the mercantile. With a voice message, it would be a particular article; should there be a visitor, it was to be a different item. In the event that a paper message came, it was to be firmly secreted; if oral, then remembered well by at least two Landry loyalists.

It was after sundown and nearly dark when the lieutenant, although dusty, fatigued, hungry and thirsty, made sure the three remaining enlisted men of the detail were fed, and his mount was cared for by the garrison horse stewards. He had admonished the troopers to keep to themselves, under penalty of courts martial, the essentials of what they had done and seen that day, and to advise those who had returned with the wayward crate to do the same. They would all, on the other hand, receive additional pay and be granted special leave for their cooperation, a promise Beckner made without authority, but which he was sure he could gain from Middleton with little ado. He admonished them that to thwart his wishes and those of the United States Government could play against all in the form of general insurrection, even warfare, and for them personally, certain pain.

Jorgensen had rendezvoused with the party that afternoon with the advice that, in his considered opinion, the renegades had most likely headed south over the great Glorieta Cuesta. They had heard his single shot and caught up with him as he headed back. Beckner felt sure they had re-routed the arms to Albuquerque, and that Sergeant Tandy and Private Milton would haunt them to their destination.

In his barrack room, he removed his shirt and trousers, washed his face and hands in the bowl on his night stand, dressed in mufti, and left for the headquarters building. He determined to eschew the officer's mess, in part because little besides cold scraps would be left at this late hour, and because he felt he deserved and needed the company of rowdy civilians in a noisy, smokey *cantina* where he would find solace in hot, spicy food, strong drink and the roving, interested eyes of rosy-cheeked *señoritas*. But on his way, and by agreement, he would report to Major Middleton. Almost as an afterthought, he detoured to the desk of the duty officer. There was indeed a message for him. Someone connected with Jesse had shown up at the house.

Middleton came to the door of his quarters wearing nothing but his uniform trousers, suspenders down, loose white undershirt, socks, and he carried a book. His initial frown turned to a smile when he saw the lieutenant. "Ah, Beckner. Enter."

Beckner thanked the senior officer, then took the straight-back chair indicated.

"So, what'd you find, Beckner?" Middleton sat on the edge on his bunk and put the book aside, pages open and down.

"The renegades were gone, of course. Men and guns, both. The single crate of carbines they lost is within our midst. And safe. I dispatched Sergeant Tandy and trooper Milton to watch the canyon east of Albuquerque. In case our quarry traveled that way."

"Good. Fine strategy." Middleton nodded his assent.

"To me it appeared they were headed that way. They're to follow the renegades discreetly and wait for me at the western outpost. The dragoons."

"Excellent, Lieutenant." Middleton swiped at his wayward hair.

"Sir, any news from Townsend or Carruthers?"

"Our watchers? Only that our man is still here. He took his midday meal and supped at the hotel. No visitors as far as they could determine."

"I see." Beckner stroked his chin. "Is he watched now?"

"They're spelling each other. I don't know which. Could be difficult at night."

"Yes, indeed, sir."

"What do you expect?" The major cocked his head.

"If he leaves for Albuquerque, it might confirm my notion about the destination of the arms and their purpose."

"Yes, yes. Most likely so." Middleton paused and nodded sagely. "Then what?"

"If Tandy can track the armaments, we may be able to find who—here in the territory—is working with our friend."

"Mm, yes."

"It appears as though someone has arrived with a message from Jesse Landry. I should speak with him." Beckner rose. "I'll check with our man at the hotel first."

Middleton stood and stretched by raising his arms above his head. "All right, Beckner. Keep me posted."

"That I will, Major."

Despite increasing hunger and desire for a stiff drink, Lieutenant Beckner crossed the plaza and entered the lobby of the inn. Two women and an equal number of men were seated in velveteen chairs as they conversed above the chatter. Across from a gambling table, a gaggle of people, principally men, were gathered about the bar and an upright piano, which was being hammered by a man who, in Beckner's opinion, could stand a few more lessons. From another room, he heard the click of billiard balls and a shout from a man who had apparently made a good shot. He looked about, but was unable to see either of the two junior officers. Then he felt someone tap on his shoulder. He turned.

"Hello, sir." Carruthers smiled. He was slight, an inch shorter than Beckner, with smooth, light brown hair that swept down to his collar.

Beckner scanned the noisy room briefly, then looked at Carruthers as he received his hand preparatory to shaking it. "Evening, Carruthers." He lowered his head, leaned into the other man and spoke softly. "Let's avoid using military greeting." He then raised his head, stood back, and shook hands broadly.

"Of course." Carruthers also looked about self-consciously. "Of course. A libation, perhaps?"

"Although I have a goodly thirst, not now, Carruthers. Another engagement awaits." He spoke in competition with the cacophony, then lowered his voice again. "But tell me; what of our mark?" He peered hard at the younger man.

Carruthers drew in a deep breath. "Stays put, as far as we can determine. Eats in the mess—restaurant—here. No visitors we could ascertain."

"Is there not a back door to this place?" Beckner jerked his head to point roughly.

"True, but that's the only path to his room." Carruthers pointed with his chin toward a hall door.

Beckner turned, glanced, then returned his gaze. "No rear way? Sure?"

"Only for the latrine—the necessary." Carruthers shook his head.

"Mm. When are you to be relieved?"

"At midnight." Instinctively, he pulled a chain-draped watch from his vest and flipped it open.

"All right. I'll leave now. I'll have a peek at the back of this place."

They clasped hands again as Beckner surveyed the faces in the room for any sign of interest. He detected none. Carruthers moved nonchalantly to the hallway and looked in, then away.

Beckner walked around to the rear of the hotel where it became increasingly dark as he approached the narrow alley, save for flickering amber light from an occasional lantern carried along the street at either end, along with damped light from two hotel room windows along the alley that separated the main structure from the stables and the outhouses. Despite the deep shadows, he was able to make out an indentation in the long adobe wall. After ensuring he was alone, he tried the thick wooden door. It gave inward easily, and without noise. Inside, a short passageway was lit with a wall-mounted taper. He was instantly assailed by the vague, but distinctive, odors of corn meal, hot animal fats and strong liquors. Voices, part jabber, part laughter ricocheted down the hall. He looked back, then tread carefully to the end of the passage way. A kitchen, pantry, modern wood-fired cook stove and aproned workers, greeted his eyes. Carruthers' information appeared to be correct.

The lieutenant made sure he was not followed or watched as he circled behind the massive east wall of the Romero manse to the north side access at the rear of the Landry compound. He waited a full minute in the starlit darkness, then carefully slipped through the personnel door cut into the wagon gate. There, he waited again to assure himself he was not observed. From there, he went to the back door of the mercantile and rapped on it.

Incarnación Serna opened the door slowly and timorously, enough to see who had knocked, then wide as he recognized the visitor. He held up a finger with a smile to signal the military officer to wait, then doused the counter lamp and led Beckner to the house, the portable lantern in hand.

Serna opened the outer door to the kitchen and stood aside to let Beckner in. Across the room, Francesca worked diligently at what she liked best, preparing food. Her sleeves were rolled back, and her portly midriff and ample chest were protected by a large apron. She turned, an apprehensive look on her face as the door opened, but broke into a broad grin when she saw who followed Serna.

Beckner acknowledged her wordless greeting and returned her smile as she made a bee line for him. She nearly crushed him as she rose on her toes to award him a warm hug and a kiss on the cheek. Tears welled in her eyes as she stepped back.

Seated at the big table centered in the room with food in front of him, was a man Beckner did not recognize, but whom he suspected was the messenger. Francisco, who chewed with a big calico cloth napkin draped from his collar, looked up, nodded, then scraped his chair back, stood and waited as Lieutenant Beckner strode to greet him.

"Lieutenant Beckner, U.S. Army." He took Maestas' hand as both men reached across the table.

"*Soy Francisco Maestas de Bernalillo. Con mucho gusto.* I am pleased to meet you."

Beckner waited as he expected Francisco to say more about why he was here, but he was silent. "Do you come with word about Jesse? Jesse Landry?" He looked around as Serna quietly closed the outer door to the courtyard.

Maestas nodded. "Yes."

Francesca interrupted. "Lieutenant Beckner, sit. You must be hungry. You must eat. Sit. Please." She pointed to a chair near their visitor, a matronly look on her face, then turned to Serna. "Wine. Get some wine for our guests."

Serna left the room for the *atrio*, the cool wine room and the wooden barrels and bottles inside.

"Thank you, Francesca, I will. I'm famished. Thank you." Beckner sat, then realized as he did that he was most likely the only one in the room who understood the word he had used for hunger beyond the ordinary.

Maestas took the opportunity to take another bite, then said, "Along the way, below La Bajada, I met Baca, the sheriff, and three of his men. They had guns. They are looking for Jesse Landry. They did not say his name, but I knew. They called him *coyote*." He looked up at Francesca, who tried to suppress a worried look as she placed a plate, bowl and utensils in front of the army officer.

Beckner ruminated for a second, then said, "It figures."

"*¿Qué?* What?"

"It was not unexpected. I expected that to happen." Beckner created a hand gesture for emphasis. "The word *coyote*. What does that mean?"

"Ah. *Grácias.*" Maestas nodded in understanding. "*Coyote* is for someone who is both gringo and Hispano. Spanish. Mexican." He nodded.

"I see." Beckner began to tuck into one of Francesca's chicken enchiladas as Serna entered with a jug of red wine and set it on the table along with two crockery mugs. When Beckner had consumed a second helping and drank most of a glass of red wine, he sat back, sated. He looked at Maestas with a satisfied smile and shook his head. "Wonderful. I like it better every day."

Francesca, busy cleaning up and her back to the army officer, cleared her throat self-consciously.

"Thank you, Francesca. My intent was to dine at a *cantina*, but this is superior." He talked to her back. "Far better." He followed with the Spanish, "*Mejor.*"

Maestas looked at Beckner, then Francesca, smiled and looked down at his empty dishes.

Beckner had been in the region long enough to know that among the native Hispanics, there was an unwritten rule about when to talk and when not to. Although anxious to learn about Jesse, he waited until he felt that both he and Maestas were warm, calm and connected enough to discuss the problem at hand. He pushed his chair back several inches, sipped at the last of his wine, then said, "So, Francisco, please tell me of Jesse."

Maestas related everything he knew, including the fact that Jesse was concerned about his own safety and that of the Maestas family for harboring him. Beyond that, he was intensely curious about the events that led to Jesse's flight and his fear of capture. Maestas' final words concerned Jesse's father, Evan, and his funeral. Incarnación, Cipriano and Francesca assured Maestas that they would follow Jesse's wishes and arrange for a decent funeral in his absence. Evan was to be interred next to his deceased wife.

Beckner wasn't sure how much he should take this stranger, or the others in the room, into his confidence. Thus, he feigned a certain amount of ignorance, but told of the circumstances leading up to Jesse's escape. It was predominantly honest, because he himself was unsure of the dynamics which had led to the tragedy in which they were now embroiled. What he couldn't say was how he truly fit into the picture, or that he now had suspicions about the elder Landry's involvement with the man whom they were watching at the hotel. In the recesses of his mind, that also led him to have doubts about Jesse and those around him as well. He tried to perish those thoughts. He would wait and see.

Maestas was interested in why Beckner was not in the blue uniform of the army, and why he was willing and able to help in this case. The lieutenant explained that although the sheriff had jurisdiction over Santa Fé and environs, the army, which represented the U.S. Government, was required to look into all potentially criminal cases that occurred within the Territory. That went double for any that exceeded the authority of sheriffs. Beckner, when telling this, hoped his partial lie would not be betrayed by his body language to the stoically clear and steady-eyed Francisco Maestas. He added emphatically the fact that he was Jesse's friend, and that counted for much. Maestas merely nodded and appeared satisfied by the explanation, but Beckner knew full well that suspicions ran deep and wide with the locals when it came to gringos of any stripe, especially those who were part of what they considered an army of occupation.. Beckner would have to earn this man's trust.

They both agreed that haste was imperative; Maestas, in no small part because of his encounter with Baca and concern for his family; Beckner for professional reasons having to do with the arms shipment, and a genuine worry for his friend. They would meet as soon as possible the following morning after exiting the town independently. Maestas would wait on the plain before the trail dropped onto La Bajada. Beckner would be there after taking care of certain business at the garrison.

Francesca Anaya arranged for a bed for Maestas for the night, then fed him breakfast and provisioned him for the ride south. He was out the rear gate after Serna and Cipriano Anaya checked for spies, then, with the Landry employees' advice, Maestas circled north of the town. He kept low to avoid the curious. The sun was barely above the mountains.

Beckner arose at dawn, took breakfast in the officer's mess, then strode off to the inn on foot before reporting to Middleton. Second Lieutenant Townsend stood in the shadow of the entrance. He wore a long coat against the morning chill, when Beckner approached him.

Townsend, a tall, thin youth with a shock of blonde hair swept back from his forehead, stepped out to greet Beckner. "Sir, I think he's slipped away."

Beckner held up his hand and checked the empty streets and plaza behind him. "First, Townsend, no military greeting!" He took in a sharp breath. "Now, how do you know he's gone?"

"Not absolute, Lieu—Mr. Beckner—but we haven't seen 'im, and I sneaked over to his room and listened."

Beckner took two steps away, hand to chin, then returned. "That wouldn't prove much. Could be asleep."

"Correct. But I also talked to the room maid. She said he'd checked out." Townsend held out his palms in a plaintive gesture and swallowed hard.

"Damn, Townsend! Why didn't you come to me with this?!" Beckner screwed up his face.

"Because you said we were to stick with it regardless. Sir." He looked around to see if anyone could have overheard him.

Beckner sighed. "Right. Indeed, I did say that." He shook his head in self-disgust, looked down at the dirt street, around, then back at the youthful officer.

"However—"

"Yes?!"

" I was able to sneak a look at the register."

"You did!? Yes? Unobserved?"

"Yes."

"And?"

"A man named Rodman checked out around two this morning."

"Rodman!?" Beckner paused, frowning. "Where were you!?"

"Outside. The necessary. Didn't figure I'd be missed for ten minutes at that ungodly hour."

"Indeed. And of course we don't know where he went."

"No, we don't. I surely don't." Townsend rubbed his weary face.

Beckner looked at the other officer hard, his mouth compressed in frustration. He reached out and squeezed Townsend's shoulder. "Good job, Townsend. Get some rest. You're relieved."

"Lieutenant Beckner, what's going on here? I'd like to help."

"Yes, of course. Look, I can't tell you everything at this time, but you can help. You and Carruthers. Continue to stay in civilian clothes. Move around town. Watch for this man. If you see him, get that information to Major Middleton immediately."

"And you, sir?"

"I must be off. Should return in a matter of days. You and Carruthers will have to be my eyes and ears. Does that suit?"

"Indeed it does." Tired but happy, Townsend smiled broadly.

"Townsend."

"Yessir?"

"Before you eat and take to your cot, report all this to the major. And tell him I'm off to the south, and of my instructions to you."

"Indeed I shall, Lieutenant." Townsend started to salute, then restrained himself.

Francisco Maestas was where he said he would be, at the top of the trail before it dipped down into the wide, sweeping Rio Grande rift valley along the treacherous, lava rock-lined La Bajada. He sat on a large black rock, his hat down over his eyes as he nibbled a piece of jerky. His patient horse stood near him, reins draped on the dun-colored grassy ground.

The two men nodded to each other, then Beckner dismounted, reached into a saddle bag and pulled out a holstered pistol on a belt. He handed it to Maestas, who had risen and gathered his horse's leathers.

Francisco took the gun with a frown of surprise, studied it for a few seconds, then looked up. "¿*Que es este?* What is this?"

"*Para ti.* For you. We may run into trouble." Beckner was surprised at his own ability to remember that much Spanish, abbreviated as it was.

"But—"

"For you to keep, Francisco. I want you to have it. It's not new, but it shoots." He turned to the saddle bags. "It's loaded. More ammunition here." He removed a small pasteboard box and handed it to the astonished man.

Beckner avoided Francisco's gaze for awhile, since he realized the man was overwhelmed with the valuable gift and was speechless. He hoped he hadn't insulted him somehow, and didn't know if he should say anything else in a clumsy attempt to offset the perceived feelings. He mounted, and without a look back, clicked his horse forward.

The two men rode for the first hour with few words, first at a walk as they descended to the Rio Salado. Then they picked up the pace, alternately at a gallop and a walk, so as not to tire the horses. It was in the second hour, after they had taken sips of water and a few bites of the plentiful food provided by Francesca, who had instructed Francisco to share with Beckner, that they began to relate their life stories to each other.

Maestas told of his parents' loss of two children before his arrival, how they had struggled in the early years, but how Evan Landry and his business associates had elevated them from poverty. He had learned what little English he spoke by helping with his father's business and his dealings with the "Americano" traders who came more often to be called gringos after the Mexican War.

Beckner peppered him with questions about the local lore, the geography and climate of the land, and the nature of the towns and villages. He was especially curious about the Pueblo peoples who lived along the Great River and its tributaries. Maestas offered to introduce the lieutenant to two or three of the Pueblo people he knew and with whom he did business.

Beckner's new and growing closeness with the Landry staff and Francisco Maestas was fostering an increased admiration of, and affection for, these tough, resilient people, many of whose ancestors had come with the Spanish *Conquistadores*. He felt comfortable in telling Maestas of his family, childhood, upbringing and schooling, and how he had come to join the army. Maestas listened raptly, and asked questions about the rest of the country, what the lieutenant had seen on his way to the Territory, and about the cities, towns and people of the East. By the time they reached the heights above El Llanito, both men felt comfortable with each other.

Maestas was anxious for his family to meet this "good gringo" as he secretly caressed the firearm he now wore proudly on his hip, even as he still harbored suspicions about all of these taller, fair-skinned people with the fast-roving eyes and impertinent ways.

They had passed two wagons headed north with hay and other produce, as well as three moving in their direction. Francisco talked with both north-bound parties, then translated what had been said. Both drovers had told of how they had heard of the sheriff and his men. One had been accosted by Baca and grilled about the young *coyote* from Santa Fé. They had honestly related to the peace officer that they knew and had heard nothing of such a man. Typically, something Francisco related to Harold Beckner, was that his friends and neighbors would never give over someone, even a *coyote*, who had snuffed out the life of a gringo *Tejano* without good and powerful reason.

It was mid-afternoon when they came within sight of the Maestas house.

Beckner stopped under a cottonwood and beckoned Francisco. "Francisco, it's best you go on ahead. I'll hang back and wait for you to let me know when to come to the house. May be better if I wait until dark."

Maestas studied the ground, then looked up and nodded. "Yes. See that road there?"

Beckner looked. "Yes."

"Go along there, to the *bosque.*" He pointed with his chin. "There is a small *edificio* where we store some of our crops and keep horses." He rocked in the saddle as his horse moved. "You will be safe and no one will see you. There is water and feed for your horse. I will come for you." He started to move off, then reined his horse around and returned to Beckner's side. He reached into a saddlebag, pulled out a small, cloth-covered bundle that had been provided by Francesca, and handed it to the officer. "Should you become hungry. *Si tienes hambre.*" He nodded and clicked his horse away.

Beckner looked after him, his face marked with pure amazement.

12

Beckner found the little *edificio* Francisco had described as he lead his horse on foot and watched his back periodically. It was at the edge of the cottonwood *bosque*, composed of an adobe hutment adjoined to a stripped cedar corral. The adobe portion, the tops of its walls worn from rough use by large animals and the ravages of weather, was covered, lean-to fashion, with more stripped cedar chocked with mud and covered with six inches of dirt, netting a protected area the size of his own mean barrack cell. In that shaded space, the lieutenant spied an ample mound of hay.

He unsaddled his mount, after which the horse made his way to the water trough carved from a single thick split of mountain pine trunk. He took hay to the animal, then entered the hut and lay back on the feed. In less than a minute, he was asleep.

His welcome, dreamless slumber was interrupted by the faint sound of the approach of someone or something other than his horse. Although he found it difficult to open his eyes, and was surprised at himself for not leaping to his feet, Colt's pistol at the ready, he sensed somehow he was not in danger. The next sound was that of rustling cloth and the faint smell of something that smacked of women's perfume. He felt something press into his calf.

He blinked open both eyes, jerked his head up and away from the straw, as his knees came up and his arms pulled back to support his weight on the raw earthen floor. Bent over him, with enough light from the late afternoon sun to illuminate her, was to him in that instant, the prettiest girl he had ever laid eyes on.

"¿Señor?" Mercedes' eyes were wide and her mouth opened in a stance combined of fear and curiosity. She straightened and took a step backward, arms defenselessly at her sides.

"Hello," was all Beckner could utter. He gathered himself after a pause during which he shook his sleepy head, then leaped up, kept his eyes on the girl, and brushed himself off self-consciously, which produced puffs of dust and pieces of falling straw. He blurted, "Beckner. Lieutenant Harold Beckner. At your service, ma'am." He immediately felt the fool. At least, he didn't salute, he thought.

"*Soy Mercedes. Maestas.*" She folded her hands across her hip line and awarded him a faint, demure smile.

Beckner could only nod and smile, his voice gone, as he stared at her. He recovered, then looked around as though searching for something. He realized there was nothing for hin to find, looked at her again, and said, "Well—"

"I have come to take you. To the house." She pointed vaguely as she looked the gringo officer over, and found herself engaged in emotions she was unaware were possible. "*Mi hermano, Francisco*—My brother, he asked me for you to come. To the house. He is away. He will return. Soon." She stood stock still for a few seconds, then turned and said, "Please, come." She waved her beckoning hand at waist level.

Beckner walked beside her to the house, along the narrow wagon trace that paralleled the corn and chile field. At first speechless, he tried to make small talk as they went, and was nearly destroyed each time he looked at her, taken with her genuine, open smile and the manner in which her eyes lured him. By the time they reached the house, Harold Beckner had nearly forgotten why he had come to this place. What he did know, subconsciously and instinctively, was that he would never return to his east coast home—at least to remain. He was where he belonged; rooted.

Mercedes Maestas also realized, subtly if not overtly, that her life had changed. Her initial encounter with this handsome outlander had affected her in a way nothing had before. She felt an urge the burgeoning woman in her understood full well, but that the child—the girl—in her did not. Jesse's image, although fresh and intriguing, faded against this new one. Should she tell her mother, her one true confidant? No. She must not. For the moment, no one would know. It would be her delicious secret. More to the point, it would become her goal. Why were these thoughts racing through her mind? She felt momentarily dizzy with these realizations.

Filomena Maestas, Mercedes' mother, stood in the doorway as her daughter and Beckner approached the house. Beckner slowed and hesitated as he braved a smile. Mercedes advanced, then looked back at him. Filomena, her female and maternalistic antennae out and respondent, perceived immediately that something was transpiring between Mercedes and this tall, young gringo. On the one hand, it did not please her, yet there was also a side of her, something very fundamental, that approved. She shook the thought off quickly, and moved her cogitations to more mundane issues.

Jesse stood in shadow behind Filomena, and when she stepped aside after allowing Mercedes to enter and pass him, the two young men greeted each other with enthusiasm. Their instincts were to hug and slap each other, but decorum prevailed, and they confined themselves to a hearty handshake. Beckner backed away while Jesse introduced him to Filomena in Spanish. Her husband, Sabino, aroused by the commotion, entered the room with a broad smile. He, too, shook Beckner's hand with gusto.

Beckner mumbled the Spanish phrase for greeting, but felt awkward. He also found himself studying the elder Maestas for another reason, and that invoked an odd, but not unpleasant shock to his innards.

As they were half way through their evening meal, the kitchen aglow with candles and a modern oil lantern centered on the table, Francisco returned. Beckner rose and shook his hand as his mother served him from the stove. Before sitting, Francisco unbuckled the gun belt Beckner had given him and laid it on a side table.

"The sheriff and his men are in Albuquerque." Out of age-old tradition and respect, he looked first at his father, then Jesse, then Beckner as he leaned forward, a spoon close to his mouth. "The sheriff has a room at the inn. His men are camped just outside the town."

"Francisco," Beckner began, "did you happen to see a man—a gringo— wearing a leather jacket. With fringes. The strips of—" He gestured.

Francisco interrupted him, nodding emphatically. "I know. Fringes." He then shook his head. "No. I did not see such a man."

Beckner ruminated for a moment, then cleared his throat. "Did you perchance see a *remuda* of mules? Three ? Two or three men? Texicans, probably?"

Again Francisco shook his head. "What is this *remuda?*"

In that moment, Beckner realized he had said something not easily explained to anyone in the room. He pondered as he touched his cloth napkin to his lips, glanced around the table, then said, "The commandant suspects that supplies were stolen from the garrison in Santa Fé." He shrugged, and hoped no more would be said about the matter, and continued to eat.

Jesse cut in. "I will leave in the morning. There are associates of my father in *El Rio Abajo* who will house me. Albuquerque."

"The sheriff," Sabino said. "You must wait until he passes this way. He will tire soon. Wait here."

Jesse looked down at his plate, then Sabino from under his eyebrows. "No, if I should be seen here with you, the sheriff would accuse you of hiding me. It would bring you trouble." He glanced at the rest in turn. "I will go."

Sabino shook his head and frowned in frustration.

Francisco said, "Who are these people who would help you, Jesse?"

"Tápia. In Los Chávez. Noriega. In Albuquerque."

"And you trust these people?" Francisco cocked his head.

Jesse jerked his head to one side, eyebrows raised. "I shall see."

"Mm," Francisco muttered. "I will go with you. I know a better way than the Camino."

Beckner, who had avoided looking at Mercedes during dinner, and more so after her older brother's arrival, who sat across from him, unable to contain himself longer, looked at her. She, who had been likewise struggling, caught his glance at the same time, which resulted in mutually locked eyes for three seconds before they broke away with embarrassment. Mercedes' chest heaved as she looked down and away. Beckner looked at the ceiling, drew in a breath, then stared at Jesse, as though his young friend could somehow save him from an awkward moment.

Everyone at the table, save one, caught the transaction, subtle as it was. Francisco was torn, given his new-found appreciation for Beckner, while Mercedes' parents were in quandaries of their own. The teen-aged Javier, who sat at his sister's side, was oblivious. Jesse, for his part, wanted to smile and nod approval, but decided discretion was the best choice. In ordinary circumstances, he would have been drawn to Mercedes, but with his on-going problem, romance would have to wait. Oddly, he felt glad for his military friend, although there was nothing to assume. Not yet.

Francisco, although divided, wanted to de-fuse a potentially nasty situation between their visitors and his family, as well as move forward with the problem at hand. Driven by curiosity, he looked at Beckner. "This man in the fringed jacket. Who is he?"

Beckner was thankful that the momentary silence, which felt to him as though it would go on for a very long time, had come to an end. "Well," he began, formulating as he spoke, "we are not aware of the man's name. He may be involved with the thieves. We are not certain." In that short span, he had decided that saying the man's name was too much, and might serve to interfere with his investigation.

Francisco, who sat next to Beckner, turned in his chair to face the lieutenant, eyes friendly but narrowed. "Why are you not in uniform?"

"Simple reason, Francisco. If I were in uniform, and I spotted these men, they would run. They don't know me. This way, if they see me, they probably won't become alarmed."

Francisco stared for a few seconds, then nodded.. "*Bueno.* Good."

Beckner, bravery returned, chanced another look at the pretty teen-aged girl across from him, but executed the action with haste.

She responded briefly by returning his glance, then averted it, pushed back and stood. "*Mama, vamos á limpiar la cocina.*"

Her mother, who wore a suppressed smile, rose as well, and the two of them began clearing the table.

"I'll ride with you. Dark now. Too late to travel?" Beckner looked at Francisco, then Jesse.

Francisco stood and dropped his napkin on the table. "In the morning." He picked up his newly-acquired firearm, then turned, looked at Beckner, who had risen as well. He shook his tilted head in a short, jerking motion. "I asked you before, but I ask again, why do you help this man?" He raised his chin in Jesse's direction. "You are the army, yet you are not in your uniform." He gestured to indicate Beckner's clothes.

"Francisco!" Sabino jumped from his chair and faced his elder son. "You insult our guest!"

Francisco glanced at his father, then returned his gaze to Beckner. "No! I want to know! You give me this gun, yes. I am happy. I am grateful. But I wonder. Why? You are not the sheriff. You are not the law here. What can the army do? What can you do?!"

"Francisco," Sabino pleaded.

Mercedes and her mother turned to witness Francisco's barrage.

Francisco kept his eyes on the army officer, but took a moment to roll his eyes away from the lieutenant toward his sister and back, a gesture not lost on anyone except Sabino, who watched his back, and his younger brother, who only watched and wondered.

Beckner's steady regard on Francisco shifted to Jesse, who had also risen, then to Sabino, then settled on Francisco again. He released a long sigh and nodded. "You deserve to know. It is true. I am not the law. The army is not to interfere in civil matters in the territory. Unless there is insurrection or massive disorder." He awarded Mercedes a sidelong glance as he thought how some—or most—of his words were likely lost on all in the room but Jesse.

Francisco held out the palms of his hands in frustration. He shot a glance at the others in the room as though asking for compliance.

"But," Beckner continued as he gestured in Jesse's direction, "this man, Jesse Landry, is my friend. His father was my friend. He did not murder the man at the inn. He killed him, yes, but not without cause. He defended himself. He defended his father's honor." He paused to collect his thoughts, glanced at Mercedes, then returned his steady gaze to Francisco. "There is more. But more I cannot tell you. I have not told Jesse, nor will I, until I find out certain facts. I told you of a man in a fringed jacket and of mules with stolen goods. These are armaments—guns and ammunition. He and the guns may be related. That is all I can say. I ask you to trust me. I am not here to hurt you or your family. The uniform? What I told you before is the truth. You know how we—the army—are regarded." He pointed at the holstered pistol in Francisco's hand. "That is a gift. From me to you." He pointed at his own chest, then at Francisco. "You are Jesse's friend. You have proved that. All of you have. That makes you *my* friend. The pistol was—is—a gift to a friend. You came to Santa Fé to help Jesse, Francisco. So, from one man to another. Not to buy your allegiance. Not to buy your friendship. A gift. I am here to help. Please ask no more. Now." He took a step back and released his breath as he avoided Mercedes' approving eyes.

Francisco, affected, turned slowly to look at his father, who nodded somberly, then at Beckner. His eyes had softened. He then moved the pistol to his other hand, reached out and took Beckner's as he looked steadily into the officer's eyes. "*Mañana. En la mañana.* In the morning."

As they held each other's outstretched hand firmly, neither smiled openly, but both nodded with looks of male acceptance and understanding.

13

Although Jesse could have slept in the Maestas house, he declined in favor of bedding down with Lieutenant Beckner, who, despite a similar invitation, insisted on spending the night on a bed of hay in an unused alcove of the animal shed next to the house. As it was, what with a large supper and an extra glass of local red wine each, they slumbered well, despite various sweet-rank animal smells and the sounds of a nearby snorting pig and a gaggle of noisy cooped chickens.

Beckner's motive for such a primal sleeping arrangement went beyond common courtesy. He felt that if he stayed in the house, he would be keenly aware of the young woman who commanded his attention and every drifting thought in a nearby room. He was also certain in his desire, that she, too, would be thinking of him nearby. As these thoughts rambled through his mind, he considered that all but the youngest among them would also be holding such thoughts. He drifted into deep slumber, warm in his new-found certainty.

Francisco woke them both before dawn by shaking their feet under the blankets that Mercedes and her mother had provided. They buckled their trousers after relieving themselves sleepily but discreetly behind the structure, then headed for the house and the warm kitchen. There, Mrs. Maestas and her teen-aged daughter both held sway over an effluvium of cooking odors that had the two travelers salivating as soon as they entered.

The senior Maestas joined them, as did Francisco and Javier, while Filomena and Mercedes bustled about, ensuring that the men's plates, bowls and cups were filled and stomachs sated. It was obvious to all, though, that Mercedes was more than attentive toward Harold Beckner, who found himself increasingly smitten, yet embarrassed by the attention. More than once, Mercedes, when she felt as though the others concentrated on their own particulars, brushed her sleeve against the lieutenant's arm.

Sabino Maestas, in part because he was aware of his daughter's interest, but also out of concern for the young men about to embark on what he considered a dangerous mission, sat back and began to dish out advice. Although his eldest son had already decided on the same plan of action, he suggested they head west, ford the river, then thread their way through the *bosque*. Thick with cottonwoods, salt cedar and Russian olive, they would be difficult to spot from the better-traveled eastern bank. That, in turn, rose to the piedmont, then the sharp escarpment of the mountain known as the Sandia, or watermelon, which allowed a better chance of being seen by potentially adverse eyes.

Beckner announced to his traveling partners that he would report to the Union encampment overlooking the village of Albuquerque and the flat river valley on the heights above the river to the west, but would arrange to rendezvous later with Jesse and Francisco Maestas. Mercedes, close to bursting, her English tortured, blurted the question about the lieutenant's return, then, red-faced, revised her question to include all three men, as she looked away, head down. Beckner started to answer, then held his tongue as he looked around the room at the others. Only Francisco looked at him, his head lowered, his eyes penetrating below his eyebrows. Beckner sensed that the look was not entirely filled with warning. At that, without a word, Jesse cleared his throat, scraped back his chair and stood, wiped his mouth in the process, and the other three men followed suit.

The horses were not charmed by the task of fording the shallow, brown waters of the Rio Grande, and had to be goaded. Francisco's animal, used to the crossing, after brief hesitation, provided the example for the other two, after which the maneuver moved more quickly, single-file. The brutes were happy to be on the other side, and demonstrated their pleasure with snorts and shakes of their huge heads, as though in a demonstration of self-satisfaction and relief at the success of their task. All three men congratulated the feat with fond pats to their steed's necks, along with soothing words and clicks.

A bright smile took over Beckner's face and spread to Maestas and Jesse as sunlight beamed over the crest of the mountain and struck the *bosque*, almost instantly warming the verdant surroundings with sharp shafts of light carved by the foliage.

Despite the crashing of the horse's hooves on dried cottonwood leaves and fallen twigs along the path through the trees created by many years of animal traffic, the men heard a different sound that came from the track in front of them. They perceived women's voices, but proved to be those of three sub-teen Pueblo Indian boys, each dragging small bundles of drift wood with ropes made of indigenous plant fiber. When they saw the men on horseback, they cowered and moved off the path and behind trees with large trunks in an effort to hide.

Francisco Maestas waved his hand in a friendly gesture and spoke to them in a language neither Jesse nor Beckner had heard. The boys looked at each other for support, then returned to the path with their heads bowed submissively. Maestas smiled, spoke again, then reached around to his saddlebags and withdrew three pieces of jerky, which he held up. The boys smiled coyly, then slowly advanced to Maestas' side, as they dragged their collections behind. Both Jesse and Beckner followed suit with more jerky, while Maestas offered up a couple of his mother's tortillas. Although there were no words whatsoever from the three foragers, their smiles and nods were communication enough. As they began to consume their morning windfall of victuals, they hurried away north.

With their horses at a stand-still, all three men watched the boys retreat.

"I didn't know you spoke their tongue, Francisco," Jesse said.

Maestas glanced at Jesse. "A few words only." He clicked at his mount and the horse reacted by nodding his head and moving again.

"Where do they live?" Beckner asked.

Maestas jerked his head over his right shoulder. "Santa Ana."

"That where Chávez made a deal with them?" Jesse asked.

"Yes. And the cousin, Cabeza de Baca."

Their trek along the river bank and through the dense *bosque* led them near the village of Corrales, then south to the outskirts of Albuquerque. On their way, they encountered only a covey of pheasants and two disinterested men leading a bare-backed horse, both of whom merely nodded and touched their hats. As they came within sight of the high banks immediately west of the town, Maestas reined his horse to a halt and pointed.

"Up there. The army post. They call themselves dragoons."

Beckner shaded his eyes beneath the broad-brimmed hat he wore and squinted. "Much obliged." He looked a Francisco. "Have you visited the encampment?"

Maestas shook his head. "No, but as many here do, I have had a look. They don't want us near." He smiled.

"I see," Beckner said. He looked at the ground, then up. "See here, I will report to the officer in charge, then meet with you later." He squinted at the sun. "I reckon it to be close to midday. Before sundown? And where?"

"I don't know Albuquerque," Jesse said.

"There is a place—a *cantina*—behind the church. The soldiers do not go there. Nor do the *ricos*. It will be safe." Maestas nodded as he patted his impatient mount which had begun to agitate his legs. "They are not happy with gringos. Or *Tejanos*. But they stay silent and serve them." Maestas awarded each of his partners with a straight look of affirmation of his message.

Beckner eyed Maestas, then Jesse with concern. "I will watch for you. One or both. I speak only a few words of Spanish."

"You will be safe with us," Maestas said. He clicked at his horse, and the animal started off. "*Vaya con diós.*"

"Fair well," Beckner said.

"*Hasta la vista,*" Jesse said.

The encampment lay enough distance from the escarpment along the western bank of the Rio Grande to allow a watch over the valley and the approaches below. From that vantage point, an observer with a field glass was afforded a view of the east-side *bosque*, portions of the town *plaza* and a smattering of buildings surrounding it. These were predominantly brown, flat-roofed adobes amid farm fields, small orchards and animal pens. The twin spires of the adobe San Felipe de Neri Catholic church situated on the north side of the plaza was the most prominent feature.

The dragoon bivouac consisted of two dozen tents, arranged in four neat rows, the largest of which was headquarters for the detachment. Horses were corralled on the western side, not far from the latrine trench. A flag was planted immediately to the left of the impromptu entrance, centered against the rows. The banner of the United States flapped at its zenith, while just below was the dark blue and gold streamer of the unit. A sentry in blue, his carbine at parade rest, stood casually on the tent side.

As Beckner approached the perimeter from the north on horseback, another sentry challenged him as he brought his bayonet-equipped weapon up and angled from his hip. "Halt! What business, sir?!"

"I carry a letter of introduction from the 3rd Infantry Provost, Private. One moment." Beckner pulled an envelope from his inside jacket pocket, removed a sheet of paper, leaned down from the saddle and handed it to the sentry.

The soldier maintained his weapon clumsily, then accepted and opened the folded document. He scanned it quickly, handed it back to Beckner, and changed his posture to parade rest. "Do you wish to see the CO, sir?"

"I do. The officer in charge." Beckner returned the letter and envelope to his jacket.

"That would be Captain Marchant, sir. In the headquarters tent, sir. Just there." He turned half-way and gestured with his chin. "With the flags, sir."

"Thank you, Private. As you were." This last remark Beckner instantly regretted. Although, as he reflected on it, he realized the young picket most likely did not realize its import which could indicate his true calling.

The sentry, upon reflection, also found the command odd, as it issued from a man in civilian clothes. After a moment, he dismissed it.

Beckner continued on his horse between two tent rows. Several troopers, most of whom lounged outside their tents, looked up at him as he passed, curious at the "Anglo" man in civilian clothes. He dismounted near the headquarters tent, which stood midway along the second row from the western perimeter, tied the reins to a hitching rail which restrained one other horse, and walked to the tent opening. The makeshift door was open, so he rapped twice on the frame, then entered to an empty tent.

"Not here, sir."

Beckner swung around to see a small soldier with red hair, his suspenders draped down to his knees, but above his dusty, black boots.

"The captain?"

"Yessir. Be back shortly. Nature call."

"I see."

"You have business with Captain Marchant?" The soldier squinted at Beckner.

"I do. Does it suit if I wait inside?" He gestured.

"You do that, sir. I'm Kennedy. Cap'n's aide. Corporal."

"Fine, Corporal Kennedy. I'll take a seat and wait." Beckner walked deeper into the tent. He found a folding wooden chair, sat and looked around.

Corporal Kennedy exhibited deep curiosity by peering into the tent, stared for a moment, then disappeared.

The floor of the collapsible shelter consisted of wooden planks with varying width gaps apparent. A simple military field desk was situated near the rear, opposite the opening. Behind it was a wooden swivel chair. The desk's surface held a lantern, several books, scattered papers, a pen and ink set, and a rocker-style blotter. A heavy wooden file cabinet listed to one side of the desk, and a cot with a pillow in need of laundering and blankets lay along one edge of the canvas wall. A foot locker and a pair of black leather boots occupied the underside of the cot. A small table with personal belongings and a lamp stood at the head of the simple bed. A tintype of a young woman was angled so it was visible from the desk as well as the bed. In the corner nearest the foot of the bed was a carbine, butt down. Hanging from a strap next to it was a holstered pistol.

Beckner turned as he heard the sound of heavy footwear hit the wood floor. He turned to see a man in his same age bracket enter. He was an inch shorter than Beckner, slim and beardless, and was without his jacket, which was draped over the back of his desk chair. He wore a look of deep wonder as he eyed the visitor. He stopped for an instant, then continued, without a word, to the desk. There, he stopped, cocked his head, nodded as he worked to form his words, then spoke. "Corporal says you want to see me. Who are you, and what are you doing here?"

"My name is—"

"This is an outpost of the U.S. Army, and we are not here to—"

Beckner reached for the envelope in his jacket pocket, removed a second letter, leaned forward, and laid it on the desk. "I'm Lieutenant Harold Beckner. Assigned to headquarters, Santa Fé."

Marchant peered at Beckner for a few seconds, then picked up the paper and read. He made a face, nodded, handed the letter back and sat in the swivel chair. "Why in mufti?"

Beckner adjusted his posture. "Special assignment. Moving among the civilians in uniform would make my work more difficult."

"And what is that work?" Captain Marchant leaned so that he rested his chin in his right hand, his elbow on the chair arm. He raised his eyebrows.

Beckner hesitated for a count of three. "Has a Sergeant Tandy or a Private Milton reported to you?"

"Here?"

"Yes, here." Beckner controlled his irritation at the inanity of the question.

Marchant dropped his arm and leaned against the desk. "Why would they, Lieutenant?"

"I instructed Sergeant Tandy to report here. Two days past. If he should appear, it may or may not be with Milton."

"Explain, please."

Beckner hesitated again. "I am here—in the Territory—under orders from the War Department, Captain, and I am not at liberty to reveal precisely what my mission is."

Marchant stared at Beckner as he drew back, sucked in a mouthful of air, then released it. "And why should I believe any of this poppycock?" He leaned back and scowled, his chin to his chest. The dry, loose wood of his chair squeaked.

"Because if you do not, and should you choose not to aid me and any of the men under my command, your actions—or lack thereof—will be duly reported to the provost in Santa Fé. I dare say you would prefer to avoid that happenstance, Captain." Beckner nodded, his mouth severe.

"I see." Marchant swivelled in his chair such that he looked away. He stretched his legs out straight and folded his hands across his midriff.

"The consequences would be yours to suffer."

"Of course." The captain brought both hands up to his pursed lips. He was silent, then he turned and straightened to face the lieutenant, "So, you are not obliged to reveal your mission, Lieutenant?"

"I am under orders not to, Captain. Only as the need arises, and only to those with a requirement. Now, as to Sergeant Tandy and Private Milton, who are on assignment under my orders, I repeat; I expect one of them to report here. It should be Sergeant Tandy, if not both."

"Mm."

"When Tandy arrives, I am to be notified."

"Where were they, and what was their assignment?"

Beckner thought a moment, then, "They were ordered to intercept and track a party with mules."

"What does this party carry that requires tracking? If I may ask." Marchant had calmed.

"Contraband."

"Am I not to be made aware?"

Beckner was pensive, then, "I ask you to be patient in this matter, Captain Marchant. It is better that this be kept quiet. For now. We do not wish for this to be known, since we want to know the destination of the shipment. In good time. Your cooperation in this matter is essential."

Marchant stood and paced slowly around his desk and to the crude opening to the outside. He folded his arms across his chest and stared out into the sun-drenched day. "And if this mission were to affect this unit?"

"Depending upon conditions, then I would be obliged—"

The captain wheeled to face Beckner. "To inform me, Lieutenant?"

"Most certainly. And perhaps to alert your troopers to action."

Marchant smiled at this remark, moved quickly for his desk and stood behind it. He jerked his head down, then up in a quick nod of approval. "Fair enough, Lieutenant. But mind you, if I find that you—"

Beckner stood. "I understand, and you won't."

"You are welcome to bivouac here, Beckner. We have officer's quarters. A tent, to be sure—"

Beckner shook his head. "I appreciate the offer, Captain Marchant. Better that your men remain unaware of my identity or purpose, so I will seek lodgings in the village. If I'm unsuccessful, I will return. Thank you." He paused, then, "I shall leave now, but I ask that if Tandy, Milton or both appear, that you give them this and hold them here until I reappear." He reached into his jacket and retrieved a sealed envelope. "This is to identify me to them. I plan to be here once a day if possible."

Marchant nodded his assent as he took the envelope and laid it on his desk.

"If you lend me paper and pen, I will leave a note for them."

Marchant opened a desk drawer, retrieved a single piece of paper, handed it to Beckner, then shoved the ink well and blotter toward him. Beckner leaned forward, wrote, blotted the ink, folded the message, then handed it to Marchant.

"You are welcome to read it, Captain."

Marchant merely nodded and set the note aside.

Beckner rose. "And do me the favor of not asking them details of their mission."

"You have my word as an officer, Lieutenant."

The two men rose, shook hands and Beckner left with Captain Marchant staring after him, motionless behind his desk.

After parting with Lieutenant Beckner, Jesse and his companion, Francisco Maestas, rode past the escarpment below the military encampment, then well beyond the western edge of the village of Albuquerque, until they were more than two miles south. There, they found a wide place to ford the river to the opposite bank, where they encountered more thick cottonwood *bosque*. Maestas' reasoning was that if alarm had been spread that the sheriff of Santa Fé was chasing a fugitive from the north, they would be less likely to be regarded as suspicious arriving from the opposite direction.

They were forced to negotiate the flat, swampy terrain of the eastern bank, mainly by following animal trails, until they emerged into the open and the fields that lay to the south of the town. There, they were able to move along dry wagon paths and irrigation ditch banks. Their mounts snorted and pranced at the odor of green plants and water.

"We need to feed them soon," Jesse declared.

Maestas strained in the saddle as he cast his head about. "Look for a trough. They will be happy to eat grass." He pointed to an open field.

The two men sat on a ditch bank under a tree as they ate jerky and *tortillas* while their mounts ripped happily at the nearby grass, their reins free on the ground.

Jesse's horse, Campeón, raised his head, snorted, and took off at a rapid walk.

Maestas stood, pushed his hat back and stretched his arm out. "Look. A trough. Over there."

After a few seconds delay, Maestas' mount followed eagerly.

"Good," Jesse swallowed. "I want to find Noriega's house."

Maestas looked down at Jesse. "That *cabrón*?! ¡Es pendejo! ¡Oquete!"

"Francisco, he is my father's partner." Jesse held out both palms.

"I'm sorry." Maestas shook his head. "He has a bad reputation here. The entire valley. He cheats his friends and mistreats his workers."

Jesse studied the ground at his feet. "Perhaps, but I think he will protect me. He and his family have known my father a long time. Never have I heard my father speak ill of him."

Maestas looked away silently as he bit into another piece of jerky.

"Do you know the way?"

"To where?"

"To the home of Noriega."

Maestas looked down at Jesse. "You don't know the way?"

"I was a mere boy when last there with my father."

Maestas hesitated as he looked first one direction, then another. "We need the main road first. I don't remember from here."

On their mounts again, after coaxing both animals, Jesse followed Maestas single-file along the high, west side bank of the *Acequia Madre*. This was the "mother ditch," the main irrigation canal which fed muddy Rio Grande water to lesser *acequias*, and thence to the fields of corn, chile, squash and orchards that lay in patches in and around the village of Albuquerque. Shortly, they dropped down onto a wagon trail that wound through the thinning, eastern edge of the cottonwood *bosque*. On either side, scattered, were simple houses of adobe, nestled close to animal pens, all grouped according to their extended familial relations.

At a cross roads, Maestas drew up and waited for Jesse. He turned in his saddle. "This way." He pointed north, toward the town.

"I recall a large house."

"Oh, yes; it's large," Maestas said. "Many rooms. On the plaza."

Jesse squinted. "I thought you didn't know how to find it."

"As I told you, back there, no. Here, yes." He jerked his thumb behind himself. "Had to find the road." He waited a beat. "I do not normally sneak into Albuquerque from the south with fugitives from the law." He threw Jesse a quick smile.

Jesse shook his head in a good-natured manner.

As they made their way north, their horses were forced to follow the southern extension of the famed Guadalupe Trail, the high-ground path created by cattle, sheep, draft and other, feral, animals that traversed the swampy, undulating Middle Rio Grande Valley, as they had for millennia. The land was predominantly flat, saturated by the high water table provided by the meandering river, and that which lay underneath in layers for thousands of feet. Either side was covered by occasional small ponds, reeds, willow and cottonwood. Ducks, and an occasional pheasant, flew up and away with their passing. Water-dwelling animals, such as beaver, and muskrat were in evidence. The air was damp, redolent of the flora that abounded. Soon they approached higher ground, above the irrigated fields.

The manse was large, its thick adobe walls, designed to thwart attacks by the Apaches and other plains tribes, including Navajos from the west, and the infrequent Comanches from the Llano Estacado, who in earlier times poured through Tijeras Canyon from the east. Its high outer walls were punctuated with windows protected on both sides by thick, native pine shutters fastened with hand-wrought iron hinges and latches. Integral with these were animal pens which stretched to the south until they met with open produce fields. To the east, separated by a wagon road, was an orchard of mixed varieties, most of whose trees were only now beginning to bear fruit.

As they approached from the south, the two men encountered a bustle that Maestas rarely saw, but with which Jesse was all too familiar. Several children ran, shouted and played in an open area behind, to the side, and in front of the house, which fronted on the plaza. As they walked their horses closer to the village square, Jesse noted silently that both men and women were dressed less formally than in Santa Fé. Most of the men wore ponchos and wide straw *sombreros*, a style common in El Paso del Norte and to the south of that town. A horse-drawn farm wagon moved from one end of the square to the other, then disappeared into an alley between two buildings. An old man who lead a burro laden with *piñon* and cedar branches passed in front of them. Across the plaza, two women in long, dark dresses, their heads covered in equally black shawls, moved toward the San Felipe de Neri church which dominated the north edge of the rectangle.

Maestas brought his mount up short, looked around, then angled himself in the saddle such that his right leg came up high as he turned to look at Jesse, who studied the scene. "What now?" he asked.

Jesse heaved a sigh, looked at Maestas and tossed his head in a shrug. "I don't know." He peered behind, then at the big house, then at the sky. "Midday. Perhaps I wait. Think this over." He paused. "But I want to go to Noriega. I think he can help me."

Maestas made a face. "What about Baca? Does he know you? If he sees you here—"

Jesse shook his head violently. "I don't know! Perhaps. He knew my father. Not well. Maybe at the store—"

Maestas was silent for a few seconds as he roved his eyes over Jesse, his horse, saddlebags and everything that hung from the saddle and straps. He jerked his chin. "Those guns. How many men wear a pistol and have a saddle carbine? He could be looking for someone who is well armed. Such as you. A *coyote* to boot." He made an upward gesture with his rein-free hand.

Jesse stared at him, at first blankly, then nodded and looked at the dirt street beneath Campeón. "You're right." He looked around. "He may not know my face, but he might know my horse. And these guns."

"You need to make yourself invisible, my friend." Maestas looked back toward the Noriega stables. "Take your horse over there." He pointed. "Put the pistol in your bags and give the carbine to me. I will keep it until you are safe. Go to the house and introduce yourself."

"Where will you go?" Jesse frowned.

"To my cousin's. Archuleta. He is reliable. Then I will wait for the gringo. Where we told him to go." He craned his neck as he darted his eyes at the milling people in the plaza. "Now."

Jesse looped Campeón's reins to one of the cedar rails that constituted part of the corrals at the rear of the Noriega place, put his pistol and belt in a saddlebag, then removed it, the carbine and its scabbard, and handed the latter up to Maestas, who was still in his saddle.

"Come to the meeting place soon. I will ask my cousin if he has heard anything. *Adiós.*" With that, Maestas reined his horse around and headed away.

Jesse watched him disappear, then made his way on foot to the plaza and the long *portal* that shaded the entire length of the big, north-facing house. He stood at the corner for a minute and looked around as though he expected to see something or someone, but not sure of what. He was anxious, and wanted nothing more than to leave, to return home.

He took a deep breath, turned and headed for the big, counter-sunk entrance, past three large, deep-set windows, so typical of the houses of the well-to-do. There, he found a pair of thick, hand-hewn, unpainted paneled doors hung with over-sized iron hinges. At the centered vertical joint was a heavy, hand-hammered iron latch assembly. To the right, from a hole bored in the frame, was a leather pull-string. He grabbed it and pulled. He heard a bell ring inside.

14

Trooper Amos Jorgensen had spurred his mount into a gallop. He felt that, given the fact that his quarry was moving ahead of him with heavily-laden mules, they would be easy to come upon shortly; certainly before sunset. He reasoned as well that they would likely not stop, and for more reasons than one. They would be anxious to get as far away as possible from any run-in with the U.S. Army, and since they might be non-Spanish-speaking gringo Texicans, would be singled out by the local population, only too willing to relieve them of their contraband, personal belongings; even their lives. On the other hand, they would need to carry water for themselves and the animals, and allow time for rest and grazing of those beasts.

After he had decided that his quarry had not taken the steep climb to the Glorieta questa plain, he had ridden down into the Pecos River Valley in pursuit. He stopped near the hamlet of San Juan, an important way station on the Santa Fé Trail, alert along the way. There had been many tracks, such that he could no longer tell the difference between those left by east-bound hooves and wheels and all the others which sliced ruts in both directions. At the edge of the Pecos River, he remained in the saddle as his grateful mount partook of the cold, clean water that flowed from the mountains to the north. He scanned the ridge ahead, then the heights to his right, where the low-lying adobe houses of the village perched. Two men, carrying bundles, stopped to look at him, suspicion in their eyes, then moved on and climbed the trail to the little town. He opened the canteen that hung from the pommel and took a mouthful of water.

He forded the stream at a place where it spread out such that the water was shallow enough that it rose no higher than his horse's fetlocks. On the east bank, he walked his mount up the side of a rocky ridge which rose high above the river plain. He could have followed the trail, but decided he might be able to spot the contraband caravan based on his findings in Glorieta better from a high vantage point. At the top, after he goaded his reluctant mount, he stopped, pulled his campaign hat off and wiped his brow with his kerchief. In front of him was the great, verdant sweep of the valley between the rolling and variegated Rockies piedmont and the Glorieta questa structure to the south. It was at that moment that he felt the sudden rush of air close to his right ear, followed closely by a second, then the tell-tale reports of gunfire. The last one he knew was meant for him. He was hit in the side by a large-caliber carbine ball, and his reaction was to twist to one side, drop the reins, lose his balance and fall from the saddle. As he fell to his right, his right boot became stuck in the stirrup. His horse whinnied in alarm, paced forward, and dragged him several feet before he was able to loose himself. His side was in great pain.

Below, behind a set of boulders, Gerald Rodman and a black man had positioned themselves such that they could survey the river bank and the trail. The three men, a contingent which included another white man, the co-drover, had watched the road behind them, and had seen the lone trooper. Rodman had reasoned that there could only be one reason for such a sight; a blue coat on a good army horse, with arms, often at a full gallop, coming in their direction. They had rested their carbines on the boulders, at the ready, when the black man had suggested that Rodman look to his left, up the slope to the top of the ridge. It had been then that they both took aim and fired.

Rodman had joined the outlaw drovers after he felt sanguine that he was not watched or followed. He had left the *fonda* in the pre-dawn hours, taken to horse and made his way, at first slowly, in the dark, then quickly after sunrise. He had rendezvoused with his new trail partners south and east of the village of Pecos along the river. Now, he found himself to be, in effect, a desperado, an outlaw, at risk for being arrested and held at trial by the Army.

Sergeant Tandy and Private Milton had moved as quickly as they could, ahead of Lieutenant Beckner and the army detail out of Santa Fé, up out of Glorieta, down through the Apache gap, then south toward the Sandia Mountains and Albuquerque. They had stopped only occasionally, once to water their horses at a rancher's well, then to sup on their military rations, and to relieve themselves. Sgt. Tandy figured they would be well ahead of the contraband, should it indeed be circling around to the city on the Rio Grande. Pvt. Milton, although a loyal and steadfast soldier, but not the brightest of troopers, pestered Tandy to tell him where they were headed and the reason. He had confessed he was glad to get away from the cursed Mexicans and their strange ways and victuals, and to be on an adventure of sorts, but he was also nervous, not knowing what they were heading into. The latter concerns Milton did not confess to his superior, but Tandy, a seasoned campaigner, knew all too well. Tandy, for his part, was not certain of their mission, but was delighted to be involved, and felt alive. It had been sundown on that first day when they reached the eastern slopes of the great Sandia uplift and made camp.

Despite the time of year, they awakened stiff, sore and cold. Tandy decided that to build a fire might draw attention from those with an interest in doing them harm, and they were, after all, on a secret mission. They ate a cold army field breakfast, drank precious water from their canteens, saddled their mounts and joined what little trail there was that skirted the mountain's eastern slope. As the sun rose and warmed them, they felt better, although Milton allowed as how he missed his hot coffee in the mess. Since they were riding single-file, Tandy merely grunted a response without looking around.

A little more than two hours passed when they came to a halt on a prominence that looked down into the wide cut the locals called Cañon de Tijeras—the scissors. Below, to their right, they spied blue-gray smoke emanating from several adobe house chimneys. To their left was more smoke, a single column from amongst *piñon* and scrub oak that dotted the landscape. Ahead, the land rose into more mountainous terrain, but to a lesser degree than that behind them.

Tandy pulled a brass spyglass from a saddlebag and raised it to his eyes. He scanned the east-west trail that wound down from the rise on the east, along the steep *arroyo* that defined the canyon, then west, through the western cut, onto the piedmont that led to the valley of the Rio Grande and the village of Albuquerque. He focused on the smoke to his left, and was able to discern human activity. A small party of men dressed in leathers, covered in what appeared to be colorful symbols, moved about between horses, or crouched next to the fire which had been laid in a circle of rocks.

He handed the glass to Milton, who was beside him. "Comanche. Gotta be. Seen 'em 'afore." He pointed.

Milton raised the brass tube to his eye, moved it around, then stopped. "Ya' think? I never seen 'em 'afore."

Tandy moved his head back and forth as he scoured the scene and took its measure. "I reckon. They don't like towns, and town folk don't cotton to them, neither."

Milton lowered the glass and looked at Tandy. "Long way from the town, ain't they?"

Tandy reached for the glass. He cocked his head to the right. "Down there. That's a town. Heard tell it's there for this purpose."

"Like a guard post?"

"Yep." Tandy raised the telescope and focused on the village.

"Hot damn." Milton screwed his face up into a furrowed-brow grin.

Tandy lowered the glass and returned it to the saddlebag. "We settle here for now." He raised his arm and made a sweeping gesture. "If the mules come down that trace, we'll see 'em from here." He dismounted and dusted his breaches.

Milton pulled back on his horse's reins, talked to his mount, then slid onto the ground. "How long we tarry?"

Tandy held his horse's reins. "Don't know." He shrugged. "If they come this way, should be today. Most likely tomorrow." He handed Milton his reins. "Here, take 'em down to that crick and see if there's water. Let 'em graze a bit."

Milton took control of Tandy's horse together with his. "Right. Hope none 'o them Injuns spot me."

"You know how to move. Stay low 'an slow. I'll watch from here." Tandy pulled his carbine from his saddle scabbard, then, on second thought, reached for the spyglass instead. "I'll keep a sharp eye. Don't linger, Milton."

"Yep, Sergeant. You'll see me presently. There's grass up here, too." He gestured, his brow furrowed.

The two men whom Jorgensen had seen along the Rio Pecos had made the top of the trail and the rocky ledge where the village of San Juan lay when the shots from two carbines rang out and echoed across the little valley. They looked first toward the sound, then at each other before returning their gaze to the sudden racket. One of the men pointed to the ridge line across the river. They saw a man fall from a horse, then watched as horse and man disappeared below the ridge line. They gibbered at each other, pointed and waved, before one ran toward the low earthen houses, and the other scurried down the trail to the river, then up to the top of the ridge.

Within a half hour, Trooper Jorgensen was lying on a pallet, semi-conscious, in a small, dark room. The men who had seen him and three women stood over him as they discussed the problem at hand. Another, older woman, entered, ordered the others to make way, then began to inspect the trooper's wound. She pulled his bloody, long-tailed shirt from beneath his belt line and loosened his suspenders. She inspected the gory hole in his side, raised her eyes, put her hands together, and uttered a plea to *Diós*. Discussion amongst the others led to one of the men taking to horse and riding off at a fast clip toward Glorieta Pass and Santa Fé, some forty miles distant.

Rodman and his accomplices had scrambled away moments after watching the trooper fall. All three were on horseback, while the three burdened mules slogged along behind at the ends of rope leads. They increased their speed along the rutted trace until they reached the cut in the hog-back ridge along the road that led to the town of Las Vegas, then north and east along the Santa Fé Trail. That was also the place where Apache raiders made their decision whether to head west to Pecos Pueblo and on to the canyon named for them, or south for the path to Albuquerque.

The Texicans turned south through the hog-back ridge valley, toward the dreaded and dangerous plains. That trail was rougher yet, but passable. When they reached the Comanche Trail that led from that tribe's traditional home on the Llano Estacado, now a part of Texas, where the so-called Texas Rangers had been given carte blanche to clear the ancient tribes out, they headed west. All three kept a constant lookout, fearful lest a stray Comanche or Apache band might suddenly appear and wrest their food, liquor, firearms and lives from them. As often as not, they moved away from the trail until they came to the cuts that rose onto the plain of the Glorieta cuesta and down into the Valle de Estancia. When they pulled to a stop to attend to bodily needs, it was in a swale some distance from the main trail or among black rocks at the base of a mesa.

When they stopped, it was without fire and resultant smoke. The black man, who went by the name of Cat, and the other drover, Pulver, a white man, sat together, silent, across from the self-important, but secretly worried and low self-esteemed Gerald Rodman. Both middle-aged plainsmen, who had developed a true friendship despite on-going conditions for the "darkie," knew, without discussion, but with uncanny non-oral communications, that the man sitting across from them, their ostensible leader, was a scoundrel, fake and most likely a racist. They also knew, without mutual speech, that they would sacrifice the man in the fringed jacket in a trice should their survival depend upon that outcome. They sensed Rodman would return the favor, should the need arise.

With some trepidation, they greeted two young Comanche men, more teen-aged boys, riding bareback on pinto horses. The Indians were east-bound, and carried weapons capable only of taking a rabbit or small deer. They had been successful in their hunt to the extent that each had small animal carcases tied with sinews draped across their horse's backs. They didn't show their emotions, but if the Texicans had known, the young bucks were terrified of the armed gringos. That included the strange black one, and they were only too happy to raise their hands stiffly in their traditional sign of peace, move on and look back every few seconds to savor their good fortune. They knew their flimsy arrows were no match for lead balls that were swifter than diving birds of prey. For the little contraband-moving group, they were also relieved, happy to see the native boys fade into the distance with their meager catch.

As they dropped down from the cuesta into the sprawling Estancia Valley that rose on its western verge to the Sandia-Manzano range, all three were glad their journey was nearing its end. They were also gladdened to see patches of grazing sheep both north and south of the trail. At one point, mid-valley, Cat called out that he had spotted a pair of antelopes. They had a full day ahead of them, and would have to camp one more night.

Fifteen miles away, others awaited their arrival.

15

Jesse pulled the leather thong a second time. He heard the bell again, followed by silence. Then, the side of the closure on his right opened slowly with a distinct squeaking sound broadcast from the iron hinges. A small boy, barefoot, garbed in loose-fitting white breaches and like shirt, stood in the hall as he reached up to hold the iron latch. Jesse reckoned him to be no more than five or six.

The boy looked up at the visitor with big, brown suspicious eyes. "¿Quien es?" he piped.

Jesse replied, "Soy Jesse Landry. Para señor Noriega. ¿Está en casa?" He looked over the boy's head.

The boy shook his head. "No está."

Jesse heard a second voice, female, mature, but young. A second later, a girl in her late teens turned the corner from the right cross-hall. She stopped for a moment, took two steps toward the door, then halted. The boy looked around at her, his hand still on the latch, then back at Jesse, a boy portraying a man.

The girl smiled at the boy, went to him and touched his small, round head, then looked at Jesse after sobering. "¿Quien es? ¿Que quieres?"

Jesse was unable to see her face clearly in the shadows of the somber hallway, but he sensed she was pretty. He barely made out two, long, black braids that hung onto her back. Petite, she wore a long skirt of what appeared to him to be fine cloth, the sort of material his father's mercantile carried for people of means. Above that was a white bodice with long sleeves, firmed across her bosom with thin, X-crossed black ribbons, a style he had not seen before. He noticed a pendant on a gold chain that hung from her neck and rested across her chest, which was bare above the bodice.

He repeated, in Spanish, the information and question he had told the boy, who moved away from the door and against the girl, where he took her hand. Jesse held his hat in his hands.

"My father is not at home. What is your business?"

"Perhaps you don't recognize my name. Landry. My father did business with your father."

"Oh." She edged closer to the door, into the light, as the boy released his grip, slipped away and ran off. She peered at him through the partially open door.

Jesse saw her face. A long oval with a small chin, her smooth, tight skin was light olive, her eyes green. He smiled at her beauty. "I'd like to speak with him."

"You said your father 'did' business with my father. He does no longer?"

Jesse waited a beat. "He has died. He was killed." He bent his head to one side and flopped his hat against his pant leg to control his rising emotions.

She cocked her head and frowned. "Oh, I am so sorry. When did this terrible thing happen?"

"Only yesterday. No—two days past. He was shot." Jesse nodded his head and sighed.

The girl stood still with her hands folded across her front, her head bent in distress, her brow furrowed. "Ay, God. So terrible." She was silent for several seconds as she stared at him, then she held out both hands in a welcoming gesture. "Please, come in. You may wait for him. I will show the way." She turned and moved off.

Jesse shoved the big front door closed and followed.

The room where the girl led him was large, with a high, beamed ceiling with herring-bone pine *latias*. The thick walls were adorned here and there with stiff, formal oil portraits of men and women, most beyond their middle years; mostly poorly rendered. A large, cloth tapestry hung over the space opposite the wall where a formal, mantle-topped fireplace dominated. It featured a castle turret surmounted by a warrior's tufted helmet. Behind the crenelation, was what appeared to be an angel, while below, a knight on horseback rode by from right to left. On the face of the turret was a huge bird, its wings spread wide. The castle, with its accompaniments, were surrounded by leafy rubric. Beneath it all was a scroll with the name "García de Noriega." It hung loosely, with minor bugles, dips and stretch marks. Jesse was certain he recognized silver and gold threads in the theme portion.

The floor was of new wood, where square, large-head nails were in evidence. Centered was a spacious, low table with a heavy wooden top. It sat on a huge Middle-Eastern motif rug. Large, heavy armchairs of wood and leather were arranged around it. A pair of dark wood book cases stood against the walls at the opposite ends of the room, replete with cloth- and leather-bound volumes. Two large, wrought-iron candelabra hung from the ceiling beams. More, smaller, iron candelabra rested on the table. Two of the windows Jesse had passed on the *portal* allowed muted light in from the plaza, reduced only by thin, white, lace-edged curtains drawn closed. He wondered what room lay beyond, a room with one window. Given his own experience, he imagined an office for the master of the house.

A few feet inside the room, the girl wheeled to face Jesse, who had stopped and was busy taking everything in. "My father will soon return. Please have a seat." She gestured.

He looked at her. "May I know your name?"

"Apolonia." She smiled. He sensed a certain strength and assuredness in her. He thought of the child, and wondered if he were hers.

"Apolonia. I believe I have heard my father speak of you." This he invented, since he had no true recollection. He held his hat in both hands.

She smiled. A pause ensued while they looked at each other.

Jesse broke the reverie as he moved for one of the chairs arranged around the table. "I will wait, then. Thank you."

Apolonia moved toward the hall door. "I will tell him you are waiting. He won't be long." She disappeared, then reappeared a few seconds later. "May I provide you with something? Perhaps something to drink?"

"I appreciate the offer. I would be grateful for some water. It has been a long, dry ride."

"Of course. Momentarily." She disappeared again.

Jesse sat and looked around the big room. Two minutes passed, then the boy entered the room carrying a cup very gingerly. He stood far enough away from the visitor such that he had to proffer the cup with outstretched hands. As he did, he watched Jesse's face with intense wonderment. Jesse smiled and thanked him. The boy said nothing.

"Did your mother send you with the water?" Jesse sipped at the liquid.

The boy shook his head. "My mother died."

Jesse put the cup on the table. "I'm sorry." He found himself saddened, yet relieved. The boy was not Apolonia's offspring. He smiled at the child, who, after a short pause, brought himself to return a smile. "What do they call you?"

"Roberto." His tone was of embarrassment as he looked down at the floor.

Jesse nodded. "A good, strong name, Roberto."

At that, Roberto managed an embarrassed grin, turned and raced from the room. Jesse stared after him.

He waited several more minutes, then stood and strolled about the big room. He realized that except for random noises coming from the earthen plaza, the huge, thick-walled house, at least in his part of it, was silent. It was not unlike the Abréu-Landry house where he grew up. He went to one of the windows and pushed the curtain aside. The plaza was occupied with the normal activity of the day. A man on horseback here; a farm wagon there; small boys running; women in long skirts carrying baskets. He allowed the curtain to close, then walked slowly across to the book case on his right. As he reached the tall piece of furniture more accustomed to rest in east coast houses, he heard a sound from behind. He turned.

The man in the doorway stood not as tall as his father had, but was much thinner; almost slight. His face was thin as well, and angular. Jesse was reminded of a line drawing copy of an El Greco painting of a Spanish Grandee he had seen in a book about art. His hair was full; greying on the sides. He wore a fine shirt over pants and boots suitable for riding horseback. His facial expression and demeanor was that of a man in control, one who knew who he was, and was happy to let others, who in his view were beneath him, know. Jesse reckoned him to be in his sixth decade; his father's age. "Good day, sir," he said, in Spanish. "I am Nerio Antonio García de Noriega. This is my house."

Jesse answered in the same language. "Good day." He sensed tension in the man.

"My daughter told me that you awaited my return. What is your business? What may I do for you?" His voice was icy as he remained in place, a step inside the big room. His hands were clasped behind his back.

Jesse allowed a small frown to cross his brow. "She did not tell you my name?"

Noriega raised his head in an imperious pose as he waved his hand. "No. She did not. Should she have?"

"My name is Landry. Jesse Landry. Of Santa Fé. My father—"

"Oh," Noriega said, softening immediately. "Please forgive me! Of course! How thoughtless of her! She should have told me." He advanced, held out his hand, then grabbed Jesse's outstretched hand and covered it with his other. "How is your father? Well, I trust. You favor him." He looked Jesse in the eye.

Jesse shook his head. "I am sad to report that he is dead. He was killed."

Noriega, while his hand still held Jesse's, looked deep into the young man's eyes. "No! When—how did this terrible thing happen?! Tell me!" He was genuinely shocked.

Jesse started to speak when Noriega released his grip and walked toward a sideboard that stood against the hall-side wall.

"Please sit," Noriega said.

Jesse took the chair he had occupied when Apolonia left.

Noriega returned with a cut-glass carafe and two matching tumblers. He moved one of the chairs and angled it such that it was close to Jesse's and sat. He put the glasses on the table, pulled the glass stopper from the carafe, and poured brandy into each. He then handed one to Jesse and held the other up. "To your father." He sipped.

Jesse took the glass, but hesitated.

"Drink. Please. To your father. You are under duress. The brandy will calm you. Please." Noriega emptied his glass, then gestured to encourage Jesse to drink. "Now tell me."

Jesse touched the glass to his lips, enough to taste the strong alcoholic beverage, then lowered it. His eyes looked away. "He was shot."

"Shot?! Ay! No! Shot? By whom?!" Noriega slammed his empty glass onto the table. "Tell me, and I will have this criminal arrested!"

Jesse glanced at Noriega, then looked away. "The man who killed my father is also dead."

Noriega was silent for two beats, then, "He is dead? How? How—?"

"I shot him." He looked at Noriega as he nodded his head, then sipped the liquor.

Noriega cocked his head at Jesse. "You—!"

Jesse looked directly at Noriega. "Yes."

"But how—?"

Jesse told Noriega everything he knew, about the incidents that led to his being in Albuquerque, and how he could not understand why his father had been shot. He was careful to modify the story enough to keep Lieutenant Beckner's role out of his narrative, at the army officer's request.

Noriega rose from his chair, agitated, then paced about the room as he repeated his disbelief. He sat again and peered closely at his visitor as he shook his head slowly. "He was a thief, this man? You believe he was a *Tejano*? I will meet with Baca and tell him. You say there were those who saw you shoot this brigand?" Noriega continued to stare at Jesse.

"Yes." Jesse stared at the floor as he shook his head. "I should not have carried my—the pistol." He looked up.

"No. No. You did the correct thing, my son." Noriega shook his head, reached over and touched Jesse's hand. He was quiet, then, "You will stay here. With us. My wife is at the church at this moment, with her elder sister." He managed a sideway glance, as though to indicate the church across the plaza. "They attend mass each day to pray for all our souls and to speak with the priest." He looked away, then said, barely loud enough for Jesse to hear, "The old fool. They are required to pay. He has a profitable business himself, and drinks and carouses each night." He calmed after his minor outburst, stood and generated a smile. "You will meet her." He paused, reflected, then said, "Come, I will have Ermelina show you to your room. You are now a part of my family. You will stay as long as need be. We will talk business, now that you are a man of commerce. But later, after you have rested. Come." Noriega slapped Jesse on the knee, stood and strode for the door, then stopped and turned. "May I assume that the white steed tethered to my corral is yours?"

Jesse stood. "Yes. I—"

Noriega raised his hand to assuage his visitor. "No matter. I will have Ustacio quarter, feed and water him. He will bring your belongings to you."

Jesse followed his host as he disappeared past the wide door frame into the hall.

As he caught up to him, he saw Noriega stand in the hall and turn his head to look in both directions along the passage.

"Ermelina!" He shouted. "Ermelina!" He waited stiffly.

From one end of the hall, a trim, middle-aged woman with gray hair appeared. She hustled toward Noriega as she wiped her hands in a white apron tied around her waist. "¡Sí, patrón!"

"Ermelina, take this young man to the guest room—uh—nearest the rear entrance. Make him comfortable." Noriega, whose demeanor had changed to a more distant, austere tone, waved his hand majestically.

"Sí, patrón." She advanced in hesitation, looked first at Noriega, then smiled briefly at Jesse, who returned the silent greeting.

Noriega turned to face Jesse. His manner changed again as he smiled with what Jesse detected to be managed. "Ermelina will bring you what you need. If you have further requirements, do not hesitate to ask. We sup immediately after vespers." He paused and looked at the floor. "My dear wife requires it." He lifted his head. "At six. And now, my boy, I must leave you. Business calls. Welcome." With that, he marched off down the hall, entered a room two openings away, and shut the door.

Ermelina approached Jesse and looked up at him. "Come. This way."

The room was half the size of his in Santa Fé. In one corner was a narrow wooden bed with a modern, but thin, cloth mattress, a small pillow at its head. At the foot was a small hand-made locker. Under the bed was a brass *orinal*, for use in the dead of night or winter. Centered, was a throw-rug over a modern, tiled floor. Across from the bed, against the opposite wall, stood a tall *ropero* for closeting clothes. Beyond the end of the bed was a small chest of drawers with a plain, white ceramic wash basin and pitcher. In one corner was a beehive-shaped fireplace. At the exterior-facing end of the room was a deep-set window, smaller that those along the front of the manse. It looked out onto the enclosed courtyard, or *atrio*, smaller than the Landry's, which was capable of encompassing freight wagons and their draft animals.

Jesse stood a few feet inside the room. He turned and nodded to Ermelina.

"I will return in a moment."

She went to the dresser, took the pitcher, left, and was back in less than five minutes. She carried bedding and the pitcher, heavier with wash water. She laid the pile of cloth and a blanket on the bed, then placed the pitcher in the basin.

As she began to make up the bed, a small, wizened man with bow legs stood in the door. In one hand he carried a pair of leather saddle bags that Jesse recognized as his own. "I'm Ustacio," he said. He held them out at arm's length. "Here are your bags."

Jesse went to him and took the bags. "Thank you." He started to reach into his breaches for a coin.

Ustacio held up both hands and shook his head. "No, no. You must not. The *patrón* pays us well." He shot a glance at bustling Ermelina, who ignored him. He then turned and disappeared after executing a small bow.

Finished with the bed, Ermelina stood and faced young Landry. "The necessary is out through the door that way." She pointed.

"Thank you," he said.

Without another word, the woman hurried from the room and was gone. Jesse looked about again, then opened one door of the tall, narrow wardrobe and dropped the bags into it. He was satisfied that the heft of one of them meant that it contained his sidearm. He would leave the house without it.

He entered the hall, looked both ways, then re-traced his steps to the room where he had met Noriega, and on to the foyer and front door. On the way, he noticed the pictures that hung from the walls. Most were oil portraits of mature men and women, along with a few religious depictions. One *nicho* contained a painted wooden rendition of the sad Virgin Mary. He thought of the *Guadalupana* on the Maestas house, and how there was none on the porch wall of the Noriega estate, something that puzzled him, given Noriega's statement about his wife's apparent piety. Perhaps it was beneath the dignity of the Noriegas of Albuquerque.

As he opened the big front door, he sensed he was being watched. He turned to see little Roberto, who stood with most of his body hidden around the corner to the hall. Jesse, who had donned his hat, doffed it to the youngster, who smiled coyly, pulled his head back and ran away.

He stepped out onto the long, shaded *portal,* stopped and looked about the sunny plaza. He saw no one or anything he might perceive as a threat. With a certain amount of anxiety, he headed across the bare, rutted dirt expanse in the direction of his rendezvous.

16

Lieutenant Beckner rode away from the Union Army's tented encampment overlooking the town of Albuquerque at a walk, and headed south along the ridge of the escarpment on the west edge of the Rio Grande. He maintained that path until the land dipped to a trail that led onto the littoral plane paralleling the wide, shallow and muddy, meandering river. He studied the myriad of animal and carriage tracks, selected the most likely, and navigated the stream with ease.

On the east bank of the river, he followed more tracks through the thick willow and cottonwood-choked plane. A few young boys and girls, along with several women, looked up with idle, but passing curiosity at the gringo on horseback as he rode by. He smiled at all in general, and touched the brim of his hat to a pair of women, one of whom deigned to smile in what he reckoned to be an open, appreciative way.

Beckner noticed a certain rusticity to the town of Albuquerque versus the relative sophistication of Santa Fé. The principle daily pursuit in this town along the stream named by the Spanish as the "big," or "grand" river centered more on agriculture and animal husbandry, rather than the commerce, tariff collections, banking and politics of its neighbor to the north. The effluvia carried that fact in abundance to his nostrils. He was reminded of his sojourns with the Union cavalry in the field, but these odors were different. The smell of various animal types were interwoven with the tangy aroma of fruits, vegetables and hay. Ultimately, he discovered that he approved of the experience.

Francisco Maestas had told him to go to a *cantina* a short distance north of the town plaza, along the main north-south thoroughfare, the Camino Real. This was a place where gringos, or "Americanos," might be, although grudgingly, accepted, especially if accompanied by recognized locals. That included trail-weary *Chihuahuensos* not in a murderous mood. Preferably, those who might be engaged in business with the brash, light-skinned outlanders with a promise of profit.

As he rode through the plaza at a walk, he encountered little interest in his presence. He reasoned that the people were used to seeing outsiders of his ilk. He may have been helped, he realized, by the clothes he wore, which both Jesse and Maestas had recommended. They were less like those worn by him before his foray into the army, and more like those worn by men of the Territory. The nervousness he felt as he crossed the river and entered the town was dissipating. He was taller than the average man, and that had been a point of curiosity from the outset, but even that seemed to be wearing thin.

He found the *cantina*. It was a modest adobe structure without a porch, so common in Santa Fé. The swept dirt approach in front featured a pair of hitching rails a few feet away from the single entrance. Two thin, flat native stones, one lying flush with the ground, the other upright, were placed in front of the opening, a novelty for the patrons upon which they could make a pass at cleaning mud and ordure from their boots should they be sober enough to care. Two small windows, one on either side of the door were sunk deeply into the brown earthen walls, more or less balanced. The one on the north canted to one side a few degrees, a sign that the wall was shifting, a condition Beckner had noticed in other buildings that used the ancient construction techniques brought from Southern Europe. Along the south side there was an empty, flat, Murphy-like wagon, its tongue at an angle to the ground. Three horses, their reins tossed over one of the rails, stood patiently. A wagon, drawn by a single horse, moved slowly by from the north. The old man driving it nodded to Beckner and mouthed a greeting as the Union officer raised his hand in greeting.

The lieutenant dismounted next to the nearest rail, threw the reins over the crude, de-barked pine branch horizontal bar and headed for the door. As he stepped onto the fancy stone entry, prior to passing through the opening, he noticed that at least one potential patron had taken advantage of the ad hoc boot cleaner. He was sure the donation was not mud or any other form of dirt. It appeared well-aged.

Beckner stepped no more than three feet inside and stopped. The interior was somber, such that the four oil lamps that hung from the ceiling were aglow. Their energy was for the most part wasted, because all but one of the five men who populated the single large room that constituted the *cantina* appeared lost in their own thoughts and required no light. One sat upright against his chair back, eyes half-open, while another, at a table near the entrance, lay on the table, apparently asleep. The fifth seated man, who appeared alert, he recognized. It was Francisco Maestas.

Maestas raised his cup to Beckner, turned to look toward the bar, then back.

Beckner went to his table. "Have you been waiting long?" He pulled a chair out as he eyed a woman approaching.

"Not long," Maestas replied. He looked up as the woman stood next to the table.

She smiled at both men. "What do you want?"

Francisco looked up at her, then at Beckner. "*Pulque. Dos.*" He shot a questioning glance at the lieutenant.

Beckner shook his head in a short, jerking motion and frowned.

Maestas leaned toward him across the table. "Better we pretend to drink than not at all."

Beckner nodded assent, and Maestas looked up at the waitress, who moved off.

"Tell me, my friend, how are the *Americano* soldiers up on the bluff?"

"Well. They stand ready."

Maestas frowned. "Ready? For what? To attack us?" He smiled.

Beckner shook his head. "They do their job." He looked down at the table, moved imaginary dust, then looked up.

"Why do they not come into the town? Are the gringo soldiers afraid of us?" Maestas bent his head to one side.

Beckner scratched his head. "Of the women. Not the men."

Maestas hesitated two seconds before he broke out in laughter. That drew the attention of the man across the room who fought off sleep from the alcohol in his system. Maestas slapped the table. "Good! Very good, my friend!" He paused and sobered. "And why are they afraid of the women?" He tilted his head again.

Without hesitation, the army officer said, "Because they are beautiful, and they become weak at seeing them." He raised his chin in a triumphant gesture.

The waitress returned with two small, crude glasses and set them on the table while Beckner reached for coins.

"Ah." Maestas picked his drink up and held it out to his table partner. "Well said. Here is to you and our friendship." He sipped as he watched Beckner over the glass.

Beckner picked up the other glass and raised it. "To you, to your family, and to your lovely sister." He tasted as he watched Maestas' face.

Maestas set his glass down gently, then rotated it slowly. He was silent for a time, then, "I could not avoid seeing that which transpired between you and Mercedes."

Several seconds passed before Beckner spoke. He shook his head and toyed with the small container in front of him. "She is beautiful. And sweet."

"And she is young and in the bosom of her family. And you are a gringo. In the army. And you will go home some day. A long distance from our home. Her home." He looked straight into Beckner's eyes.

Beckner did not avert Maestas' gaze. He shook his head. "That I will in time leave the territory is not certain, Francisco. It is not certain that I will remain in the army. It is true that I do not know the language or many of the customs. But I am learning and willing to become a part of this place."

Maestas shook his head and looked away.

"You love your family. Your ways. Your sister. I also have a sister. If you were to see her, you might feel as I do toward Mercedes."

Maestas concentrated on Beckner again. He was very still.

"Our friend Jesse Landry. His father was a gringo. His mother was from this place. Your people. Study him. Does he not fit in?" Beckner narrowed his eyes with the question.

Maestas sucked in a deep breath, released it, and took another swallow of the strong drink.

"Francisco, I have no ill plans for you, your family, and least of all, Mercedes. I don't know her. She doesn't know me, but I do know this, Francisco: I have never met a girl—a woman—who has captured my feelings as has she." He paused. "Perhaps I will ride away without speaking another word to her, but I tell you this as a man, an officer, and a gentleman, that I want to know her more. And if it takes a year. More—"

Maestas turned his head to follow Beckner's gaze as he stopped and looked toward the door.

Jesse stood near the opening. He looked around the room, recognized Maestas and Beckner, removed his hat, and went to their table. He pulled out a chair, sat and looked at each man in turn.

"How did you fare?" Beckner asked.

"I have a room at the Noriega house." He looked from Beckner to Maestas. "Where you left me."

Both men nodded in approval.

"Did you meet the great man?" Maestas queried.

"I did. We spoke for a time, then he had other business. I am to return at meal time." He looked at Beckner. "Did you go to the encampment?"

"Yes."

"What now?" Maestas asked.

Jesse asked, "Have you seen Baca or his men?"

Maestas shook his head. "No."

Jesse rubbed his chin. "I told Noriega of my problem. He said he knows Baca and will speak with him on my behalf."

Maestas, without moving his head, rolled his eyes first at Jesse, then Beckner, then down at the table top. He sipped his drink.

Jesse studied Maestas' face. "You think he lies?"

Maestas cocked his head to one side. "No, he does not lie so much as he promises too much."

"You know him well?" Jesse frowned at Francisco, then shot Beckner a glance.

"I have not met this man, but I know of him. As I said. He is powerful. He is among the richest of men in this valley. He can hurt people, and he has done so." He toyed with his glass. He looked up as he saw the waitress approach. "Do you want to drink?"

Jesse shook his head. "No."

Maestas waved the waitress off as she neared the table. She scowled at him before she turned away as she wiped her wet hands on her dress.

"The Hawken?" Jesse asked.

Maestas looked at Jesse. "Hawken?"

"The carbine. You took it from me."

"Ah. It is with my cousin. He is a good man. It is where it will not be found." Maestas paused. "And your pistol. Where is it?"

Jesse jerked his head toward the town center. "It is also hidden. In my room."

Maestas patted the gun at his side, smiled at Lieutenant Beckner, then at Jesse. "Mine is also safely hidden. At my side."

All three men laughed. Maestas raised his glass to Beckner, who responded in kind, and both men drank.

Maestas moved his head about, sniffing the air. "I detect the tang of roasting meats. I believe we should see what this filthy place has to fill our bellies."

"The two of you eat. I have been invited to sup with the great man and his family," Jesse said.

Maestas made a bowing gesture with his hand. "Of course. You dine with those who have the most to share. I applaud you." He smiled.

Jesse looked down. He shook his head. "It is not my intention to remain long. But if this man can help me—"

Maestas sobered. "Of course. I meant no disrespect. To you or your father, who was our friend. Or to Mr. Noriega and his family." He closed his eyes in a solemn way.

"No offense taken, my good friend. I will remain with you while you sample the fare."

"Yes, let us try their food. It smells good from this vantage," Beckner said.

Maestas looked toward the bar expectantly.

Jesse looked at Beckner. "Where will you sleep?"

"If there is no lodging here, then I have a billet at the encampment." He pointed vaguely.

"You, Francisco?" Jesse turned toward Maestas.

"With my cousin. Archuleta." He winked. "His sweet wife likes me, I think." He paused. "I believe they will welcome the lieutenant." He looked at Beckner expectantly.

All three men smiled at each other.

While Sergeant Tandy lay on his stomach, his spyglass to his eyes, Milton, four yards away behind a cedar next to a large rock, tucked into the last of his rations. Behind him, their two mounts stood patiently, but uncomfortably, under the shade of a ponderosa, having been saddled again earlier should the two soldiers need to depart in a rush. Tandy said nothing, but he found the noises Private Milton made while enjoying his repast more than annoying, even across the space that divided them.

Tandy came up on his elbows and grunted as he raised his head in sudden increased concentration.

Milton, his mouth full, looked up and grunted, "Huh?!"

Tandy waved at Milton to stay down as the private started to stand. "I think I see 'em! I think it's them!"

Milton wiped his mouth on his sleeve and crawled to Tandy, then looked first at the NCO, then the direction his telescope was pointed. "Hot damn, looks like the lieutenant was right?!"

Tandy scratched his forehead, then adjusted his hat. He shot Milton a scowling glance. "'Course the lieutenant was right!" He looked into the glass again. "Gotta' be them. Three on horses and three packers."

"Kin I see?" Milton asked.

Tandy handed him the telescope. "Take a gander, then hand it back."

Milton held the glass up to his eye, moved the instrument around, then settled. "Hot damn! It's them. Who else? Yup." He gave the spyglass back to the sergeant. "Whatta' we do now?"

Tandy took several seconds to answer. "We watch 'em pass, then get on their tail." He crawled backward instinctively to stay out of sight, although the maneuver was unnecessary.

Below, in the canyon, Rodman and his partners, Pulver and Cat, struggled down along the steep, rock-strewn, badly eroded path that constituted the Tijeras cut that divided the high Sandia mountain from the lower Manzanos to the south. The pack animals brayed at the manner in which their loads had shifted on their sore backs, and they tensed up on the ropes leading to the two horses the drovers rode behind Rodman. The contraband load on one brute had moved so far that it threatened to fall off. Cat, the black man, turned at the cries of the victimized animal, and shouted the alarm. Rodman turned in his saddle as a crate broke lose, fell to the hard ground and splintered open on one side. The barrels of two of the weapons protruded through splintered wood. The mule panicked, brayed, reared its hind legs and stumbled. As it went down, its right front knee cracked against a sharp rock.

Cat was off his horse in a flash and alongside the suffering mule as it panted and hyper-ventilated, eyes wild with the pain. The black man stood, pushed his hat back and shook his head as he stared down at the incapacitated brute. "Shee-ut! He's a goner. Hot damn!"

Rodman whipped the reins around and loped back to the stressed mule. "Goddamn it, you stupid nigger! I told you to keep a sharp eye on these animals! What the hell's wrong with you!" He made a wild gesture with his hand, his eyes aflame.

In a flash, Cat whipped his long-barreled .44 pistol from its holster, wheeled, angled it up at Rodman on his mount, and cocked the hammer, all in one swift move. "And goddamn you, ya' stupid lily-white prick! It twarn't me wit' the dumb-ass idee to load up dese here brutes wit' this armament and traipse all over kingdom-come! It was a accident!"

Rodman, his jaw slack at first, recovered. "How dare you point your weapon at me! Lower it this instant!"

Cat's eyes burned as he stood his ground. "Listen to me agin', an' y'all listen good, white jackass. We's out' the middle o' only God knows where, an' I ain't takin' no shit fum' you or nobody! I could shoot yo' silly white ass here an' now, and nobody but nobody would know or care!" His six-shot revolver had not wavered an inch as he squinted. "So, here's how it works. We works together, or we don't work 'tall. I don't owe you nothin', but I am willin' to expend a single bullet on you to prove it!"

Rodman looked at Pulver, who had also halted and turned. Pulver leaned forward on his saddle horn, hat low over his eyes, a thin smile on his face. His eyes darted between the two other men. He was motionless as Rodman implored his assistance with his eyes.

Rodman angled his head arrogantly at Cat. "Listen, you—!"

Pulver, his voice low, but audible, said, "I prefer, Mr. Rodman, sir, that you take heed to my friend's serious 'nough words. 'Cuz, ya' see, we jist don't give a shee-ut 'bout you or what you think, say or do." He paused and fired off a long, noisy, dark line of spittle to one side. "My strong feelin' here is we oughter' git them thar fowlin' pieces up an' outa' here afore we're spotted for what you, me an' him are all about." He intensified his gaze at Rodman. "See, we figure in this neck o' the woods, you an' me jist barely are tolerated. These here Messcans an' Injuns would jist as soon slit our throats as look at us. An' him?" He pointed at the black man who had yet to lower the hammer or his weapon. "To these folks, we're all the same. Ya' know?"

Rodman allowed himself a long silence as his face screwed up with the anxiety he felt. He lowered his head, then looked up. He cocked his head to one side in contrition. "Look. I'm sorely regretful. I—I lost my temper. We're all tired, and this has been a tough jaunt." He pulled his hat off his head, smoothed his hair, then put it on again. His voice softened more. "Let's get this crate back up. I'll help." With that, he dismounted and went to the damaged wooden box.

Cat hesitated, then pointed the long-barreled revolver away and at the ground as he lowered the hammer. His voice was barely audible, but Rodman and Pulver heard him. "Dis here po' mule ain't gonna' make it. An' we cain't carry 'im. He's gotta' go to his ree-ward." He looked first at Pulver, who nodded sagely, then Rodman who merely shut his eyes and jerked a "yes."

Cat pointed his .44 at the mule's head, cocked the hammer and pulled the trigger. The revolver kicked in his hand, the mule shivered for four seconds, then settled into death.

Cat holstered his gun, but stayed in place. "We oughta' give 'im a decent burial, but dis here terrain, along wit' the time we ain't in possession of means we gotta' leave 'im fer the cahy-otes an' the buzzards. Amen."

"Amen," Pulver said.

On the ledge that overlooked the canyon, Sergeant Tandy, prone, continued his surveillance of the three men and their animal-only caravan. "What the—?!" He pushed up, balanced on one hand. The spyglass was still to his eye.

Milton, busy packing the remaining victuals and camping gear, turned. "What'd ya' say?"

"Somethin' goin' on down there. Hear that?!"

Milton joined Tandy as Tandy stood up. He dusted his breeches as he did. "Shore did! Whattaya suppose?"

Tandy pointed. "Take a look." He handed the glass to Milton.

Milton put the brass piece to one eye and squinted the other. "Looks like they dropped somethin'. Sure does."

"That's what I say. But the gunshot."

"Shit, loading up them poor ani- mules with all that hard, heavy baggage. No wonder." Milton handed Tandy the telescope.

Tandy peered through the glass for a few seconds. "I reckon they lost a mule. Yep. I think they had to dispatch a mule. Lyin' down. Likely dead. That'll make it harder." He paused. "Well, we'll wait 'til they pass, then get behind 'em."

Milton looked at the sergeant with a deep frown. "I don't git this, sarge. Why come we not just go down there an' arrest them renegades?"

Tandy looked hard at Milton. "Cause Lieutenant Beckner gave us orders, that's why! You know, Private Milton, you're good at soldierin', but sometimes I wonder 'bout you. We got orders, an' I intend to follow 'em. We wait an' we follow. An' we report. Got that?" He slid the spyglass closed and walked away as he tossed his head.

Milton cocked his head. "Yeah, I figure." He turned and trudged back to his duties.

As Trooper Milton walked away, Sergeant Tandy turned toward the lower-ranked man, removed his campaign hat and scratched his head. "But I'll tell you this, Private. All of us, includin' them down there, is mighty lucky."

Milton stopped and turned toward Tandy. "Why's that, Sarge?"

"'Cause them injuns are gone. Yessir, plumb disappeared. Apaches gone. Gone. Hm."

"Now, how about that?" Milton asked.

In the canyon below, Rodman, Cat and Pulver managed to bind the damaged crate together, divide the load and spread it to the two remaining mules. During that time, which encompassed almost half an hour, Rodman avoided Cat's glances as he engaged in the sort of work he had never had the displeasure of experiencing before. At one point, given his inexperience, he managed to acquire a small splinter from a crate slat. Cat pulled his six-inch, antler-handled hunting knife and offered to dig it out, but Rodman thanked him all the same. The black man and Pulver traded amused glances as Cat shrugged, raised his eyebrows and twisted his mouth.

All three kept an eye on the trail in both directions, happy to note that they were, in their view, alone and unobserved, considering the loud report from Cat's pistol. Although both Pulver and Cat occasionally scanned the ridges and tree lines for possible intruders, they did not detect the two troopers several hundred yards to the west and a hundred feet above them.

Cautiously, and in silence, they regained their trek westward. Once again, Pulver and Cat held the lead ropes. The difference lay in the fact that the chastened and worried Rodman took up the rear. This was, in part, because he feared reprisal and betrayal on the part of his companions, and because he did not want their eyes on him, even his back. He also nurtured the idea, one that appealed to his cowardly sense, that the animals and their precious cargo required a close watch, and he had assigned himself that important duty. So he told himself.

As they passed the section where Tandy and Milton lay in wait, the trail, although at an incline, leveled out to a degree, thus becoming more passable and less of a strain on the overtaxed beasts.

The two soldiers who crouched above them watched as they moved slowly by. When the contraband caravan was at a distance from the trooper bivouac where Tandy reasoned they could remain behind, keep pace and observe without detection, the two men, glad to be on the move again, slipped down from their aerie onto the rutted trail. They guided their mounts on foot. Tandy opined that they should stay behind, such that what their quarry might observe would be seen only as figures in the distance. He reckoned that they should hug, as much as possible, the steep rocky cliffs along the route.

As they approached the long sweep into the Rio Grande Valley from the rugged Tijeras, the contraband team and their followers encountered occasional people, wagons, and horses that trafficked between the outpost village in the mouth of the canyon and the town on the river. They saw small bands of sheep grazing the beige grama grass that covered the piedmont.

Tandy calculated they could close the gap some, not only because they would be less noticeable, but because he feared losing them in the increasing population mix. The troopers were amazed at the sight before them. They had been surrounded by mountainous terrain from Apache cut south, then through the spectacular canyon, now they faced an open, sloping plain until it seemed to rise again in the distance. The town of Albuquerque, not yet in view, lay below the crest of the piedmont, along the flat litoral of the broad meandering stream.

Ahead, the three men from Texas had the same reaction.

Rodman developed increasing concern over his locale and the approach to the town. More people meant more suspicion and the possibility of an unwelcome challenge. The two men who headed up the group were less concerned, for the most part, because they were not fully informed of their mission. They knew they were transporting contraband, and they knew what it was, but they assumed it was for sale, possibly surreptitiously for some reason, and that beyond their caring. If they had known they were carrying weapons for a potential insurrection, they might have refused the journey. They were armed, a rarity among the populace, paid in part with gold coin, and had only their own skins to protect. They did, however, look back at Rodman more often.

The sun was mid-high in the west when the three men saw the vast north-south sweep of green cottonwood *bosque* that blanketed the flat flood plane built by the brown silt-bearing, meandering stream. They were unable yet to see any of the scattered, flat-roofed, adobe houses in the outskirts of Albuquerque.

Rodman, who had ridden in the rear the entire distance from the dust-up in Tijeras, sped up and pulled up alongside Cat and Pulver. "Let's hang here for a minute, boys," he said.

Cat pulled his hat off and slapped his knee. "Boy, howdy! Will you look at dis?! Hot damn!" He leaned his head to the side. "Ah don't see no houses..."

Pulver leaned forward and moved his head back and forth as he scanned the ribbon of green that lay below. "You ain't wrong there, Cat. Some sight. Who'd a-known? They's probly 'tother side the forest. You reckon?" He ranged his head back and forth in attempt to see signs of structures.

The horses reacted to the stop by nodding and moving their great heads about and stomping their forelegs, while the mules remained gratefully silent.

"They smell water," Cat said as he looked at Pulver and patted his mount's neck.

Rodman ignored the remark. "It's a sight for sore eyes." He paused. "Here's the deal, boys." He hesitated as he reached inside his loose-fitting shirt to retrieve a piece of paper. "There's someone I'm to meet up with down there." He unfolded and looked at the paper. "Before I do, these crates'll have to be safe from prying eyes." He peered at the paper, frowned, looked up, put the note back inside his shirt, then glanced at his companions. "Now, the way I look at it, these animals and these crates attract too much attention." He waved his finger at the loaded mules. "So, let's get 'em down to them trees, drop the load, an' get the animals to water." He paused. "One 'o you stay with the boxes while the other takes 'em." He looked at Cat and Pulver in turn. "Does that suit?"

"An' where'll you be?" Pulver asked. He touched his hat.

"Seeking out my contact."

"An' what we say's in dese here crates if'n we're challenged?" Cat asked. He squinted at Rodman.

"To those with the proper skills, the words on the boxes read 'wagon parts.' If they can't read, then so state."

Both Pulver and Cat turned to look at the crates, then at each other.

"An' if some local bandit covets them wagon parts?" Pulver squinted at Rodman.

"If they can't be convinced with kind words, show 'em the iron on your hip," Rodman said. "But we'll secret them amongst those trees for now." He pointed to the cottonwood *bosque* below. "Soon's I connect with this fellow, we'll move 'em to safety and away from the curious."

"Thing is, Rodman, neither Cat nor me relish the thought o' swinging from one o' them trees yonder fer what we're up to, so my advice to you is to make great haste." Pulver awarded Rodman a look the man could not mistake for kind rebuke.

Rodman held up his hand. "I'm in the same danger as you gents, which ain't a lot, considering because these 'er for sale. But—an' here's the rub. It's the god-damned army don't like it. So I contrive to move quickly. Remember, you have more gold and specie coming your way." He nodded to both men. "It's take care and caution and the lips sealed." He saluted to the brim of his hat.

"Be assured we plan to receive it promptly 'an in full measure," Cat snarled. "'An you can fergit the specie. 'Specially that bank 'o San Antone paper."

"Rest assured." Rodman smiled nervously.

Cat sniffed and looked away.

The three of them on horseback lead the hungry, thirsty and weary mules, followed the depressed track of gravel-rich, sandy loam to the plain created by the ancient, shallow, muddy meandering river. There, they moved southward along dense, soft, sandy ground among thickets of Russian olive, willow and infant cottonwoods struggling for a place in the sun.

The mules were unloaded in an open space far, and hidden from, the nearest house and planted field beyond the thick cottonwood *bosque*. It was decided that Cat should remain, given the color of his skin. He reclined on one of the crates after lighting up a cheroot, while Pulver, still in the saddle, led Cat's mount and the two happy burden-carriers away. Rodman's pace was quicker, and he soon disappeared through the trees and back to the trail. His admonition to his traveling companions was that, for now, he must appear separate from them.

While Pulver lead the animals to water trough hewn from a single tree trunk a few yards outside the southeastern plaza entrance, Rodman angled away on a separate route.

From a vantage point well behind, Sergeant Tandy and Private Milton watched the trio with the contraband as they dipped down into the verge of the forest east of the town.

Tandy spurred his horse to a trot, as did Milton, but when the troopers reached the steep cut of the trail that dropped to the plain of the river, their quarry had disappeared from view. They stopped and looked.

"Shit," Tandy said under his breath. "Lookie this. It's like a jungle down there."

His horse pranced at the sweet, pungent odor of moisture transpiring off the cottonwood forest beneath.

Milton reined his horse around as he scoured the land below. "Shore is. Hot damn!" He paused and looked up. "An' look-a them peaks yonder. Look like tits! Damn!'An them mountains back that-a-way. Sheesh." He turned to point.

"Somethin' fer sure. Wide open, it is." Tandy paused and stroked his chin. He turned in the saddle and looked behind at the Sandias. "An' we was on that thing. God!"

Milton turned as well. "Shee-ut. Mighty high." His voice was almost a whisper; reverential. "Wonder how high." He paused, becalmed, then returned his gaze to the greensward below. "They had to go midst them trees."

"Reckon you're on to somethin'." The sergeant spoke without a hint of the sarcasm he intended as he also returned his attention to the problem at hand. He removed his worn campaign hat, scratched his head and the back of his neck, then settled it on his head again.

"What now?" Milton asked.

"We needs be nimble, Private Milton. They got mules, an' they got crates. Neither's easy to hide. Long as they're in the open. So, we go down and start lookin'. Now they'er midst them trees—"

"Right, sarge." Milton clicked his mount and started down the cut.

As the troopers rode slowly through the dense cottonwood forest, they saw no sign of their quarry or any locals. They followed the trace onto the animal-created wagon-wide trace bordered by shallow, swamp-like land on either side. They were startled when a pair of pheasants rose up and flew away from the underbrush alongside the trail, as their wings flapped noisily.

"Hey! Birds?!! How 'bout this place. I thunk it was total desert!"

"Guess not, Private," Tandy opined. He smiled.

A quarter mile later, the trail widened onto higher ground surfaced with sandy dirt and gravel. Then came the first of farm fields, houses and outbuildings. Small groups of the curious, men, women and children appeared, drawn to halt their endeavors long enough to watch the two men in blue uniform as they rode by, side-by-side, campaign style.

Nervous, Tandy turned to Milton. "Wave at 'em, Milton. An' smile."

Milton, who took Tandy's suggestion to heart, said, "They ain't runnin' at us with guns 'er nothin'."

"A good thing it is, Private. If the opposite, we'd be inconvenienced, an' that's the truth." Tandy gave a two-finger salute to a woman wielding a wooden hay fork.

As Tandy and Milton approached the town proper, they made their way through hard-packed dirt streets defined by simple, crude adobe houses that rambled in a semblance of order, some obviously interconnected after original construction. More people were in evidence, and more came to doors, the few windows that existed and alley corners as word spread of the sighting of the two soldiers west-bound on horses with saddle bags, camping gear and firearms. For the most part, their observers were silent women and children. As they passed, the murmurs, though non-threatening, rose.

Milton leaned toward to Tandy. "This watchin' makes me plumb nervous, sarge."

"You ain't alone. Least ways, we ain't seen no gun barrels pointed our way."

The two men continued to smile, nod their heads and salute as they moved slowly along. They both wanted desperately to turn and look behind, but both resisted the temptation.

When they came into an open area past a row of houses, Milton reined his horse in, caused it to circle toward Tandy, and halted. "Shit, sarge! You see what I see?!" He kept his voice low and gestured with his chin.

Tandy looked in the direction Milton indicated. "I do, indeed, Private. Pay dirt."

He nodded, his lips compressed in a confident smile.

More than two houses away, one of their quarry, Pulver, stood next to two saddled horses and two mules. The animals were crowded together at a horse trough. The renegade was unaware that the Union Army duo had spotted him.

"We gotta git outa' sight," Tandy said. "Over there." He reined his horse to the right and clicked.

Milton followed suit. At the trough, Pulver looked around a few seconds after the soldiers left his line of sight, unaware that he had been spotted, but secure, in his own mind, that he had not.

Rodman rode slowly and warily into the plaza of the little farming village after he followed the trail that crossed the swampy area between the piedmont rise and the village. To his right stood the San Felipe de Neri church, with its thick, earthen walls and arches that fronted the east side addition. The Texican agent expected the natives he encountered to scowl and point, but he was pleasantly surprised to note none of what he expected. He halted immediately inside the square, beyond the edge of the first house, dismounted and stood with the reins held loosely in one hand. Two young boys walked past, one who carried a sack laden with fruit. Rodman hailed them.

"¿Sí señor?" They stopped and spoke in wide-eyed unison.

Rodman held out the piece of paper he had pulled from his shirt. "Uh, this place? ¿Éste?" He pointed at the paper.

Both boys crowded in to see. One shook his head slowly. The other considered, then stretched his arm out and pointed. "Pa' alla. Esa casa." He looked up at the gringo and nodded, his mouth agape.

Rodman, who had leaned down, stood up straight and looked at the place the boy had indicated. He dug into a trail-dusty trouser pocket, pulled out several coins, selected two of them, and handed each one. With large grins, the youths looked up at the outlander, thanked him, then studied the little round pieces of metal as they moved happily on, jabbering about how they should spend their windfall.

He looked first at the church on his right, then around at the few low buildings that defined the plaza, then studied the minimal bustle in its open space. He led his horse to the building identified by the boy, looped the reins to a hitching post in front, then went to the door under the *portal*. In little more than a minute, the interior bell brought a small boy to the big, double door.

17

Roberto, at the age of six, loved answering the door, or more to the point, loved the bell that led to answering the door. For him, the little, oddly-shaped metal object with the long leather string attached was a wonder; an innovation like none other he had experienced in his young life. He could not imagine what lay before him, that one day he would look back on the wondrous, sonic thing and puzzle why it held such fascination for him. To investigate the ringer of the bell, the visitor responsible for pulling the leather string, however, in some way caused him to feel a part of that magical process. In some inexplicable way, it rounded him out, gave him a sense of importance; a part of the larger world. The awful part, though, was the fear that overcame him, a fear of the unknown, when he took that final step as the vibrations died, and he struggled to open the heavy wooden closure and looked up into the face of a visitor. That feeling varied. It depended upon the person he confronted.

The man who now stood at arm's length outside the door affected him as monstrously as any had before, such that he stepped back at the visage in front of his small, spare body. He was unable to speak his usual phrase, "*¿Quien es?*"

Rodman's smile, which seemed to Roberto more like a grimace, did little to offset his raw feelings.

Ermelina momentarily rescued Roberto from his panic as the gringo at the door looked up. "*Si, señor?*" She laid a kind hand on the youngster's head, smiled down at him briefly, then looked up at the Texican as she lost her pleasant aspect.

Rodman reached inside his shirt pocket, retrieved a small envelope and offered it to the woman. "For—" He started to say.

"*¿Que es este?*" Ermelina frowned as she glared at him. She made no attempt to take the envelope.

Roberto twisted away from Ermelina's kind hand and traipsed away.

"For the man—the gentleman of the house. Your master?" Old psychological wounds welled up from Rodman's subconscious, a feeling which would later anger him; cause him to question his own sanity. He was not used to being challenged by those he felt were inferior. This woman's abrupt manner would never pass in the South, from which he hailed.

"*¿Quien?*" Ermelina peered at the folded and sealed piece of paper without budging.

"*Para el hombre. El hombre de la casa,*" Rodman, exasperated, breathed his words. They came out, although distorted by his own accented English and his difficulty with Spanish, as understandable. He turned his head for a moment to look beyond the long *portal* into the plaza. He saw only a smattering of disinterested parties going about their business.

Three seconds ticked away before Ermelina relented and took the envelope from his outstretched hand. She looked at it, up at Rodman, then said, "*Espere. Aqui.* You wait."

Rodman cracked a relieved grin and nodded emphatically. "Certainly. Yes. Here. I will wait." He gestured at the porch floor.

Ermelina closed the outer door noisily.

His nervous hands at his side, Rodman turned around fully to survey the goings-on in the big open space between the house where he stood and the church across the way. He saw nothing more than the usual, certainly no one with any suspicion about him or his nefarious mission. He paced to the edge and looked along the length of the house in both directions. He waited six minutes, and wondered about the drovers and the contraband, when the front door opened behind him. He turned.

Ermelina stepped onto the porch, closed the door, looked around before settling her eyes on the Texican, then gathered her skirts and started off for the east end of the portal. She whipped her head around to look at Rodman, but walked on. "*¡Venga!* Come!" She gestured. Her long outer skirt trailed.

Rodman, stunned, stood stock still for a moment before realizing what the woman wanted. He set out behind her, then quickened his pace to catch up. She quick-walked to the edge of the porch, turned at the corner of the building, then marched along in the high-angle shadow of the eastside. Behind her, Rodman struggled to keep up with her commanding stride. When they reached the far corner of the corral behind the house, the woman stopped, turned and pointed. She waited until Rodman caught up to see where she had indicated, then moved away.

He stared after her. "What?!" He frowned and threw his frustrated hands out.

She stopped and peered at him. She pointed. "*¡Adentro!* Inside!" She turned and hurried away.

Rodman looked along the southern-facing rails of the corral. To the right, toward the house, more than half was covered with lean-to roof covered with thatch. Several horse stalls lay underneath, three of which were occupied by animals. One was white. An open space, covered variously with animal ordure, hay and other bits and pieces of vegetable material, lay ten feet between the stalls and an outer fence. Beyond that was another covered area, a smithy with a forge. He walked slowly along the rails as he craned his head around. When he came to a gate set mid-way in the fence line, he heard a voice; that of a man.

"*¡Aquí!* Here!"

Rodman shaded his eyes and peered into the dark of an empty stall to the left of the gate.

"Come here. Inside," the voice said.

Rodman looked for the crude, leather-hinged wooden latch, lifted it, entered, and closed the gate. He stopped and peered into the shadows of the stall after scanning the area surrounding the structures for any interested on-lookers, of which he saw none.

"Come."

The Texican moved slowly for the voice. He thought of reaching for the small pistol secreted in his belt line and hidden by his jacket. As he moved closer, he saw the end of an eight-sided pistol barrel appear around the edge of the stall. He stopped. His heart rate up, he said, "I'm not armed. No gun. *No pistola.*" It was a lie he would soon regret.

The pistol waved him into the little space. As he came around the corner, a middle-aged man stepped closer and brought the weapon he held in his right hand close to Rodman's midriff.

"Open the coat!" the man barked. His voice was muted; a half-whisper.

Rodman hesitated an instant, then did as he was instructed.

Noriega spotted Rodman's pistol and relieved him of it. "*¡Mentires!* You lie!"

Rodman raised his hands. "I—"

Noriega reached out with his left hand and yanked the pistol from the Texican's belt line. "*¡¿Quien es?!* Who are you?!" Noriega, his voice low and hoarse, stepped back and looked around frantically, his brow tight.

Rodman thought the man had seen something or someone, so he turned briefly to look out again into the empty road and field south of the house and outbuildings. There was no one. He momentarily wished there had been, a bulwark against his sudden feeling of edgy loneliness and abandonment. He moved sideways into the shadow of the animal shelter and pointed to his chest. "I'm Rodman. I'm here from Texas. I been in Santa Fé. Waiting. Are you Gavilán? If so, we need to talk."

Noriega lowered his head and gave the Texican a piercing look from under his eyebrows.

"Where did you hear that name?" He had calmed.

"In Austin. I have somethin' to say. Called it a password. They did."

Noriega dropped Rodman's gun to his left side, and relaxed the angle of his own firearm. "Tell it to me."

"Let the eagle pass?"

Noriega nodded his head. "The eagle flies." He lowered his pistol more. After a short silence, he said, "Why are you here? I thought—"

Rodman started to speak.

"How did you find me?!"

"A message from Austin. A description of the house. And you. No name."

Noriega peered at the Texican fiercely. "Who—?!"

Frustrated and nervous, Rodman held out his hands. "I don't know! I don't—"

Noriega turned away, then back. He held up his hand. "Yes. Of course. *Calmate.* Calm yourself. I understand."

Rodman slowed his hyperventilation and shook his head. "There is a problem. I wouldn't be here else." He continued to shake his head. His eyes were narrow and furtive.

Noriega's jaw weakened. He frowned, "*¡¿Que?¡* What?!"

"Guns. I Have guns. Arms." Rodman leaned forward into his message.

Noriega moved briefly into the afternoon light and looked around. "Let us go. Inside.

Come." He started to move.

"My gun, please."

Noriega turned. "Of course." He handed Rodman his pistol.

Ustacio, behind a wall in one of the horse stalls, watched as Noriega lead Rodman past the animal containment area, and walk toward the house to a side door. When his employer and master had padded out to the horse stalls, Ustacio had been below the sight-line of the structure, cleaning one of the stall floors. When he heard Ermelina and the gringo come to the corner, he had stayed low to watch and listen. When he felt he was alone, he moved cautiously out of the stall, through the gate and onto the road. He stood for a moment in a state of puzzlement, then walked slowly away, a crude wooden rake in his hands.

The room where Noriega took the Texican was at a far corner of the house. It was smaller than any other room in the house, used principally for storage of odds and ends, including an occasional empty wine cask. Its furnishings were no more than boxes, crates and a broken chair. The sole window, small, high, dusty and dominated by spider webs, stared uncurtained to the west. A roundtop wood and steel-banded trunk sat in one corner, locked.

Noriega walked in front of Rodman, waved him in silently, then looked outside before closing the door. He moved to the center of the somber room, turned to his visitor, folded his arms across his chest, as the pistol dangled from his hand. He gauged the Texican who remained near the door. "You know this is dangerous."

Rodman adjusted the recovered pistol in his belt to a comfortable position as he watched Noriega. He tried to identify the odd, but not unpleasant odor that dominated the small space. It was a blend of dust, old wood, tallow and wine. "We have a problem."

"We?" Noriega cocked his head.

Rodman nodded with a frown. "I. And the cause." His voice betrayed annoyance, but he realized as quickly that he would have to be careful. He was in no position to cross this purportedly powerful man in an unfamiliar place, on his turf.

"This 'problem'—what is it? *Señor* Rodman?" There was sarcasm in Noriega's question.

Rodman took in, then emitted a long stream of air from his nose. "I—we—have crates of arms. Out there." He pointed. "Where the trail comes into the town. From the mountains. The other side of the swamp."

Noriega took three seconds to digest what he had heard. "What town?! This town? Albuquerque?!"

"Yes—"

Noriega's regal bearing disappeared, as his body lost the rigidity he had maintained to this point. "You have arms—here?!" He un-folded his arms loosely, effectively waving his firearm around with near abandon.

"Yes. Here! I need help. I had nowhere—" Rodman angled his body forward in a pleading manner, his arms outstretched. He bobbed his head.

Noriega brought his pistol under control and laid it on a crate, as his mind swirled. He looked intently at the Texican. "From where are these armaments?! And why?!" He held his arm outstretched.

Rodman, his anxiety lessened from the pinnacle it had reached earlier, related the story surrounding the guns, saving some parts of the tale, including the death of Evan Landry. He did report that they had stopped a Union trooper who seemed to be tracking their movements near one of the towns along the Santa Fé Trail. He explained his role, how he had been wrangled into the position of spy-in-place, although he did not relate it that way. No, he had not ordered the guns; that had come from factors in Austin, in part because they were under the impression that "The Hawk," he, Noriega, was ready with a small army of insurgents.

Noriega shook his head and moved two paces across the room. He turned and looked at Rodman, his distressed palms out. "You were followed by a Union soldier?! ¡Jesús, María y José!

I should go to the commandant on the hill and report you!" He turned away and lowered his head as though in pain.

Rodman watched Noriega's movements. He frowned deeply and took a step toward the other man. "What?!"

Still faced away, Noriega put his hand to his chin and raised his head in concentration. "But I will not." He hesitated, turned to face Rodman and pointed at him. "No, I will not. Because to do so would hurt our cause. Indeed, it would bring into question my role." He lifted his eyes to study the crude, open- beamed ceiling of round *vigas*. "I sell to this army. Their officers and some of the *soldados* have been to my house. They are crude. They think they own this country and everything in it. They remain out of town and aloof because they think they are better. We must rid this country of them." He paused as he twisted and un-twisted his body, then, "Where are the guns?"

Rodman, fully recovered, pointed vaguely. "Amongst the trees. Yonder, where the trail drops into the valley. Beyond the swamp. I got men with 'em. Two men. Two mules. Six crates." He paused. "We need to move 'em. Hide 'em." He cocked his head to one side and clenched his teeth.

Noreiga moved again and turned toward Rodman. He lowered his voice as he thought. "Yes, yes. They must be secreted; hidden." He frowned at the packed earthen floor, then looked up at his guest. "They are in the *bosque*?"

"Boss-key?"

"Forest. The forest." Noriega flared briefly with his angst.

Rodman nodded. "Yes. Yes, the forest."

"Two men?"

"Yes."

"Are they reliable? The men?"

In an instant, Rodman reviewed his experience with the pair who had aided in the recovery of the arms and their escape. On the one hand, he was astounded by them; even fearful of them, yet overlaid with abiding respect. He knew, despite his encounters with them, that he could count on them—both of them—in a contest. He surprised even himself as he admitted silently that Cat, the Negro, would be the better of the two in a fight. "Yes, indeed, sir. They are reliable." He nodded emphatically.

"Mm, that is good." Noriega studied the Texican's face and nodded slowly. "Good." He paused, then, "Go back to them. Stay with the arms until dark. I will send a wagon. You will come here. I will find a place for the cargo." He hesitated, looked away, then back. "I will send food with you." He swivelled toward the inner door that led to the house interior. "Your horse. Is it on the plaza side? Near the house?"

Rodman nodded. "Yes. At the house rail."

"Wait here. I will send someone to tell you when you may leave. Soon." He picked up his pistol.

Rodman nodded. "Thank you. *Grácias.*" He offered his hand to Noriega, but Noriega ignored the gesture, turned and moved toward the door to the interior.

Noriega stopped and turned again. "When you return, I will arrange for a place for you. And your companions." His voice trailed off. "*Muy buena suerte.* Good luck." With that, he disappeared into the house and closed the door, leaving Rodman to stand alone with a returning sense of anxiety.

Tandy and Milton had dismounted their grateful, but impatient horses and stood between a small house and a corral, waiting for the man they saw with the horses and mules to finish watering them.

"Wish that feller'd git done what he's about," Milton said, as he soothed his horse with strokes to his bobbing head. "Seem's they'd had 'nough by now. An' these horses cain't wait much longer. They'er 'bout to stampede."

"Yep, " Tandy answered. He looked around nervously. "Listen here, Milton, when he goes, take the horses to the trough and water 'em. If there's any trouble from the locals, give 'em some o' that coin the lieutenant gave us. I'm gonna' follow this character on foot an' see where they's planted."

Milton turned to Tandy, his face screwed up. "Give 'em money? Why for? Water's free!"

"Goddamnit, Milton, use your brain-pan! Sure it's free, but we need to keep matters calm hereabouts! You may not have to, but do it if you have to! Here, take some 'o mine." He reached into his tight breeches pocket, selected two coins and handed them to the private.

"Well, I s'pose." Milton accepted the money and pocketed it. He stared at Tandy and frowned. "Say, it ain't gonna' be easy, you sneakin' about in army blue."

"Yeah, I do reckon that, Private. But I ain't got a choice." He spoke as he tried to calm his mount with a soothing hand.

"Lookie. I do believe them animals is sated." Milton gestured toward the watering trough. Across the way, Pulver led the horses and mules away to his rendezvous with Cat and the crates.

"Okay," Tandy said. "Here's the plan. I'll follow best I can, you water the horses, then head back the way we came. I'll meet up with you quick's I can. If I don't show in a half hour, head on up 'tother side o' the river to the encampment an' stay there. Tell 'em what the lieutenant said and wait." He handed the reins of his horse to Milton and began to move away as he watched Pulver disappear behind a house.

"Right, Sarge. Hey, you take care now. Hot damn, I don' wanna' lose ya. I'll be where ya say."

"Good man, Milton." Tandy glanced at the private and moved off.

As Milton, in a faked blasé fashion, started to whistle as he moved the thirsty horses to the crude trough, Tandy made his way back along the trail, east, moving, when he could, between and behind rambling adobes. He watched as his quarry, Pulver, angled away from the houses and fields as he skirted irrigation ditches and damp fields toward the narrow earthen bridge through the swamp to the eastern *bosque*.

Milton stood alongside his brute charges while they noisily slaked their thirst. He glanced about furtively from time to time, relieved at the lack of challenge. Soon, a few small children, boys and girls, appeared to stare with open curiosity at the gringo soldier in blue. Milton smiled at them, but they merely stared, wide-eyed. One little boy, frightened, ran away. A teenaged girl showed up and began to berate the children and order them away from the potentially dangerous stranger. Two of the smaller waifs obeyed, but the older ones hesitated to move. Milton looked at the girl, and she returned his gaze. Struck by her simple beauty, his sole response was to allow his mouth to go slack, then gulp and swallow hard. She stopped, looked at him, then lowered her eyes with a coquettish smile. It was then that an adult woman appeared and loudly proclaimed all fraternization was at an end, and the other children vanished in a rush.

The girl hesitated, looked away, then again at the army private with the horses.

Milton, lost in the shock of the moment, also looked away, then back more than once. His sole response was to nod his head in a crude attempt at a bow, as though the girl were sub-royalty. The next time he looked in her direction, she was gone. Frozen, he stared at the dappled, leaf- and twig-bearing water in the crude dug-out and shook his head. "Jee-zuz Christ. Jee-zuz Christ almighty," he proclaimed under his breath.

Tandy, as he moved away from earthen structures, onto the dry trail and into the *bosque*, removed his campaign hat and began to crouch, fearful he might alert the man with the four animals.

Pulver, for his part, was unconcerned, and had no idea he was being followed. This misconception was reinforced by the knowledge, as Rodman had assured him and Cat, that the U.S. Army encampment was well to the west of the town, and that he, Rodman, had information that their patrols, if any, were few and far between. Aside from that, why should he worry? The crates were well camouflaged, and it was true that the territory was hungry for farm equipment.

He found Cat stretched out as he dozed across two of the re-arranged crates. As he approached, Cat's horse whinnied, and the black man sat up.

"Hey, Pulver. Yo're a sight fer sore eyes. Didja find water?"

Pulver sat on one of the crates after he dropped the horse reins, pulled tobacco and a pipe from his vest pocket, and began the ritual of stuffing the pipe and lighting it. "Yep. That I did. Trough near the edge 'o the town." He gestured with his chin as he put fire to the tobacco and sucked. "Water had leaves, twigs an' such, but the animals enjoyed it."

"Well, good on you, you po' white boy, you." Cat stood, stretched, straightened and looked around.

"Want a puff?" Pulver asked.

"Smells mighty fine, there, Pulver, and I thank ye kindly, but no. Makes me cough an' hack. My preference is a good cheroot. Guess I'm jus' a weak nigger."

Pulver smiled and looked away. "Never say I didn't offer."

"I won't." Cat grinned and studied the ground. He picked up a stray cottonwood twig and scratched the dirt at his feet. "I could eat."

"I'm ready fer that lilly-livered, rooster-posin' Texican to re-appear with some grub an' whiskey." He paused. " I got some jerky."

"Yep. Sorry as he is, we're tied to 'im fer the duration." Cat looked around. "I'm gonna' mosey yonder to that stand o' bushes and engage in a nature task. When I return I'll take you up on yore kind offer 'o dried meat."

"I'll be here. Smokin'."

Tandy watched all this from behind a large cottonwood tree, but heard little. He looked about, pondered, then crept away.

Ustacio rapped on the inner door of the room where Rodman and Noriega had met, opened it enough to see into the room between the jam and the door edge, then moved slowly into the room. Bent forward as though his back ailed him, he kept his suspicious eyes on the Texican as he entered.

Rodman turned, then nodded in greeting.

"*Su caballo.* Your horse. *Está listo.* Ready." Ustacio kept his voice low and gestured.

"*Grácias,*" Rodman said. He imitated Ustacio's voice control.

Ustacio hesitated, then moved for the outer door, opened it and peered out. He looked both ways, then turned his head to Rodman. "*Bueno. Está bien. Puede ir.*" He gestured with his head, then stepped aside for Rodman to pass.

Rodman nodded thanks to the old man, moved into the door frame, looked out, then walked briskly away.

Behind, Ustacio watched the man from Austin disappear around the corner, then shut the door quietly and retreated into the house. As he moved, he asked him self silently why it was that his master, Nerio García de Noriega had asked him to behave in such a secretive fashion. He had no immediate answer for himself.

Although Sergeant Tandy expected nothing less, he was gratified to find Milton at their agreed rendezvous, and at the appointed time. Milton, mounted, held the reins of the sergeant's horse, which reacted to the appearance of its owner and rider with a small dance by shaking his shaggy head with attendant snorts.

"How'd it go, Sarg?"

Tandy, his brim-back hat on his head again, mounted, then turned the reins west. "I spotted 'em. They're in the trees 'oer that a-way."

"Whatta' we do now?"

"Report." Tandy paused. "Do what the lieutenant said. Report."

Milton, confused, frowned at the sergeant. "How? Where?!"

Tandy gestured with his chin, reined his horse around and clicked it into motion toward the town. "Encampment 'tother side 'o the river. Yonder. Remember? There."

"Right," Milton replied. He fell in behind, then pulled alongside. "I'm with you."

"So I seen, Milton. So I seen." Tandy smiled to himself.

Rodman, anxious and frustrated, rounded the Noriega house for the plaza side. As he approached his tethered horse, he realized that one of the saddle bags bulged with the promised provisions. He mounted, wheeled around, and headed out of the plaza, east-bound.. When he came to the horse trough Pulver and Milton had used, he watered his mount. He moved again along the trail until it spread out past the swamp, then angled into the dense, cottonwood-dominated forest below the soft, rolling, river-carved piedmont cliffs. He found Cat and Pulver seated on two of the crates. He coaxed his horse to a halt, swung off and dropped the reins to the ground. Without looking, he said, "Gentlemen."

His horse idled away to join the other animals grazing on the intermittent grass under the trees.

"Howdy," Pulver said.

Cat looked to one side and spat.

Rodman pulled the saddlebags off his horse and handed them to Pulver. "Victuals," he said. "Courtesy of our new-found friend."

Pulver pulled the leather strap from the bulkier of the two bags and looked inside. "Shee-ut oh, dear! Lookie here! A bot-tle of wine!" He stretched the word 'bottle' out into two distinct syllables. "An' some o' them boo-reetohs." He turned to Cat, grinning widely. "Here, Cat, you dumb nigger, have one whilst I partake o' this fine red wine, which I will share with you shortly." He held his arm out toward the black man.

Cat took the corn husk-wrapped *burrito*, opened it and bit into it. "Mm-mm!" He exclaimed.

Rodman paced away a few feet, as he disingenuously avoided becoming part of the impromptu picnic. "We wait until dark. Someone will come to guide us back. With the crates. We'll have a place to bunk down." Privately, Rodman wondered where Noriega would put his trail partners.

When Jesse decided he should return to the Noriega house, he had watched Francisco Maestas and Lieutenant Beckner eat and drink more than they had intended. He pushed his chair back and stood. "Francisco, will you be with your cousin? The one who has my carbine?"

Maestas looked up as he wiped the corner of his mouth, first with his finger, then a cloth napkin from the side of his plate. "Yes. I will look after your property."

Jesse shook his head. "I'm not worried, Francisco." He looked at Beckner. "And you to the encampment?"

Beckner put his fork on his plate, then wiped his mouth. He looked at Maestas. "Francisco, would you come with me? I want to ask around to see if sheriff Baca has arrived and what's being said. Are you willing?"

"Of course, my friend. We must be careful." He pointed at Beckner, then looked up at Landry. "Sup well, Jesse. And sleep well. When shall we see you again?"

"After dark?" He looked at both seated men. "I want to know if Baca is here."

Beckner and Maestas nodded to each other in agreement, then looked up at Jesse.

"Where?" Beckner asked.

Jesse thought, then Maestas interrupted, "The church. The arches."

Jesse nodded. "Good."

Beckner acquiesced as well, and Jesse was off.

Beckner and Maestas both mounted their horses and rode toward the plaza. As they rounded the corner of the last building on the northwest corner, Beckner brought his horse to an abrupt stop.

Maestas looked back, then reined his horse around. "*¿Que pasa?* What's the matter?"

Beckner paused, then said, "Those two troopers there. I think I should speak with them." He gestured with his head. "Would you wait here?"

"*Como no.* Of course."

"Thanks, Francisco; I'll be right back." With that, Beckner spurred his horse forward.

Tandy and Milton, in tandem, moved through the south side of the plaza on their mounts at a fast walk.

Milton saw Beckner first, and he raised his arm in reaction as though to wave. "Hey, Sarg!" Across the way, Beckner shook his head violently in a 'no'.

Tandy looked as well. "Shut yore trap, Milton! Don't say or do nothin'!"

"But—"

"Goddamnit, don't you see the lieutenant don't want to be recognized! Jeezuz! Don' look. Keep on ridin'."

"Okay, Sarg, okay." Milton, chastized, lowered his head and looked away.

Both men continued through the plaza and beyond. Beckner rode south across the plaza while Maestas looked after him with open curiosity.

The lieutenant followed the two Union troopers around the southwest corner of the plaza, then another two houses beyond. Tandy was keen enough to the situation to order Milton and he continue.

Beckner caught up to them and rode alongside. "You don't know me, men. Don't call out my name or recognize me." He couched his words by moving his head in such a way that an observer would believe them strangers.

"Right, Lieutenant," Tandy said. He faced forward.

Beckner rode a distance of two horses away, then, when he realized they were unobserved, pulled in close. "Sergeant, did you see anything of our quarry?"

"We did, indeed, sir, an' we know where they are at this very time."

Beckner, hardly able to contain himself, managed, "You don't say. And where might they be?"

"Opposite side o' the town, Lieutenant. In the forest. Past that swamp. They's two of 'em. One's a darkie. They got six crates and two mules 'sides their horses. There may be more, but I didn't see 'em." He maintained both hands on the reins and gestured with his head.

"Two? Not a third man?" Beckner tightened up his face.

"No, sir. Just the two." Tandy continued to focus forward.

Beckner hesitated, then, "Well done. Excellent work, men." He paused to think. "Now, we gotta' track 'em to where they cart the arms." He paused again. "You can't, being in blue, but I can."

"Say, Lieutenant—sir—maybe I could git some mufti, some civilian clothes an' help." Milton had more on his mind than contraband armaments, a renewed interest in his assignment.

Beckner looked behind, then at the young soldier. "I agree, Private Milton, but where would you get mufti?"

"Well, sir—Lieutenant—I could buy some at a store, or maybe one 'o them soldiers on the hill'd let me borry some." He nodded his head emphatically, proud of his idea.

Beckner was quiet, then said, "It's a couple of hours 'til dark. Go on up and see if Milton's idea is good, Tandy. If you manage to find suitable clothing for both, come back. But remove as much evidence you're on army horses as possible. Meet me behind the church. Wait there. Stay out of sight." He pondered. "Go south from here. You'll find a crossing not too far. Look along the bank. You'll see the tracks." Beckner started away, then halted. "Tandy."

Tandy stopped as well and turned in the saddle. "Yes, Lieu—"

"Tandy, see if you and Milton can obtain sidearms."

"Right," Tandy said. He and Milton pulled their reins to the left and moved off as Beckner wheeled around for the plaza.

As Beckner rejoined Maestas, Francisco asked why the lieutenant had wanted to speak to the troopers.

"See if they knew anything of the sheriff, or heard anything. They asked about the encampment. They didn't know much. Came in from Las Vegas." He smiled. "Shall we begin?"

"We'll speak with my cousin first." Maestas clicked his horse forward and Beckner followed suit. "They will welcome you."

18

As Jesse walked from the *cantina*, where he had met Lieutenant Harold Beckner and Francisco Maestas, to the sprawling Noriego manse, he was careful to keep his face shaded by his broad-brimmed hat, which he had pulled lower in front. Rather than move directly across the open expanse, he skirted along the edges of the few low adobe buildings that ringed, and faced, the plaza. He used his peripheral vision and occasional side-long eye movements to scan the nearly naked area for potential trouble, principally in the guise of the dreaded Sheriff Baca of Santa Fé or one of his deputies, most of whom he knew. Only a few local people going about their daily routines were about, and he passed unnoticed.

Little Roberto opened the door to the Noriega house. The child was glad to see Jesse, and expressed it with a broad grin and opening a one-way conversation as he described his day and its activities. After closing the door, Jesse knelt down, put his hand on Roberto's shoulder and joined the conversation. The boy rambled on about some of the small animals he cared for, and a hand-made wooden toy he cherished.

Until Roberto looked up, Jesse didn't notice Apolonia standing behind him as she watched their innocent tete-a-tete. He turned, looked, then stood. He started to speak, but she interrupted him.

"Roberto, Mr. Landry has other things to do besides listen to your chatter." She smiled beatifically at the boy.

Roberto ducked his head and took a step back, wracked with embarrassment.

Jesse kept his eyes on the boy. "Oh, no, Roberto and I have been discussing very important world affairs. I have learned much in a very short time." He shook his head and glanced at the girl.

Roberto didn't understand what Jesse said. He looked, wide-eyed, between the two adults, then went to Apolonia and took her hand. He looked up at Jesse and smiled sheepishly.

Jesse smiled down at him. "Roberto, we must continue our talk at another time. Perhaps you would show me your animals and toys."

The boy wrapped himself partially in Apolonia's skirt, then ran off.

Jesse looked at Apolonia silently.

"My father wishes for you to meet my mother and my aunt. They are waiting in the drawing room." Apolonia locked her eyes with his, then her mouth went slack as she resisted a smile and looked down at the floor.

In the moment of silence, Jesse was at a loss for words. He recovered and blurted, "Of course. I want to meet your mother and aunt. Thank you."

She hesitated again, then moved off. "This way, please."

Nerio Noriega's wife, Efigenia, sat self-consciously perched on the edge of a huge, ornately-carved, throne-like chair centered at one end of the large drawing room. She wore a black lace shawl, and her small hands were folded in her lap, which was, in turn, adorned by a black, silken dress that fell to her ankles. Her tiny feet, wrapped in equally black, leather lace-up shoes, barely touched the floor. Behind her, on the high, white-washed wall, were two large religious oils depicting full-length, sad, reflective saints in the mode of El Greco.

Opposite her, across the room, twenty feet away, her husband, Nerio, sat in a wood-and-leather chair of similar make. Unlike his wife, he sat back, as both of his arms rested on the leather-wrapped arms of the expensive furniture. His legs were un-crossed and he tapped his fingers impatiently on the arms of the chair. His face revealed a tight, forced smile.

Between them, at an angle of ninety degrees, close to the outer wall, was a settee, also of leather and carved, angular wood. This was occupied by two people; one, Apolonia's brother, Bonifacio; the other, his aunt, his mother's sister, Chavela.

Bonifacio, in his early twenties, lithe and supremely self-confident, sat erect, the patrician, one leg thrown over the other, while one arm rested on the arm of the settee. His face was tilted upward in a disdainful pose. Jesse suspected that he was play-acting for a sympathetic audience.

At the other end of the settee, closer to her sister, an old and tiny Chavela hunched forward on the seat, her head down as she worked her fingers nervously in her lap and mumbled to herself. She was dressed in a fashion similar to that of her sister, but somewhat rumpled and disheveled, as though she wore nothing but a loose bag. Her feet dangled an inch short of the floor, and she swung them back and forth, under the settee, then back into the room.

Jesse, after no more than a few seconds reflection, felt embarrassed and out of place, as though he had somehow caused this odd scene to unfold before him in a strange dream. He was instantly reminded of a puppet show he had seen as a child. He nodded to Señora Noriega as he hunched his shoulders forward in the suggestion of a bow, then looked at Noriega and nodded. He merely glanced at the imperious son, Bonifacio.

Apolonia, behind Jesse, sensed his discomfort, and moved alongside him and began to speak. "*Mi madre—*"

The elder Noriega, still semi-regal in his chair, interrupted. "*Mi esposa, la señora Noriega.*" He lowered and cocked his head as he gestured toward his wife.

Jesse took his cue and went to the stiff woman in black. She held out her right hand limply, which bore two expensive rings, one of gold, the other silver, for their visitor to kiss. Jesse obliged, then stepped back a pace. "*Con mucho gusto.*"

The lady Noriega emitted no more than a low-register growl, her lips in a stilted attempt at a smile.

Apolonia seated herself in one of the right-angle ladder-back chairs across from the settee and to one side of the entrance to the hall, then gestured for Jesse to take a seat. He obliged by moving to the twin utilitarian chair on the opposite side of the door.

When this awkward moment passed, an experience for which Jesse seemed an eternity, Noriega spoke. He looked first at his daughter, then Jesse. "*Sientate, mi hijo.* Sit my son." He threw a glance at Bonifacio, a moment of grace to ensure that his arrogant, temperamental male offspring would contain himself, then continued, "Our dear friend and associate, the father of this young man, Evan Landry, has been killed. Murdered by a gringo ruffian." He paused long enough to lower his head in a gesture of sympathy, then looked up and around, as though speaking to a vast crowd. "But this brave young man has settled the score. This after being threatened by this same man. Yet, he is sought by the authorities from Santa Fé." He paused again. "I will intervene on his behalf. In the meantime, he is our guest, and we welcome him into the bosom of our family."

Noriega threw Bonifacio a severe look as his son shifted in his seat and changed the position of his booted legs such that it made a thud against the floor in the nearly quiet room. Bonifacio responded with a look of childish petulance toward his father, then looked away, his chin again raised.

Efigenia Noriega acknowledged her husband's announcement with a slow nod of her head, but without awarding the subject of their concern a direct look. Apolonia, her hands demurely in her lap, lowered her head, smiled and threw a glance at the young visitor across from her, then lightly brushed her auburn hair. Her aunt, the unresponsive Chavela, remained in her own personal, unaware domain, as she mumbled and worked her hands.

Jesse rose halfway from his chair in response to Noriega's comment about his father, then regained his seat. *"Grácias, señor Noriega."* He lowered his head in a bow.

Noriega glanced at the open doorway to the hall, where he spied Ermelina, then looked at Jesse. "Let us sup." He rose, crossed the room to his wife, took her hand, and moved for the door. He gestured to Jesse as he passed.

Apolonia went for her aunt, took her hand, and guided her out of the room, while Bonifacio waited, his eyes fixed on Jesse, who stood and waited for the others to clear the room.

Constant Ermelina, without benefit of a time piece, who seemed to sense all the movements and requirements of the house in all directions at all times, waited immediately outside in the hall. As the dinner party exited the sitting room, she wordlessly turned and lead the way.

The dining room was on the opposite side of the entrance hall, with the same outline as the sitting room where Noriega's guest had met the remainder of his family. It also had a wide, deep-set north-facing window against the *portal* and the plaza beyond. A large, heavy wood table dominated the big space. Along the long edges were four elegant, straight-back chairs. At each end were two, larger, more elegant seats, with arms, in the same motif. All featured dark leather seats and backs, secured with large brass hammered tacks, and had high, steeple-like rear posts, in the Spanish style. The four thick edges of the grand table were decorated with carvings of food-related religious inscriptions. Tapestries that featured scenes of imperious, elegant, over-sized horsemen, baying hounds among the horses' hooves, chasing down robust deer, hung from two of the walls. The other vertical surfaces were decorated with depictions of wan, pious saints interspersed with fancy wooden crosses. Two large, wrought-iron candelabra were placed strategically at balanced ends of the table on white lace cloth which stretched nearly the length of the board, which allowed the dark, lustrous wood surface to show through. Its fringes fell short of the tables edges, which provided space for plates, bowls and utensils. The three tapers in each candelabra were aflame. They flickered and danced with the light breezes caused by the entrance of the diners. Five places were set; at both ends, two along the north side nearest the window, and one across the table for Jesse. Large pewter under plates supported thin, decorative china plates at each position.

Noriega first led his wife to one of the large arm chairs, positioned her, then went to the opposite end, nearest Jesse, who was to his right. Apolonia arrived last after taking her aunt Chavela to the kitchen where she was to be fed separately. Once seated, Noriega reached for a cut-glass decanter of red wine, poured for Jesse, then himself, then handed it to his son, who poured for himself. The two women, who would have declined, were ignored.

Noriega raised his glass. "To the memory of my dear friend and associate, Evan Landry."

"Thank you," Jesse responded. He raised his glass toward Noriega.

Bonifacio nodded and pointed his glass toward Jesse, who responded in kind. Apolonia and her mother lowered their heads reverently.

A sub-teen Navajo girl, Jacinta, entered with a large wooden tray, followed by Ermelina, who carried a kettle of soup. The girl laid the tray on a sideboard, then distributed soup bowls. She left, then returned with a platter holding a pork roast and placed it in front of Noriega, along with a bone-handled carving knife and two-tined roast fork set. Ermelina, after serving the soup, placed two more serving dishes with vegetables onto the table.

Noriega picked up his soup spoon, eyed the others, and began to eat.

Little was said during the meal, and that, small talk of the Landry business and the sadness of Evan's passing, virtually all from Noriega. He ate quickly, with an air of impatient abandonment, wiped his mouth with a large cloth napkin, and stood. "My apologies, but business calls. Certain problems with the south fields which must not wait, and a situation at the *tienda*." He looked at Jesse. "Please relax. Make yourself at home. My son and daughter will entertain you." He crossed the room to Efigenia and helped her out of her chair. "My wife will retire now."

Efigenia nodded graciously to Jesse.

He stood abruptly, his napkin held awkwardly in both hands. "*Buenas noches, señora,*" he said.

Jesse sat as the shy Navajo girl appeared with a tray of fruit and *natillas* custard for dessert.

Apolonia, who, during the meal, had glanced in Jesse's direction as often as she dared, given her fear of her parents' possible disapproval, looked at him directly. "What are your plans? What will you do?" Her spoon hovered over her dessert dish.

Bonifacio, who had eaten with a certain studied élan, but gusto, and who had slurped up half his dessert before either of the other two had started, shoved his chair back noisily and looked at the dark, rectilinear ceiling beams. "Father will get the sheriff off his back, and he will return to Santa Fé to continue his father's business." He wiped his mouth and threw the napkin onto the table. He looked at Jesse, his mouth set in a wry half-smile. "Is that not so, Señor Landry?"

Jesse, taken by surprise, began, "I hope your—"

Bonifacio ignored Jesse and looked at his sister. "And you, Apolonia, dear sister, will continue your marriage plans with Federico Navarro, your intended. Is that not so?"

Apolonia glared at her brother. "You can be so crude, Bonifacio!" With that, she rose, gathered her long skirts and hurried from the room, her mood dark and her emotions close to tears.

Bonifacio got up slowly, went to the big arm chair where his father had sat, and draped himself over it, one booted leg up over an arm. He picked up a spoon and toyed with it, then moved the tip across the table cloth. He watched the utensil create an imaginary pattern, then spoke. "My sister can be quite emotional, Señor Landry. She is weak, and has fantasies. She is in need of protection, you see, and my father and I watch over her—watch closely. We keep her close to us. I'm sure you understand. No?" He looked up at Jesse, smug and self-assured.

Jesse waited several beats. "I do, Señor Noriega; I do. Your sister is a beautiful, charming young woman. It is fortunate that I have so many demanding tasks that occupy my time and efforts, such that I do not present a threat to the sanctity of your home, her chastity or her reputation." He paused. "Now, if you will please excuse me, I must leave. I have more pressing concerns."

Bonifacio, his mood a cross between surprise and confounded fury, stopped moving the spoon, dropped his leg to the floor, and straightened in his chair. He bored in on Jesse and went silent.

Jesse stood, looked at young Noriega and held up his hand, palm out. "Please. Don't get up. I suggest you have another glass of that very fine Mexican wine." He pointed at the decanter, turned and left the room.

Bonifacio slumped in his chair and fumed as he gripped the spoon until his knuckles went white.

Nerio Noriega had left the dining room and made his way directly to the rear of the *hacienda*, where he encountered the faithful Ustacio, waiting in the hall near an outside door. As Noriega approached, his servant held a glowing oil lantern up high.

Without looking at his servant, Noriega said, *"Vamos,"* then opened the door.

The two men exited the house, Ustacio closed the door quietly, then followed his master to the stables. Noriega, who had in his youth performed this task often, helped Ustacio lead a draft horse to a four-wheeled wagon that stood in the road behind, and hitch the brute to it. Ustacio had hung the glowing lantern to a rigging post at the front of the vehicle. Before climbing up into the driver's seat, he turned to his employer expectantly. Noriega checked his surroundings briefly, closed in on Ustacio, then whispered to the man. Ustacio nodded, mounted the wagon, took the traces, and clicked the horse forward.

Jesse went to his room, closed the door, found his pistol and strapped it to his waist. At the door, he peered up and down the hall to ensure he was unobserved, then moved quickly along the hall and left by the rear door nearest his room. He made his way along the dark east side of the great house, then stopped at the corner of the *portal* and looked about the plaza. It was faintly lit here and there by scant yellow-orange light coming from some of the houses that edged the square and aided by faint blue-white light of the rising moon. Across the space, he made out the somber outlines of the Catholic church. He saw no one, so stepped out onto the big, open space of scarred earth and strode to the church.

19

Sergeant Tandy and Private Milton had made their way across the shallow, silt-laden Rio Grande and up the bluff to the army encampment. Their mounts, not used to walking in water for some time, complained by stalling, shaking their shaggy heads about and snorting in protest as they neared the water's edge. Both troopers assured them, however, that they would not drown with the application of low words of encouragement, neck stroking attendant with forceful tugging on the reins, constant clicking sounds, and heels to their bellies.

The young, green sentry, his bayonet-fixed weapon taller than he, was shocked to see two dusty, uniformed, but disheveled veteran soldiers appear out of nowhere, especially from the direction of the forbidden village below and across the broad, shallow river. Their appearance drew out more young soldiers who had been lounging about their tents, and they, too, were in awe of the site. For them, their terrible, boring assignment brought a semblance of excitement.

Pvt. Milton sensed this, and felt a wave of pride sweep over him. His sudden change in posture in the saddle would have been noticed by, and surely amused, more mature observers. For his part, Tandy, the veteran trooper, was concerned solely with Lieutenant Beckner's request, and how he would frame it to the camp commandant, thus he ignored their impromptu audience.

After he dismounted and began to walk amongst his new admirers, his horse's reins in hand, Milton found himself consciously strutting like a cock in a field of clucking, compliant hens. "Ah cain't tell ye ever' thang," he crowed, "but Ah kin say we been trackin' some bad fellers." He looked about, eyes askance, taking in the awed reaction. "An' we ain't done yet." This last remark he emphasized both orally and physically with an outstretched arm.

More than one suggested they should attend this outing. Milton's reply was to say that it wasn't up to him, but that they would be welcome if it were reduced to battle.

Captain Marchant was less disposed to open excitement, and harbored what there was of it well when he spoke with Sgt. Tandy. He sat at his make-shift desk while Tandy stood at a proud parade rest, as he explained in couched terms the needs Beckner had requested, second-hand, at Pvt. Milton's rash suggestion. Marchant saw in Tandy what he secretly desired in the way of a trooper; a true soldier of the Army of the United States, performing a potentially dangerous mission, on sweaty horseback, firearm at the ready, adrenalin rushing, eating little more than jerky and hard tack, sleeping fitfully and going lean and hard in mind and body. Yet he was forced, he felt, to argue against what Tandy mouthed as a front. After all, he was in command, yet here he was, doing the bidding of under-lings. He knew he would cave in, but played it out. His resistance was worn down easily, though, because he saw in Tandy's eyes and demeanor the mild contempt he felt for himself, the unspoken truth they both understood but kept internalized. He gave Tandy the note that Beckner had left for him, and waited for the sergeant to read it, fold it, and stuff it into his trouser pocket.

Eager to extricate himself from what was developing into a embarrassment, Marchant bounded from his chair. "Come with me, Sergeant!"

Civilian apparel was found in a rag-tag way for both Tandy and Milton, but what few horses were available bore the same Army brand on their flanks. It was decided to cover the marques on Tandy's and Milton's mounts with a pair of odd blankets not of government issue.

Despite some grumbling on the part of the man who donated his pants to Sgt. Tandy, he was still proud to do something for the cause. Both trackers were fed along with the encampment soldiers, during which time, new friendships and false promises of future meetings were assured. They took their leave at dusk, in part to ensure safe passage across the ancient, meandering, silt-bearing stream, as virtually every man, most with their suspenders dangling from their waists, watched jealously.

At the place where Lieutenant Beckner had left them off, Sgt. Tandy and Pvt. Milton sat astride their patient horses, waiting in the grey half-dark. After no more than a half hour, Beckner rode toward them from behind, at a walk, his mount's hooves barely audible in the quiet of the evening.

Milton was the first to hear, then turned his head. He said, his voice low, "The Lieutenant."

Tandy turned as well.

The lieutenant came alongside, then all three horses, bearing their riders, faced each other in a three-point daisy pattern.

"How'd you make out, Sergeant?" Beckner's voice was low as he leaned forward in the saddle.

"The cap'n an' others found us some clothes. Pants an' shirts, sir. No horses, but we got the brands covered. Wrangler's hats we got, too." He pointed to his wide-brimmed, felt hat in the half-light.

"Good. Good. Sidearms?"

"Yes, sir. They's the same. Army issue. But we're packin' e'm in our belts." He gestured in the dark.

"All right, Tandy. Good enough. Best you could do. Good job. Both of you." He sat up and looked around. He saw no one. He faced around again. "Did you eat?"

"We did that. Not bad fare, considering." Tandy hesitated. "What now, Lieutenant?"

"You and Milton make your way back to the place you saw the two men and the crates. Stay back, but keep watch if they're still there. Skirt the town if you can. If they move, follow as best you are able. But Tandy; don't risk being discovered. If you are, talk your way out of it and leave. Understand?"

"Yes, sir, Lieutenant. An' where'll you be?"

"In these parts. Near the plaza here. I'll watch for you." He mulled, then, "Listen, Tandy, no; I'll be over there around the church. When you get back—or you, Milton—strike a match near the corner of that big house." He pointed. "We'll meet for your report." He turned his horse to leave, then stopped. "Two hours should do it, but I'll wait."

"Next to that there place?" Milton asked. He pointed in the near dark.

"That's what the lieutenant said, Private." Annoyance carried in Tandy's voice as he cocked his head toward the young soldier in a side-long glance.

"Yessiree, Sarge! Geez!" Milton pulled the reins of his horse, which caused the animal to nod his great head up and down and side-step in confusion.

"Right, Milton." Beckner turned his horse again and rode back in the direction from which he had come, behind a house which extended beyond to a series of small houses that stretched in a northerly direction along the west side of the plaza. He called back in a loud whisper, "Good luck, men."

Tandy urged his mount forward, and Milton, in a sallow mood, followed dutifully.

Beckner rode slowly in the dark, his path exposed to his sharp eyes only by muted, orange lamp light effusing from random windows in houses along the west side of the plaza. He worried about the two men he had a few moments before sent on what could be a dangerous mission, but reasoned that he must determine where the illicit arms shipment would go. He trusted Sergeant Tandy and Private Milton, and that the two men would behave dutifully. He was comfortable with their teamwork.

At the corner of the last of four houses in the series, where an open space led to the plaza, Beckner turned his mount in that direction, brought his horse to a halt and surveyed the big open area. Two teen-aged boys ran past, unaware of his presence. They said nothing, but panted as though in a hurry, possibly from a deed that would not bode well for them or others. He saw three men across the way, as they stood near the center of the public place. He heard their voices and intermittent laughter. One of them smoked. The end of his cigar glowed bright red as he sucked on it. A few seconds later, they moved off in a direction opposite the church, his destination.

Beckner spurred his horse forward a few steps, then stopped him again, brushed his neck and spoke softly to him. He scoured the plaza once more, then turned his attention to the church. He saw no one nor any movement. Leery of approaching the rendezvous from the plaza, he turned his mount toward the north, and walked him slowly around the rear of the big adobe religious structure. He saw nobody on the east side of the church, so he dismounted, then wrapped his horse's reins around the branch of a small tree. He stood for a few moments to listen. He heard random voices at a distance, then music from a guitar, then a voice raised in song. His horse shifted his position, huffed, then stomped a hoof as Beckner looked north. He saw and heard nothing. When he turned toward the plaza, he sensed a figure at the corner of the building, then heard a low whistle from the outline of a man. He touched the grip of his pistol.

"Beckner! Francisco! Here!"

Beckner recognized Francisco Maestas' distinctive voice, with its lilting Spanish-language overtone. Relieved, he moved quickly toward the corner as Maestas turned to look out into the plaza to check for curious on-lookers. He walked around the corner into the deep shadows offered by the high, arch-invaded wall. In the dark, he sensed the presence of a third person, Jesse Landry.

"Lieutenant," Jesse whispered.

"Jesse. Good to see you." Beckner turned, thought a moment, then, "Although I can't." He smiled, and sensed Landry's smile in return.

Maestas, who ignored both and peered out into the empty, barely visible plaza, said, "I believe Baca remains." He sniffed.

"I have not seen him," Jesse said.

Beckner was silent.

"I know one of his deputies. Martinez. My cousin said he stays with a friend at his house."

"There were more, no?"

"Yes. When I met then at La Bajada, Baca was with three others." He emitted a short laugh. "They are afraid of you, Jesse Landry. They need four armed men to subdue you."

Jesse shook his head, an action neither Beckner nor Maestas could see. "I am a dangerous coyote." He sniffed.

Maestas laughed again.

"Ah, yes, coyote." Beckner mused. "Where are the other two? Did they return?"

"No," Maestas replied. "They are camped near the house of the other."

Jesse moved a step beyond the archway into the plaza. Without turning, he said, "Señor Noriega said he would speak to the sheriff on my behalf."

"Pah! That scum!" Maestas spat. He spun around and angled his head angrily in the shadows. I don't trust him any more than a chicken could say a prayer!"

"He was my father's partner," Jesse said. His voice was low.

"A pity," Maestas retorted. "Still, I do not trust him."

"Why?" Beckner asked.

"Because," Maestas shot back, "he makes pretty to those with whom he does business or who can help him, but spits on those he thinks beneath him. He has done so to our family. To my father!" He marched away two steps and stood at attention, his annoyance palpable in the gloom. "Perhaps he did not know that your father was my father's partner. No matter."

"I understand," Beckner chimed.

"Look," Jesse whispered. He pointed.

The three men watched as a wagon emerged from the rear of the Noriega house, a lantern with yellowish, oil-fed light streaming from it as it dangled from a post at the front of the vehicle. The wagon was pulled by one horse, and one man sat in control at the reins.

"Late for a trot," Beckner said.

"That's the Noriega house." The other two could not see Jesse frown.

Maestas stared at the moving wagon. "You were there. Do you know him?"

"That may be the old man, Ustacio. I can't see from here, but it must be Ustacio. He cares for the horses. The forge. Performs chores about the house. I ate with them this evening. Noriega, his wife, son and daughter. The aunt."

"Where does he go this time of the night?" Beckner asked.

"I have no idea," Jesse said. "Why? Is it important?"

"Curious; no more," Lieutenant Beckner replied. Privately, he wondered about the wagon traveling in the same direction Sergeant Tandy and Private Milton had gone. He turned to Maestas. "Francisco, do you think your cousin can find the sheriff? Or find where he is?"

Maestas turned toward Beckner. He was silent for a few seconds. "It is possible. But—what are we to do if we find him? What is Jesse to do? If the dog, Noriega can help—"

"Noriega is related," Jesse said.

"Look," Beckner said. He pointed toward the Noriega house.

The three men watched as the front door opened and light from a lamp appeared. Jesse realized the figure holding the lamp was Ermelina. A man of large bulk then interfered with the light. Another man was outlined against the wavering light, next to the first.

"Baca," Maestas said.

"Do you recognize the other man?" Beckner asked.

"No."

Maestas moved close to Jesse. "You should go. Back to my house. It is not safe here."

Jesse paused, then shook his head. "No, Francisco. I will stay. Thank you. I will wait. After Baca has left, I will go back and speak with Noriega. Many thanks, my friend." He touched Maestas' shoulder.

"I worry. These are men who live only for themselves. But you are brave to face this problem in such a way. I will remain." He looked at Beckner. "And you, my other friend, who has been so generous, and who thinks of my sister?"

Beckner chuckled and looked at the dark earth at his feet. "I, too, will remain. I saw what happened, and want justice for Jesse."

"Good," Maestas said. "Look, they have entered." He paused. "And the wagon has disappeared."

"There is something I must see to," Beckner said. He started for the corner of the building.

Both of the other men looked in Beckner's direction as he started off.

"What?" Jesse asked. "I will go with you."

"I, also," Maestas offered.

"No, my friends. This is something I must do alone. Stay here and watch for the sheriff. I will return soon."

"Army business?" Maestas called after Beckner as he rounded the corner to his patiently waiting horse.

"A task for the troopers on the hill," Beckner answered.

"Hm," Maestas muttered. He looked at Jesse, then away, as he fingered the gun at his hip.

"You have little trust for the lieutenant," Jesse said.

"I trust him. I do not trust the gringo army."

Maestas found a place to sit, and Jesse followed suit. Both men fell silent, their eyes focused on the big adobe house across the plaza.

Lieutenant Beckner rode as fast as he could, given the dearth of light that fell from occasional small windows along the winding path between houses and weak moonlight. His horse, unhappy at his master's demands, snorted and jerked, as he fought against the reins and tip-toed as only a horse is able through the dark alleys of Albuquerque.

He had lost sight of the wagon with the beacon light, but felt sure he knew its destination. Then, past the last house before the narrow path that lead across the swamp, he spied a pinpoint of dancing, swinging light in the distance. In less than a minute, it disappeared, then shown again, then was lost again. Uncertain of his ground, he halted and waited, as he hoped to see the light again, to no avail.

To the east, past the narrow swamp bridge, Tandy and Milton were positioned along the trail near the *bosque* clearing where Tandy, through the cottonwoods and tamarisk, had seen the two men guarding the contraband crates earlier that day. They had dismounted, and were careful to keep their mounts quiet. Although they listened carefully, they heard nothing more than occasional rustling of leaves, bird calls, crickets and the movements of small animals and land-birds. There were no lights.

After nearly an hour, Milton saw something that appeared to be deep in the woods and back toward the village, not in the expected direction . He whispered, "Sarge! Over there! Lookie the light."

"Yeah, I see it. What the hell happened to the sods who were here? Ain't nobody." Frustrated, he took several steps toward the light, then turned back.

"Whatta we do now?" Milton asked.

"Stick it out fer now. No choice, as I see it."

"Someone's comin'." Milton crouched as he whispered.

The two soldiers clicked their horses off the trail and into the cottonwood forest, leading them with their reins, then watched and waited silently. Soon, they heard the sound of horse's hooves, then the strong pant of the animal. The rider moved on at a walk, then stopped and returned.

"Tandy? Milton?" Beckner cried out in a hoarse whisper.

"Hey! It's the lieutenant," Milton whispered to Tandy.

"Yeah, I thought so," Tandy said. "Here, hold the reins. I'll go stop 'im."

Tandy sprinted to the trail. "Lieutenant! It's Tandy! Over here!" He spoke as loudly as he could without shouting.

"Tandy," Beckner replied. He stayed in the saddle. "What's going on? Where are the men you spotted?"

Tandy spread his arms out in a shrug in the dark. "They're gone, sir. Disappeared." He swung his arm out and pointed. "We seen a light a bit ago, but that's it."

"Damn!" Beckner spat. "They got smart on us." He reflected, then, "Listen, Sergeant, see if you and Milton can find that light and follow it. I'll look around a bit." Several seconds passed, then he said, "Sergeant, if you find 'em, don't encounter. Try to follow unseen, then get back to me. I'll be near the plaza. Along the western edge, where we met earlier. Understand?"

"Yessir," Tandy said. "I'll get Milton." With that, he turned and made his way back into the *bosque.*

Beckner, with increased frustration, removed his hat and wiped his brow. He then dismounted, dropped the reins of his well-trained horse to the ground, and picked his way carefully through the underbrush and between cottonwoods. When he came to what he sensed as a clearing, he struck a match and looked around. He saw what he considered evidence that someone, or more than one person, had been there recently, and that there had been boxes or crates as well. These were accompanied by boot and hoof prints, which led away through the dense foliage. The match flame died and he made his way back to the trail.

Because their horses were creating too much noise, Tandy and Milton moved back to the trail. In the process, they found themselves in shallow swamp, but were soon out of it and onto the trail with their nervous mounts. Tandy decided they should hitch them to a tree and proceed on foot.

As they got closer to the outskirts of the village, they saw a moving light they thought they had seen earlier. It was intermittent, and bounced, sometimes wildly. Neither man could discern the distance, so were wary of getting too close. They were prepared to use their pistols if necessary, but that could prove very troublesome, especially should they wound or kill an innocent. Then the light disappeared. Moments later, they heard Beckner approach.

"Tandy?" He called out.

"Here, sir. Me an' Milton."

"Your horses back there?"

"That's a fact, Lieutenant. Makin' too much of a racket."

"Nothing, eh?" Beckner asked.

"That's a fact, too, sir. I'm regretful—"

Beckner held his hand up in the dark. "Okay, Sergeant. You did your best. Both of you." He paused. "Don't worry; we'll find 'em. They're bound to surface."

Tandy removed his hat and swiped at his thinning hair. "Yessir. Sure hope so. Cain't let this progress. That's fer sure." He turned to Milton. "Better get our horses."

20

It was after dark when Ustacio, with Nerio Noriega's assistance, had put a horse in the traces, lit a lantern and set out in the direction Noriega had ordered, east, toward the mountains. A man past middle-age who almost never became nervous over anything, he was somewhat so this night, because he sensed his mission was not strictly legal, and possibly dishonorable. As a man of deep and certain faith, he crossed himself several times along the way in an effort to shield himself against the possibility of harm that might ensue from his otherwise innocent deed. He performed the simple act as insurance for his imagined eternity, that which had been taught to him so many times from early childhood on, that which he must constantly monitor and guard. A simple soul, faithful to his master and the house of Noriega of Albuquerque, none the less, he did his duty without open question.

His journey was slow, given the scant flickering, orange light from the oil lantern held by the angled pole at the front corner of the wagon as he moved through the crazy-quilt paths between the squat earthen houses until he reached the eastern edge of the village. The faithful horse he controlled was afforded little light, but through instinct and a certain familiarity, found the way.

Ustacio was told he should watch for a signal composed of a light that would blink on and off in a three-step sequence with dark between; that he would spot it on his right, beyond the beginning of the *bosque*, and that it might be east of the swampy area. He was to answer in kind, to rendezvous with three men attendant with a pair of mules. To do so, he was required to take the lantern from the post.

Earlier, after Gerald Rodman had arrived at the impromptu depot and provided Pulver and Cat with refreshment, he had distanced himself from the two men he needed, but whom he had come to dislike and mistrust on a personal, although not professional, basis. This was in no small part because of the bond he realized existed between the two drovers, despite their differences in skin tone, cultural and ethnic backgrounds.

Cat had stood, looked around and then paced a bit. He came back to Pulver and looked down at the man as he ate, one eye squinted. "I ain't com- for- *table* with this here situation, Pulver. I believe we should move this here heavy stuff right along."

Pulver, his mouth full, dribbled crumbs from the corners of his full mouth. His voice muffled, asked, "What? Where to, Cat?"

Cat turned and pointed toward the town and a denser part of the woods with dry ground. "Yonder. Dang harder to see. Know what I mean? This place's too easy. Too close to the trail."

"Yep." Pulver cleared his mouth and stood. He brushed discarded bits of food from his breeches. "Good i-dee. Let's move."

When Rodman heard the commotion a few yards behind him, he turned and saw the men in the fading light, goading and coaxing the mules to drag the crates with ropes tied to their harnesses. He hurried back, his face cloudy. "What the—?!"

Pulver glanced at the Texican briefly. "We're movin' in case."

Rodman spread his arms. "In case 'o what?!"

"Cat reckoned it better to be there a pace, where it's thicker. Harder ta' see." He pointed with his chin as he worked with a leather strap.

Rodman paused, dropped his arms, took in and blew out a long breath. He scratched his cheek and looked about. "Yeah. Good," he answered, his tone one of defeated acquiescence.

Re-stationed, ready and nervous with anticipation, the three contraband couriers didn't wait long after dark before they heard the thud of horse's hooves, the creak of the wooden vehicle, and saw the wavering, flickering light of Ustacio's lantern. Rodman struck a match and touched it to the wick of the lantern Ustacio had provided along with their supper, then raised it. He covered the lens facing the on-coming rider with his hand, opened it, then did so twice more. He lowered the lantern, then raised it and repeated the signal. The on-coming light halted, followed by a similar signal generated by the lamp the old man held.

Cat and Pulver struggled the crates onto Ustacio's wagon, then, with leads to the grateful mules in the rear, followed the wagon on their horses. Rodman quenched his lamp, placed it on the wagon, mounted and rode ahead of the wagon. As they moved, the three outsiders each craned his neck to stay aware of potential trouble that might spring from the dark. When they had traveled a few hundred feet, Ustacio extinguished his flame, and they continued in the dark.

Rodman, Pulver and Cat had not spoken to Ustacio, nor he to them. For one thing, Ustacio didn't want to know what was happening, and could only guess as to the contents of the mysterious boxes and the unusual manner in which they were being delivered. He comforted himself with the notion that they were no more than articles his *patrón*, a gentleman of commerce, had purchased as a matter of course, and merely wanted to protect them from the prying eyes of competitors and thieves. For another, he was short shrift with English, with only a few words in his lexicon. He knew how to work for his keep, and more than that, he did not want to know or care.

They by-passed the plaza, and rounded the village on the southern perimeter. Of the one or two stray young men carousing that night, no interest was displayed toward the shadowy caravan.

The simple adobe house where Ustacio led them was three large rooms in an Ell pattern. It featured two outside doors, with interior openings between three rooms. One room was dense with grain sacks, barrels, crates and other odds and ends, storage and overflow from Noriega's business and the management of the family land. Mixed with the dank smell of feed and rough cloth, it reeked of soured wine; red by Rodman's reckoning. Ustacio bade them store the contraband crates in a corner of that lair. When accomplished, he covered them with grain sacks and a blanket of Mexican origin, per Noriega's orders. He shut the outside door, pointed to the *común*, and showed Pulver and Cat the room they could occupy, complete with floor-bound mattresses consisting of large, lumpy sacks of straw as well as food and water for a day. The mules, along with the horses that belonged to Pulver and Cat, were lodged in a corral next to the secondary house, while the empty wagon was driven back to the main house.

After completing these duties, Ustacio turned to Rodman, who had stood and watched the other men work. "*Venga.* Come." He gestured with his chin, then started away on foot.

Rodman nodded. "Yes, of course." He began to lead his horse.

Ustacio looked down. "*En su caballo.* On your horse." He waved with a note of irritation.

The Texican reflected a moment, then pulled himself up into the saddle and followed the Noriega servant in the dark, illuminated faintly by starlight and stray lantern light from nearby houses. Five minutes later, after moving slowly through the empty plaza and past the church, Ustacio moved through a narrow passage between two houses, then into a yard through a gated opening in a high, rock and adobe wall. The space spread out widely within the walled area, on the opposite end of which was a substantial house. Yellow light fell from two of its windows under a *portal* that ran the length of the building.

In the half light, Ustacio stopped at a hitching rail parallel to the porch, then beckoned Rodman to lash his horse's reins to the rail. He signaled the Texican to bring his baggage.

Rodman removed his saddlebags and the stuffed carpet bag tied to it and followed the old man to the front of the house.

Ustacio rapped on the heavy door. A few seconds passed before it was opened by a young Pueblo Indian girl. Ustacio said something to her, and she stepped aside. As Ustacio went in, followed by Rodman, he removed his hat, while the girl lowered her head and looked at the floor. Rodman also doffed his head cover.

Ustacio said something to the shy girl in a low tone, as a middle-aged woman entered the room.

She was lithe, dark-haired, cloaked in a long, black dress, her hair in a severe bun, her lips compressed in the age-old set of someone with ownership; in charge. She looked at Ustacio.

"*Gracias, Ustacio,*" she said, then at Rodman. "*Venga conmigo.* Come with me." With that, she turned and moved for the hall from which she had issued.

Ustacio executed a dip of his head in respect to the woman and returned his hat to his head.

Rodman looked at Ustacio. "My horse. *El ca*—"

Ustacio glanced at Rodman. He raised his hand. "*Está bien.* I take care." He then turned and left the house. From there, he went to Rodman's horse and led the animal away in the dark.

At the Noriega house a short time later, he sought out his *patrón* and discovered him with Jesse.

21

Jesse arose the morning after his talk with Noriega to the aroma of the house breakfast fire and resultant fare that wafted along the hall and into his exiguous room. He sat up sleepily, shook his head, fingered his errant hair, and peered through the lone window at the *atrio*. Encircled by the big house, it was flooded with early sunlight past steep shadows cast by the east wall of the enclosure. In response to the urgency in his innards, he hastily slipped on his britches below his floppy, gray nightshirt, left the belt loose, and hurried from the room and the house on stocking feet to the small *el común* nested in a corner of the inner square.

Relieved and in his room again, he squared up his clothing after performing modest ablutions with the bowl of fresh water and towels. They, in turn, had been provided by Jacinta, the Navajo girl, under the supervision of the invariant Ermelina. From there, he followed the effluent trail to the warm, welcoming kitchen.

Ermelina was bent over the corner fireplace as she tended to a kettle of water suspended from an iron tripod. Ustacio stood behind her with an armload of seasoned split cedar, cottonwood and *piñon*. Little Roberto stood at the big table situated in the center of the generous room, both of his little hands gasping a huge wooden spoon as he stirred the contents of a locally-made clay bowl. Apolonia sat on a stool, also at the table, a knife in one hand as she prepared vegetables. Her long dress flowed close to the hard-packed, ox-blood sealed, earthen floor.

She looked up at Jesse, smiled and brushed at her face with the back of her wet, vegetable-stained hand. "*Buenos días.*"

"Good morning," he said, in Spanish.

When Ermelina and Ustacio looked around, he nodded at them.

Ermelina awarded him a faint smile, then returned to her task. Ustacio nodded his head, then looked down at Ermelina's back, as he waited patiently to place the new wood on the fire.

Roberto turned to Jesse. He blurted, "I'm going to show you my toys!" He took in a deep breath of excitement and returned to his serious task, his tongue out, clamped between his teeth in concentration.

"I await with pleasure, young Roberto." Jesse smiled and nodded.

"I think Roberto likes you," Apolonia said in a low voice. She looked at the boy, then the visitor.

Roberto glared at her. "I do not! He is my friend!" He stirred more vigorously, his tongue out farther in an expression of superior effort.

Jesse compressed his lips, looked around, then down at the small boy. "Yes, Roberto, we are friends, but I like *you*." He grinned widely and winked.

Roberto looked down, embarrassed, but said nothing as he wielded the big spoon, his little arms extended up and over the bowl as it rocked precipitously near the edge of the table.

Ermelina straightened from her management of the kettle and turned to watch the boy. She and Apolonia both laughed.

"Come, *señor* Landry, sit and partake of our modest *desayuno*," Apolonia spoke as she rose and went to long wooden shelf attached to the wall with ropes. She returned with a plate and a bowl.

Jesse went to a stool and sat. He looked up as Apolonia put food in front of him. Their eyes locked for an instant before Jesse looked away. He was relieved to see that neither of the two other adults in the room had noticed the brief transaction.

"*Gracias*," he said.

"*De nada*," she replied. "There will be hot chocolate soon. Ermelina is preparing it." She moved back to her work station, picked up the knife and busied herself.

His mouth full, Jesse uttered a satisfied grunt.

Ermelina retrieved the vessel from the fire and took it to the work table.

Ustacio unburdened himself of the wood, brushed his hands and clothing, adjusted the fire with a poker, then went to the counter. He took a still-warm, fresh corn tortilla, wrapped a piece of meat, a chunk of cheese, a slice of green chile and a spoonful of beans into it and left the room. As he did, he flashed a side-long glance at Jesse, who concentrated on his victuals.

Ermelina finished preparing a breakfast tray, hefted it, and exited into the hall, but not before pouring a cup of chocolate and delivering it to their guest.

Roberto dropped the spoon and jumped away from the table. He looked at Apolonia with a serious, excited expression. "Chavela!" He shouted. He jumped up and down once and slapped his sides.

Apolonia put her hand to her mouth. "Oh, my god! *Gracias, Roberto!*" She dropped what she was doing and rushed from the room.

A few minutes later, she re-entered with her aunt Chavela's hand in hers, then led her to a chair at the table around the corner from Jesse.

Roberto followed this action with his eyes, then looked at Jesse dolefully as he resumed the unnecessary stirring.

Apolonia fussed over Chavela for a few seconds. She smoothed her dress and pushed back her errant hair. She then turned and fixed a bowl for the forlorn woman. Together with a spoon, she placed both in front of her. "*Coma,*" she said. "Eat."

Chavela, her feet bare and suspended a few inches off the floor, the bowl in front of her, looked up at her niece with no apparent emotion, then slowly took the spoon and began to slurp food into her frail mouth. Apolonia stood up straight, wiped her otherwise clean hands on her apron, then turned to Jesse and smiled sadly.

Jesse returned her smile, nodded, and continued to eat, eyes averted.

Finished, Jesse bussed his dishes to the sideboard, thanked Apolonia and said goodbye as she again tended to her aunt. The girl did not turn, but answered in kind. As he walked back to his room, he wondered where Ermelina had gone with the laden breakfast tray. The rooms along the hall with open doors where he had met family and conferred with Noriega, he noticed were unoccupied. All other doors were closed.

In his room, he donned a leather vest, put on his hat, considered, then rejected, the notion of strapping on his pistol, and exited through the back door. From there, he went to the stables, where he found Campeón. The animal recognized him and executed a dance with his head, stomped a tattoo with his right front hoof and snorted. Jesse patted the faithful animal's great head, and looked about as he did, as he expected to see Ustacio nearby. Thwarted, he murmured to Campeón, then walked away, around the rear corner of the house and stables, toward the plaza. The sun was nine o'clock high.

As he stepped beyond the Noriega house porch line, he spotted Francisco Maestas across the open space, crouched next to his horse, smoking. His hat was low over his eyes, such that he did not see Jesse as he approached. A moment later, he looked up, saw Jesse, stood, spiraled the burning fag away, and nodded, chin up in instant recognition.

"Francisco," Jesse said as he walked up. He held out his hand.

Francisco took Jesse's hand, looked at him squarely, then nodded toward the big house across the plaza. "How goes it?"

Jesse glanced in the direction of the Noriega place. "Well. I talked with Noriega. Last night."

"And?"

"Señor Noriega spoke with Baca. He has promised to forget what happened."

Maestas leaned into Jesse. "What?!" He stood straight, marched away several steps, then returned. He scowled at his friend. "I don't believe it. No."

Jesse shrugged. "He said he told Baca he would pay him well. To forget. To leave me alone."

Francisco shook his head, looked at the ground, away, then at Jesse. "I don't trust them. I don't know Baca, but I know Noriega. I don't trust him. He lies."

"Francisco, he wants me to stay here for a time. He is to include me in his business. Now that my father is gone. I have the business up north. You know that." Jesse threw his friend a look of frustration.

Maestas was silent for a time. His eyes went wide and he shrugged. "*Bueno*. I will find the lieutenant and inform him. Do you want me to remain?"

"No, Francisco. I am treated well at the house. I will stay for a time and work with *señor* Noriega. It is important that I learn more about my father's business. And Noriega's. Go home to your family. I will see you and your parents—your sister and brother soon." He paused, then, "I will speak with your father about our business."

Maestas nodded, disappointment apparent on his face. He smiled. "You do well, Jesse Landry. But be careful!" He wagged his finger in Jesse's face.

"I will, my friend. I will tell you and your father what I learn. We will continue to trade." He tapped Francisco's shoulder with his fist. "Tell your father. This I promise."

Lieutenant Beckner had returned to the place where Francisco Maestas waited for him at the Catholic Church after Jesse left for the Noriega house. Beckner welcomed the idea of a shot of *aguardiente* before returning to Maestas' cousin's house. In the morning, following a generous breakfast prepared by the lady of the house and served by her daughter, Beckner insisted he pay for his lodging, thanked his hosts, and left. Maestas saw him off after promising to check with Jesse.

Since everyone who approached the army encampment on the bluff overlooking the Rio Grande and the village of Albuquerque was spotted early by more than the lone sentry, Sergeant Tandy and Private Milton, attended by a small contingent of curious soldiers, were there to greet their superior officer as he rode up. Captain Marchant, upon hearing the news, stood expectantly in the opening of his tent.

Beckner dismounted, Milton took the reins of his horse, and the lieutenant made his way to the command tent.

In deference to Marchant's superior rank, in part to stay within bounds of military discipline, but also to soften Captain Marchant up, he halted, then saluted the officer in command. Marchant was mildly surprised, but pleased, as he belatedly and awkwardly returned Beckner's military salutation..

"Good morning, Captain," Beckner said.

"Good morning, Lieutenant Beckner." Marchant held out his hand, and Beckner took it. "Come in, please."

Beckner followed Marchant inside, where he was offered a chair.

Marchant took his seat behind the small, impromptu desk. "So, Lieutenant, I now have three of you here from headquarters. I'd appreciate a report. I'd like to know why you, the sergeant and the private are here." He leaned back, his arms folded and his chin on his chest, his demeanor a cross between his knowledge of his position, but more a sense, that in a way, he was actually out-ranked by a junior officer.

Beckner pulled his chair closer to the desk. He looked behind and through the door briefly. "I agree, Captain. I intend to tell you why we are here, and what we are about. I ask, however, that we take a walk, away from this area such that we cannot be overheard."

Marchant dropped his arms and leaned forward. His face pinched. "Really. It's that serious? That confidential?"

"Indeed, Captain. Indeed it is. Is this a good time?"

Marchant hesitated a few seconds, then rose. "Certainly. Follow me."

Beckner stood. "I want Tandy and Milton with us."

Marchant turned, his curiosity even greater. "Oh?" He shook his head. "Are you implying that they don't know?" He spoke in a lower tone.

"I am so implying. They know only to the extent of their direct orders. Now, they must be brought into full knowledge. I suggest we hail them and take our walk."

Beckner, Tandy, Milton and Marchant walked away after the captain admonished the sentry and a sergeant to maintain order, and for all troopers to stay within the confines of the encampment while he and the three others were away.

When they were well away and out of earshot, Beckner drew a letter from an envelope he carried in his breast pocket and handed it to Marchant.

Marchant peered at Beckner, read the contents, then looked up. "This declares you are here under orders of the War Department." He paused. "That you, in effect, out-rank all others, including superior officers, in the Department of New Mexico, when your activities apply to your mission." He dropped his hand with the letter in amazement, then raised it to return the letter to Beckner.

As Beckner put the letter in the envelope and that to its hiding place, both Tandy and Milton stared first at Beckner, then Marchant, then back.

Marchant screwed up his face. His voice was close to a whisper as he looked at his three visitors in turn. "What—what *is* your mission?" He shifted his weight in anticipation of the answer.

Beckner shook, then nodded, his head, looked at the ground, then at the other three men in turn. "We know—we have knowledge—the United States government has knowledge—that there are attempts by the government of Texas, to include land to this river below us in their new republic. To that purpose, they have sent agents here—to this region, to help that plan." He stopped and looked at the shock and surprise of his audience. "What these two men, Sergeant Tandy and Private Milton, have been doing—and they have been successful to now—is to track a shipment of arms intended to aid in the overthrow of *this* government on behalf of the plotters in Austin." He pointed at the ground. He waited while Marchant, his face a mask of disbelief, shook his head and stared at the lieutenant.

Tandy turned a short circle and shook his head with his hand to his chin.

Milton stared at Beckner. "Shee - ut!" He exclaimed out loud, then, "Hot damn," under his breath.

Beckner waited for his words to sink in, then continued, "Last night, these men and I lost track of that shipment. It was last seen by the sergeant and the private here on the other side of the village. Last night, it was removed, to what hiding place we know not." He paused. "But this I believe; that there is someone, or more than one person, in that town below us, who is in on this." Again, he pointed.

"God bless," Tandy whispered. He looked askance at Milton.

Milton went slack-jawed.

Marchant nodded, looked away, then, "How do we aid in this effort, Lieutenant Beckner?" His voice and demeanor carried new respect.

"I have brought you into my confidence because you need to know what we are up against. I require first, that you accept this challenge, and that you—" He looked at the two enlisted men, "all three, maintain confidentiality in this matter. This is essential. If this information should leak out, it could jeopardize our efforts to find the perpetrators, the agents, and their local conspirators. Even amongst the men in this army." He paused. "There is one other who is aware of this and of my mission here, and with whom I have complete confidence. That is Major Middleton, the Provost in Santa Fé. He has my full cooperation." He looked closely at each of the men facing him.

All three nodded emphatic assent.

"Secondly, Captain, I require that you be willing to lodge these two troopers when and if needed. Further, if and when the perpetrators are discovered, and military action is imminent, you and your men be ready to act."

"Yessir. Uh, yes, Lieutenant. I welcome the opportunity and the challenge." He nodded again with a new, positive look of appreciation. He folded his arms across his chest.

"Hot damn," Milton repeated.

Beckner smiled at Milton, then Tandy, who beamed back at him with new pride.

"I must return to the village to speak with someone there. Upon my return, Tandy and Milton will return to Santa Fé with me to gather civilian clothes, horses and guns, and will then return. When I return, I cannot be certain, but I will soon thereafter. We require a half day's provisions if you can meet that need."

"We can indeed, Lieutenant Beckner. As to these troopers, we welcome them back, and we welcome the challenge." Marchant held out his hand, first to Beckner, then Tandy and Milton in turn, excitement and energy in his action.

Tandy stepped forward. "Lieutenant, what about that shipment we was trackin'? We lost it last night. No idea where it is. How we gonna find it?" He pointed behind himself toward the river below and the village. "Hell, we ain't welcome there, even in civilian clothes."

Beckner nodded, paced away, then back. "Most astute, Sergeant. You are correct. At this moment, I have no answer as to how to proceed. But I may have soon. Something we need to work on. We may have friends down there. Not all are against us. These people know we keep marauding Indians and outlaws at bay. They also trade with us. Along the trail and down into Mexico. Gringos, as they call us. What's more, if you listen, you will hear words of distrust toward Texicans and Texas. We will discuss this further."

Tandy kicked at the dirt with his boot. "Yessir."

Beckner, after asking Marchant, Tandy and Milton to report to curious troopers that their wilderness tete-a-tete had been no more than about such mundane topics as chasing bandits common in the territory, he hauled himself into the saddle and made his way down to the river. He was half way across the silt-laden stream when he spotted Francisco Maestas coming from the town. They stopped mid-way.

"Are you going home?" Beckner inquired.

"I am," Maestas replied. "I met Jesse. He is free of the sheriff. I came to find you."

"What?!" Beckner frowned.

Maestas shrugged. "He told me the *pendejo* Noriega sent the *cabrón* Baca away with promise of riches. It is true." He shrugged again.

Beckner looked down and away, then back. "Jesse told you that?"

"Yes, he did. He said Noriega convinced Baca that Jesse was innocent and to go away. Made him promise to make no charge. Money changed hands."

"Do you believe this?" Beckner squinted.

Maestas shrugged again. "I do. I watched as Baca and his men went away this morning."

"So you are leaving?"

"He told me to tell you he will be working with the *rico* in his business for a time. That he needs no more protection. I came to tell you."

"Hm." Beckner paused. "Thank you. Francisco, I need your help. Let's go to the bank. This way, away from the town."

The two men crossed to the west side of the river.

Beckner dismounted and led his horse away toward a copse of river willows. Maestas followed on horseback, then got down.

"What do you wish? If it is my sister, I may have to kill you." He smiled and slapped Beckner on the shoulder.

Beckner blushed, looked down, then up. "I wish it were that simple. I would fight you for her." He smiled.

Maestas nodded, shut his eyes in understanding, then went quiet. He cocked his head, curious.

Beckner then launched into an explanation for his travel with Jesse Landry, his disappearance the night before, and his reason for being in the Department of New Mexico out of uniform. He went on to say that because of the relationship Francisco's family had with Jesse and his deceased father, that he felt he could trust him with his secret and looked to him for help.

Maestas stared silently, dumb-struck, at the gringo army officer for a long time, then paced away as he mumbled to himself. He swung around and, stock-still, looked hard at the lieutenant. "You—you tell me these things because you trust me?" His voice was low, serious, but not menacing. "You say these *Tejanos* want our land? They are here, with guns, to start a fight, a war?" He jabbed his finger at the ground.

"I am. I do. Yes."

Maestas walked a tight circle, then came back to Beckner and looked him directly in the eye. "I believe you, you damned gringo army man!"

Beckner held his tongue as he waited for Francisco's emotions to run their course.

Maestas turned away, stooped to pick up a twig, then began breaking it into little pieces. Without turning back, he said, his voice nearly inaudible, "I will help you, gringo. I will help. What do I have to do?"

Beckner talked to his back. "First, no one else may know. Not your family; no one else. Too dangerous."

Maestas nodded, his bent back still to Beckner. Then he turned. "I want to tell my father. You can trust him, Beckner. I need his help."

Beckner and Maestas looked into each other's eyes.

Beckner spoke as he nodded. "Yes. You tell your father. But Francisco, please, no one else at this time. Do I have your word?"

"You have my word, gringo." He held out his hand.

They shook.

Beckner looked down, then up. "I need you here, in Albuquerque. You can move about freely. You can see things. Hear things. I cannot, nor can my men. But you must be careful. We must find the guns. We must find who hides them. Even if it is your friends or family, we must know."

Maestas turned and threw the remains of the twig away. He shook his head.

"I swear, it is not my friends or family, but if it is, I will kill them myself," he growled.

Beckner nodded. "I don't think it is, Francisco."

"Jesse Landry. You have told him?"

Beckner looked away briefly. "No, Francisco. I have not. He does not know."

Maestas raised his head to peer at Beckner down his nose. "Why is this?"

"Because, my friend, I do not know who to trust. The fact is that I trust you more than I trust Jesse."

Maestas shook his head with a pained look.

Beckner took a step closer to Maestas. He lowered his voice. "Francisco, I believe the man Jesse shot was the man who killed his father. I think that man killed his father because he knew something—was somehow involved with this dastardly plot. If Jesse knows something, and I tell him these things, I think it will go badly for our plan. He must not know."

"What is the word 'dastardly'?"

"It means something very bad."

"You think my friend—our friend—is with these *Tejanos*?"

"No. No, I don't, Francisco." He shook his head adamantly. "No. But he was close to his father. Now he is close to Noriega. And we don't know who is involved." He shrugged.

"I understand."

"Good."

"Maybe I will not interfere with my sister, gringo."

Beckner chuckled. "Thank you, Francisco. We shall see. She may not care for me."

"Oh, yes. Oh, yes, gringo. I know the look. My mother knows the look." He shook his head and pointed his finger at Beckner's face. "¡Jesús, María y José! Coyote nieces and nephews!" He laughed, then took a step closer to the lieutenant. "One thing, gringo. Don't ever take her away from here! I will have to chase you and kill you! With the pistol you gave me!"

"You're getting ahead of yourself, Francisco. It may never happen. But let me tell you this: if it happens between your sister, Mercedes, and me, I would never ask her to leave here. I swear that."

Maestas nodded in silence for a time, then, "Good, gringo. ¡Vámos!" He grabbed the reins of his horse and sprang into the saddle. "I must return to my home now, but I will come back. I will help you and the gringo army rid this place of the dastardly *Tejanos!*"

Beckner remained on the ground. He looked up at Maestas. "One more question, Francisco. What will you tell your family? To explain your absence?"

"I come to this place often. For business. To see friends. I will think of something. Do not concern yourself." He shrugged as he awarded Beckner a knowing smile.

Beckner nodded in satisfaction, mounted his horse, and the two men rode up the embankment and onto the western escarpment of the Rio Grande.

22

Marchant had added a second picket in reaction to his new-found mission, and both reacted at seeing Beckner's rapid return with another man, he with a sidearm, and obviously not a gringo.

Beckner and Maestas halted a short distance outside the encampment, where Beckner sent for Tandy and Milton, who had both easily become an integral part of the dragoons. He introduced the two soldiers to Maestas, and explained that Francisco Maestas was now a part of their group, with full knowledge and cooperation. Tandy and Maestas, through some mysterious, unspoken channel, took to each other almost immediately. The two men sensed in each other some elementary kindred spirit of manhood. Beckner then took Maestas to meet Captain Marchant, who although feeling chilly in his presence, accepted Maestas as well. The commandant felt an aura of strength surrounding the young Hispanic he could not deny, and was attracted to it at the same time he had a visceral fear of it. He would later discuss it with himself in the privacy of his restless dreams in this foreign, but intriguing place.

The four men rested overnight, and partook of the camp food, which Francisco Maestas found odd, but fulfilling. Marchant ate with them, and at one point, Maestas offered to bring the troop the carcass of a deer or perhaps an elk from the mountains to the north. Marchant declared his desire to attend in this primal endeavor, to which Maestas was charmed enough to invite him to accompany him.

The following day, with cheers and hat-waving as a send-off, the four men set out for the Rio en Medio.

It was late in the day when they crossed the river at a shallow place where the river spread thin between sand and silt bars several dozen yards upstream. They then made their way south through the flat, sandy *bosque* and across a river-fed irrigation ditch to the edge of the Maestas family property.

The elder, Sabino, was in the field with his second son, Javier, and looked up in surprise when he saw the four horsemen approach. Francisco rode up first, followed by Lieutenant Beckner, who raised his hand in greeting. Javier waved, then Sabino, although in a more muted gesture. Francisco dismounted, went to his father and greeted him with a hug. He was half a head taller than the older man. He then did the same with his younger, stouter, brother. Soon, all were introduced. Sabino was flustered and somewhat discomfitted by the presence of Tandy and Milton, especially upon recognizing their profession as delineated by their dusty and trail-worn uniforms. He played the gracious host, though, and walked alongside as they all made their way to the corrals and house, as they lead the horses on foot.

The happy animals were unsaddled, then led to water and feed. Beckner handed Sabino spendable specie, which surprised and delighted the elder Maestas, an act which further warmed Francisco and his father to the army officer.

As the men completed the job of putting the horses up, Mercedes emerged from the house. When she realized what ensued and who had arrived, she picked up her pace to a run toward the stables, skirts flying, then slowed to a walk, then stopped and looked away, embarrassed. Her face bright, she stared at Lieutenant Beckner's back. When he turned and saw her, he also froze. They looked at each other for a long moment with open smiles, some fifteen feet apart, then Mercedes broke off and looked down and away, uncertain as to what to do with her hands as she twisted back and forth. Beckner also looked away and turned his body, his face red. There were two who did not observe or understand this brief transaction. One was Mercedes' younger brother, Javier, who gibbered on about the event surrounding him as he dealt with arranging horse tack; the other, her father, Sabino.

Beckner braved a glance at the other men around him to find knowing faces with suppressed smiles, save for those of Sabino and Javier. He dared to turn again, and watched as Mercedes strode back to the house. She threw her long braids back over her shoulders, hips in motion, head high, driven by primordial female instinct.

Filomena, Mercedes' mother, Sabino's wife, emerged from the house as her daughter approached. Upon seeing the girl rush toward her along with a group of men with her husband and boy near the corral, she threw her hands into the air in alarm, with the thought that something terrible had happened. A few minutes later, she believed that something truly terrible had happened with the arrival of the gringo lieutenant. But at the moment, she screeched at her daughter to inquire as to the emergency she thought she witnessed. Mercedes brushed past her wordlessly and disappeared into the house, then to her bedroom. Filomena turned to see the men ranged in an arc across the yard, all quiet, all in awe of the unfolding drama. Beckner waved at her.

Francisco was the first to move, and advanced on his mother to give her a hug and a kiss on the cheek. He turned to the others, his arm held lightly against his mother's midriff. "*Ven acá*. Come." He motioned.

Beckner came up to his suspicious hostess and greeted her with a loose bow from the waist. Then he took her hand and kissed it, an act so daring and brazen to her, she became flustered and could not help but smile and roll her eyes. The lieutenant then held out his arm to Tandy and Milton, who, taking a cue from their superior officer, imitated the bow in unison as he introduced them.

Soon, they were all in the kitchen. Tandy and Milton stood close together at one end of the room, hats in hand, near the window that looked out toward the front orchard and the Santa Fé - Albuquerque road, the Camino Real, beyond. Beckner stood in the middle of the room, while Sabino and Francisco bade them all sit at the table. Javier rushed into another room to retrieve a stool and a chair to fill out the seating. Filomena folded her hands in front of herself near the stove. As the men began to scrape seats back to sit, Sabino offered that he had only that day sacrificed a pig, and allowed that he needed to butcher the animal. Milton jumped up and proclaimed his skill at such a task, at which Sabino was only too glad to have him help. Javier went with them, ready to bring the chops, shanks and ribs for his mother to prepare. Francisco went for wine, and Filomena put out cups and tumblers.

As she stood away from the table after setting the drink containers down, Filomena looked toward the door to the hall. "Mercedes? Mercedes! *¿Donde estás? ¡Ven acá, hijita!*" She made a sound of displeasure to herself, then returned to the wood-fired stove and the counter close by.

A minute later, Mercedes appeared in the doorway. At the same time, Francisco returned from outside with the wine and went directly to the table. Beckner looked up, then stood and made a small, awkward bow to the girl. Tandy stood as well on his leader's cue. Milton followed suit.

"*¿Sí, mama?*" She sneaked a glance at the lieutenant, then away. She blushed. Her mother turned. "*¡Ayúdame!*"

Mercedes donned an apron and went to her mother.

Beckner found the opportunity to defuse the strained moment by offering to help Francisco with the wine.

An enthusiastic, gibbering Javier burst through the hand-made outer door, followed by Milton, then his father, all carrying the results of their efforts with the unfortunate hog.

That evening, they supped on a pork stew put together by Filomena and Mercedes, spiced with green chile, onions, corn and pinto beans, and washed down with a local red wine for the men and water for the two women and Javier. Mercedes sat on the other side of her mother, angled away from the gringo army officer, who sat at the head across from Sabino. Her head was down demurely much of the time. Francisco made sure what little conversation ensued steered clear of any implication of impropriety on the part of his new friend or of his sister.

The following morning after being fortified with more stew, eggs from the family chickens and some of Filomena's tortillas, Beckner, Tandy and Milton took to horse. Javier helped the saddling process along with discussion about it with Tandy, while Beckner conferred off to the side with Francisco. Mounted, they mouthed their goodbys. Francisco nodded to Tandy as he touched the rim of his campaign hat, each other in total unspoken understanding of themselves and each other.

As they removed themselves from the Maestas land, Beckner sneaked a look back toward the house. The pretty, teen-aged Mercedes stood close to a corner and stared after the troopers. Her long, dark braids framed her well-proportioned bosom. When she realized the lieutenant had turned, she held up her hand at waist level and moved it to and fro in a muted wave. Beckner saluted to the rim of his hat, then faced forward. A moment later, he looked back, but she had vanished.

As the three troopers made their way north along the Camino Real, to the right, the sun rose against the northern escarpment of the Sandias and the rounded peaks of the Ortiz mountains. On their left, along the broad, shallow river valley, smoke rose from the breakfast fires of the Pueblos. They rode abreast, at a walk, not anxious to tire their well-fed and watered mounts.

Milton reached back and slapped his leather saddlebags. "Got some hot-damn good tor-tee-ahs that lady made. Gonna' save 'em. Yessir!" He paused, then, "Ahm a-goin' back there after I git outa' this man's army and raise hogs with ole' say-bee-no. He said he'd wait fer me. Yessir! I never knew!" Then, under his breath, "Hot damn."

Beckner and Tandy both maintained their faces forward, but each wore a secret smile and a squint of pleasure in their eyes at the private's declarations.

Later, at midday, when hunger overtook them, they stopped below La Bajada along the Rio Salado, to eat and slake thirsts from their canteens. As Milton continued to openly outline his future in the hog-raising business, Tandy sank his teeth into one of the fat burritos Filomena had manufactured.

When Beckner opened his saddlebag to retrieve his victuals, he discovered a little yellow flower, crushed by the unyielding leather of the pouch, but still aromatic. He looked at it for a few moments, smelled it, then carefully inserted the stem of the sad, half-destroyed bloom into a button hole in his vest. He smiled, then bit his lip and looked away, his eyes moist.

Tandy, seated on a large rock and masticating, saw the action out of the corner of his eye, but did not react, as Milton carried on, lost in his own fantasies, oblivious.

23

After a brief breakfast in the Noriega *cocina*, attended only by the stalwart Ermelina, Jesse left the house for the stable behind the house. There he found Ustacio tending to part of his morning chores. He noticed that the forge had been fired. He greeted the old man, who nodded and smiled in return.

Jesse went to Campeón. The animal raised his great head from his feed and snorted as Jesse spoke to him and brushed his mane.

"He is a fine horse," Ustacio said from the next stall.

"He is, indeed," Jesse answered. "I am proud of him. He is a gift from my father. He came along the trail from a place they call Missouri. Across the great river."

"Ay, how wonderful," Ustacio said.

Jesse took a brush from a nearby shelf and began to smooth the animal's flank. "Have you seen the *patrón* this morning?" He looked at the servant over Campeón's huge back.

Ustacio shrugged. "No, I have yet to see him today."

"I was to meet with him today. This morning. On business matters."

"Of course," Ustacio said. "He is a man of his word. But he is also quite busy."

"Of that I am sure," Jesse said. "I can wait."

He spent another ten minutes currying his horse, then left on foot and headed for the plaza. As he came around the corner of the great house to the right of the porch, he spotted Noriega and halted.

Noriega wore a beaver felt flat-topped black hat with wide brim. On his feet were black high-topped leather boots over tight riding breeches. He carried a riding crop that moved in a great arc as he swung his arms confidently. He moved quickly across the open space toward the northeast corner, near the church. Jesse started to hail him, but as quickly decided against the notion. Something about the man's demeanor and stride caused him to think his host was not in an accepting mood, and would not welcome discourse, despite his earlier promise.

Jesse adjusted his hat down closer to his eyes, looked about, saw that no one seemed to be interested in him, and moved in the direction the *patrón* was taking. He followed as Noriega rounded the corner of the church, then angled toward a narrow alley that led eastward. Jesse hurried to follow as Noriega disappeared on the edge of another building. As Jesse entered the alley, he saw Noriega go through a high wooden gate, then close it. Jesse looked behind, saw no one, then approached the gate. He put his eye up to a small inquiry window in the thick wood. Noriega had stopped in front of a big house inside a large, walled-in compound, and appeared to be in conversation with another man.

The man was taller than Noriega by half a head, and was smoking a cheroot. He wore a tan deer skin jacket with fringes on the cuffs and hem. He nodded, spoke, and gestured with his cigar, at one point, toward the sky, then held his arms out wide. Jesse was unable to hear what was said.

He watched as the two men conversed, then move toward the house. As they reached the edge of the porch, he saw Noriega turn and look toward the gate. Just as quickly, he joined the other man, and they disappeared into the house.

Major Middleton sat on a short, three-legged stool outside his office, his tunic unbuttoned, suspenders exposed, hatless, socks alone covering his feet, as he laboriously polished his boots. Lieutenant Beckner approached and stopped six feet away, silent, his hands folded across his midriff. He was not in uniform.

After a wait of five seconds, Middleton, startled, looked up. He sat up straight and set the boot he was working on aside. "Ah, the return of the prodigal." He squinted and smiled. "And it would seem, none the worse for wear. Indeed."

"Good morning, sir." Beckner executed a sloppy half salute. "How are you, sir?"

"Well, Beckner, well." He returned the military courtesy in the same manner, stood and arched his back as though in pain, then gestured toward the open door to his office. "Come in. Come in and tell me your tale. I trust it will excite me." As he entered, he padded along in his stockings, and took an embarrassed swipe at his unruly hair.

Beckner followed and took the seat in front of the major's desk as Middleton lowered himself into his high-backed swivel chair.

Middleton ran his fingers through his rebellious locks again as he sobered into his official demeanor. "So, Lieutenant, what news?" He paused. "Second thought, Lieutenant. What of our man, Jorgensen?"

"Ah, yes, sir. He mends well. In the infirmary."

Middleton frowned. "What happened out there?"

"He testified, sir, that he came up on a ridge behind the men he was chasing, they spotted him, and he took a lead ball."

"And he was treated by the locals?"

"Quite so, sir. And one of them took to horse to sound the alarm. Quite a distance from the village. San Juan, I believe. I reckon some forty miles."

"Astounding. Did our men see anything of the cowards when they retrieved Jorgensen?"

"Sorry to report, sir, no. But—"

"But?"

"In my view, it confirmed that they were trafficking the arms either back to their origin or around to Albuquerque. And now we know."

"Indeed?" The major attended to his errant hair in a nervous gesture again as he peered at Beckner.

Beckner moved in his chair. "The arms arrived in Albuquerque, Major, but we lost track of them."

"You were able to track them? Excellent. But lost track, you say. Hm." Middleton rocked back, both his palms flat on his desk as he peered intently at the junior officer. "Why did you lose track, Lieutenant?"

"My men, Sergeant Tandy and Private Milton, did fine work in spotting and following the contraband, but lost them at night when the armaments were moved to another location. I had admonished them not to expose themselves."

"Of course. Quite so." The major sat forward and looked down at a pen on his desk.

Beckner adjusted himself. "We will find them, sir. We have allies."

"Allies?" The major looked up and frowned. "Who, pray tell?"

"Sir, I met with certain friends of the Landry son. Jesse. Jesse Landry. Actually business associates of the Landry firm. One of the family—these friends—the eldest son, to be exact, accompanied us—Landry and me—to Albuquerque. He is called Francisco. They are strongly opposed to any interference on the part of the Texicans in the territory and are only too glad to help." He paused. "I also enlisted the aid of the outpost above the town. Captain Marchant and his dragoons, to be precise."

Middleton pushed back. "So, they are unaware of your true mission." He peered at Beckner.

Beckner shook his head and sighed. "No, sir, they are aware."

Middleton paused as he shook his head, then cocked it to one side. "I see. You feel that is safe, given the circumstances?"

"I do, Major. It was—is—a gamble, but I feel worthwhile. The enthusiasm was high. Palpable." He paused, then, "Among them all."

The major stared at Beckner. "I see..."

"To a man, they are anxious to aid in this effort." Beckner spoke with new confidence. He had not been sure as to Major Middleton's reaction, and was relieved.

Middleton looked down, reflected, then up. "What about the Landry boy?"

"Sir?"

"Is he with them? The cabal?"

Beckner looked away as he squirmed in his seat, took a deep breath, released it, shook his head and answered, "I don't know, sir. He remains in the town. Albuquerque." He shook his head again. "With the family of his father's partner. He was concerned about the Sheriff."

"We can't interfere, Lieutenant. Civil affair." Middleton cocked his head and raised his finger.

"I am aware, Major." He looked at the floor. "It appears the man there—they call him the *patrón*—Noriega, is housing and protecting him—Jesse Landry—for now." He paused. "But I was informed that ths man, Noriega, has forestalled the sheriff's actions against the Landry fellow."

"Really? Odd business, this. Well, what's next, Beckner?"

"Tandy and Milton will be on temporary duty at the outpost encampment. They returned with me to collect personal belongings and civilian apparel. I, to report to you and to send a message to Washington. I will return to Albuquerque. It may be wise to wait for advice from Washington." He reflected, then, "They will accompany me. Francisco—his last name is Maestas—is keeping a sharp eye for me. In Albuquerque. He blends in, of course."

"Of course." Middleton nodded and subconsciously moved a small note-book on the desk as he gathered his thoughts.

Beckner stood. "Will that be all, Major?"

The major looked up at his subaltern. "Where will you billet? In Albuquerque? When you return?"

"Captain Marchant has been very accommodating. I will operate from there. I feel, at least for now, to be seen in the town a great deal would be unwise. I feel the situation can be resolved with dispatch, but caution is paramount."

Middleton rose. "Good. Satisfactory, Lieutenant. Carry on."

Jesse turned away from the gate and went back the way he had come. As he entered the plaza, he encountered what he thought for him to be a strange site: a black man in trail clothes walking beside a white man; both men with sidearms strapped to their legs. He had seen black drovers, but always attached to white men who either owned them or paid them for their services, but never in such a way as this. He had seen, once, a black drover with a long gun within easy reach as protection from marauders, but until now, not walking along as a free man with a gun at his hip.

He watched as the two men strolled across the plaza, then accost and talk to a local man. The pair seemed to be asking questions, then the local man gestured, turned his head and pointed. As the pair nodded and waved at the man, Jesse felt a hand on his shoulder.

He turned to see Noriega beside him. In reaction, Jesse doffed his hat. "¡Señor!"

"Good morning, my son. My apologies for not meeting you at the time I told you I would. Some urgent business to conduct. I'm sure—" Noriega abruptly stopped talking and shifted his eyes away.

Jesse turned his head to see what had taken the older man's attention. He realized it was the two armed men, one black, who had finished talking with the local man, and were walking toward the northwest corner of the plaza. They were apparently focused on a destination, which he reckoned would most likely be the *cantina* where he, Francisco and Lieutenant Beckner had met. He glanced at Noriega, who seemed transfixed, a hardened expression of concern on his face.

Noriega recovered, returned his attention to Jesse, and smiled. "Ah, yes, young Landry, we must now discuss business matters. Let us go to the house." He tapped Jesse's shoulder again.

Jesse walked with Noriega to the big house and to his office, where the *patrón* offered his young guest a seat. Noriega went to his desk, opened a large, leather-bound book, turned several pages, then sniffed loudly and went to the door to the hall. He shouted, "Ermelina! Ermelina!"

Ermelina appeared in the doorway momentarily. "¿Sí, señor?"

"*Mi hijo. Bonifacio. ¿Donde está?*"

Ermelina shrugged and raised her eyebrows. "*Pues, you no sé, patrón.*"

Noriega looked away, then back. "Find him and send him to me! *¡Pronto!*" His voice was a low growl.

"*Sí, señor.*" Ermelina turned and walked away, unaffected by her master's anger.

Noriega stared at the floor for a moment, then reached for a wine decanter on his desk. He took two small flutes off a wall shelf, filled both, and handed one to Jesse without looking at him. He drank half, lowered his glass, and emitted a long breath. He nodded.

Jesse sipped at his wine. Embarrassed, he cleared his throat.

Noriega emptied the vessel, set it down and spoke, again without looking at Jesse. "When my son arrives, we will make plans."

"Plans?" Jesse looked at Noriega from under his eyebrows. He held his wine glass in both hands, still virtually full.

Noriega finally deigned to look at Jesse. "Yes. I have much business to conduct, and as I promised, you are my partner." He paused. "One of my partners." He lifted his glass and looked at it as he rotated it. "You will meet one of them soon."

Both men reacted to the sound of boots on the hard floor of the hall by looking in that direction. Three seconds later, Bonifacio strode into the room.

He stopped, looked at his father, then Jesse, then at the wine decanter. Without hesitation, he reached past his father, grabbed the cut glass container and looked about for a glass. He spotted one on the shelf where Noriega had found the others, stretched to retrieve it, then poured wine into it. He set the decanter down, gulped the entire contents of the glass, then slammed the empty container onto his father's desk.

Noriega sat with his hands peaked together against his mouth as he watched his son. "Where have you been?" His voice was low and steady.

Bonifacio spent the next three seconds rolling his eyes, and made a face as though to convey boredom and a certain resentment at his father's question. "Mm. I was with Perez. He has a good horse I want. I think I will purchase it from him." He nodded, turned and took two paces away.

"You were to be here for our meeting, Bonifacio." Noriega spoke quietly.

"Yes, indeed, father, as were you. Yet I watched as you left the house at the very time you had prescribed. Earlier. I adjudged you had cancelled—or forgotten—the very obligation you had ordered. So—"

Noriega took in and released his breath. "It is true. You are correct." He paused. "No matter. We shall proceed at this time. No harm has been done." Noriega looked away for a second as he drummed the surface of the desk with his fingers and thumb.

Bonifacio looked down at his seated father, turned, and walked to a nearby chair. Since entering the room, he failed to look at or acknowledge Jesse.

Jesse found himself studying the patterns in the floor at his feet. He remembered the wine, sipped at it three times, then drained it as a defense against his rising anxiety.

Noriega raised his eyes and looked at the two young men across from him. "Now," he said, "We are to discuss some business." He paused and cleared his throat. "The two of you—with your permission, of course, Jesse Landry, as my partner—are to travel to the border, to Mexico. El Paso del Norte. You will represent me, deliver goods and make a purchase for me." He looked from Jesse to his son and back.

Bonifacio raised his head and cocked it as he shot a quick glance at the man from Santa Fé, but said nothing.

Jesse nodded to Noriega, then to Bonifacio. He looked at his host. "May I ask—what we take and with what will we return?"

"Yes, of course. I will send bales of wool, some dyed. Sheep skins. From there, glass for windows. From the Americanos in a place called Boston. There will be some furniture, and of course, wine. Finished goods, such as *camisas*, *pantalones*, socks, shoes. Farm implements. Other small goods such as hand tools and cloth. It is true, that many of these same items come to us along the trail, the north, but these, you will find to be in many ways superior and less expensive. I believe you require goods for yourself—for the—your—mercantile." He paused and looked at the ceiling, then down. "You will go by horse and wagon to El Paso, and will there perhaps be met by certain parties from Chihuahua, although of that I am not sure. You will be provided with a new freight wagon. It is a part of the purchase." He paused, then smiled and moved his head in a gesture of sincerity.

"Was this an order placed by my father, and how am I to pay for my goods?"

Noriega nodded and shook his head in succession. "Yes, indeed, these are of your father's request, that is true. We will concern ourselves with payment at a later time, my boy. I will provide a letter of credit to cover your goods. Do not worry yourself. In good time." He shot a glance at his silent son. "Bonifacio will share the responsibility. To represent me, that is. I have charged him with carrying my letter of credit." He cleared his throat, then helped himself to wine.

Bonifacio stood and paced slowly to a window that faced the plaza. He spoke without turning. "Who will accompanied us?"

Noriega turned to deal with some papers on his desk. "I am sending Paco and Rafael. They are good trackers and know how to deal with Indians. You may well need their services." He mulled for a second. "They will be armed."

"And I?" Bonifacio turned to face his father.

"You, too, will carry a weapon," Noriega said, but with no small amount of irritation. He looked at Jesse. "I believe you have a weapon? A pistol? Perhaps that with which you dispatched the cowardly *Tejano?*" His voice was low; almost conspiratorial.

"I do," Jesse replied.

"And do you have another? A long gun, perhaps? A carbine such as the gringos carry?" Noriega turned his head to peer at Jesse in a side-long manner.

Jesse started to answer in the negative, then the thought of the distance between the two cities and the dangers that lay there, he hesitated.

Noriega continued to watch him. "You hesitate."

"My apologies. Yes. Yes, I thought of what faces us. There is the carbine I have carried on guard mount. It is at the home of my friend. I do not have it here." He shot a glance at Bonifacio, who looked at him from under his eyebrows, but dispassionately

"They are valuable on the road," Noriega said. "Why did you not bring it here?"

"I was not sure it would be welcome. The women..."

Noriega smiled, looked at the floor, then up. He shook his head, then shrugged.

"I will fetch it," Jesse said.

"Good." Noriega glanced at his son.

"When do we depart?" Bonifacio asked. His tone had softened.

Noriega turned to face into the room, but looked at the floor with his hands across his midriff. He drew in a deep breath and exhaled. "The agent from Chihuahua is to be in El Paso in ten days time with some of the cargo. By the river route the entire distance, you can be there in one week. You leave in three days time." He paused, then, "I would speak with my son in confidence, Jesse. Affairs of family. I trust you understand." He smiled.

Jesse stood. "Of course, sir; of course. I must prepare. See to Campeón." He looked briefly at Bonifacio, then back at the still-seated Noriega.

"Will you sup with us?"

Jesse pondered. "I hope to, sir, but if not—"

"Of course. Should we not see you, then may you pass the night in peace and comfort." Noriega looked up as he reached out to touch his young guest's hand.

Bonifacio tilted his head and looked askance at the transaction between his father and the man from Santa Fé, then raised his head and turned to face the plaza through the window as Jesse left the room.

24

The sun had risen no more than five minutes when the faithful Ustacio approached the run-down, but serviceable adobe house where he had left the two drovers, Pulver and Cat. Cat emerged from the *común*, the outhouse behind the edifice, hitched up his pants and looped his crude leather suspenders over his arms as he came around the corner. When he saw Ustacio, he stopped.

Ustacio halted as well. He held up a small piece of paper. "*Para tí*. For you."

Cat stared for a second, then moved slowly toward the old man. As he took the paper, he looked behind the servant, suspicious, but saw no one. "Hey, thanks. I guess. *Grácias*." He pronounced the word, "Grah-see-ass."

Ustacio stared for a moment at the man with the very dark skin and unusual features, which featured thick lips, a broad nose and short, kinky hair. He then blinked, nodded, turned and hustled away.

Inside the small house, Cat kicked the toes on Pulver's still sleeping foot.

Pulver jerked awake with a start, stared at nothing, then sat up on one elbow. "What the hell, Cat—! Goddamnit! Cain't y'all see ahm a-sleepin?!"

Cat threw the paper down at Pulver. "See what's there, ya' fuckin' sleepy head! Ah cain't make it out!" Cat was not easily persuaded to admit his illiteracy.

Pulver reeled with half-sleep and the effects of too much *aguardiente* the night before. He shook his head, looked blearily after the retreating black man, then grabbed the paper and nearly destroyed it by closing his fist over it. After he brought himself to a state of relative wakefulness, he unfolded the paper and blinked at it. "It says—it says—"

Cat, who had regained his makeshift bunk to sit and fiddle in annoyance, said, "Says what, goddamnit?!"

"Shee-ut. Says we's ta' meet that goddamn Texican."

"Yeah? The one what owes us?"

Pulver strained to turn his head and looked at Cat with a deep scowl. "Now which ever Texican would it be, ya' sorry nigger, you?!" He waggled his head in fake anger.

Cat took a moment to look at the dusty, cobweb-decorated ceiling, with bits of dirt that leaked between the *latias*, short, round tree branches that served as ceiling, set straight between the beams. "Well, lemme see now. How many o' them cowardly bastards do I know. Lemme ponder upon it." He grinned in the half-light of the dusty, cluttered room.

Pulver studied the wrinkled paper again. "Shee-ut; now listen to this here!"

Cat, again without looking at Pulver, said, "What?"

"Hot-damn. We're to haul along one o' them fowling pieces we brung."

Cat looked at Pulver. "Yore daft, mule-driver! That's plumb crazy! Yore readin' wrong! Yore eyes is crossed!"

"Ah ain't, Cat." He looked away, then peered at the message again. "Wants us'ns ta' hide it in some fashion, so's we ain't exposed."

"Ex-posed?"

"Seen. Discovered. Like that."

"Hot damn."

Rodman, known by some to be slow on the uptake at times, had considered meeting the two drovers at or near the place where they had first entered the Rio Grande Valley and rendezvoused with the illicit arms shipment in the *bosque* east of the village. Further consideration brought him to the notion, the possibility, that that place might be unsafe; might have been watched during and since, and that there might be officialdom of some nature in wait, presumably the dreaded United States Army of the West. That was especially prominent in his tattered thinking because of Cat, all too obviously not of this region.

It was more than a mile north of the outskirts of the town, in the cotton-wood forest, or *bosque*, not far from the river, with no dwellings or people within sight, where Cat and Pulver waited. Pulver lounged astride his horse. Cat prowled around as he inspected the ground and looked up at the leafy trees as his mount waited patiently.

Pulver chewed on a piece of jerky. Without looking at his partner, he asked, "Watcha' lookin fer, Cat, ole man?"

Cat, also without engaging Pulver's eyes, replied. "Nuthin. Jus' lookin.' I kinda' likes dis jere country." He peered up at the blue sky through the cottonwood leaves.

"Well, now, ain't that some amazin' bit o' tidings. Happens Ah do as well." Pulver spat a piece of gristle off to one side as his horse shook his great head.

Cat turned to look toward the south. "Well, howdy, lookie here. There approaches our bountiful ben-o-factor."

Pulver looked up. "Seems kinda' tardy, don't he now?"

"He do indeed. He do indeed." Cat continued to walk slowly around as he took in the ancient, leaf- and twig-covered river plain.

Rodman rode up and coaxed his mount to a halt. "My apologies, gents. Nature problems. My gut does not agree with the local fare. I long for that of home."

Cat mumbled, "I kin understand that, given yore attitude. It ain't the grub, it's yore slimy insides."

Rodman, although aware that Cat had spoken, neither heard nor understood what he said, ignored it, and would have done so regardless. "Gentlemen, if you would deign to gather, I have words to dispel."

Cat returned to his horse. "Dispel away, then, goddamnit." He mounted his horse, then brought the brute under control as it falsely detected a signal to move off.

Rodman, aware of his history with the black man, ignored Cat's rant. "Yes, yes. Of course. Well, it seems I am off to Texas; El Paso, to be precise. I will be assisting in the purchase of cargo for our partner. And, of course, to aid and abet the guarding of same as well as all and sundry along the trail." He cleared his throat.

Both drovers realized that the Texican was relieved and happy to report this event. Both internalized the guard part as a joke and did not react, although Cat shook his head and spat.

"And of us?" Pulver asked. He took another bite of the dwindling jerky.

"Yes," Rodman answered. "It is important that you remain. To oversee the safety of our special cargo. The crates. Indeed." His horse pranced, and he spoke a soothing word to the beast. "Until they are removed to safety or sold."

"Well, now, that does appear to be excitin'," Cat said, barely loud enough for the other two to hear. "Would you not concur with me, Mr. Pulver?" He looked at his friend.

"Does, indeed," Pulver replied. He expended another unwanted piece of jerky to one side.

Rodman continued, and again ignored the anecdotical bait offered by the free-wheeling, independent drovers. "And as to that special cargo, I assume that long object strapped to your rigging to be that which I requested?"

"It is, indeed," Pulver replied. "Y'all want it at this time?"

"Yes. Please." Rodman hesitated, then, as he realized he was required to make the hand-off, dismounted, approached Pulver, and took the carbine-containing scabbard.

Pulver looked down at Rodman from the saddle. "What's the i-dee? You got a sale, do ye?"

Rodman stopped half-way to his mount and took in a short breath as he calculated. "Yes. A possible sale. I must be cautious, however. You understand. A sample, you see." He broke his gaze at Pulver and shot a glance at the Negro. "Our friend is not an easy man." He cleared his throat.

Pulver muttered an "Mm."

Cat remained silent.

Rodman spoke as he affixed the covered carbine to his horse rigging. "Our friend has arranged for you to be taken care of in a fine manner. You are to be provided with the best of victuals from his own family kitchen." Finished with placing the firearm, he swung up into the saddle.

"And of our gawd-awful lodgings?" Pulver squinted at Rodman.

"They are being improved as we speak. Real beds. A table. Chairs. Lamps. Blankets." Rodman looked at each of the men with a satisfied grin.

Cat raised his eyebrows. "Well, ain't that somethin'!" He made a face and rolled his eyes.

Pulver pushed his hat back and scratched his head. "Give that man our thank-yous, then."

"How 'bout some hard coin or least-ways some spendable specie so's we can wet our whistles while y'all 'er traipsin' about the country?" Cat asked.

"Glad you mentioned that, boys. I have here at this time good, hard cash moneys for you. Part o' your pay, plus extra." Rodman reached around and pulled one of his saddle bags open.

"Now yer talkin'," Pulver remarked. He leaned on the pommel of his saddle. Though the dried meat had disappeared, he continued to masticate.

"I leave in two days," Rodman said. He walked his horse over to Pulver and handed him a small leather pouch. "I expect to return in three weeks time." He swung his horse around so he could see both men, threw his finger up to the brim of his hat, and moved off at a walk.

Cat and Pulver looked at each other. Cat shrugged and Pulver held the pouch out high and shook it up and down. The sound from inside was that of hard metal.

The mules Rodman, Pulver and Cat had used to pull the contraband-laden freight wagon from Glorieta Pass to Albuquerque stood patiently in harness in front of a flat-bed wagon alongside the stable and forge lean-to behind the Noriega place. The wagon floor was burdened principally with bales of wool and stacks of sheep skins. The remaining space was taken up by containers of food and water, bed rolls, blankets, cooking and eating implements, ponchos, and items favored by sometime hostile Indian tribes, especially the Apache.

Jesse sat astride his horse, Campeón, as did Bonifacio and Paco on their mounts. Rafael was up on the wagon bench, ready to drive the mules. His horse was on a lead at the rear of the transport. All saddlebags bulged with extra trail food, ammunition and select personal items including, in the case of Paco and Rafael, religious talismans. All four men were armed with pistols. Paco had his carbine at the ready alongside his saddle, as well as a knife sheathed at his belt line. Rafael's carbine was beside him on the wagon. Bonifacio, also with a carbine and knife, had a straight Spanish sword in a scabbard lashed to his horse's rigging straps.

Ustacio stood nearby as he waited for any more instructions from the group before he returned to his usual duties.

Apolonia appeared with little Robert, his hand in hers. She walked over to Bonifacio's horse and patted his leggings. "*Muy buena suerte, hermano mio. Vaya con Diós.*" She crossed herself as did her brother, who remained unsmiling.

Roberto crossed himself in imitation of the adults, then looked up at Apolonia for approval.

She then went to Jesse's horse and repeated the ritual. He reached down and touched her upraised hand, which she grasped for two seconds. They smiled at each other as Bonifacio looked away with a disapproving curl of his mouth.

At that moment, her father came on foot around the corner of the structure from the direction of the plaza. He was followed by a man on horseback who wore a tan, fringed leather jacket and a broad-brimmed, plantation-style, head cover. Noriega stopped, looked at the four mounted men, then at Rodman, who had reigned his horse to a stop.

"This, gentlemen," Noriega began, "is *señor* Rodman. He will accompany you to El Paso del Norte. He carries certain letters of introduction and credit for merchants there and from Austin, Texas." He paused. "As you may readily observe, he is also carrying a weapon. This will help to ward off attack."

During a pause in Noriega's speech, Jesse looked at Bonifacio, then the other two. He detected surprise by Paco and Rafael, who alone shrugged moderately, but Bonifacio appeared the opposite; as though he had been aware of the fellow traveler. He, alone, looked down and away, to avoid Rodman's eyes.

Rodman lifted his hat and nodded with a smile to all, including Apolonia. He said nothing.

Jesse nodded to Rodman, held up his hand in greeting, then acknowledged Noriega, who looked from man to man. Jesse took note of the long gun in a leather scabbard alongside Rodman on his right. He wondered momentarily why he did not see a side arm on the man. Only Noriega was aware of the fact that the Texican carried a small caliber pocket pistol secreted in his vest.

"*Bueno, señores;* Be on your way," Noriega said. " Safe journey and may God be with you. Avoid *Los Apaches* if you can, but desist from a fight if you should encounter them." He removed his hat and used it to wave. "But survive if you do!" He shouted.

Apolonia ducked her head, tugged at Roberto's hand, and turned for the house while Ustacio and her father watched the five men ride away on and behind the trundling wagon.

From a safe distance, unbeknownst to the gathering, Pulver and Cat watched the scene with no small amount of trepidation.

25

Bonifacio Noriega moved to the head of the party, not because he knew the route to be taken, obvious to all who plied the Santa Fé-Chihuahua Trail, but out of his self-aggrandizing sense of self-importance which he wore like a badge, and which, if he were to reveal in truth, was in reaction to a burning insecurity. He was not in his father's image, nor that of his father's father, or of his uncles and cousins, men who were strong; men who took what they wanted, as men of generations before had taken, giving them rise to heights of fame and glory, such as had conquerors, kings, emperors and popes. Rather, Bonifacio wanted nothing less than to partake of this trek, but to his self-given credit, bit his tongue and agreed to take his father's direction and travel under a secret cloud of fear and angst. He was also leaving behind that which he loved the most, the affection of another human being not of the family. But had the family, or anyone else in his circle, known of his desire and passion, they would have been, at the very least, outraged, and at the very most, driven to action. His love was not that of a woman, even a low-borne wench, but that of a low-borne boy; a young man, a farmer by occupation, close to his age. He thought of him now, and fantasized that his lover watched in awe at him, tall in the saddle, the image of masculinity and power.

Immediately behind him rode Paco, a seasoned man in his mid-thirties. Up on the wagon, was Rafael, the approximate age as Paco, both hired by Bonifacio's father, Nerio, as helpers and guards. Paco, for one, sensed the problem with their temporary master, but he kept his suspicions to himself. They were engendered by the feelings that arose in him when Bonifacio looked at him. Subtle, but revealing. It nauseated him, but he kept his own counsel, lest he lose this temporary employment. Behind the wagon were the three on horseback. These men rode single-file, with Jesse Landry bringing up the rear. Jesse, in part, because he felt the lone outsider, in part because his sense of Rodman was less than healthy, and in part because he was divided in his enthusiasm for the venture, despite its potential rewards. He had yet to absorb and digest the idea of being the head of a successful commercial concern.

Rodman rode alone at this juncture in part because he was at sea. He was out of his element, but in reality he had been out of his element since leaving his ancestral home. Here, it was worse. He had begun to regret taking on his nefarious assignment. He had thought it would gain him something; now he realized those possibilities were distant, if at all. He was also unnerved by Jesse's presence—not that he connected the dastardly deed performed by the diminutive Blakely to Jesse—but more that the fact that the young man a-horse behind him was from that city where the infamous event occurred. Although he knew better, he felt as though he wore the filthy knowledge on his sleeve.

The small party moved south along the old, well-traveled, trail, on the east side of the river, through the primitive forest of cottonwoods that lined it, past occasional farms and nascent orchards. When they reached the area north of the Pueblo of Isleta, they skirted it the best they could, which resulted in being greeted with a band of thick willows as they reached the river's edge. Bonifacio wisely held back while Paco took the lead and selected the best place to ford the shallow, brown water beyond the thicket. Rafael came next as he guided the complacent, obedient mules that pulled the wagon into the gently flowing stream. The axles of the squeaking wooden wheels were exposed above the water as it crossed.

Bonifacio hung back farther while Jesse and Rodman passed. He was not observed as he gazed longingly back toward the village beyond the *bosque* and his favorite pastime. His petulant mouth was down-turned in anguish.

The trip to El Paso del Norte was uneventful, in that it meant stopping periodically to eat, sleep, and tend to the animals, all peaceful, uninterrupted pursuits. However, that included watching for danger, which they mercifully avoided, although more than once Paco and Rafael spotted what they believed were Apache outriders. The Apache, as they watched the party pass, saw nothing of value that would tempt them to risk a battle over. They did not need wool and sheep skins; those they possessed. They took collective mental note and would wait for the return passage.

The Noriega-sponsored party felt safer as they entered the broad valleys north of the city, where the population grew, and where the nomadic Indians were more likely to face the firearms of the local militias and more particularly, the might of the United States Army.

By this time, the party had learned, to a degree, to warm to each other. Rodman and Jesse engaged in conversation minimally, although somewhat stilted and guarded for the most part, given their mutual, guarded suspicions. Paco and Rafael, with their muted resentment to the presence of the Texican, said little to Gerald Rodman beyond advising him that victuals were ready for consumption, to advise him of an intruding insect, or to make way for a rattlesnake to slither past.

Bonifacio, who, after two grueling days, had lost much of his bluster and pretense. It had reduced to controlled petulance, and he said little more than was necessary to anyone. That was usually to the two hirelings, toward whom he felt he must still behave as surrogate *patrón*, despite the fact that he and they knew better. Through unspoken mutual understanding they maintained the ruse.

Jesse was comfortable helping Paco and Rafael gather firewood, prepare their stingy dry meals and maintain trail etiquette by seeing after the four-legged brutes and aiding in other chores. He felt comfortable with the two earthly men not only because he spoke their language, but because he liked and respected them.

Bonifacio, on the other hand, felt that such demeaning tasks were beneath him, while Rodman was merely marginally helpless. The mutual distrust between Jesse and Bonifacio served to keep them respectfully distant from each other.

Their contact, one Señor Silviano Márquez, met the tired and somewhat bedraggled party at the town plaza, this after a lookout on his payroll, spotted, then confirmed, their identity, and raced off on foot to advise his employer. The portly and affable Márquez returned with the servant, also on foot. He panted from the exertion as he wiped his florid face with a kerchief and greeted all but Paco and Rafael equally with smiles and loud banter. He explained the reason for the unexpected public rendezvous. He wanted to allow them to unload their wagon quickly and at the same time show them the goods and materials stored in his nearby warehouse. He explained that one part of their order, that for kegs of a certain wine, had yet to arrive. He went on to say that others, also suitable, were available.

Bonifacio dismounted, approached Márquez, reached into an inner pocket of his deerskin vest, and withdrew a sealed letter. He held it out to *Señor* Márquez.

Márquez took the letter, broke the seal, opened it, studied it for three seconds, then, with the letter in his left hand and dropped to his side, he executed a small flourish with his right arm. "*Señor* Noriega, I value the business of your father, and that you come with these gentlemen."

Bonifacio closed his eyes and executed a small bow, then instinctively swept his arm with a flourish as well.

Jesse, quietly amused at the scene, glanced at Rodman, who seemed bewildered at the formality being exhibited in this place he considered primitive.

The wagon was unloaded quickly by three employees as Márquez ticked off each item on a tablet.

While Paco and Rafael lounged outside with the faithful mules and the horses, their burden greatly lightened, Jesse, Rodman and Bonifacio stood immediately inside the large, barely illuminated store room. Below its low, dark ceiling were regiments of boxes, crates, barrels, sacks and a myriad of odds and ends. There were tools, furniture, lamps, horse tack, stacks of tanned leather, raw animal hides, rugs, carpets, bolts of cloth and religious items. The load from Albuquerque was added to it.

Seated outside were two armed men who brandished long guns. The younger of the two was in his late teens. They eyed Paco and Rafael, also armed, with undisguised suspicion.

A fact none of the travelers from Albuquerque knew at the time, but would come to conjure surprise and appreciation upon their return trip, was that they had been followed and watched the entire distance. The stalkers were two men, Pulver and Cat, who, at Cat's insistence, they follow the untrustworthy Texican, who they reckoned would cheat them of their meager trail pay. Now they hovered on the fringes of the Mexican town interspersed with discreet penetrations to observe their quarry. They bided their time, worried that the Noriega party would move deeper into a land about which they knew little, and would prefer to leave with haste, given the unknown dangers that lurked, in their minds, in every direction.

26

When the wagon was cleared and Márquez had finished with the list, he turned to his guests. "Let us go to my family's residence to rest, sup and partake of the local wine before we continue our business." He looked at Rodman, Jesse and Bonifacio in turn. "This we will do on the morrow. You gentlemen are the guests of the Márquez *hacienda*. ¡*Vamos!*"

As they all left the warehouse and walked onto the street, the two warehouse guards stood. Each nodded his head out of respect for their employer. Márquez failed to acknowledge their passive greeting, rather he looked straight ahead as he moved in demonstration of his self-importance. Paco and Rafael, attendant to the horses and the mules, stood aside as they eyed the members of the business party. They both prudently withheld their feelings about the pomposity being exhibited. Jesse looked at them, cocked his head and nodded with a caged smile.

It was then that a breathless young boy ran up to Márquez. The *patrón* bent down, said something to him, and the boy ran off in the direction from which he had come. His sandaled feet kicked up dust and pebbles as he ran.

Márquez turned and smiled at his visitors who had also halted. "My youngest son. He will alert the house to our arrival." He turned to Bonifacio. "I will arrange lodging and meals for your men." He gestured vaguely in their direction, but did not look at them, something both men suffered all too often at the hands of those who saw themselves as superior. "My house is only there." He gestured. "Close to my business. I have other lands, of course, but it suits me to be near." He looked at his close audience of three, moved off, then turned his head. "No need to mount up as you can see. The animals will be cared for."

"Thank you. Most kind," Bonifacio answered.

Jesse and Rodman each mouthed a positive response, unheard by Márquez.

Bonifacio looked at both of the warehouse guards, but concentrated on the younger of the two for several seconds. The young man colored when he returned Bonifacio's gaze. Bonifacio raised his head, drew in a deep breath, looked away, gulped and shook the purse that hung at his side, which caused the coins it contained to jingle. The young guard looked away, then back. He smiled, eyes wide, then looked away again to hide his response. Although no one else noticed, Jesse took note of it, unsure of what he was seeing, but curious. The group moved off at their host's insistence, *Señor* Márquez in the lead.

The great Márquez *hacienda* sat more or less centered within a two-acre compound surrounded by high walls of adobe, rock, and in some places, bark-covered wooden stakes. As the tall, double gates at the front that faced the main road opened, the group encountered three people; one, a man well into his sixties, nicely-dressed in servant's attire, and two teen-aged boys in lesser clothing, both without footwear. The old man, the majordomo, lowered his head to his *patrón*, then approached him. Márquez spoke to him, gestured toward Paco and Rafael, then moved on as the troop followed.

The majordomo beckoned one of the teen-aged boys and pointed at the two Noriega travel guards, after which the boy went to them. He gestured, and they followed as their horses trailed. The other boy walked behind the outsider group as they all moved for the front of the big house.

A man appeared , who, without instruction, attended to the mules.

"*Espedanse*," Jesse called out. His request was directed at the boys who had taken charge of the horses.

The entire party stopped as Jesse approached his horse, now held still with his reins in the hands of one of the boys. He unleashed the bedroll behind the saddle and released the bindings on the leather saddle bags, then threw all three over his shoulder. He also removed the carbine from its scabbard. "*Gracias*," he said to the boy, then fished a coin from his vest pocket and gave it to him.

Bonifacio and Rodman followed suit by also retrieving their personal belongings and arms from their mounts. That included the gesture of the gratuity on the part of both. Rodman made his offering without any outward sign attended by a mumbled thanks. Bonifacio allowed his face to crease into a frown as he glowered at Jesse after handing the other boy a coin without a word.

Most of the scene as the party moved into the Márquez compound was observed by Pulver and Cat, who watched from their vantage point at a corner of the Márquez mercantile warehouse next to a large tree, prudently out of sight of the guards. The two drovers looked at each other, then at their surroundings as they contemplated their fate for the night and following day.

That evening, Jesse, Bonifacio and Gerald Rodman were hosted at the Márquez family dining table by Silviano Márquez, his wife, and his two eldest daughters. Their remaining five younger children ate in an ante room close to the big kitchen. Jesse and Bonifacio found them selves being eyed by the two girls who had been placed strategically opposite the young male visitors. They were none too attractive, but demure and alluring in their own way, closely-honed by family tradition with guidance from the Catholic priesthood and local convent nuns. Jesse reacted positively, maintained a polite smile, and engaged in polite conversation. Bonifacio did his best to do the same, although it became clear to both young ladies that he externalized little or no interest. This was determined by them both through their inborn female instincts, and would become the subject of conversation and analysis later in their closeted chambers over late-night candle-light, rustling bedclothes and giggles.

It was at the appropriate time as the meal came to a close, accompanied by the ringing of a bell by *Señora* Márquez, that she and her daughters rose, and two male servants arrived with cigars and brandy for the men, who then arose in unison to bow to the women as they exited.

Márquez insisted that the ensuing conversation, in part because of Rodman's presence, in part because Márquez was uncertain about Jesse, the coyote, that the conversation avoided not only business, but politics, given the presence of remnants of the United States Army on Mexican soil.

Subsequent to a toast to all present, and after less than half an hour since the disappearance of the female contingent, Márquez commanded his house servants to guide his three guests to their rooms with lanterns held high in the lead.

Jesse lay atop his bed in the dark, half-dressed, as he drifted in and out sleep, when he heard what sounded to him as though someone were knocking on wood. He realized that indeed someone was rapping on a nearby door. He froze, then rose and went to his door, boots off, and put his ear to the old, thick wood. At his feet, he saw orange lantern light leak through the crack between the bottom of the door and the rock-paved floor. It rose, undulated, faded, rose again, then flickered and faded away until the dark took charge. He found the door latch in the blackness, pulled up on the handle, and opened the door slowly. Once the gap between the door and the frame was wide enough, he poked his head out into the hallway. He saw what he was certain was the Texican, Rodman, outlined in the lantern glow, boots in hand, as he followed someone. Three seconds later, the man disappeared around the corner at the end of the hall, as did the soft lantern light.

Jesse closed the heavy door slowly, carefully, and without noise. He stood in the dark a few inches from the thick wood, as he attempted to fathom why Rodman, who spoke only a few words to Márquez in his, Jesse's presence, would now be beckoned from his repose in the night, here in this Mexican house.

Then another sound came through the door, that of another, closer door opening. Jesse, still awake and puzzled, re-opened his door and looked out into the hall. In the faint light from a hall window, he spied who he believed was Bonifacio, move tentatively into the hallway, then carefully close his bedroom door.

Jesse thought for a moment, then sprang to his bed, started to grab his boots, then thought better of it. With as much stealth as he could muster, he returned to the door and entered the hall. Bonifacio had disappeared.

Jesse looked both ways, then moved in the direction from which they had come earlier after supper. When he reached the corner that separated the bedroom wing from the main hall, he looked in both directions. At that moment, he saw faint light come from his right, partially blocked by the figure of a man. He realized instantly that the figure was that of Bonifacio Noriega.

Bonifacio hesitated, then stepped out into the night. As he did, Jesse saw that he held his boots in his right hand. Bonifacio pushed the outside door partially closed, then moved away. Jesse, in his stocking feet, moved quickly for the door, then flattened himself against the wall near it. When he reckoned that Bonifacio had moved away from the building, he peered around the edge of the door. From his vantage point, he saw Bonifacio go to an arched gate in the perimeter wall. He watched as the young Noriega hesitated, look toward the building door where he had exited, then pull his boots on. A few seconds later, he opened the gate and stepped through. In the grey light, Jesse saw the gate close. He heard a faint metal-to-metal sound as the latch settled home.

The following morning, after his rustic ablutions aided by one of the young servant girls, Jesse made his way to the kitchen. He found that an easy task, since he smelled the fine cooking odors that wafted along the main hallway, and followed them to their origin. There, he saw two middle-aged women bustle about as they prepared the morning meal, along with a young girl and a boy, servants, who moved dishes and utensils into the breakfast room. He reckoned the girl to be Indian, possibly Apache because of her facial structure and swarthy skin. All in the room gibbered in moderate tones, and all were surprised at his entrance.

Jesse looked briefly at each of the people in the room in turn with a humble grin as he dipped his head and held up his hands in a gesture of appeasement. His voice muted, he said, "*Buenos días.*"

All four workers stopped what they were doing and faced him; all uttered a nearly silent "Good morning," and offered a small genuflection.

The boy and the girl looked toward one of the women whom Jesse supposed was in charge, as though to ask what they should do. The woman, who began wiping her hands in the apron that hung from her ample waist, tossed her head at them and said, "*¡Anda!*" Both resumed their duties and hurried from the room.

The second cook then turned back to her chore as the head cook stepped toward Jesse. She told him breakfast would be served shortly in the formal room for that purpose, and indicated the way.

He looked at the big table in the center of the kitchen. Five wooden stools were set scatter-shot about it. On the table's surface were bowls, plates, tumblers, carving knives, large holding forks, eating utensils and various raw vegetables. One plate contained a portion of raw pork, while another a de-feathered chicken.

He peered at the big kettle that hung from an iron hook over the open fire. "Stew?" he asked.

The cook glanced in that direction, then back. "*Sí. Y frijoles.*"

"Is it Ready?"

"*Sí.*"

He pulled out a stool and sat. "May I partake?"

Both cooks looked at each other, aghast, mouths ajar.

The head cook replied, "Of course, sir."

The young servants re-entered the kitchen at that moment. They both gawked at Jesse, who was seated at the table, eating. The head cook berated them for stalling, then ordered them to serve their impromptu guest.

After satisfying himself with the offered fare, Jesse wandered into the breakfast room and then to the sitting room. He turned as he heard footfalls behind him.

"Good morning to you, sir."

Jesse turned to encounter Márquez. "And a pleasant day to you, sir. Thank you." Jesse nodded.

"Shall we sit for our morning repast?" Márquez gestured.

"I would, sir, but I am sated. I have only now left your wonderful kitchen, where I was fed."

Márquez, taken aback, hesitated, then said, "You ate—?"

"In the kitchen, yes. My sincere apologies if I have trampled upon house rules. I certainly would not want to—"

Márquez waved his hand and shook his head. "No, no. Certainly not. In no way—It is only that—the kitchen?"

"Again, I apologize, sir. I was up with the roosters, and the perfume that came from the kitchen was too much to resist. And since I seemed alone—"

"Wonderful," Márquez said. "I am delighted. Surprised, but delighted. And charmed." He waited a moment as he studied Jesse's face, then, "Will you join me while I take my morning repast?"

Jesse made a side gesture with his head. "I'd be delighted to do so. After you, sir."

He sat at a long side of the dining table, while Márquez sat at the head as the two young servants met his needs. Jesse was offered more food and drink, but declined.

Márquez, who had essentially ignored Jesse in favor of Bonifacio, the son of his main trade partner in Albuquerque, delved into Jesse's relationship with Noriega. As he heard more about the young Landry's story, he became more intent on discovering as much as he could. He soon realized that a marked difference existed between Jesse and Bonifacio; that Landry appeared, to him, more serious and business-like than Bonifacio. He had detected in Bonifacio a certain careless nonchalance; that he seemed more interested in appearances than business tactics. He told himself he would reserve judgment until they actually got down to business; that he would gauge each of these young men when faced with business and trading decisions.

Márquez, his questions for Jesse exhausted, changed the subject. "I wonder—"

As he started to speak, Gerald Rodman entered the room, stopped, and looked from Márquez to Jesse and back. "My apologies, he said. I overslept."

Márquez got up part way, a white cloth napkin in one hand, and greeted the Texican with a brief handshake. "Not all, sir, not at all. Please, sit and join us. Any time. Your time is our time." He swept his arm toward a chair at the table directly across from Jesse, and turned toward the door that led to the kitchen. "¡Chico! ¡Margarete! ¡Vamos! ¡Pronto!" He clapped his hands loudly, then turned and smiled at Rodman and Jesse.

Moments later, Chico, the young servant boy, peered into the room, then disappeared. Within a minute, Rodman was served by the two lackeys.

Márquez, with a fork close to his mouth and his napkin tucked under his chin, looked at both his guests. "You see, I run an efficient house." Then he popped the morsel into his mouth, sat back and masticated with smug satisfaction.

As this was playing out, Jesse wondered why Bonifacio had yet to appear, and moreover, where he had gone the night before.

Márquez put his fork down, wiped his mouth, looked around the room as though that would aid him in his quest. "Where's that young Noriega? Does he still sleep, perhaps? We have work to do." He stood, went to the door to the hall, peered out, then returned to the table. "You need to travel. The road north will soon see rain." He sat and picked up his cup.

Jesse found it odd that Márquez and Rodman seemed to avoid speaking to each other, let alone allow their eyes to meet for more than brief moments. He thought about this as well. Why was Rodman led from his room in the night? That event could have been engendered only by the master of the house himself.

Jesse realized that for some reason Márquez had ceased talking to him as well, possibly because the man was loath to converse in one direction only. On the other hand, he reasoned that Márquez may have wanted him out of earshot, giving him leave to discuss something with the Texican for that man's hearing alone. Based upon that thought, he got up and pushed his chair close to the table. "Gentlemen," he said, "I give you leave. I must see to my horse and admire the early sun." He nodded his head at both men.

Márquez got up and offered his hand, which Jesse took. Rodman, his mouth full, awarded Jesse a deep nod and a grunt without rising.

In the hallway, Jesse walked several feet, stopped, and with stealth, moved back to stop and stand close to the edge of the door. After a moment of silence from the room, he heard low, intense male voices emitting from the breakfast room. He recognized first that of Márquez, then Rodman, then both again in turn. He waited, but unable to discern what was being said, continued to the main outside door.

Márquez, Jesse, Rodman, Paco and Rafael had foregathered at the Márquez warehouse shortly after Márquez and Rodman finished breakfast. The new wagon provided by Márquez was loaded with most of the goods on the Noriega and Landry lists. Two warehouse workers were in the process of completing the order.

Márquez found that Jesse was capable and business-like in his handling of the transactions, not only for the Landry mercantile, but for Noriega's requirements in Bonifacio's absence.

Bonifacio arrived almost an hour later. As he approached, the others noticed his appearance was somewhat disheveled, and his face wracked and puffy as though he lacked sleep. His gait was slow and tentative, and he looked at the three businessmen in turn sheepishly. He looked about as though for someone or something, then at his feet. He stopped a short distance from the assemblage. "Good morning," he said. His voice betrayed fatigue. He cleared his throat.

Jesse and Rodman answered in voices raised only minimally above a mumble.

Márquez answered Bonifacio in kind, then looked about. He turned to the older of his two guards, the only one present. "Where is that young cur?!" He gestured with both hands.

The man merely shrugged and raised his eyebrows, mouth firm.

Márquez returned his gaze to Bonifacio. "Are you well, young sir?" He frowned with concern. His irritation showed.

Bonifacio moved his head in a jerking fashion, from 'yes' to 'no,' then back. He attempted a smile, but it resulted in a look more of anguish and pain. "Sí, señor. Sí."

Jesse looked at the ground, embarrassed. Rodman looked at Jesse, Márquez and Bonifacio, then away, unsure of what he was witnessing. Márquez' lone guard made a face, looked down and away, then feigned interest in his firearm, which he stroked as though it required close inspection. Márquez looked at him, curiosity apparent, then back at Bonifacio, his mouth agape. Paco and Rafael, both expressionless, remained aloof a few yards away as they stood, along with their horses, ready for the trail north. The mules were in harness.

It was then that the three horses belonging to Jesse, Rodman and Bonifacio, led by the same young boy who had taken them to the Márquez barn the night before, hove into view. Each animal was properly saddled, along with the individual travel packs and saddle bags. The latter had been gathered from the respective sleeping rooms and placed there by house staff.

Paco led his horse to the rear of the Murphy and placed the animal on a lead to the vehicle. He then mounted the wagon's bench and prepared the leads to the mules.

Márquez watched Paco, then turned to Bonifacio. "Bonifacio," he said, "Master Landry and I have filled your father's order as well for his mercantile in Santa Fé. I trust you approve. The letters of credit have been verified, and all is well." He paused as he held up a piece of paper, looked about and shifted physically in a tight circle as he displayed the document. He stopped and focused on Bonifacio, the paper yet held up. He raised his eyebrows in a question.

Bonifacio swallowed, lowered, then raised his head. His voice cracked, which caused him to clear his throat again. "I am well satisfied that my father's business has been satisfactorily represented by our esteemed associate, *Señor* Landry, the younger. All is well and we shall make our way. Many thanks to you. And to your fine family for the gracious hospitality rendered upon us." He executed a half bow.

Rodman snapped his head in Jesse's direction as Jesse lowered his head and looked at Bonifacio.

Jesse went to Campeón, took the reins, inspected the saddle, the carbine, trappings, bedroll and bags, which he tugged to check the bindings.

Rodman followed Jesse's lead and saw to his mount.

Márquez returned Bonifacio's bow, lowered the paper, and inserted into his inner vest pocket.

Bonifacio stood for a moment, then, as increased embarrassment set in, made for his horse. When he was astride the saddle, he pulled the reins such that his horse made a circle, then came to a stop. He looked at the Murphy wagon and the canvas that covered its contents. "What is that?" he asked. He pointed. His voice had recovered from his fatigue.

"To what do you refer?" Márquez asked. He moved his head in a jerking fashion as he pretended to study the Murphy.

"There. The large crates. In the center. Two." He pointed his shaking finger. Irritation carried in his voice, in large part as a diversionary cover for the scene he realized he had created.

"They are mine," Rodman said.

Bonifacio whipped his head around and peered at the Texican. "What?! What are they?! We have no room—!"

Rodman prodded his horse forward several steps to be nearer young Noriega. He leaned aside in his saddle and looked at Bonifacio directly. "You will see that they contain implements for farming. Shears, shovels, hoes. Scythes and pruners." He held out his arm toward the wagon. "As ordered by your aunt. I do this for her."

Márquez moved to stand between the horses upon which the two men sat. He looked up at Bonifacio. "Indeed, *Señor* Noriega. I arranged for these implements for our friend here. They are from the best iron and implement workers in Zacatecas and Michoacán."

Bonifacio, although half sick from a night of little rest and nothing for breakfast beyond a cup of hot chocolate, pushed himself to take, what he imagined, was charge of the situation. He peered at Rodman, his head dipped in a gesture of contempt to peer at the Texican from under his eyebrows. "And where is she to employ these implements, *Señor* Rodman? She does not farm."

Rodman arched his back, gathered himself psychologically, and looked hard at Bonifacio. "I confess. I have farmland to the north and east, in Texas, sir. Your father and *Señor* Marquez recommended that I purchase these implements, as they are among the finest available. In these demanding days, it is difficult to obtain such items from beyond the Mississippi River, and we are here, and they are as well." He paused, then, "I mis-spoke only now. Although, it is true that your aunt Alma has vouchsafed for me in this matter. This purchase. If I have caused you or any of this assemblage harm in any fashion, I will gladly pay a toll. Perhaps I should purchase another beast to aid in our travels." He went quiet, looked at all in turn, then back at the fuming Bonifacio. "I await your pleasure, sir."

Bonifacio, his head fixed forward, moved his angry eyes from side to side, enough to take in the men around him in his peripheral vision. He drew in a long breath and exhaled. "If this is satisfactory with my father, his partner, *Señor* Landry and my dear *tia*, then it is satisfactory with me. Please accept my apologies. Let us proceed." He pulled his horse's reins, clicked his tongue at the animal, touched its flanks with the spiked rowels of his spurs, and moved off at a half-gallop.

Paco whipped the reins attached to the mules, and the group moved off, leaving Márquez and his sole guard to watch them as they moved away.

True to form, Pulver and Cat watched from a safe distance as they prepared to follow the Noriega trade party north. Their collective demeanor was much improved from the preceding evening, however; that because in their endeavor to find a safe and comfortable place to set out their trail camp, they found themselves in an interesting and intriguing situation. They had been invited to sup and drink with three women and two men who had spotted them, and curious as to their identity, position in life and appearance in their territory, saw to their care and feeding for the night. They had been amazed that the language barrier caused no problem when it came to food, wine, music, laughter and flirtations. This, in turn, had led both men to revise their thinking about this strange land along the Great River, to the extent that they vowed to return when presumably flush with the money the Texican owed them.

27

Unknown to him, Gerald Rodman's armed trail partners, drovers and erstwhile protectors, Pulver and Cat, waited until the Noriega Murphy-type wagon, loaded with goods bound for Albuquerque and Santa Fé, had rolled well beyond the northern outskirts of El Paso before they set out to follow it and its attendant party.

With Paco up on the buck board, a long gun handy, and Gabriel riding his horse on point, the caravan moved slowly due to the heavy load and the nature of the placid beasts that pulled it. Bonifacio rode between Gabriel and the wagon to be alone for the time being, in no small part because he felt his solitude might aid in washing away the embarrassment he had suffered with Márquez and the others. He was distracted by thoughts of the events of the night before, something that would haunt him for a long time, and eventually tear at the fabric of his faux personality.

Jesse and Rodman rode several yards behind the wagon, roughly in parallel, but not close to each other. Each said little, save for an occasional comment about the weather or the rough terrain.

Rodman continued to feel estranged from the group, much out of his element, and longed for his own people. He wanted to be away from these who spoke almost entirely in a foreign tongue, save that of his present trail partner, who was capable in his native tongue as well. The major reason for his relative silence, however, was tied to his real mission in the territory. He feared that with even normal conversation with those who were unaware of his true identity, they might ferret out his true self. In addition, he was bothered, aside from his homesickness, by his concern over the high possibility of skulking Apaches at the periphery of their route. He turned to look behind from time to time, as he sensed they were being watched, by whom or what, he knew not. He saw nothing and no one of interest, but faced forward each time, concern written on his features. This was only vaguely sensed by Jesse, who gauged him as merely tense and alert.

Jesse, for his part, watched in every direction, but with minimal movement of his head. His concern was for the Apache, who would surely arrive in their own good time, most likely at a safe distance from the travelers, in places where ambush was favored, far from populated areas.

The noise from the trundling wagon included a set of metal drinking cups that hung from hooks that protruded from a short platform, and that in turn, which extended from the side of the wooden vehicle. Atop that was a short barrel of potable water, with the consensus that the precious liquid would not be used for washing; even filthy hands. Aboard the wagon were extra victuals, raw and prepared, from the Márquez household, which would suffice for no more than a day or two.

They moved north through the flat river valley north of El Paso, undisturbed as they passed outlying farms, fields, a few orchards in various states of maturity, and scattered dwellings, most of which were set close to the nearly universal outdoor labor. Most of these were low adobes huddled together or conjoined in familial or clan groups for mutual convenience and protection against weather and physical attack. They met travelers in both directions; most of whom were engaged in carrying field produce, small animals, firewood or finished foodstuffs for market. Two men on horseback guided a recalcitrant, half-hobbled bull south bound at the end of a chain.

Bonifacio chose to ignore most of them with no more than sidelong glances or an outright display of haughtiness, although in some cases, he strained to look more closely. Rodman performed no more than an occasional smile, a dip of his head or a touch of the brim of his hat, given his paucity with language. Jesse, Paco and Rafael, to the contrary, engaged in limited conversation more than once. In those instances, the discussion, although touching once or twice on issues regarding the local economy, centered principally on whether hostile Indians had been spotted or talked of, which might signal the possibility of attack.

In the latter case, *Señor* Márquez had provided extra small casks of wine and bottles of brandy as a potential aid in warding off the Apache desire for combat and theft in favor of drunkenness and sick hangovers. Paco and Rafael looked askance at such a tactic, having experienced encounters with the brave and fearless native peoples from the mountains of the southern territories and northern Mexico.

Pulver and Cat carried extra rations. That included water and fiery *aguardiente* liquor, provided them by their new-found, but erstwhile friends. They followed well behind, stayed close to irrigation ditch banks, the cover of trees and sometimes houses. Both men were somewhat sleepy and sated, which caused both to stop more than once to clear their bowels and bladders. They ate bits of food and drank water as they rode, and over time, regained their natural response to the trail.

They passed by a group of houses where the locals peered at them as though they had arrived from outer space, but made no reaction beyond a nod of the head or a wave, mostly from small children.

Cat spoke up. "You see that?"

Pulver, without looking at the black man as he rocked along in the saddle, his hat down over his eyes, replied, "See what?"

"That Texican, Rodman. I do believe that man keeps a-lookin' back this-a-way." Cat executed a sweeping, dismissive gesture with his arm.

Pulver, who lifted his head enough to see the path ahead, but maintained his gaze forward, waited a full five seconds before he growled, "How on God's green earth do you figure that? I think that fire water got to ya."

"Watch 'im, goddamnit! Keep yore eyes peeled." Cat frowned and re-adjusted his tattered broad-brimmed hat.

There was silence between the two of them for several minutes.

Pulver spoke up, his voice low. "I do believe ya' got somethin' there. He does act that a-way."

Cat waited, then, "Whattaya think it means? Think he seen us?"

Pulver drew in a breath and let it out. "Don' know, Cat. Mebby so." He patted his horse's neck, and the animal reacted with a snort and a toss of his head.

Neither man slowed their pace, which mimicked that of the Noriega group ahead.

"Here's the way I see it, Cat. If'n that cheatin' rotter thinks we're trackin' 'im, then he'd be back here real quick-like."

Cat nodded.

"On 'tother hand, if that was so, he might just see us and pretend he *don't* see us, and let it go. You ponder on it. He's that sort."

"I will say, Pulver, y'all got a head on those weak shoulder's o' your'n." He smirked.

"Why, I do thank ye, you pore 'ole black bastard, you, for recognizing smarts when you sees it."

234

Both men smiled without looking at each other in enjoyment of their camaraderie.

That night, the first after leaving El Paso, the Noriega party established camp near the river, while Pulver and Cat camped on a slope well above the valley floor, with a clear view of those below. They eschewed a fire, in part because of a lack of wood; in part because they didn't want to be discovered and possibly investigated. The black man and his companion dined on donated *tamales* and sugar cookies.

After Paco and Rafael unharnessed the mules, established a picket line for the horses and saw to their food and water, they scattered to scout for firewood. All were surprised to see Bonifacio lower himself to help start the fire and secure some of the food and utensils, while Jesse walked to a high point to scan the western horizon for signs of parties interested in their movements.

Rodman watched Jesse for a few minutes, then strolled up to join him while Rafael, who assumed the role of chef, saw to the evening meal.

The Texican stood three feet distant from Jesse, who nodded to him. "See anything?" He roved his eyes, then focused on young Landry.

Jesse took a step downslope, and without looking at Rodman, said, "*Nada*. Nothing. Yet." He glanced at Rodman with a brief half-smile, then adjusted his hat.

Rodman sensed that Jesse either didn't approve of him, or had other negative thoughts that might, in time, thwart his true mission. He decided he should get closer to this unknown factor whose presence seemed to be a near constant among the Noriega clan. "Do you expect trouble?"

Jesse nodded, paused, then, "Most likely. Most likely north. Narrow spaces. Valleys across the river where they hide. Southern Apache." He pointed with his chin, still faced forward, his arms folded across his chest.

Rodman nodded, turned half way around, then back, as he surveyed the area.

"What do the crates contain?" Jesse asked. He looked askance at the Texican.

Mildly shocked by Jesse's question, Rodman turned and faced Jesse. "What—what do you mean?! You heard! Farm implements!" His eyes danced as he realized he would be required to bluff. He instantly regretted appearing defensive. "I apologize. I didn't intend to shout. It's an honest question."

Jesse altered his stance to face Rodman. "Curious. You come to Albuquerque, then travel to El Paso to buy farm tools. You said to begin that Alma had ordered them, then that they are for you. Why? You could have traveled directly to Chihuahua or Nuevo Leon. Why the long way through New Mexico?" He pointed vaguely with his thumb.

Rodman swallowed hard, gathered his thoughts, then said, "That is certainly true, Mr. Landry, but there is more than one reason. The trail across Texas is treacherous; more treacherous than the one we're on, and indistinct. The Comanche appear from nowhere. And I have business with *Señor* Noriega. Since he had business here—in El Paso—I took advantage of the opportunity." He paused. "You are a business man. Surely you understand." He paused, then, "His sister agreed to add to his credit on my behalf. I expect monies from my bank to re-pay her."

Jesse turned his head to one side. "Of course. Forgive my intrusion into your business."

Only mildly relieved, Rodman cleared his throat. "Quite acceptable, sir. Quite acceptable. And I might add that perhaps you and I can do business one day." He paused. "You are welcome to inspect the crates." This was a huge risk, for it was the last thing he wanted to happen.

"No need. Your business is your business. Not mine."

"Thank you sir. You are a true gentleman." He dipped his head respectfully.

Jesse nodded. "Most kind of you to say. My thanks." He waited, then, "Who are the two men following us? Are they associated with you? Protectors, perhaps? Concerned over your safety."

Rodman, again in shock, dropped his mouth open, twirled around to peer south into the gathering dusk, then faced Jesse with a blank stare. "What?! What men?! What are you saying?!"

"You are unaware? You have not seen them?" Jesse cocked his head and awarded Rodman a knowing smile. He swung his head to look south, then back to look at Rodman.

"I have not!" He paused to catch his breath. " Where—where and when have you seen men following?! And further, why would these apparitions be associated with me?! Or—or with us?!" Once more, Rodman realized he was reacting suspiciously, and cursed himself with a pinched face.

"To the south. They move at our speed. On horseback. One is a Negro. I am certain I encountered them—saw them—in Albuquerque."

Rodman's heart rate jumped as he turned to look southward again. He was agape.

"You won't see them. If they are tracking us, and skilled at that, we will catch only a glimpse of them at odd times." He waited. "I have no doubt that they watch us even now." He tossed his head.

"Preposterous!" Rodman exclaimed. He knew Jesse was probably correct, but his mind swirled with questions as to why and how. He cleared his throat again, uttered a forced laugh and forced himself to lower his frantic voice. "I know of no such men, especially a Negro." He dismissed Jesse's comment with a wave of his hand. "With my apologies to you, sir, I think not. You must be witnessing a mirage, but if true, they have no truck with me, nor I with them." Internally, Rodman grew more panicky. He had sensed someone following, yet he had not been the one to verify his suspicions. Again, he wished he were almost anywhere but where he was at the moment. His mandate had become more complex. He had assumed he was among lesser beings and in control, something that was being disproved more each day. How would he explain away Pulver and Cat should the need arise?

Jesse shrugged. "Yes; perhaps I am mistaken." He looked up, then down at the encampment. "I for one, am hungry. I see that Rafael signals for us to go and partake of his fine fare." He unfolded his arms and strode away.

Rodman recovered, but only minimally. "Yes, indeed. Let us sup." He was hungry; less so as he followed Jesse down the slope.

Paco was the first awake at dawn the following morning. As he looked about to check on the camp and the animals, he spotted the tops of high, dark clouds beyond the tops of the mountains to the southwest. These, to him, forebode thunderstorms over their path in a few hours. He pulled on his boots, then kicked Rafael wordlessly, who popped awake with a guttural grunt, and joined him. He and Paco led the animals to the river for water, and let them graze on what they could find, before readying the patient mules for wagon harness.

Jesse was next to rise soon after. He realized why the two servants were already busy, and leaped into service as well. Rodman and Bonifacio also awoke with the rustle of work, but out of confusion and early morning daze, did little to aid. They realized shortly that their breakfast would not be hot.

Up on the piedmont of the Organ Mountains, Pulver and Cat woke up almost simultaneously, relieved themselves, then bridled and saddled their sleepy mounts, unsure of when the group they were tracking would move.

Before setting out, the Noriega group slurped the remains of cold coffee and gnawed on jerky, while Rodman's followers swallowed a gulp of water and sipped *aguardiente*. When they figured they were no longer in danger of being observed by Rodman or his traveling companions, they led their horses to the flood plain and waited until the animals had sufficient breakfast at the river's edge to move on. While they delayed in anticipation of their mounts raising their shaggy heads, they dug into their saddle bags for green chile-laced meat wrapped in corn tortillas, the last of the provisions from their brief sojourn in El Paso. Both developed tears and took a swallow of the powerful liquor in an attempt to wash away the heat in their mouths, a sensation new to both, but not unappreciated.

The wagon remained on the east side of the broad river, while Cat and Pulver forded the brown stream to the west side. They both agreed they would be less likely to be seen with the river and its verges as cover.

Three and a half hours later, and a little less than thirty miles north of their overnight bivouac, the storm caught up to them. They were pelted first with hail, then heavy rain, as lightning struck around them. Within a matter of a few minutes, they, the animals and the canvas-covered Murphy were soaked. All dismounted to lead and calm the horses made nervous by the bright, flashing strikes and the resultant thunder. Paco got off the wagon to be in front of the mules and lead them. The downpour lasted eighteen minutes, tapered off, and a few minutes after that, the sun shone bright out of a clear blue sky as the thunder heads scudded in an easterly direction.

Pulver and Cat, across the river, also dismounted in favor of their horses. They covered themselves with ponchos, a process with which they were familiar in their travels.

The Noriega party faced muddy ground interspersed with sandy loam which had absorbed much of the rainfall, thus they hied as close to the river's edge and that condition as possible. An hour and a half later, they halted to eat, all hungry following a hasty retreat from breakfast. Jesse suggested, with concurrence from Paco and Rafael, that they eat cold offerings and move on, given the potential threat from Apaches on the west bank. They pointed out that the storm would have hampered the movement of local tribes as well. The sooner they left the more desolate areas of the river basin and came closer to towns with, although sparse, local militia, the greater chance there would be to avoid conflict. As they stood around, consuming rations, all variously scoured the opposite side of the river.

Jesse approached Rodman out of earshot of the others. "Where are the two?"

"The two." Rodman answered. He swallowed a morsel, then answered, "I'm sure I don't know. I have not seen them. Nor, in truth, does it concern me, although I have been alert to them. Out of curiosity, mind you." He hesitated, spat a piece of gristle onto the ground and looked away. "However, it would be amusing to know who the devil they are and what their game is." He paused again. "Perhaps they plan to rob us." He looked at Jesse with an imperious smile as he worked diligently to recover the self-aggrandizing patina of the noble upper-class man, in reality distant from his origins.

Jesse looked around, then back at the Texican. "I reckon the reason we haven't seen hide nor hair is because they're on the other side." He pointed with his finger at waist level, then looked away again as he masticated.

Rodman frowned and swung his head to peer at the *bosque* that followed the river along its length. "You—" He returned his gaze to Jesse.

"I do believe. Makes sense. If they follow us with purpose, the west side is best. We can't see them. Not now. Later."

"Of course," Rodman said. He lowered his head with the thought that he was once more coming across as stupid and unthinking.

Jesse finished chewing, then took a slug of water. "They might be Rangers but for the black."

"Rangers?" Rodman squinted.

"They show up along the north trail. Across the plains—other side of Santa Fé." He gestured. "Outa' Texas. Outlaws. They and the Comanche, Kansa and Arapaho." He paused, burped, put his hand to his mouth, then continued. "Want the same thing as the Indians. They're thieves, except the Indians are hungry and they're angry with us. We're stealing their land and their way of life. Rangers, they're just outlaws." He looked hard at Rodman. "These men. Following us. Maybe they want the same thing." He looked at the *bosque* again, then at Rodman. "Maybe not." He nodded, started off, then said, "Best be moving."

Paco traded with Rafeal, who climbed up onto the wagon bench, while Paco rode point. Again, the mostly silent and lone Bonifacio rode between the wagon and Paco, off to one side. Jesse came a few yards behind the wagon, and Rodman hung back farther, surreptitiously watching the opposite river bank in hopes of seeing Cat and Pulver. For the time being, he was unsuccessful. That caused him to wonder about the young Landry from Santa Fé, who had claimed he had seen two men who fit the description of his sometime trail partners and hired help. Was he telling the truth, or was it some sort of ruse? Paranoia rose in him, and he wondered about Landry's veracity. If that were the case, why? What did he know, how and why?

His questions would be answered soon, but not in the best possible manner, although that event would allay to a great extent the paranoia and doubts he harbored about Jesse Landry.

It was the following day and a few miles north of the westerly bend in the river when the problem occurred.

Neither party, the wagoners nor the followers, had seen or met anyone on the trail to that hour, mid-morning. The Noriega party had forded the river at Angostura, roughly the same place they had executed the traversal on their journey south, a wide, shallow place where the animals were unlikely to bog down in the silt and gravel beneath the gentle, brown stream. The storm they had suffered through had slid east, denying the river of overburden to the north, thus the relatively calm and stable state of flow.

When Pulver and Cat saw the wagon and the five men in attendance cross the Rio Grande to their side, they slowed to a stop and guided their mounts into the bordering Russian olive, reeds and young cottonwoods, and waited until they felt they could continue undetected and remain on the same side.

Bonifacio, who remained faithful to his isolated position in the slow-moving file, was the first to feel the brunt of the attack; that with a well-aimed arrow that lanced into the left side of his torso immediately above his waist and into the soft flesh of his belly. He cried out with the pain, leaned to his right in reaction, dropped the reins, tried to right himself by compensating to the left, then fell from his horse after involuntarily removing his foot from the right-side stirrup. His horse, panicked, started off at a gallop, first to the right, toward the river, then left, then straight north, as his reins trailed.

Rafael, up on the wagon, was the first to see his temporary master fall. He did three things; one, he shouted the alarm, two, he pulled the mules to a stop, and three, grabbed the long gun at his side. He then dropped to the floor below the bench, stretched out, and took aim. What he saw were six young Apache warriors racing toward them, all on foot, who had emerged from behind a cluster of barren rocks at the mouth of a narrow canyon some fifty yards from the river bank. Two of them were armed with carbines, while the others carried bows and arrows at the ready. Silent but for the sound of their deer-skin covered feet on the ground, they had long learned that crying out battle yells served only to give their victims added time to mount a defense.

Paco swung around and pulled his long gun from the scabbard as an arrow penetrated his horse's rump, something the young Indians avoided, since they wanted the animals as much as anything. He raised the weapon to his shoulder and took aim, as did Rafael, at one of the two attackers who were aiming in their direction with firearms. Both men fired within a second of each other, and both shots missed their targets. The Apache gunmen also fired. One aimed at Paco, the other Rafael, because they also knew that the greatest danger came from the fast-moving lead balls of the long guns. One ball whipped past Paco's ear; the other thudded into the side of the Murphy below the bench.

Paco rolled off his horse, and in nearly a single movement, removed the arrow, whose tip had barely penetrated his horses' tough hide. He slapped the brute, and he obliged by following Bonifacio's horse at a gallop.

Jesse reached for his Hawken carbine, raised it, aimed at one of the Indian gunners who had stopped to reload, and fired. The slug hit the man in his upper right arm, glanced off the bone and settled into his right side, to which he reacted by tossing his gun away and grabbing his injured chest with his left hand. He then raced toward the rocks from which they had come. Three seconds later, he staggered to a halt, reversed his movement and returned to the battle. He continued to nurse his arm and side, then dove onto the ground and grabbed his dust-covered carbine.

Rodman's reaction to the attack came in the form of a yelp and a jerk of his horse's reins, which caused the frightened, agitated animal to rear up. Rodman loosed the reins as he felt for the pistol hidden at his right belt line, and he tumbled backward, slid off the horse's rump and onto the ground. He rolled over, stabbed the muzzle of his pistol into the soft earth, then arched up to a half-stand at the same time as he waved his pistol to decide on a target. It was at that moment that an arrow caught him in his lower right belly. He fell back, dropped the pistol, grabbed his stomach area, lost his hat, and rolled away in pain.

Jesse dismounted and slapped Campeón, who then ran away to follow the other horses, which then included Rodman's. Jesse dove for the cover of the wagon as another shot was fired by one of the Apache Braves, and more arrows arced toward the wagon.

Pulver and Cat required several seconds to realize what was taking place ahead of them.

"Jee-zuz! Lookee that, Pulver!" Cat exclaimed.

"I see it! Let's go!"

Both men kicked their mounts into a gallop. As they rode, they leaned forward in their saddles, and with deft hands, readied their revolvers. When they were no more than fifty feet distant from the skirmish, both fired at nearly the same moment, having taken aim at the bowmen. One of the arrow slingers was hit, twirled in a momentary dance, then fell to the ground. The other three, shocked by the appearance of another white man and a black, and the death of their companion, froze in place, cocked arrows down. Both Apache riflemen lowered their weapons when they realized that five men, including Jesse, Paco and Rafael pointed weapons at them.

Several quiet moments ensued, then Jesse lowered his gun, looked around at everyone, then found the spare wine and brandy that Márquez had included in the shipment. He held up two of the small, web-covered containers, then walked around the end of the wagon to the Apaches, who stood silently with deep suspicion written on their faces as they stared at the approaching white man.

Rafael gestured to them to put their weapons on the ground, to which they complied. Jesse walked up to them and held out the bottles to the man he perceived to be the eldest. There was no immediate reaction, so Jesse gestured by putting the mouth of one of the wine vessels to his mouth. The Apaches looked at each other, then the man took the bottles tentatively.

Cat holstered his pistol, looked down at Rodman, then dismounted and approached the Texican. He knelt down beside him and spoke in a near whisper. "What the hell did you do, Rodman? Looks like you got in the path of an Injun arrow, by God."

Rodman looked up at the Negro. "God, yes, Cat. I'm hurtin' bad." He moaned as he squeezed his eyes shut.

Cat started to rise. "I'll git somethin' to cure that. It don't look to be the end o' yore life."

"Cat!" Rodman said, his voice a croak.

"Yeah? What?"

"Cat, don't know me. Don't know me. You and Pulver. You don't know me. Please."

Cat frowned, looked around, then settled his gaze on Pulver. He looked back and down at the wounded man. "Okay. That's what you want."

"Yes, please. I'll make it worth your while, Cat." He winced, then, "Oww..."

"Hang on. I'll git some aid to ya."

Rodman slumped again in his misery.

Cat stood up to see Pulver who stood close by. He walked close to him, pushed him back two feet, leaned close, then whispered, "He's not in terrible shape, but he wants us to not know 'im."

"Not know 'im?!" Pulver cocked his head with a deep frown.

"That's the truth. Think on it. What we brung 'an all. Let's humor the feller. All we care 'bout's the money. He's promised more."

Pulver peered around Cat at the man moaning on the ground, then looked at his partner. "Okay, hot damn it. If it works..."

Cat returned his gaze to the injured Texican, then back to Pulver. "I'll git some cloth to make a bandage. Stop the bleedin'. You have a look at 'im."

Paco went to Bonifacio and knelt beside him. Wordlessly, he inspected the wound, then stood up and looked toward Jesse and Rafael, who remained dealing with the Apaches. Jesse noticed him, then turned and walked toward him as Paco nodded to the unconscious man on the ground.

Jesse knelt down to look, then up at Paco. "Let's get him onto the wagon." He stood.

Paco ran to the vehicle, threw back the tarp and began re-arranging cargo.

Cat had taken a cloth from his saddle bags to Pulver, who ministered to the downed Texican, then approached Paco. "Kin y'all make room for that 'un?" He pointed.

Paco glanced in the direction Cat indicated, and although he didn't understand Cat's words, he understood his request. He nodded in the affirmative, then Cat delved into helping him move crates, barrels and sacks.

Jesse looked at Rafael, who held his long gun leveled at the defeated, but confused Indians. "Hold them, Rafael. I'll be back." He went to the wagon and asked Paco what was going on, then looked at Cat. "Who are you? You've been following us."

Cat replied, "Yessir, we have. No trouble." He held up both dark hands. "We didn't want to interfere with y'all. Mm-hm."

Jesse took a moment to answer. He doubted Cat's veracity, but saw no reason to challenge it at the moment. "Well, thanks for helping out here. You're welcome to ride along. Better for all."

"Thank you most kindly, sir." Cat raised his finger to the brim of his hat, then returned to his task with Paco.

Jesse looked about, then at what Paco and Cat were doing, and since he understood the reason, said nothing. He then removed a cloth that contained tortillas and another with jerky, and returned to the Indians. He handed the bundles to one of the surprised, disarmed bowmen, then knelt down to look at the deceased man who lay on the ground. He shook his head, then went to the wounded and bleeding Indian who sat, dejected, on a large rock. He looked at the wound, then quickly retrieved bandage cloth from the wagon with which he bound the man's chest and arm.

He rose and went to Rafael, who still held his carbine pointed at the defeated attackers. "Do you speak any Apache?"

Without looking at him, he replied, "Not much. A few words only." He awarded Jesse a quick glance.

"Can you tell them to take their weapons and go?" Jesse cocked his head.

Rafael frowned at the man from Santa Fé. "Let them go?! After what they did?!"

"None of us is dead, Rafael. One of them is. Look at them. They're hungry, thirsty and scared." He looked at the Indians, then at Rafael. "They have nothing, We have everything. Let them go."

Rafael shook his head, then nodded. He lowered his firearm. "I suppose. *Jesús, María y José.*" He executed the sign of the cross over his broad chest and looked heavenward.

Jesse turned to the Apaches and made the eating and drinking motions, then went to the wagon for water. The Apaches looked at each other, then sat and tore into the tortillas and jerky. One of their number opened a wine bottle and took a long draft from it and handed it to the next one, who shook his head and passed it on. Soon, water was provided by Rafael, which was more widely accepted. They all sat, ate and drank, then began to speak softly among themselves. All their weapons were stacked nearby.

Paco, Cat and Pulver managed Bonifacio and Rodman onto the wagon, both on their backs, then covered them with a portion of the tarp to their necks, the remainder of which went over the intact goods that had been piled to one side. In the traces, the placid mules stomped and moved their heads around, dumbly curious at the human activities.

Paco, Rafael and Cat looked for the errant horses. They were located a quarter mile north, where they all enjoyed a spate of freedom as well as grass and other flora watered along the edge of the river. None of the well-trained animals mounted a resistance against their capture, and were all safely returned to the site of the conflict. Paco's horse, with the barely bloodied arrow wound, was found to be well enough for travel, but was unsaddled and tethered to the wagon to follow, while Paco rode Bonifacio's.

Two days later, as the seven-man caravan continued to wend its way north, it was mid-afternoon when Pulver raised his voice enough to alert all to a scene on a high ridge to the west. All, save Rodman and Bonifacio, who remained ailing, but conscious in painful recuperation on the wagon, turned their heads. A dozen Apache men stood in a row as they looked down at the passing group, but made no sound, or move to drop down into the flat river valley. Jesse reflected for a moment, then raised his arm, palm open, fingers splayed, to them. One, then two, of the Native Americans, raised their arms in response. Rafael, then Cat, Pulver and Paco followed suit. A few seconds passed, then all the arms on the ridge were raised. No weapons were evident. Another thirty seconds elapsed, and the Apaches faded away.

Cat shook his head. "Son-of-a-bitch. Son-of-*a*-bitch."

Pulver, who rode alongside, without looking at his black friend, mouthed a guttural, "You said it." He pinched his lips, shook his lowered head, his brow shaded by his hat, then raised his head to sweep his gaze along the empty ridge line in sheer disbelief.

28

During the trip north and toward home, Paco and Cat looked after Bonifacio and Rodman, both of whom remained on the wagon. That meant stopping the wagon often to quiet the pounding of the wheels on the trail so their wounds could be looked after. Although in pain and with intermittent bleeding, Rodman was able to sit up and take food and water occasionally, his bloody, make-shift bandage obvious, while Bonifacio stayed on his back, half delirious.

Sepsis had set into Bonifacio's wound, and puss appeared. Paco and Cat managed to drain the area that bulged out from the area near his belly button as the patient cried out and mumbled a combination of religious sayings and unintelligible remarks about people and places that neither, especially Cat, understood. Both stand-in nurses felt his forehead and agreed that he had a fever. They gave him sips of water several times an hour in an effort to offset his mounting temperature. Cat wet a rag and laid it across his forehead more than once.

Jesse came up alongside the wagon on his horse and looked on as both men tended Bonifacio and helped Rodman, in better shape, in minor ways. "How does it look? With Bonifacio?" He directed the question to both men in both languages.

Paco shrugged and made a face, while Cat swung his head back and forth in a negative gesture.

Jesse looked at the mules, then north along the trail. "We'll go to Isleta. Only a short distance." He pointed, then goaded Campeón into a trot and moved ahead of the caravan to reconnoiter.

Pulver decided to attend him, and clicked his horse to follow.

On the east side of the river, after Jesse, Paco, Cat and Pulver had ensured that the precious wagon, with its human and goods cargo had crossed successfully, Jesse pulled his horse in close to Pulver's. He kept his eyes front. "Do you know the Texican, Rodman?"

Pulver, taken aback at the question, required three seconds to frame an answer. "Do now." He also kept his gaze forward.

Jesse sensed that Pulver's answer was cagey. He decided to press. "Did you know him before? Before this journey?" He pursed his lips in annoyance.

"Seen 'im in Albuquerq'." Pulver shot Jesse a momentary glance.

Jesse looked down and away with a knowing smile. He waited a count of five. "What were you and your partner doing in El Paso? Why were you there? Long way from Albuquerque."

"That is true," Pulver answered. "Aside from the *señoritas*, we was seein' the sites."

Jesse nodded. He felt he knew the truth, but maintained the ruse of innocence. "So, it was a coincidence that you and Cat followed us until the Apache attack."

"Quite so. We had no desire to interfere with y'all, but stayin' close meant some protection."

"Of course. A fine plan." He paused. "I noticed how your partner, Cat, was quick to get to Rodman when he was shot."

Not to be trapped, Pulver removed his trail-stained, bedraggled hat, scratched his pate, then settled it on his head with care. "That black feller, he's good at helpin' folks. Known 'im awhile now. He was well thought of back where he come from. He's real good at tendin' wounds an' such." He looked at Jesse with wide-eyed sincerity, then spoke in a high-pitched voice. "Why, hell, he did as much for me once 't." He was silent, then, with his voice far lower, "Shore did." Another short silence, then, "Hell's a-fire, he saw that feller back there sick-like, 'an off he goes!" He cocked his thumb in the direction of the flat wagon behind them for emphasis.

Jesse decided he was getting nowhere with Pulver, but added, "We owe a great deal to you both for showing up. It could have gone worse for us if you had not. Much obliged." He looked at Pulver and touched his finger to the brim of his hat.

Pulver cocked his head to one side. "Glad to help. Glad to help."

They entered the Pueblo's southern boundary between closely-set dirt-roofed, adobe dwellings, and into the main square. At the north end, set well away from the huge, bare ceremonial dance area, facing south, was the big, earthen double-spired Catholic church. To the south, at the opposite end of the plaza, was the main Kiva, the ancient, secret below-ground ceremonial center of the tribe.

Soon, few people, mostly women and children, busy with their daily routines, noticed the wagon and the men on horseback. Most stopped and looked silently as more people emerged from houses and between the buildings. Another minute passed when men appeared, yet all were silent. Jesse doffed his hat and nodded his head in greeting. The other men followed suit.

Jesse turned in the saddle and pointed to the wagon. "He spoke in Spanish. "We have wounded men. Apache attack."

It was then that a young, cassock-robed priest exited the church and moved toward the intruders. An older Indian man joined him and they both approached Jesse.

The priest stopped and looked up at Jesse as the other man went to the wagon.

"What is the problem? What brings you here?" The priest asked. He eyed Pulver on his horse next to Jesse, then past them both at the mule-hauled wagon, Cat, Paco and Rafael. He settled his eyes a moment longer on Cat.

"We have two wounded men. Apache attack south of here." Jesse gestured. "One is quite ill. He needs help."

The priest moved to the wagon with haste, as the swish of his long, restrictive black robe preceded him. He and the Isleta man looked at both Rodman and Bonifacio, then concentrated on Bonifacio. The Indian turned and said something to an old woman who had moved tentatively toward the wagon. She turned and walked to a nearby house. An impromptu conference was held by the priest, the elderly Indian and two more men who came forward, and Bonifacio was carried to a house on the west side of the plaza. Rodman was led there upright, with a pronounced limp, as well.

The interior of the old room, with its mud-plastered walls and low ceiling, was somber, but soon lamps were lit. Rodman was led to a chair, while Bonifacio was placed on a pallet. Soon, water appeared as the elderly Indian woman who had come to the wagon inspected the young Noriega's festering wound. She began a low chant as she and a second woman carefully pulled away the bloody clothing and rags that Cat and Paco had applied.

The priest stood aside as a shaman entered. He also began a chant as he performed a slow, rhythmic dance. He held sprigs of sage and corn stems in both hands, then pulled a chicken egg from a waste pouch and slowly moved it over Bonifacio's entire body and touched the skin in select places. Bonifacio was barely aware of what transpired, so did not react. A young girl came into the room from a place deeper in the house. She carried a decorative pottery bowl, held out at arm's length, in both hands. The older woman took it from her and turned to Bonifacio's stricken belly, where she began to apply the contents to the outer fringes of the ragged, arrow-inflicted gash.

The shaman went to Rodman and reached out to touch him with the egg. Rodman reeled back and uttered a "What ?!," then settled back and allowed the ceremony to take place as the priest nodded to him, warning him silently that he should accede.

The priest moved to Bonifacio's side, removed a small, black wooden Christian cross from his cassock, raised it over the lad and mumbled a short prayer, then crossed himself. He went to Rodman and did the same thing, then leaned in and spoke. "The egg is to remove evil spirits." He nodded.

In a low voice, Rodman responded, "I see."

A third Isleta woman entered, also through the same interior door. She went to Rodman, leaned down to peer at his lesser wound, then invited him to move to a pallet, where she began to aid him in the same, calm, methodical manner with which Bonifacio was being treated.

The priest, satisfied that the incidental patients were in good hands, went outside.

Jesse, Paco, Cat and Pulver had dismounted, and Rafael had stepped down from the wagon bench. As the others saw to their horses by leading them to a trough at the edge of the open earthen plaza, Rafael began to rummage through the wagon food stuffs for jerky.

Pulver and Cat, fascinated by their surroundings, looked about the plaza and the squared periphery of adobe dwellings. Small children, then older, moved in small groups to peer in wonder at Cat, the man with the very dark skin. One small boy dared to approach Cat, and touched him. Cat smiled tolerantly as two women moved forward through the line of silent watchers carrying baskets of food. Wordlessly, they went first to Cat, then Pulver and the others and held them out. Jesse, Rafael and Paco, experienced with the Indians, expected such hospitality and generosity, but both of the men from Texas were taken aback, in part because of the white man—Indian hostilities in their home territory. They quickly warmed to the situation, and accepted the offerings with muttering of gratitude. The women merely smiled coquettishly.

The baskets included bison and deer jerky, parched, dried corn, beans, squash, berries, bits of green chiles, and a round, thick, tortilla-like bread. Water in tin cups, bartered from traders who plied the Santa Fé Trail, followed.

The women laid the baskets on the tail of the Murphy, then backed away to watch the men help themselves to more.

Inside the make-shift infirmary, the women and the shaman who had volunteered their services with Bonifacio and Rodman, continued their labors.

Given that the time of day was late and close to sundown, all the men aside from Rodman and the young Noriega, who remained under health watch, camped outside the confines of the Pueblo. They unhitched the mules, watered and fed them along with the horses, and established a picket line. The wounded patients were afforded overnight accommodations where they had been treated. Several times a pair of women, accompanied by the shaman, looked in after the two. Bonifacio was on the mend, and slept relatively peacefully.

In the morning, Jesse, Cat and Rafael, came to collect the two wounded men. Jesse offered the impromptu physicians coin, as did Rodman and Bonifacio, but they refused. Jesse took the priest aside and gave him the collection and asked him to spend it as he saw fit.

When the travelers returned to the wagon, Pulver and Paco confirmed that two Isleta women and two young girls had brought more food and placed it silently on the wagon, then as quietly, turned and disappeared.

29

When the wagon pulled into the Noriega family compound, Cat and Pulver were no longer present. They had peeled off and headed for the temporary quarters afforded them by the master of the house. Bonifacio, nearly healed after the nursing by the Isleta women and Cat and Paco, rode on the bench with Paco, who was at the reins that controlled the draft mules. Their horses followed on leads at the tail gate. Rafael rode alongside Jesse, then slowed as they entered the gate that Ustacio opened for them. They dismounted, ready to unload the cargo that safely arrived from a more than five hundred mile trip.

Jesse continued on horseback to the horse stalls, where he dismounted, removed the carbine from the saddle scabbard and set it aside. He removed the bedroll, saddle bags and started to remove the saddle, when Ustacio appeared.

"Would that I look after your horse, young sir?"

Jesse smiled at him. "Yes, I would like that very much, Ustacio. I am much obliged." He dug into his pants pocket for coins.

Ustacio frowned. "No, sir. You must not." He shook his head and looked away.

"Yes, I must, Ustacio. I insist. You will take it, or I will toss it into the middle of the plaza."

Ustacio hesitated, then turned and looked at Jesse with sad eyes. "You are too kind, *Señor* Landry." He extended his open hand, elbow at his waist as he looked around to ensure no one observed.

"Good," Jesse said as he placed the coins onto Ustacio's palm. "This is as it should and must be." He nodded deeply in affirmation of the transaction.

As Ustacio took on the task of removing the saddle, Jesse looked toward the wagon and the others. Paco and Bonifacio had gotten down off the drive bench. Paco went first to check on the faithful mules, then to the tail of the wagon, while the younger Noriega moved slowly toward the house, his hand to his sore midriff, along the path that split the animal stalls and the forge. Rodman, off his horse, lead it to a rail, where he looped the reins. Rafael was in the process of removing the tarpaulin that covered the goods on the flatbed wagon.

Don Nerio Noriega, master of the house and Bonifacio's father, rounded the corner of the stalls from the front of the house, that which faced the plaza. He was no more than two yards from the wagon, when he stopped to watch the scene taking place. Bonifacio halted and looked at his father, took a tentative step toward him, then stopped and turned to look at the men with whom he had been associated for two weeks.

The elder Noriega looked at his son, then moved quickly for him. "You're wounded! *¡¿Qué pasó?!* What happened?!" His face took on a expression of horror as he looked from Bonifacio, to Jesse and the others, then back at the wounded youth.

"Papa," Bonifacio began, but was interrupted.

Jesse stood between the two Noriegas. "North of San Marcial. We were attacked by Apache. We fended them off, but, as you can see, we suffered a casualty." He hesitated, then turned and looked in Rodman's direction. "Two casualties."

Noriega went to his son, stood an arm's length away, and looked him up and down. He swung his head around to look at the others, who had stopped their labors to bear witness to the scene. He frowned at Bonifacio. "Did you fight them?! Did you fight back?!" He flapped his arms against his sides and glared.

"Papa, I—"

Noriega looked hard at Jesse, then at Paco and Rafael. "Well, did he?!"

Paco and Rafael stole glances at each other, then looked away and down with pained expressions as they continued their labors. Neither man wanted to betray to their employer what they considered his son's poor performance in battle. They both knew, as all did, that Bonifacio had no real chance to defend himself when the Apaches ambushed them.

Jesse took a step in Bonifacio's direction. "The Apaches attacked without warning." He swivelled to face Rodman and gestured in his direction. "They shot *señor* Rodman, and—" He looked at Bonifacio again, "An arrow took your son before he knew they were there." He looked Noriega in the eye. "He fell from his horse and was knocked unconscious."

Noriega looked at the ground, then up. He uttered a guttural sound as Paco and Rafael both added their confirmations of Jesse's explanation with strong head nods.

Rodman cut in, "Quite true, *Don* Noriega. Bonifacio had no chance."

Noriega threw up his hands in acceptance, then went to Bonifacio and awarded him a restrained hug. He backed up, then said, "Go to the house, my son. You must take care of that grievous wound."

Bonifacio turned and took two steps before his father spoke again.

"Son—ah—the invoices. The bills of lading." He held out his hand.

Jesse said, "I have them. They are here." He reached into one of the saddle bags he had removed from Campeón, pulled out a sheaf of papers, and held them out for Noriega.

Noriega, with a deep frown, looked at Jesse, then the retreating figure of his son. He shouted, "Bonifacio!"

Paco and Rafael, neither of whom wanted further involvement with the proceedings, turned away to apply themselves to the load, some of which they transferred to a temporary storage room attached to the house.

Bonifacio stopped and turned. "*Sí, Papá.*"

Noriega took a stride in his son's direction. "Why?! Why does our guest and partner, *señor* Landry, possess these papers and you do not?! You were to represent me!"

Jesse moved toward Noriega, whose face had reddened. "I have the papers, *Don* Nerio, because your son was wounded and bloody!"

Paco, Rafael and Rodman heard the lie, but said nothing. Rodman went to the wagon, while Paco and Rafael glanced at each other with tiny smiles.

Noriega went silent, looked down, then up at Bonifacio and Jesse, shook his head and moved slowly to Jesse to receive the papers. As he took them, he nodded his head in silence, and walked toward the house behind Bonifacio.

It was at that moment that Apolonia appeared along the path to the main house. Although her braids that tumbled down her back were perfect, she was dressed more for house duties than her role as daughter of a wealthy man. She stopped and dropped her mouth open as she surveyed her brother's condition.

"Bonifacio! What—Are you not well?! I see blood!" She held out both hands in alarm, then looked past him at Jesse, then her father.

"I'm wounded," Bonifacio said. He attempted to move past her in a state of annoyance at the attention he was receiving.

She grabbed his arm. "Tell me what happened! You are wounded!"

He glared at her with a combination of anger and shame. "Yes! Yes! Of course I am wounded, silly girl! Ask the others! Let me go!"

Apolonia dropped her hand and stepped back. "Bonifacio, you are so callous! I was only trying to—"

"I know. I know," he replied. "I want to go to the house. Let me by."

Bonifacio continued to the house as his father, after observing the clash, turned and went to the wagon to inspect the goods. He stood next to Rodman, who surveyed the dwindling inventory.

Apolonia moved to the edge of the stalls and stopped. She looked at Jesse, who had remained stationary after dealing with her father and brother. He smiled and touched the brim of his hat as he mouthed a greeting. She took a step toward him, stopped and turned half way, looked down, then raised her head to look at him squarely with a pert smile. They both stared at each other for another five seconds before Jesse broke it off.

He looked at the ground, then at her. He gestured. "I must help with the wagon."

"Of course," she said. Her voice was muted. She looked in her father's direction, and was glad he had not seen the interaction. She tossed her head, which caused her braids to swing wildly, then retreated to the house with haste.

Jesse watched her go, then moved slowly toward the wagon.

Noriega, who stood next to Rodman, spotted the large crates the Texican had acquired in El Paso. "*¿Herramientas para la Quinta?*" He pointed.

Rodman, in an effort to dodge the challenge, moved away from Noriega and avoided his gaze. He folded his arms across his chest. "Yes, *señor* Márquez recommended them. Less expensive than those from the east and what I have found in Texas. I would consider it a great favor if your men could move them to your sister's house, where she has so graciously aided me in the purchase." He paused, then said, "I will compensate your men."

Noriega was silent for a few seconds. "It will be done, at no cost to you, sir." He spent another three seconds eyeing Rodman closely with suspicion in his eyes.

Rodman ignored him, then turned and went for his horse. He loosed the reins from the rail, mounted and rode away in the direction of the plaza and the house and compound of Noriega's sister, *Doña* Salma Isabela Noriega y Castañega.

After the wagon was moved to the Noriega warehouse with the remainder of the shipment, Paco, Rafael, Jesse and Ustacio followed and cleared the wagon, save for the crates that belonged to the Texican, Rodman. Paco, under instructions from Noriega, along with Rafael and Ustacio, drove to the Castañega house with the mysterious crates.

Jesse began to sort through the crates, barrels and boxes he had purchased for the Landry Mercantile, and set them aside for later transfer. His arrangement with Noriega was that he would enjoy the use of the Murphy and the mules to make the journey to Santa Fé.

As the wagon passed the compound, the men heard the piping voice of a child. It was Roberto, who ran from the house. Breathless and happy, he shouted, "Jesseee! Jesseee!" Barefoot, he ran to Jesse and threw his arms around his legs.

Jesse raised his arms to give Roberto room, then lowered them to give the boy a hug. "Roberto, I'm happy to see you! Where have you been? What have you been doing?!"

Roberto loosed his grip on Jesse and stepped back. In little boy fashion and with breathless, gulping speech, he flailed his arms about and performed an excited little dance. He then related his adventures of the morning and of the days while the men had been on the trading trip.

Jesse knelt down to be at eye level with the boy. "That's wonderful and exciting, Roberto. Listen," he said, "I have something for you from our trip."

"You do?!" Roberto's eyes widened with excited anticipation. "You do?!"

"Yes, I do, Roberto. But it is a secret, and it's in one of those boxes there. I will have to give it to you later." He pointed.

Roberto calmed and stared at Jesse with saucer eyes. "You will?"

"Yes, I will. Can you be a big boy and wait?"

Roberto nodded with great six-year old emphasis. "Yes, Jesse. I will wait. When?"

"I must find it in all those boxes there." He pointed. "But you will have it tonight. I promise."

Roberto nodded again, then reached out and hugged Jesse again as he uttered a low hum of pleasure.

Jesse held the boy by his shoulders. "Good, now you run off and play with your friends, and we shall meet later. Good?"

"Yes, good!" Roberto shouted. He whipped about and ran away in the direction from which he had come.

Jesse looked to his left to discover Apolonia across the way, as she stood near the interior animal stall path. He looked about, saw no one, and went to her.

"I saw and heard you speak with Roberto. You are kind and good to the boy."

Jesse nodded. "Thank you, Apolonia. I have something for you as well."

She looked around. With her brow furrowed, but with a smile, she said, "Oh, you must not. What would—?"

"But I must, Apolonia. You and your family—you—you have been kind and welcoming to me."

"Thank you, Jesse Landry."

"Yes you all have, but you are different."

"Oh? In what way am I different, *señor* Landry?" She looked at him from the corners of her eyes.

"I—I—"

"Tell me, *señor* Landry. In what way, pray tell?" She raised her face to him in challenge and triumph.

"Apolonia, you are beautiful and I like you."

"I see, *señor* Landry; I see." She turned away, took a step and turned toward him again. "And I believe you are very handsome and I like you!"

Jesse, stunned, started to speak.

She moved closer to him. In a half whisper, she said, "Say nothing, Jesse Landry. Say nothing." She bored into his eyes with hers, then turned and walked away. When she was close to the house door, she turned, and with her head lowered, awarded him a penetrating look from under her eyebrows.

He stood for a minute after she disappeared, his arms loose at his side, trying to fathom what had transpired between them.

30

Jesse checked to ensure Campeón had feed and water, then took his carbine and went to his room, where he leaned it in a corner of the tall wooden *trostero*, along with his sparse collection of clothes. He thought about the pistol on his hip, and decided that it, too, would remain in the room. From there, he left the house to visit the *común*, then exited from the compound through the stall path at the rear, in order to avoid encountering family members and servants in the main part of the house. Ustacio, busy with animals, who had returned from the Castañega house, he acknowledged with a finger to his hat. Ustacio nodded, smiled, and followed Jesse with his eyes until the Santa Féan disappeared past the corner.

He crossed the busy plaza, then onto the Camino, to the *cantina* north of the church. Inside the somber room, whose typical light was provided by hanging, smokey oil lanterns, few patrons were present. He stopped, looked around, then unable to spot Francisco Maestas, approached the barkeep. The man declared that he had not seen Maestas for two days, but opined that he might show up for food and wine later, in part because of his none-too subtle interest in a barmaid who had recently signed on. Jesse asked him to advise Maestas that he had been there should he see him.

As he walked back toward the plaza, he peered above and beyond the tops of the *bosque* cottonwoods, toward the high escarpment that marked the west side of the river. The army encampment was far enough from the edge of the cliffs such that it was not possible to see. He spotted the upper body of a lone sentry as he walked along the edge, his bayonet-fixed carbine pointed at the sky, then disappear from view.

At the corner of the church, on the plaza proper, he stopped and looked in the direction of the Castañega walls, those of his host's sister. He pondered the fact that the Texican, Rodman, had requested that the crates of farm tools be delivered there, rather than stored with the main body of product belonging to the brother, Nerio Noriega. Then, fatigue from the journey setting in, his thoughts drifted away. As he made his way back to the Noriega house, he conjured up Apolonia's visage. He realized then that his interest in her was far stronger than he wished it to be. A permanent liaison between the Landrys of Santa Fé and the Noriegas of Albuquerque would be difficult for more reasons than one, yet possibly good in the business arena. He promised himself to curtail his thoughts of this young woman who looked, sounded and smelled so tantalizing. As he moved, he squeezed his eyes shut, then opened them, but the picture refused to fade along with the attendant physical twinge.

He entered through the back of the house, went to his room with stealth, closed the door quietly, and lay down, fully clothed. In less than a minute, he was adrift into sleep.

In his sitting room, Nerio García de Noriega stood next to one of the large, deep windows that looked out onto the plaza from under the long *portal* that fronted the big, thick-walled adobe residence. He held a small tumbler partially filled with an expensive French brandy in his right hand, lowered at his side. His eyes fixed on nothing in particular, he rocked forward an inch in his expensive boots, raised the tiny glass to his lips, and sipped. He pondered another ten seconds, set the still-occupied glass onto the deep, padded seat of the window ledge, turned and marched from the room.

He trekked through the house and the main rear door, then through the animal stalls. Ustacio, bent over, who managed a rake in an empty stall, stood halfway when he heard his master, and uttered a greeting, which was duly ignored.

Noriega crossed the plaza with little recognition of anyone else, despite the fact that two men and three women spoke to him as *patrón* as he passed, attendant with the ususal head-nod.

At the front gate of the house of his sister, *Doña* Salma, he stepped through the personnel door that was fitted into the high, thick wooden gate.

A moment later an Navajo boy of ten ran up to him. "*Don Nerio*," he said as he executed a half-bow.

"My sister, the *Doña* Salma. Where is she?!" Noriega knew better than to ask a yard boy such a question as he stalked toward the house, but his agitation was in control.

The boy ran alongside, his eyes wide with fear at Noriega's gruff demeanor. "I—I do not know, *señor*. Perhaps in the great house." He panted as he shook his head and tried to stay apace with the angry man.

Noriega slowed, stopped and looked down. "Never mind, boy. I will find her." He started away, then turned back to the youth, who was in the process of returning to the outer gate to close the door. He reached into his pocket, withdrew a coin and held it out. "Here, boy."

The youngster returned.

He awarded the child an insincere half-smile. "*Grácias, hijo.*"

The boy was speechless as he looked from the windfall in his small, grubby palm, then up to his well-dressed benefactor, then back at the coin. Noriega sobered, turned and marched away, deep in his own thoughts, as his heavy boots sounded on the hard-packed earth.

Although familiar with his sister's strict household, he nonetheless barged through the front door unannounced. Inside the generous front hall, with his senses recovered, he slowed, turned and pushed the heavy door to the frame as quietly as he could until he heard the hand-hammered latch tongue rise, then drop into the arresting slot. He stood for a moment to listen. There was silence for a few seconds, then he heard what he believed was first an older female voice, then that of a younger man. The sounds emitted from his left, down a hallway that led to the public rooms, opposite from the bedroom wing of the big house. He recognized the voices.

He pondered for a moment, puzzled, then, his curiosity and aggravation mounting, moved toward the adjoining hall to his left, and the voices. Three yards along, he came to the deep-framed door that led to the sitting room, whose two windows looked out onto the *portal*. He stopped in the doorway. Across the room, seated in her favorite, high-backed, padded chair, was his sister, Salma. Seated near and facing her, leaning forward on the edge of a settee positioned between the windows, was Gerald Rodman. Intent on their tete-a-tete, neither saw Noriega.

Noriega stepped into the big room. The sound of his boot heel as it struck the hard floor alerted both the man and the woman across the room to his presence, and they both looked in his direction. Rodman started to rise as he peered at Noriega, surprise written on his features.

"Please. Sit," Noriega said. He raised his right hand to reinforce his suggestion.

Rodman took his advice and sat slowly. As he resumed his former position, he looked from Noriega to Salma in an attempt to gauge their moods. He opened his mouth and uttered a sound, but was interrupted.

"I must apologize," Noriega said. He executed a small bow toward both people. His sister, who knew him well, also knew that he was insincere.

Salma gave him a sour look as she turned her face up to him. "Why should you apologize, Nerio? You never do!" She stared straight ahead, then glanced with her eyes only at the embarrassed and confused Texican. She sniffed and stiffened her back.

Noriega sighed and looked up, then down at his sister, then at Rodman. "None the less—"

Salma interrupted. "We were discussing *señor* Rodman's trip to El Paso del Norte and his business." Her hands were folded in her lap.

"Indeed," Noriega said. His voice dropped to a near whisper. "And perhaps the farming he intends to do upon his return to his home?"

Rodman, his fingers laced together in his lap, looked up at Noriega from under his eyebrows.

Salma maintained her eyes trained on a tapestry on the wall across the room. After a silence that engulfed the room for several seconds, she said, her voice also lowered, "Yes. Indeed."

Noriega looked at the seated people, then walked slowly across the room to the weaving his sister had inspected from a distance. He stopped, hesitated, then turned. "Yes, of course. Our friend from Texas will plow his fields with carbines made in the shops of Guanajuato." He raised up on his heels then back. He looked at the floor, then at Rodman, who had changed his gaze to the open door.

Salma rose slowly, went to the door and closed it. With her back to the room, she set the lock, an operation audible to the others. She stood for three seconds, then turned and faced the room, but averted her eyes from both men. "I paid for the crates," she mouthed. Still motionless, she turned her head to look at her brother. Her mouth was set in a thin, stern line.

Rodman got up and moved slowly for a window, where he looked out onto the yard. He watched the young Indian boy lead a goat into a corral.

Noriega let his mouth fall open as he stared at her with a furrowed brow. "You—!"

Salma began a slow move to her chair. Her head high, she replied, "Yes, Nerio, it was I who paid for the crates. It was I who requested of our friend, *señor* Rodman, that he purchase the implements." She resumed her seat and fixed her gaze on her shocked sibling.

260

Noriega, unable to move, shook his head in a short, jerking motion. "And are the implements for farming, Salma?!"

"Of course not, Nerio! Of course not!" She glared at her brother.

Rodman, still at the window, lowered his head. He developed a tiny smile which he was determined to hide from the man and woman behind him. The glee was, in part, because he was glad to witness the conflict in the room; in part because his role in the Territory, which he had felt was slipping away from him, was now possibly in revival.

Noriega looked at the Texican's back, then at Salma. He had gained control of himself, and his voice demonstrated that. "No, of course not, my dear sister. They are not farm implements, rather arms for insurrection. Am I correct?" He moved for the settee, then angled toward the chair that faced that which his sister occupied. He sat, and began drumming his fingers on the padded arm. "This is dangerous, dear sister, as I have pointed out to our friend and guest here." He paused. "Why was I not notified?!"

Rodman, with the evidence of his feelings erased from his features, regained his seat on the settee. He felt it prudent to choose silence.

"I am puzzled, dear brother," Salma began. "It was you who tried to convince me that we should ally with Austin. Yet, here you are, incensed, behaving as though you had changed your mind." She paused, then, "Have you changed your mind?" She leered at her brother. "You have treated our guest with disdain. He has come here, facing great danger from the army and others, and you behave as though he were a criminal. I, on the other hand, in agreement with you, have welcomed him." She smoothed the cloth of her flowing dress across her lap with her hand, and continued, "What he has brought here at great cost and danger is not enough however. I have helped to change that. I intend to change it more."

" I am not—" Noriega began.

"An alliance with Austin is in our best interest, Nerio," Salma continued. She looked at him directly and gestured. "It was you who proposed that." It was at this point that she changed to Spanish, having determined earlier that Rodman would not understand. "I did not agree with you in the beginning. Especially because of the treatment we have received from these people. But we can use them to our advantage. They have business for us. They have connections we do not possess. I now understand we need this alliance." She waggled her finger at her brother, looked at Rodman, and reverted to English. "My apologies, Mr. Rodman, for using our native tongue, but I wanted to say something to my brother that touched upon the family. I hope you understand." She dipped her head in a gesture of sincerity.

Rodman, chagrined over being by-passed in a conversation he did not understand, had stared at the floor during her speech. He looked up at her. "No need, *doña* Alma. I understand completely. No need." He shook his head, but remained unconvinced.

Noriega looked at him. "My apologies as well, Mr. Rodman. My sister can be rude at times." He paused and licked his lips. "However, I must forgive her, and I trust you will as well. You see, there are times when one returns to his or her native tongue during stress. I assure you, she was speaking of the need—nay, the requirement—for us to support you, your actions, and the plan here and in Austin." He paused. "Which I support." He looked at Rodman, his eyes wide with sincerity.

Salma reacted to her brother's statement with a flinch and a re-adjustment of herself in her big chair. She threw the Texican a hasty, apologetic smile, then looked down at her hands.

"Of course, *señor* Noriega," Rodman said. "I would do the same were the situation reversed. I must apologize for not being steeped in your language. I have every intention of learning it, especially if our mutual quest is accomplished." He lowered his head to Noriega in deference, then rose part way from his seat and did the same for Salma. "Perhaps now we could continue our discussion." He regained his seat.

"Indeed," Noriega said. He looked at his sister. "But I must know—where are the arms? Where are they stored? Under guard, I trust."

Salma raised her head, her chin prominent again. "They are safe. Ustacio placed them in the wine house. They are well hidden behind the casks. You are not to worry." She looked down, her head at a dismissive angle, and subconsciously smoothed her dress again.

Noriega shook his head. "I would see them myself," he said. He rose and started for the door, then stopped and turned to face his sister. "Who else? Who else knows of their whereabouts?" He glanced at Rodman.

Salma looked up at him. "No one! No one, Nerio! You think me a fool?!" She looked away and sniffed loudly.

Rodman stood. "*Señor* Noriega, if you would be so kind, sir, I prefer to attend."

"Of course," Noriega said.

"You will require the key," Alma said. She fished a key from a small pocket in the blouse portion of her dress and handed to her brother.

The two men exited the house through a rear entrance onto a covered *portal* that extended the length of the building, as did the one in front.

As they gained the edge of the *portal*, Noriega extended his arm to block Rodman from going farther. "*Espédase*; wait," he said. He looked around, then satisfied they were alone, gestured for the Texican to follow.

They entered the dark, cool interior of the flat-roofed adobe building through one side of a high, wooden double door, capable of passing a wagon. Rodman instantly recognized the intense aroma of wine emanating from a number of wooden barrels that lined both of the walls, in places stacked two levels above the earthen floor.

Noriega looked about, then went to a shelf, where he found a taper in a tin holder with a circle finger-handle. He lit it with a match from the same source, then returned to the door and closed it. Without looking at Rodman, he waved for him to follow, then moved for the rear of the building.

On both sides of the long room, behind the last, double-stacked barrels and racks of bottled wine, beneath scattered hay, lay the crates from Mexico.

Noriega looked at the man from Texas. "What will we find?" He pointed at the separated wooden crates.

Rodman thought for a moment, then answered, "Carbines. Ammunition." He shrugged and made a face.

Noriega took in a deep breath and released it. "And where do we find the men to use these guns? I have a few trusted men, but—"

"There are men at the border. East. And south in El Paso. A few are here. In the Territory. Hidden."

Noriega frowned at Rodman in the muted, flickering light. "Why did you not tell me this before? When we first spoke?" He frowned.

Rodman shrugged again. He felt good; complacent. He had accord with this New Mexican. "You were angry. I had no chance." He smiled disingenuously.

"How many?"

"Enough to take the troop in Santa Fé. There will be an army behind them. They are armed. The army. Of course. The first men are not. They will use these arms." He gestured at the crates.

"Santa Fé. We are a long way. Why are your weapons not there? " Noriega hesitated, then, "Yes. You told me." He stepped away, then spoke with his back to Rodman. "Some must return."

Rodman nodded, although Noriega didn't see him.

"We need a way." He paused, then faced around. "What of the men on the hill? The army outpost?" He pointed in the candle-lit half-light.

Rodman looked down, then up. "I didn't know they were there. I don't think Austin did. We will have to take care of them."

"Mm, yes. We must. I will think about it."

"*We* will think about it."

Noriega looked directly into Rodman's eyes in the flickering shadows. "Of course, my friend. We. Of course."

Rodman nodded.

"We have much to do." Noriega started for the door. "Let us re-join my strong sister. She has a good mind for trickery."

"I gathered that," The Texican muttered.

Noriega stopped and turned. "What of your men?" He frowned at the Texican.

"My men?"

Noriega attempted to restrain his irritation. "Yes, Mr. Rodman. The men who brought the crates with you."

"Of course. The men—?"

Noriega lowered his voice to a near growl. "The darkie and the other. Are they aware of the contents of the crates?"

Rodman nodded emphatically. "They know they are arms. They are unaware of their true purpose."

Noriega was silent as he pondered, then nodded. "Of course. Good." He waited another few seconds, then, "Are they reliable? Can they be trusted?"

Before he answered, Rodman flashed back to the El Paso trip and how Pulver and Cat had tracked them. In truth, he didn't know if they could be trusted to remain silent about the guns. That led him to realize, in that moment, that their reward would need to be increased. "Yes, they can be trusted. They are well paid, loyal men."

Noriega continued to look closely at Rodman. "Yes, yes; of course. Well, let us be off."

If the Texican knew the truth of Noriega's mind, he would have known that his host was not convinced of Rodman's men's trustworthiness, and had begun to formulate a plan to eliminate the need for concern.

31

Jesse awoke with a start. In his half dream state, the noise that came through the window of his bedroom sounded like the shot from his pistol when he killed Blakely. He sat up, looked through the window onto the *plazuela*, and realized that the noise was created when Ustacio had allowed a large board to fall onto other pieces of lumber.

He sat up, blinked, rubbed his eyes to clear them, and looked around. His immediate need was to relieve himself. Still half asleep, he sat for another half minute, then stood and stretched.

In the hall outside his room, he turned to leave for the necessary, when he heard a voice behind him.

"Jesse."

He turned to see Apolonia moving quickly toward him along the hall.

"There you are," she said. "I came to find you. I was worried that you had left."

His physical urgency became secondary as he watched and listened to her. "Worried? Why so?"

She stopped a few feet away. "I—I thought perhaps you had gone. To Santa Fé. To take your goods." She shook her head with a smile. Her hands were wrapped together at her waist.

"No. No." He scratched his head, looked at the floor, then up at her with a grin. "I have no plan yet. I need company. A transport. I must arrange for that. Your father offered me one of his wagons."

She took a step closer, her eyes still fixed on his. "I understand. Of course." She paused. "Will you sup with us? This evening? Or do you have other plans?"

His eyes widened. "I accept your invitation. I must find a friend first. To plan the trip north. But I will return."

She nodded, looked at the floor, then up. She had sobered. "Of course. At dusk, then. You will return?"

"I will, Apolonia. I—" He blanched as he held back in the realization he was about to say something he might regret. "Yes. I shall return." He moved his head in the affirmative.

She smiled, then turned abruptly and withdrew along the hall.

As he looked at her retreating figure, he wanted to call after her, but gained control of himself. He stood for a moment, then left.

The sun was low in the west as he crossed the plaza. A farm wagon drawn by a single horse, a man and a young boy aboard, trundled across the expanse. Firewood was the cargo, with a brown dog riding guard duty. He waved, and the boy responded in kind. The dog, jealous for attention, barked once.

As he entered the *cantina* , he estimated it to be roughly half full with men and a sprinkling of women, all enjoying the work day's end. At the same level of the chatter that filled the big room was the music coming from two men near a table in a far corner. One stroked a guitar, while the other sawed on a fiddle as they rendered a version of a Spanish tune. A man who had obviously reached a stage of drunkenness that had put his inhibitions to sleep, attempted to accompany the musicians with the lyrics. His notes sour, others shouted at him to cease, to no avail.

He stopped to scan the crowd, then spied Maestas across the room, seated at a table. He crossed to him, and as he approached, his friend spotted him, and rose from his chair. He held out his hand.

"Jesse!" He shouted above the din.

"Francisco! My friend. How are you?"

"I am well, young Landry. I am well. Sit. Let me order you a drink." He looked toward the bar and raised his arm.

"Francisco, no. No. I am expected at the Noriega house. I must not appear to be in my cups."

"So sad, my friend. Look at this reverie!" He grinned. "But so be it. Tell me of your journey." He turned to Jesse with his arms outstretched on the table, his drink held by both his hands.

Over the room chatter, which undulated lower, then higher as the consumption of *auguardiente*, wine and brandy increased, Jesse limned the high points of the trip. After some hesitation, he recounted Bonifacio's odd behavior at the Márquez place and on the travel home. Maestas was reflective, but said nothing.

From time to time, Jesse looked toward the door to monitor the daylight. When he realized the sun had crested to the west, he rose. "I promised Apolonia I would sup. But Francisco, I need to speak with you again. I have product to take north. To the store."

Without hesitation, Maestas said, "I will help. Let me know, my friend. I would see that military friend of yours. I need to keep him from my sister." He grinned and winked.

"I will that."

The two shook hands.

Jesse went out the front door of the *cantina*, turned left, and made his way toward the church and the plaza beyond. As he closed on the corner of the massive north wall of the church, he heard what sounded as though someone hissed. He stopped, looked around, then heard it again. He looked to his left, toward the alley that ran parallel to the north wall of the church. Crouched behind a large sage was someone with a hood covering their head. He surveyed the area again and saw no one else.

The figure stood, then beckoned him. At that moment, he wished he had worn the revolver that lay hidden in his guest room. "What do you want? Who are you?!"

The figure waved again, this time with agitation. Jesse looked about once more, then, with some trepidation, moved close to the figure. "I demand to know who you are and what you want!"

"Master Landry, it is I, Ustacio. I wish you no harm. I would speak with you. Please." His voice was muted beneath the hood he wore.

"Ustacio?! What—?!" Jesse looked in both directions along the narrow way.

"Please! A word." Ustacio searched the alley as well.

"What is this, Ustacio? Why—why the secrecy, man?"

"Master Landry, you must—"

"Ustacio, address me as Jesse. I am not your master. Now, what is so grave that you encounter me in this way?" He dropped his voice to the conspiratorial level the servant used.

"Ma—Jesse—I have come to see you because there is something you should know. I have no one else with whom I can confide."

Jesse screwed up his face and shook his head in disbelief. He was momentarily at sea over what the man would have him hear. "What is it, Ustacio? Tell me."

"The crates. The crates, they—"

Jesse interrupted, "The crates, Ustacio—what about them? What crates?!"

"They are guns. They are guns!" His voice dropped to a mere whisper.

Jesse furrowed his brow in a deep frown. "Guns?! Which of the crate have guns?! How do you know this, Ustacio?!"

"Jesse, when I—we—Paco, Rafael and I—took the two crates from El Paso to the house of Master Noriega's sister, I smelled something. I know the smell of gun powder." He stopped, looked around, hyperventilated, caught his breath, then continued. "After the others left, I looked inside. There was a crack. I broke away part of the wood. There are guns inside!"

Jesse shook his head as he looked up, then around.

"Jesse, I looked at the crates the man from Texas brought days ago. Jesse, they also contain guns."

Jesse was silent for several seconds, then, in a whisper, asked, "Ustacio, what kind of guns? Were you able to see?"

Ustacio nodded his head with emphasis. "Long guns, *Carbinas*."

Jesse thought for a moment, looked at the darkening ground, then up at the distressed old man.

"Why—why does this distress you? Are these guns not for sale?"

Ustacio shook his head with intensity. "No, Jesse, no! They are army guns! *¡Para la guerra!* For war!"

"How do you—what makes you think this?!" Jesse frowned deeply and shook his head.

"Because I listened! I heard them! They are not to sell! I swear this on the graves of my fathers!" He threw his arm out, his finger pointed and shaking at the shadows.

"You heard?! Who did you hear, Ustacio?!" Jesse lowered his voice as he looked around in the gathering gloom.

Ustacio swallowed hard, gulped, lowered his head, looked at the dark ground at his feet, then up at Jesse. His voice was nearly a croak, his eyes wide with fear. "The gringo *Tejano*. His horse had a bad shoe. I went to fix it. At Alma's house. I was in the stable. I heard them. The *Tejano* and the *patrón*."

Jesse paused to shake his head again in disbelief, then asked, "What did you hear, Ustacio? What did they say?"

Ustacio had calmed. He shook his head back and forth in a sweeping motion. "They spoke of men, of the guns, of attacking—I don't know...Oh..." He slumped against the old adobe wall of the church.

Jesse straightened, looked around, then turned and crouched to reach Ustacio's face. "Ustacio, who else knows of this?"

He shook his head. "No one. I alone. *Solamente Yo. Y tú*."

Still low, with his knees bent, Jesse wiped his face with his hand. "Ustacio. Return to the house. Go the back way. I go there now to sup with the family. Speak to no one of this. I will think about it and decide what to do."

Ustacio nodded, lowered his head, then stood, turned and scurried away along the north church wall and disappeared.

Jesse stood up straight, thought for a moment, then moved quickly for the *cantina*. Inside, he searched the room for Francisco, but he had gone.

Calmed, but his mind reeling from Ustacio's confession, Jesse entered the Noriega house and went immediately to the dining room.

Apolonia sat at the big table alone. When she heard him enter, she turned to look at him with an expression of concern. "I feared you would not come."

He moved around the table to his assigned seat, and pulled it out. "I'm sorry. My apologies. I was seeking help in my need to take the goods I have for the mercantile. In Santa Fé."

"Yes, of course." She smiled.

He looked around the otherwise empty table. " I see that—"

"Yes, we are alone. I must apologize as well."

"There is no need. I am happy to sup with you. Alone. I mean—"

"Of course. As am I. Father is with his sister and the gentleman from Texas. They have business to discuss. He will sup there. My mother and my aunt are being served in their rooms. Bonifacio is otherwise—"

Jesse nodded. "I see. Then we shall carry on by ourselves."

They smiled at each other in silence.

Apolonia got up from her chair. "I must see to our meal."

He pushed his chair back and rose.

"Please, sit. I will see to our supper. And some wine." She gestured for him to sit.

They had begun to eat the soup when Bonifacio appeared in the hall doorway. He looked at his sister and Jesse, then started away.

Apolonia called out, "Sit with us, Bonifacio. Eat something. You have had nothing all day. You must eat to heal, and you require cook's good food to do so." She awarded him a kind sibling smile, which he did not see, since their backs were to each other.

He shook his head as he looked at the floor. "I am not hungry, sister. I will find something in the kitchen later." He shot a glance at Jesse, and was off.

A minute later, Apolonia, who faced the window to the *portal* and the plaza, saw her brother's outline as he passed by the window onto the plaza.

It was at that moment, that the young Indian girl, Jacinta, entered with a hot, vapor-emitting platter and set it on the table between the two.

Apolonia raised her flute, half full with red wine poured by Jesse. "My father and mother disapprove of my taking wine." She grinned. "To your trip to the capitol, and your safe return."

"Thank you."

Apolonia gave Jesse a pixie look under her eyebrows. "You will not reveal to my parents that I have taken wine?"

"Upon my honor. I swear. Not a word." He grinned broadly and held up his glass.

The Indian girl stood back for a moment, then removed both soup bowls. She served Apolonia from the platter, followed by Jesse, then left the room.

They both drank again, then picked up their forks.

After several bites, Jesse put his fork down, tasted his wine, and wiped his mouth with his napkin. He looked at her. "Does your father often sup with your aunt?" He maintained a bland mask.

She chewed, swallowed, then answered as she put her napkin to her lips, "No. Rarely. I find it odd. He seemed fretful today after your return. Perhaps it was Bonifacio's injury. But he hurried to my aunt Salma's house and has not returned. One of her servants came to say he would dine there. That there was business to discuss. I believe with *señor* Rodman as well." She stared at Jesse with open innocence. "There was to be a celebration feast tonight. It makes me sad."

Jesse nodded and looked down at his plate.

"But you are here, *señor* Landry, and we shall celebrate for all. That makes me happy." She raised her glass and drank as she watched him.

"Indeed we shall, Apolonia." He raised his glass, drank, then set it down. "I have a gift for you. It is in my room. There is one for Roberto as well."

"How wonderful. And you say my name, *señor*. She put her wine aside and leaned forward against the table, which caused her bust to be accentuated.

Jesse blanched. "Why would I not say your name? I—I like it. It is a beautiful name."

"I have embarrassed you. I said it in jest." She sat back, looked down, then up as she became more solemn. "It was that—that I had not heard you say my name until now."

Jesse, recovered, countered, "And I have not heard you mouth my name often. You have been very formal with me, using *señor* Landry more often." He smiled and raised his eyebrows.

"You are correct, se—Jesse." She lowered her head as her face reddened.

He waited, then, "I like that." His voice dropped an octave and was barely audible to her ears.

"So do I, Jesse."

"Apolonia, I—"

"I know." Her smile disappeared, and she turned her head to one side.

"No. No! Apolonia, I—" As though in an involuntary trance, he left his chair, rounded the big table and stood by her side. He took her hand. "Apolonia," he whispered.

She looked up with watery eyes. "Jesse." She shook her head.

"No, Apolonia—"

"It is impossible." Her head dropped to her chest, then raised. "I'm promised."

Jesse's face showed the torment he felt. "It's not right. It's not right. I can't—"

She pulled her hand back, then got up slowly. Half a head shorter than he, she stood next to him. She looked into his eyes for a few moments, then she looked through the door into the hall. Satisfied they were alone, she put her hand to the back of his neck, pulled him down and kissed him gently on the side of his mouth. Before he could respond, she backed away, gathered her skirts, turned and disappeared into the dark hall.

He looked back at the table and the unfinished meal when he heard Jacinta approach.

She came into the room, stopped, looked from the abandoned table, then to him. She spoke to him in guttural, Navajo-accented Spanish. "Are you and the mistress finished?"

Jesse, unable to think clearly with the conflicts swirling about his head, was slow to answer. "Yes. Yes, we are. Uh, you may clear."

The girl promptly went to the table and began to gather plates and utensils.

His mind elsewhere, eyes focused on nothing on the wall, he walked out of the room in a spell-like daze. As he walked along the hall toward his room, he gathered his thoughts, and realized he had much more to do than to morn the loss of a girl he had not even won. He swore under his breath, picked up his pace, and went to his room, where he gathered up his pistol and strapped it to his midriff. From there, he exited through the rear door and moved, in the dark, through the stall complex.

As he rounded the eastern corner of the house, he encountered a figure in the shadows, standing at the edge of the front *portal*.

"Jesse!" It was Apolonia, who spoke in an exaggerated whisper.

He halted abruptly and looked in her direction. "Apolonia! My god! What—?!"

She stepped off the porch pavement and onto the dirt. "Jesse—I had to speak to you. I—I'm sorry."

He reached for her in the muted light and took her hand. "Apolonia, there is no need. I—"

"Jesse Landry, I love you," she whispered. She moved in and laid her head against his chest.

"Oh god, Apolonia, I love you." He stroked the tight hair on her head down to the roots of her braids.

She shook her head. "I am afraid. My father—"

"He will not know, Apolonia." He paused, then, "What of this man to whom you are promised? Who is he? Where is he?"

She pulled back enough so she could speak clearly, her voice moderated so as not to be overheard. "He has traveled. He travels for my father. Along the Trail. He is in Independence. He buys for my father."

Jesse listened as he looked about the empty plaza. He looked down at her. "Apolonia, how did you know I would be out here?"

"After I left the dining room, I waited, then went to your room. I saw you leave, and I hurried here, hoping to see you." She laid her head on his shoulder again.

"I'm glad you did."

She wrapped her arms around his middle. "Oh, I don't know what to do, Jesse."

He barely made out her words. "I know. I don't either." He was silent, then, "We will think about this."

She looked up at him. "Where are you going? You have your gun. Is it something dangerous?"

He dropped his arms and moved back as she did the same. "No, no. I—it's because of the night. I seek a friend. I told you, I need to take my purchases back. They need to go to the mercantile."

"Yes, of course..."

"Apolonia, go back to the house. They may see you are missing. If we are caught—"

"I know. I will go now. I won't sleep, thinking of you. I love you." She stepped back and looked at him in the dark.

"I love you, Apolonia. We will—I will—"

"I know. Goodnight."

"Until tomorrow."

She lifted her skirts, turned and moved quickly around the outside of the house for the rear door.

Jesse surveyed the plaza, which was dark, save for a few orange lights that emanated from three of the houses that sat along the edge of the open area. He strode across the expanse, past the church and up the dirt street to the *cantina*. It was crowded, smokey and loud. Francisco was not to be seen, so he went to the bartender and waited for him to notice him.

"Yes?" he said, as he wiped a tumbler.

"Francisco Maestas. You know him."

"Yes. He was here earlier." He looked out into the big room, then back at Jesse.

"He stays with a cousin. The family is Archuleta. Do you know them?"

"Yes. They are north, along the *acequia madre*. They have horses."

"How will I know the house?"

"In the dark, man?"

"Yes."

The bartender made a face. "Well, two are musicians. They play guitar and violin. Sometimes here. Perhaps you will hear them. The mother sings."

Jesse nodded, thanked him, and left.

As he picked his way slowly along the east bank of the "mother ditch," which brought brown water from the Rio Grande to the fields that surrounded the town, he wished he were on Campeón. He thought of the uncanny sense the animal had for the land and direction, even at night. He stumbled in the dark twice, and passed two houses, one with lights, the other not, then came to one with a window that revealed lamp light. He also heard the sounds of a guitar, violin and a woman's voice in song which came from the interior.

He made his way down the embankment to a low fence, then through a rickety gate to the one door he made out in the faint starlight. Several knocks on the door brought a young girl who opened it.

"Who are you?" She asked.

"*Soy Jesse. ¿Está Francisco? ¿Maestas?*"

"*Sí. Momentito. Pase.*" The girl turned and left.

A minute later, Francisco Maestas came into the room. The music continued behind him.

"Jesse! What—what brings you here?! How did you find me?" His mood was of surprise, then joy.

Jesse beckoned him in close. "Francisco, there is a problem. A big problem. I must speak with you. Outside."

"What?! What problem?"

"Please. Outside. Now." Jesse's face was stern.

Maestas looked into the dark behind Jesse, then behind himself, then followed Jesse outside.

Jesse explained to Maestas what Ustacio had told him. He could not see Maestas as the man from Bernalillo muttered swear words under his breath.

Maestas stroked his face with his hand. He leaned in close to Jesse. "This is serious, if you believe Ustacio. Do you believe him? We must see for ourselves, Jesse." He paused. "But why?! What are they for?!" His voice reached a higher pitch in his reaction.

"I believe him. I don't know. I don't know what they're for." Jesse was silent for two seconds, then, "But listen, Francisco, I have heard, more than once, from friends of my father, in Santa Fé, that the Texicans claim this land."

"What land?!"

"New Mexico. The Territory, *hombre.*!"

Maestas was silent, then calmed and said, "I believe it to be true. I believe that. But—why would Noriega—?!"

Jesse answered, in a low growl, "That Texican. Rodman is his name. He went to El Paso with us. He brought crates back. Two."

"What?! He did?! What was in them?!"

"Farm implements was written on it. Ustacio told me they were guns."

"¡Jesús, María y José! This is terrible. We must tell the lieutenant."

"But we must see for ourselves first. But how? According to Ustacio, they are held in a secret place on *Doña* Salma's property!"

"Does he know where?"

"Yes. He put them there."

"Then we will find a way. We will see for ourselves, then we will find Beckner and tell him."

Jesse lowered his head in thought, then raised it to peer at his friend in the shadows. "Yes."

He agreed with Maestas that to maintain as much secrecy as possible, Jesse not be invited to join the party in the Archuleta house.

As Jesse Landry walked away in the dark, Francisco Maestas thought of what Lieutenant Beckner had told him. Now he knew that his father's partner's son was not part of a nefarious Texas plot. He returned to the party relieved and relaxed, and more determined than before.

Jesse retraced his difficult route back along the big irrigation ditch, to the empty plaza and finally the quiet serenity of his room in the Noriega house. As he lay on his back in the pitch black, conflicting thoughts swirled in his head. His father's death, Noriega, Rodman, Apolonia, and now, mysterious guns. When he thought of the girl across the house in her bed, he crawled with desire. It was the one thing he felt positive about, but that, too, was sullied with the knowledge that she was scheduled to marry another man. That unknown became yet another concern. Fitful, he turned on his side and tried to sleep.

32

Jesse awoke with a start and a sense of panic. In the moment after opening his eyes, he didn't know where he was, When he did, he realized he'd experienced a bad dream. He was unable to recall the story thread, but the discordant feeling remained. He hyperventilated as he sat up and wiped his hands across his face and tussled his hair.

A pang shot up and through his torso and stomach as he pictured the night before after Ustacio's revelation. He knew he would have to calm himself; further, and more importantly, he knew he must carry on a pretense with Noriega, his family and the household staff. He found himself doubting his own sanity. His otherwise peaceful, happy existence had become a nightmare in a few short weeks.

He stood, went to the wash bowl, poured water from the pitcher, then splashed some on his face and through his unruly hair. After pulling on his pants and boots and using the *común*, he realized he was hungry and thirsty. His appetite at dinner with Apolonia had been reduced by the distressing news from Ustacio, then cut completely when Apolonia left abruptly.

After reigning in his hair and adjusting his clothing to a presentable state, he made for the kitchen.

Ermelina and Ustacio, the pair that constituted the backbone of the house and its operation, were there, as was the young Indian girl, Jacinta. The Indian boy, Pepe, entered behind him with an armload of wood for the cooking fire, while the girl stood at the table preparing tortillas. Ustacio stood aside from the bustling Ermelina. He drank hot chocolate, while she worked on the ingredients for *desayuno*, the morning meal.

When Ermelina saw Jesse, she awarded him a smile and a demand that he sit to eat, a command to which he readily obeyed. Ustacio reacted to the guest's appearance by holding his cup tentatively and peering at him with an expression of guarded trepidation. Jesse nodded to him, then as quickly looked away before he took a seat at the table.

Little Roberto came in, his face clouded by the remnants of sleep as he rubbed his eyes, his mouth turned down in a grumpy expression. Without a word, he went to Jesse and put his short arms around his waist before Ermelina lifted him onto a chair and placed food in front of him. Before she bid him to eat, she leaned down and whispered in his ear to see if he had relieved himself and washed his hands.

With these activities, sounds and aromas, Jesse thought the scene would meld well with those he experienced in the house he now owned in Santa Fé. Despite the tension he carried of late, he felt at home.

He hoped, on the one hand, that Apolonia would appear in the kitchen; on the other, he was glad she did not. In his conflicted mood, he wasn't sure he could behave rationally in her presence. On the one hand, his distress over Ustacio's revelation might be apparent and be misinterpreted, in the face of the relationship that had developed between them.

He finished his meal quickly, thanked Ermelina, who beamed with pride over the compliments he bestowed upon her, then took his leave. As he came to the hall door, he hesitated to look in Ustacio's direction, and shot him a glance. The old man nodded his head almost imperceptibly at the same time he flicked his eyes toward the door. Jesse caught the meaning.

He was also wary of encountering Noriega for the same reason he feared seeing Apolonia; that somehow he would give away his thoughts with facial expressions and body language. With those thoughts, he hurried to his room, where he stopped to think. A minute later, through the window, he saw Ustacio head for the animal pens. Energized, he took up his pistol belt and hat, and went to the hall door, where he looked both ways. He started for the outside door when he heard someone call to him in a loud whisper. He turned to see Apolonia half-way along the hall.

Dressed in her long night robe and barefoot, she rushed to him, and almost crashed into him. She pulled him back into his room, shut the door, then wrapped her arms around him. He responded in kind, and they kissed longingly.

"I couldn't sleep," she whispered. She lay her head against his chest.

"Nor I," he answered. His voice was low as well.

"I didn't go to the kitchen as I usually do. I was afraid you'd be there."

"I was there. I was glad you didn't come."

She looked up at him. "You were?"

"I was afraid they would see our love."

"Oh, Jesse, yes. You are so right." She put her head against him.

He massaged her warm, soft back and shoulders. "We must keep our secret safe." He paused. "But I don't know how."

She released her grip enough so she could look at him full face. "Where are you going? Your pistol—"

"Apolonia, I have yet to arrange travel. For the goods. Goods for the mercantile—" He paused, cogitating. "There are dangers, and I have yet to succeed."

She pulled him in again. "Of course. Silly of me. I just want to know everything." She leaned against him and whispered, "I want you so much. I ache..."

"I, too, Apolonia. I, too." He looked through the window at the changing light of morning. "We must be careful." He wanted to say something about her betrothal, but held back. He thought of Ustacio. "I must go, sweet love. You must return before we are discovered, while the house is quiet."

"Yes. I know."

They kissed again.

He opened the door and inspected the hallway, which proved to be empty, then looked down at her. "I will leave. Stay out of sight here. After you hear the outer door close, look carefully, then go quickly."

"If I should be discovered, I will say I was looking for Roberto."

They each released their affectionate grip and parted.

Ustacio busied himself at the forge with a horseshoe. Jesse walked past, slowed and looked in his direction, then continued. He walked away from the compound to an irrigation ditch, crossed it using the thick plank there for that purpose, and headed for a grove of cottonwoods. He found an area where he could see the house and outbuildings, but was able to duck out of sight, and waited. Ustacio carried a hay rake as a prop and followed a few minutes later.

Jesse saw that the old man was nervous as he looked back toward the house every few seconds. "Ustacio, tell me how to find the arms crates."

"As I said, they are in Salma's wine house. Behind barrels. In the back."

"Ustacio, why do you think they are there?"

He shook his head rapidly. "I don't know, but they were brought by the *Tejano*."

"Odd." Jesse paused to ruminate, wheeled away, then back. He held his hand to his chin. "I heard my father. More than once. He spoke of the possibility of better business opportunities if we were a part of Texas. That we could then be part of a nation, not a territory..." He trailed off and looked down as the image of his father's body on the floor of the mercantile came to him, then the scene in the *fonda*. "*¡Diós!* Could it be? I have been blind." He shook his head slowly as he peered into Ustacio's old face.

Ustacio nodded in silence.

Jesse spoke slowly. "They want a war." He looked away, then up at the branches of the trees. "They want the land. The Territory. They want the mountains. The river. The mines." He paused. His voice was soft; contemplative. "My father wanted business, not a war. He died. Shot. They killed him. Why?"

"*¡Jesus, María y José!* But—but why the *patrón*?!"

Jesse looked down, then at Ustacio. "I don't know, Ustacio. It makes no sense. Unless, as my father..."

"And his sister, the lady Salma?"

Jesse touched the old man's shoulder. "Ustacio, is there a way—a back way to Salma's place?"

"Yes. I can show you."

Jesse shook his head. "No, Ustacio. You stay away. Do not become involved. Describe it to me. All that you remember. I—we—will go."

"Ay, Jesse, it is so dangerous!"

"Yes, Ustacio, I know. But it must be done. We must know." He waited, then, "Tell me, then return, Ustacio. Take care not to reveal what you know or that you have spoken with me."

Ustacio nodded with worry that crossed his features. "Yes."

"Can you do this? Be silent?"

"Yes."

Ustacio spent the next three minutes describing everything he knew about Salma's house, grounds, the wine house, servants and their movements. They wished each other well, then the old man returned to the Noriega forge.

Jesse walked east through the cottonwood grove, then detoured around several houses along the eastern periphery of the village until he found a path that led to the *cantina*. He stood in the doorway to check for Francisco Maestas. Maestas was not there, but he did see Rodman, Pulver and Cat, seated at a corner table, cups and plates at their elbows, deep in conversation. He backed out, crossed to the ditch that ran parallel to the road, and stood close to the base of a cottonwood. His anxious mind spun. He ruminated for two minutes, then, when he realized the trio from Texas might see him, he moved quickly toward the rear of the church where Maestas said they should meet.

Maestas waited around the corner of the building a few feet north of the massive church structure.

Both men greeted each other soberly and quietly, and both surveyed the area carefully for anyone who might recognize them.

"I came from the *cantina*," Jesse said. His voice was low. "I thought you might be there."

Maestas shook his head.

"The three from Texas were there."

Maestas squinted a silent question. "Three men from Texas? Who?"

Jesse sighed. "They were eating. Talking. Close."

"I don't understand. What three men?"

"I think I'm going crazy," Jesse lamented.

"You're driving me crazy!" Maestas whisper-shouted. "What the devil are you talking about?!"

"Of course. I haven't told you." Jesse then told Maestas parts of the story of the trip to El Paso he had not mentioned earlier. The Apaches, Rodman and his peculiar behavior. Pulver and Cat and their involvement. He emphasized that Pulver had maintained that he and Cat did not know Rodman prior to the Apache attack.

"You say one of them brought back arms?"

"Rodman. The man brought back two crates. It reads 'Farm Implements' on the top. After what Ustacio told me, I believe it to be arms." He paused. "Ustacio also told me that Rodman came to Albuquerque with those two, the black and the white man. They had crates marked the same way." He peered intently at his friend. "They knew each other!"

"What—what does this mean?!"

Jesse looked down. He spoke slowly. "I don't know."

Maestas strolled away, then came back. "We need to see. If it's true."

Jesse nodded.

Maestas looked intensely at Jesse. "But who would use these guns?"

Jesse started to shrug and canted his head to one side. "I don't know." He looked directly at Maestas. "I have seen many gringos. Here, Santa Fé, on the road. Perhaps they hide nearby. Waiting." He gestured a question with his shoulders.

"I, too, have seen them. These *Tejanos*. They are loud. They think they are better than we. In the *cantina*—when they dare come in together—they look at us as thought we were animals!" He paused. "I agree. They come here and wait." He nodded with emphasis.

Jesse squinted at him. "And Beckner..."

"What of him?"

Jesse angled his head to one side. "I don't know..."

Maestas waited for more from his friend, but Jesse was silent. "I will return tonight. After dark. Here."

"I will be here," Jesse said.

"Wait!"

Jesse looked at Maestas, a question on his face.

"What if we are locked in?"

Jesse shook his head. "Ustacio said the lock can be opened from the inside."

"Good."

"*Hasta luego*. Until then."

33

Jesse and Maestas crouched behind the rear wall of the Castañega compound in the dark. They spoke in whispers, their heads close together.

"We can enter through the rear gate. It's not locked. I checked," Jesse said.

"Ustacio told you someone would come for wine?"

"Yes. He said one of the servants, a boy, goes there every night to get a bottle of wine for *Doña* Salma."

Maestas thought for a few seconds. "I am smaller than you. I can slip in while the boy is selecting a bottle."

"Into the wine house? You are certain?"

"If I am discovered, I will say I wanted some wine. I will bribe the boy."

Jesse pondered. "Be careful. Let's go."

Jesse went first, then Maestas, through the narrow wooden gate. Maestas closed it carefully, then both men moved cautiously in the half-light to the north side of the earthen wine house.

"How long do we wait?" Maestas asked in a low whisper.

"I don't know, but I think it is nearly time for the evening meal."

"I agree."

Tired of crouching, his knees and feet hurting, Maestas slumped down against the wall, and Jesse followed suit. They did not have long to wait. They heard a young male voice singing a familiar song out of tune as he approached the structure from the house. The singing ceased, then they heard the metallic click of a key in a lock, then the squeak of a hinge.

They got up quickly, and Maestas peered around the corner. Soon, he saw the flicker of candlelight through the open door, and crept closer. Three seconds later, he was through the door and flattened sideways in the space between a barrel and the front wall. He remained silent and still, as he took shallow breaths until the boy snuffed the candle and retreated. The servant locked the door, then walked away with the song again in his throat.

Jesse waited until he was sure the servant boy was in the house, then crept to the wine house door and rapped three times. Maestas lifted the lock in the dark, opened the door, and Jesse slipped in. Maestas put the lock back in place, then went to the shelf where he had seen the boy get a taper. Once lit, the two men moved with stealth to the rear of the building. Beneath barrels and canvas, they found the crates.

With care not to start a fire, they inspected the containers. Neither man spoke beyond an occasional muttered comment or expletive.

They had finished their inspection and returned the covers, when they heard voices outside. Jesse pinched the candle flame out, then the two of them found separate spaces in which to hide between walls and wine barrels. Half a minute later, the lock was turned, and the door opened. Soon, despite the low voices, Jesse recognized them. There was that of Noriega, then Rodman, followed by Pulver and Cat. He barely made out what they were saying, but from a word here and there, he knew it was a discussion about the crates.

Soon, the tarpaulins and wine casks were off the two crates. That was followed by the sound of steel against wood, then the high-pitched squeal of nails being pulled from dry wood as the crate tops were removed. Then they heard the clatter of individual firearms against each other as they were lifted from the crates and carried away. This maneuver lasted for ten minutes before the lamps moved toward the front of the building.

With the circle of flickering light around the door and darkness in the rear of the wine house, Jesse and Maestas both peered around the edges of the barrels that hid and confined them. They watched from their perches as the last of the carbines were loaded into a shallow false bottom of a wagon, then planks secured over them. They observed as a dozen wine casks were managed onto the carriage platform. They saw Cat and Pulver lash the load down with ropes as Rodman and Noriega held torches high. Cat climbed onto the bench, the wagon pulled away, the doors of the building closed, and the secret observers were again in complete darkness.

Forty-five seconds later, Jesse and Maestas were outside of the compound wall.

"That was close!" Maestas exclaimed. He crouched close to the wall.

"Shh! Listen! I hear the wagon." Jesse moved south along the wall in the direction of the plaza.

Maestas came up behind him in the dark. "The wagon is going east, toward the mountain. Not north along the *camino al norte*." He paused. "In the night?!"

284

Jesse pondered for a moment. "They want to move in secret. Can they go to Santa Fé that way?"

"It is far. There are two ways. The long way, through the Apache passes. The other through the cut in the mountain. With the mines."

"I will follow them."

"How?!"

"Campeón."

"*Muy peligroso, amigo.*"

"I know."

"I will go with you."

"No, Francisco. Take to horse and go to Santa Fé. By the Camino Real. Quickly. Find the lieutenant."

"And tell him what?! That you are a fool and may never return?!"

Jesse thought for a moment. "Tell him—tell him to wait and watch. Tell him I will explain what we have seen and heard. He will want to catch them all." He turned to look at Maestas in the deep shadows. "Will you do that?"

"Yes, damn you!" He shook his head, dropped it to his chest, then raised it. "Yes, Jesse Landry, I will. *¡Por Diós, hombre!*"

"Good." Jesse clapped Maestas on the shoulder. "I go now. We meet in Santa Fé." He stopped and turned to his friend. "Wait. If you do not find him, or he is unavailable, go to the house. Stay there and wait for me."

Maestas nodded in the dark. "I will. *Adiós.*"

Jesse circled the plaza and entered the Noriega manse through the back door, careful to make little sound. Inside his room, he lit a candle, then stood in thought. The last thing he wanted was an encounter with the elder Noriega, meaning he would have to eschew the interior of the house. After two minutes, he left the room, went outside and moved carefully along the south wall. As he approached each successive window, he stopped and peered in. The first past his window was dark. At the next, he saw the low light of a pair of candles, and an older woman, whom he could not identify, seated across the room, her back to him. Through the next window, he saw Apolonia holding a book as she sat close to a floor-based, three-taper candelabra. He checked his surroundings, then tapped on the wavy glass. Apolonia looked up with surprise and concern, but remained in place. He tapped again, and she rose slowly and came to the window. Her face was a mask of surprise and pleasure as she shook her head, looked behind her, then at him. He pointed in the direction of the rear door.

He waited a few feet from the exit. When she appeared, he hissed at her.

She came up to him as she held her skirts to avoid allowing them to drag on the dirt. "Jesse! What is it?! What's wrong?! Is anything wrong?!" She whispered.

He took her hand. "Apolonia, I'm sorry to meet you this way, but I wanted to let you know. I must leave. Tonight. Now."

She furrowed her brow. "Why?! What happened—?! Your goods?"

"No. No. Apolonia, I can't tell you now, but I will return. I will tell you then. You must trust me."

"Oh, Jesse, I—"

"Apolonia, *mi amor*, Please do not fret. I will return. But I ask a favor."

"What is it, *querido mio?*"

"I ask that you inform your father that I had to leave on an emergency. Tell him my friends in El Llanito need me, but that I will return. Soon. To retrieve my goods for the mercantile. Will you?"

"Of course, dear heart." She pulled in close, wrapped her arms around him and laid her head against his chest.

He encircled her slim waist with both arms. He kissed the top of her head and drew in a long breath to smell her hair.

She pulled back. "Oh, I love you. Please take care. Come back to me."

He leaned down, she raised her face to his, and they kissed.

He returned to his room for the carbine and his trail paraphernalia, then left.

Campeón reacted to Jesse with a snort and a bobbing of his great head as his master talked to him soothingly while he put on the blanket, saddle, burdened carbine scabbard, bedroll and bags. Not used to working at night, the animal was surprised when Jesse mounted and guided him around the stalls and toward the plaza. From there, he rode a long path to the *cantina*, where he purchased food and filled his canteen for the ride.

The rising moon provided more contrast between the ground, houses and trees as they rode east. He moved slowly, something his horse appreciated, fearful he would move faster than the loaded wagon, come upon them and be discovered. As he calmed after the rush and excitement of the evening, he reasoned that the men he followed would not travel far in the night after clearing the village, fearful of discovery and embarrassing questions, and would stop until morning. Given that, he brushed the horse's neck and slowed him to a walk as he peered into the dark, as he hoped to spot his quarry.

He did not have long to wait. After riding for a half hour, he sensed the bulk of a wagon attendant with large animals and perhaps men. He soothed Campeón with low words and a pat on his long neck. The horse stomped his foot in response, turned his head, then stood patiently still.

Jesse looked around, clicked the horse, and pulled the reins to the right. Soon, he found a depression behind some rocks and a cedar where he prepared for a fitful night. He coaxed Campeón to lie down without removing the saddle, something he loathed doing, but necessary, considering his self-imposed mission.

At sunrise, Cat emerged from under the Murphy wagon with its load of illicit firearms secreted beneath the floor boards, and headed for the nearest scrub cedar to relieve himself. As he buttoned his breeches, he looked over at Pulver, who was two yards distant as he performed the same morning ritual. Ruben Salazár, one of *Doña* Salma's retainers, also arose.

The three tended the mules, saddled their horses, then, with Salazár up on the bench, headed east into the rising sun. Each drank from their canteen and tore at jerky and tortillas for their opening meal of the day.

Little was said between the three of them as Salazár sat on the bench, reins in hand, effectively riding point. Pulver rode alongside the carriage, while Cat, nervous and suspicious, trailed behind. He turned in the saddle from time to time as he watched for a possible follower. He saw no one.

Jesse was up before the gun-runners. He surveyed the terrain from behind the protective cedar he had found the night before, determined the position of his quarry, then mounted *Campeón*, who had been enjoying the grama grass at his feet. He rode a wide arc around the wagon and east of it, toward the canyon named for a scissor, or cut, *Tijeras*. Behind one of the large boulders that decorated the landscape at the base of the Sandia massif, he waited. He was not disappointed. Not half an hour later, the mule-drawn wagon and the three men moved toward him at a pace that satisfied the mules as they pulled against the load. He recognized the black man and the white man who called himself Pulver, but the man driving the wagon was new to him. He reckoned he was from the

Castañega household. He noted that a third, saddled horse followed the wagon on a rope tether.

Jesse surveyed the terrain ahead and to the north, found a path appropriate for horseback, and followed it deep into rough ground that defined the side of the mountain that sloped toward the eastern plains. He was careful to maintain a low profile, but reasoned that if spotted by the trio, he would not be seen as a follower, as long as the two he knew did not recognize him. When he arrived at the valley that ran northward from Tijeras, he rode up into it and waited. His supposition was correct, because the wagon turned into it. Shortly, the transport halted, and he watched as the driver dismounted and went for the tethered horse. The man mounted, then engaged in a conversation with the other two. That included sweeping arm gestures and head nodding. After two minutes, the third man rode away toward the main canyon and the village of Albuquerque.

He watched from his hidden vantage point as the black man tethered his horse to the wagon, spoke to the other man, then climbed up onto the bench to take the reins.

He wondered what he should do next. He felt it was obvious the pair had instructions to deliver the arms somewhere else; most likely the capitol, Santa Fé. But he must make sure. And where was the older Texican, Rodman? Why had he remained behind? He decided he would track the shipment. When he was certain of its destination, he would race to join Beckner and Maestas. He opened his canteen and quaffed some water.

He would have to find a stream or pond for patient, steadfast Campeón.

Below, Cat looped the wagon tether to his horses's reins, then stood next to Pulver. "I don't like this, Pulver. Not the least of it. Look yonder at this god-fersakin' landscape. How're we supposed to make our way up here and to them camps we was 'tole 'bout?!" He pointed with his outstretched arm.

Pulver looked around, then focused on the minimal wagon and horse tracks that led north. "Well, other's 've been this-a-way, Cat. Sides, he tole us about the minin' camps betwixt. Bound to be folks 'an all."

"Yeah, and what does that mean, fer Chrissakes? We git into a fire-fight or somethin'? I don't like it." He made a face. "I don't see why we couldn't 'a traipsed up along the river. The main road, they say." He paused, looked around, then spat.

"All this fuss over some long guns. Anyone'd think we was gonna start a war, fer chrissakes!"

Pulver ignored Cat's plaint and shrugged. "Well, mebbe we can skirt the places."

"Yeah, yeah, Pulver, skirt the camps. Shee-ut!" With that, he walked to the front of the wagon and climbed up.

Pulver re-mounted, adjusted his hat and clicked his mount as the wagon creaked forward.

Noriega stood next to the kitchen work table as he nibbled portions of the breakfast food that Ermelina and the others were preparing, when Apolonia walked in. He turned to look at her.

"*Buenos días, papá.*" She went to him and awarded him a brief hug, then to one of the stools next to the table and sat.

Noriega cleared his throat. "Good morning, my child. Did you sleep well?"

"I did, *papá.*" It was a falsehood, but she covered it well. She looked down at the table that groaned with food, prepared and raw, then up at her father. "*Papá,* when do you expect Federico to return?" She looked up at him without moving her head.

With his mouth half full, he responded, "Mm—mmf—soon." He swallowed, then, "Soon, I trust." He smiled down at her. "Are you anxious, my sweet?"

Ermelina, who, with her older woman's intuition and wisdom, sensed the truth of Apolonia's desires, angled her head around to look at the girl, then as quickly looked away.

Apolonia dwelled for a moment, as she hoped to couch her true feelings in a false answer. "Of course, father." She looked down and away.

Noriega lowered his head and stared at her as he chewed a morsel. His suspicions were aroused.

She turned to look up at her father. "Oh, *papá,* Señor Landry asked me to convey a message." Her eyes went wide with contrived innocence.

"What?!"

Sensing that she might fall into a self-created trap, she was careful to sound disinterested. "Yes, he asked me to tell you—"

"Tell me what?! When?!" He glared. "You were alone with him?!"

"No, *papá,* no, I—"

"Well?!"

"No, I—we met in the hall—by chance. He was leaving. He was seeking you to speak with you. He was in a hurry. He asked me to—" Her heart rate rose at the lie.

"Well, child, what did he say?!" Noriega picked up his cup, ready to drink.

Apolonia, flush, answered, "He asked to say he had to leave quickly. Something about his friends—" She shook her head and waved her hands in a gesture of desperation. Her voice had become a whine.

Noriega interrupted again. "What friends?!"

"In—in El Llanito. I think he said El Llanito."

He stopped eating and looked aside to stare at the wall. His face was clouded with newly-engendered questions and suspicion.

Apolonia got up abruptly and rushed from the room as Ermelina followed with her eyes.

34

Francisco Maestas had made his way to the house of his cousin, Archuleta, in the half-light of the rising moon after departing from Jesse Landry. With early light the following morning, and nothing more than a swallow of water and a tortilla rolled up in his hand, he mounted his horse and rode north to the Maestas house in El Llanito. He galloped intermittently to save his horse's strength, but as they neared the house and stalls familiar to the animal, his mount chose to stretch his long legs to the fullest, an act that caused Maestas to grin with glee.

His mother, Filomena, was surprised and happy as he came through the outside door to her warm, aromatic kitchen. She shrieked with joy, wrapped her arms around him and bussed him on his cheek. She had been worried, she explained, because she had heard of all the foreigners and troubles in Albuquerque.

When they released each other, he went to the table and sat. "I am famished. Nothing but water and one of Flora's tortillas. Yours are better. I would eat, *mamá*!" He picked up the fork that rested next to the plate in front of him.

"And so you shall!" she said.

"Where is *papá*? I would speak with him."

"Oh, he will return soon. He had business with Varela." She bustled at the stove, then brought a pot to the table and served her eldest son.

After he ate, Francisco went outside. He had hoped to see his father before he entered the house. He walked toward the stalls to check on his horse when his father appeared.

"Francisco! When did you arrive?" Sabino Maestas called out with joy coloring his words.

The younger Maestas turned to greet his father. "Only this morning, *papá*."

"Have you eaten?"

"Yes."

The two closed on each other. Francisco put his hand on his father's shoulder as they shook hands. They had both decided that Francisco was too old for hugs. That was now reserved for his sister and younger brother.

"I have something to tell, you, father." He became serious as he looked at Sabino, toward the house, then back. His voice was moderated.

Sabino wrinkled his brow. "What is it, my son?"

Francisco inhaled deeply, then exhaled in the same manner. "I must ask you to tell no one of what I am about to say." He bore in on his father's eyes.

Sabino cocked his head to one side. "What is it? Has someone died?!"

Francisco shook his head and closed his eyes momentarily. "No. No. Nothing of the sort. It is perhaps worse."

Sabino's jaw dropped, then he took control of himself. He held out his palms as he waited.

Francisco told him the entire story, from the time he arrived in Albuquerque with Jesse Landry and Lieutenant Harold Beckner, ending with when he watched Jesse disappear in the dark the night before.

Sabino stared at his son, looked down and away, then back. "But why should we not raise the alarm?!"

"Because, father, to do so would alert these *Tejanos pendejos*, and that cowardly Noriega would run away. That is why."

"I see. Of course."

"We must tell the army. This Lieutenant Beckner, and let them do what they must to stop this." His voice dropped to an intense whisper.

"*Comprendo*. I understand. Of course. We must. I will remain silent. I will tell no one."

"*Papá*, not even *mamá*."

Sabino nodded sadly.

"I must go."

"Where?!"

"To Santa Fé. To find this army officer and to meet with Jesse Landry."

"He follows the shipment? The wagon?"

"Yes. He does."

"*Ay, Diós*. I hope he is safe."

"As do I, *papá*; As do I."

Francisco saw to it that his horse was properly fed and watered before he mounted up with trail food in the saddle bags, fresh from his worried mother. His sister, Mercedes, appeared as he was ready to leave. She asked as discretely as she could about Lieutenant Beckner. He told her he would extend her regards to him upon their meeting. He rode away, first at a walk to the Camino Real, then at a gallop as he disappeared from the view from his family's home and guided his mount north.

Jesse watched the slow progress of the contraband vehicle as it trundled through the uneven, rocky defile past the little mining camp named after Roque Madríd, the Spanish prospector, well north of Tijeras. He continued to ride far enough ahead of the wagon so as to keep an eye on it, yet not be recognized.

As had Jesse, Cat and Pulver found potable water in the stream bed fed by springs that leaked from the eastern slopes of the Sandia Mountain. While all three travelers drank from their canteens, the mules and horses slaked their thirst with stream water.

By late afternoon of the second day, after suffering through a fast-moving thunderstorm, the arms- and wine-laden wagon reached the outskirts of Santa Fé. They were fortunate to spend the last few miles on the last leg of the Santa Fé Trail that ran between Pecos and the capitol city. They were joined by a Conestoga wagon and a boy leading a firewood-bearing burro. In each case, Cat became a brief element of curiosity, but was unmolested, and soon disinterest on the parts of their fellow travelers set in.

With Pulver at the wagon reigns, Cat moved alongside and looked at his partner. "I tend to be nervous, Pulver. Y'all saw how them folks peered at me. Who knows what I'll run into in this town."

Pulver kept his eyes front. "You've been safe to date, Cat. I'll stand fer ye."

Cat shook his head. "I know, Pulver, and I thank yew for that sentiment, but what if we're overcome?"

Pulver cocked his head to one side. "It'll be okay, Cat. It'll be fine. You'll see. We'll show 'em our iron."

"Yeah, right." He adjusted his sweat-stained hat and faced forward, then touched the grip of the pistol at his side. "Right. That'll do it," he muttered.

"Biggest problem we got is to find this mercantile and drop this load," Pulver said.

"What's the name?"

"It's on this paper. The bill 'o ladin' or some such." He gestured toward the box beneath the bench with a head movement.

"We'll have to ask around."

"'Pears that-a-way, Cat."

As soon as Jesse was certain the wagon and its deadly cargo was headed for Santa Fé, he rode ahead. When he reached the first houses on the periphery of the town, he found a cedar and *piñon*-protected prominence where he dismounted and watched the trail traffic. He was rewarded soon after he hunkered down, Campeón's reins in his gloved hands. After the wagon passed, he fell in behind and to the side of the Conestoga to watch from a safe distance.

When the sail cloth-covered transport reached, then passed, the Guadalupe church near the intermittent stream named after the town, he was surprised when he discovered that Pulver and Cat had stopped. The distance between himself and them was close enough that he could have been recognized had they looked in his direction. He halted, tugged on the reins, and guided Campeón away to a place where he would be undiscovered while he watched after he dismounted and stood behind his horse. He saw Pulver speak with two men who nodded and gestured as he held out a piece of paper. The men pointed toward the plaza, then he saw the wagon move again as the local men stood and watched the pair move on.

With caution, he rode slowly behind the wagon as it made its way to, then across, the town center. He watched as they stopped again, spoke with a teen-aged boy, then started again. He was shocked when he realized where they were headed.

Incarnación Serna responded to the loud pounding on the north side gate and opened the personnel door to peer out. He was temporarily speechless when he saw the wagon and the two odd men in attendance. When he asked them who they were, and what they wanted, Pulver, with little more than a grunt, held out the manifest and a second paper. The Landry employee hesitated, then went to the wagon to take the papers. As he did, he stared briefly at Cat, who stared back.

Satisfied with the paperwork, Incarnación opened the main gate doors, and Pulver pulled the wagon in. As the vehicle entered the compound, pulled by the mule pair, Cipriano, followed by Francisco Maestas, came out of the house, then stopped. Cipriano expressed surprise; Maestas did not.

Pulver got down, Cat dismounted and tethered his horse, and the two unhitched the mules and led them to water.

Cipriano went to Incarnación, and they conferred. Maestas remained in the shadow of the *portal*.

"What is this?" Cipriano asked.

Incarnación referred to the documents. "It's a shipment from Jesse. These men were hired to bring it here." He turned to watch the activities in which the two drovers were engaged, then back to look at Cipriano, then Maestas. He shrugged.

It was then that Francesca emerged from the house, attracted by the noise. She wiped her hands in her ever-present apron as she went up to the two family servants. "*¿Qué pasa?*"

Incarnación explained what was happening, which brought a broad smile to the woman's countenance. "Does this mean that the lad will be here as well?"

Incarnación shrugged. "We do not know. These men appeared, but he is not with them."

"I think he still fears the sheriff," Cipriano said. He nodded in confirmation of his own assessment. "That he will be arrested."

Maestas joined the three. "He will be here. Soon."

They looked at him.

"How do you know this?" Incarnación asked.

"Yes," Cipriano said.

"My arrival was late, and I had much to say, but I was not sure of the time it would require for the wagon to arrive."

Incarnación furrowed his brow at Maestas. "You knew of this?!" He frowned at the other two, then back.

"Yes." He nodded.

"Then you must tell us," Cipriano said.

Maestas shook his head, looked at the ground, then up. "No. I will wait until Jesse arrives. Then you will know all. He knows more than I."

"Of course," Incarnación said.

All three nodded.

Francesca saw that Cat and Pulver were ready to leave. She said, "These men must be hungry and thirsty. They must eat. Tell them to come in."

"The black, too?" Incarnación asked.

"Pah! He is human, too! No?! You silly man! Tell them!" She raised her arm, waved away his remark, turned and entered the house.

Maestas started for the house. "I will wait in my room. I am angry and may say something. You talk to them." He held up his finger, then followed Francesca into the house.

Pulver and Cat were pleasantly surprised and shocked at the invitation to come into the house. They were shown where to wash their hands and faces, then to sit for chocolate-laced coffee and Francesca's breakfast fare. That included something that neither man was used to, local chile. Cat took to it immediately, although confessed to watery eyes and temporary burning mouth and tongue. Pulver was more hesitant, but warmed to it after a few bites. They both learned to follow with tortilla, not liquid, to dampen the heat.

After they finished and started to get up, at the same time they declared their appreciation and thanks to Francesca, they were asked to remain long enough for the three constant household stalwarts to pump them for news of Jesse. In their nervousness, Pulver and Cat had little to say, beyond the events of the trip north from El Paso, and that Jesse had been kind and fair. Cat professed the need for them to be on their way, his excuse being that they were to meet with another man who had offered them employment.

After they asked Incarnación to see to the mules, they rode away.

Cipriano went to Incarnación, who unfolded one of the papers he had been handed, and began to read. "What does it say?" He asked.

"I'll read it."

It read,

This shipment is bound for the Landry Mercantile of Santa Fé. When received, it is to be maintained intact, loaded, on the transport, until señor Landry, an agent of his, or that of señor Nerio García de Noriega of Albuquerque, arrives with proper credentials to allow disposition of these goods, under pain of prosecution. The contents, as well as the wagon, are to be delivered to, and lodged at, the Landry warehouse.

—N. G. de Noriega, on behalf of J. Landry.

Both men looked at each other with wonder.

Cipriano creased his brow, scratched his head and looked at the untouched wagon, then at Incarnación, who merely shook his head and shrugged.

Pulver and Cat crossed the center of the town, the plaza, then found the trail head for the Camino Real, and headed south for Albuquerque. They rode side-by-side, at a trot.

Without looking at his partner, Cat said, "Ah cain't b'lieve them folks. They treated us like we was family."

Pulver gestured with his head. "Y'all got that right. That was fine grub. Different, but mighty fine." He paused. "Not sure I understand these folks. But I like 'em." He cleared his throat. "Sure do."

Jesse had watched the movements of the two drovers as well as he could along the southern approach to Santa Fé, given that he remained wary of Sheriff Baca and his deputy. This despite assurances from Noriega that he was removed from Baca's fugitive list. He had skirted the town along the east and north sides, then settled in at a point where he was within sight of his home, the Landry compound. It was from that vantage point that he saw Rodman's men leave on horseback, without the contraband wagon.

Weary from a near sleepless trip, he unburdened Campeón, set him loose to graze nearby, then stretched out to rest against the saddle until he fell asleep.

The sun had set, the sky grey dusk, and the air cool when he was awakened by boys shouting at each other on the road that ran behind the outer city walls. This was preceded by a dream state filled with chaotic menace. He sat up, looked around for his horse, who had also napped, then rubbed his face and hair to bring himself to full wakefulness. Campeón, aware of his master's movements, also became alert and sprang to his feet.

In the growing half-dark, he threw the blanket, saddle, bags and loaded carbine scabbard onto the cooperative horse's strong back without cinching it. He then lead the horse down the slope to level ground and to the rear gate of the Landry Mercantile.

His knock on the gate brought Incarnación, then Cipriano and Francesca to his side, all of whom were joyful at seeing him in one healthy piece. Upon hearing the jubilant sounds, Maestas joined them, but stood aside until the hugs and kisses were finished, when he and Jesse shook hands accompanied by satisfied smiles. After Francesca hugged her ward tightly, she removed herself as she wept happily, to the little family chapel in the innards of the house, there to give thanks.

35

While Incarnación hastily groomed Campeón, checked his hooves, then lead him away to a stall that would be difficult to find quickly by an outsider, Francesca bustled about to feed Jesse. Cipriano trotted away, then back with wine, which the prodigal politely refused in favor of apple cider. Maestas sat with Jesse. They quietly exchanged notes over their separate trips north.

As Jesse finished the last of his belated breakfast, Francesca and Cipriano joined the travelers at the table, while Incarnación stood. They all watched and listened with undisguised pleasure as Jesse recounted his time in the Rio Abajo district. He saved the issue of the mysterious wagon until the last of his remarks. Incarnación related most of the tale of the two men, one white, the other black, the manifest, then the admonition to keep the shipment intact until instructed to move by authority as described in the side note. Maestas reinforced all that Jesse recounted where it applied.

Jesse and Maestas told them what they would most likely find in a secret compartment in the transport; that they and the territory were in potential danger as a result. The three householders were aghast. With tears, Francesca made the sign of the cross more than once as she whispered prayers under her breath. When the interview was over, she again visited the family chapel.

Jesse looked at Maestas. "Have you spoken with Lieutenant Beckner?"

Maestas shook his head. "No. I decided to wait for you. I had little proof. We have it now."

"Good. I understand." He looked up at Incarnación. "I want you to seek out Lieutenant Beckner. Can you do that? Will you?"

"Most certainly, Jesse. I will."

"Ask him to come discretely. Ask him that he not come in his uniform, but in ordinary civilian clothes." He paused, in thought, then, "Do not tell him what you know. Merely say that you have a message from me, and that you feel safer relaying it here, lest you be overheard."

"Of course, Jesse. I go now."

"You think it not too late in the day?"

"No." He shook his head. "I think I know where he may be. I have seen him in the town in the day and after sundown. If not, I will ask at the army post." He started for the door, then halted as Jesse signaled him to wait.

"Use caution, my friend. This is dangerous. We don't know who watches. Some who have been our friends may, in truth, be our enemies."

Incarnación went first to the saloon and bawdy house of *Doña* Tules, where, immediately inside the door, he craned his neck to look about the big room. He did not see the lieutenant, but did spot a man he recognized, who he knew was acquainted with Beckner. The man claimed he had seen the gringo officer earlier in the day, but not since. After checking two more likely places without success, he went to the military post in the capitol building. He was greeted with a frown and a certain air of impatient superiority by the gruff Duty Sergeant. Wary of the request, he demanded to know why a local native Hispanic would have business with a member of the U.S. armed forces. Incarnación, thought quickly, then answered that the lieutenant had left something personal at the store, and he wished to return it. When asked why it could not be left with him, the Charge of Quarters, Incarnación insisted that it was private, and that he needed to identify the recipient. The sergeant, after a short period of silent mulling, relented, and agreed to accede to the request. The visitor was asked to wait outside while a message with the name of the mercantile affixed, was sent by a runner. The Landry employee said he would wait.

Incarnación went outside onto the long *portal* and leaned against the thick adobe wall. He was there for a little more than ten minutes when Beckner appeared.

The lieutenant exited the building, looked about, then spied Incarnación. The two men shook hands as Beckner checked their surroundings for possible observers. When his anxious visitor explained who had arrived, Beckner became animated, and agreed to change clothes and follow. With that, Incarnación left.

After changing into mufti, the lieutenant made his way in the dark to the Landry place along the rear wall, then rapped on the gate where Incarnación said he would be. Incarnación let him in, stuck his head out into the alley, peered around, then secured the old wooden door.

In the kitchen, the three Landry retainers watched as Jesse and Beckner embraced. Beckner and Maestas shook hands warmly. Francesca, true to form, grinned from ear -to-ear as tears wet her face and worked her hands in her ev-er-present apron. She excused herself to retreat to the chapel, there to give thanks for the reunion, but returned after a quick prayer, lest she miss something of consequence.

Cipriano served wine as Jesse, Maestas and the army officer sat.

Jesse invited Incarnación and the others to sit as well. Then he recounted, in as much detail as possible, all that had transpired since his parting from the officer in Albuquerque. He was silent for a minute to allow Beckner time to absorb what he had heard. He spoke again. "I believe Noriega is involved with the insurgents."

Beckner locked eyes with Jesse as he nodded, thinking. "This Rodman fellow. What does he look like?"

Jesse described him.

"Does he wear a fringed leather jacket?"

Jesse cocked his head, then nodded. "Yes..."

Beckner took in a deep breath, then released it. "What I am about to say, Jesse—" He looked at Incarnación, Maestas, then Cirpiano and Francesca as they waited with rapt attention. He continued, "will shock you, and may anger you, but I believe it to be true."

All four people looked searchingly at Beckner. Jesse's concentration mounted.

"I think I know why your father was killed, and who was responsible."

Jesse stared at Beckner, while the other four traded serious glances.

"This Texican, Rodman."

Jesse was silent for a long time as he breathed deeply and his heart rate increased. His voice was deep, close to a whisper. "The man I shot—"

Beckner interrupted, "His agent." Beckner went silent, then, "The night your father excused himself. I believe he met with this fellow, the Texican, Rodman, and his assailant. Something went wrong." He leaned forward, intense, his forefinger up. "Listen, Jesse, we found a wagon—a broken down wagon in the canyon—the canyon of the Apaches. Along the Pecos Trail. It was carrying arms. Guns. Carbines."

Jesse rose slowly, took up the glass of wine Cipriano had poured, sipped, and set it down. He then stepped slowly away to stare at a blank wall. He lowered his head, then returned to the table and sat. He looked at Beckner. "I heard my father—from time to time—speak about the Texicans. Taxes. Fees. Tariffs.

Business arrangements. I thought—" He paused. "But I never heard him speak of insurrection. War." He shook his head slowly.

Francesca whispered, "*Ay, Diós de mi vida...*"

"What could have happened?" Jesse asked.

Beckner ruminated, then, "I'm not sure, but there is now a wagon in your possession with arms. I think that may be what they planned. They brought arms to be held here, your father refused, they saw him as a traitor, and—"

"And they return them now that my father is gone."

Lieutenant Beckner merely nodded with emphasis. He was silent for a moment, then raised his glass to sip his wine, and set the vessel down gently. He started to tap the table with his finger, then stopped and looked at each of the people in the room. "What I am about to say is a secret. It must not leave this room. If the army found out that I had revealed it, I could be courts-marshaled and forced to leave the army. Even imprisoned." He looked around again. "Do I have your solemn promise?"

All indicated agreement with nods and a muttered acquiescence.

Beckner sipped again and looked at Jesse. "The man who killed your father was called Blakely. Thomas Filmore Blakley. Originally from the state of Tennessee, late of the Republic of Texas."

Jesse lowered his head and peered at Beckner. "How do you know this?"

"Do you recall the day we returned from Las Vegas? The caravan?"

"Yes."

"I asked you if you knew the short man on horseback. Wearing a black vest."

Jesse thought for a moment. "Yes. I do."

"Blakely."

"But how—?"

"Here's the secret." He paused and looked at his audience again. "I was sent here by the War Department in Washington. The United Sates Government. For one job. One job." He jabbed the table top with his finger. "That job was—is—to seek out and identify an agent or agents working on behalf of the Republic of Texas to subvert the Territory of New Mexico on its behalf." He studied those around him again. "We have found such an agent. But there may be more."

"Who else knows you are here?" Jesse asked.

Beckner shook his head. "Major Middleton. Only he."

"How did you know it was Blakely? Know his name?"

"I have field reports from our agents in Texas. After you shot him, I looked through those records and found his description." He was silent, then, "And I must confess, Jesse, that I suspected you after I realized your father must have been involved."

Cipriano looked at his wife, who crossed herself and muttered, *"Jesús, María y José . .."*

Jesse looked away, then back. "Is that why you aided my escape and followed me to Albuquerque?"

The lieutenant nodded solemnly. "In part."

"What do you think now?" Jesse asked.

Beckner shook his head minimally and smiled. "You are not a traitor to the Territory of New Mexico, or the United States of America, my friend."

All smiled. Francesca clapped her hands once in glee, then held them to her face in a gesture of prayer as her eyes welled with tears.

Maestas looked at the army officer with new appreciation "What now?" He asked. His eyes darted about with excitement.

"We wait," Beckner said. "We wait."

"Wait?!" Incarnación, incredulous, glared at Beckner, then looked at each of the others.

"Yes, wait," Beckner said. "We need to find out who will come for the wagon, and—"

"And what they will do with the guns," Jesse said.

"Or who will come for the guns." Beckner moved his head to look at everyone in turn.

"It means that they unload the wagon, the wine casks, then take it away with the guns?" Incarnación asked.

There was general silence, then Beckner spoke. "I don't know, but I doubt they expect to maintain the arms here." He pointed at the floor.

Incarnación pulled the wrinkled transport instructions from his pocket. *"Espédanse.* Wait. This paper says to take the wagon to the warehouse." He held it up.

Jesse leaned forward. "Let me see that!"

Incarnación handed the paper to his employer.

Jesse read it, then waved it at Beckner. "Francisco and I watched them hide the guns from two crates. There's at least one more in Albuquerque. Maybe more."

"Who is to use the guns?" Cipriano asked.

Beckner leaned back and raised his eyebrows. "I expect there are men waiting nearby and across the border. Perhaps on their way here."

Jesse looked down, reflected, then up. "If—if my father was expected to store arms here, then what's their plan? Men—fighters—would come here?!" He shook his head with a frown.

"I don't know, but I can guess," Beckner said. "They have a plan. Of that I'm sure. That could include an invasion." He ruminated, then continued, "The smuggled arms are most likely intended for taking and securing key points. The Apache pass and Tijeras. Military and militia guard posts." He was silent, then he looked at Maestas. "Francisco, do you know reliable people in Albuquerque; people we could depend upon to watch and wait?"

Maestas screwed up his features. "What do you mean?"

"I mean people, maybe more than one, who are willing and able to watch others. Noriega, his sister, this Texican, Rodman. Possibly others."

Maestas thought for a moment. "I understand." He paused, "I think so. I think my cousins, Archuletas, could."

"Good. Let us talk about this, then I'd like you to return to Albuquerque."

"To tell them?"

"Yes. But, Francisco, it is very important, vital, that they are firmly with us and remain secret. They must tell no one. They will have to be very careful." He thought, then, "Listen, there should be watchers at the canyon. East of Albuquerque. An attacking force would come through the canyon."

"Tijeras," Maestas answered.

"Tijeras," Beckner echoed. "But no one else. Understood?"

"I understand. What of the soldiers on the west side? Across the river?"

"Yes, they need to know. But they must not do anything yet. I will see to that." Beckner looked around the room. "I must confer with the Provost, Middleton. Then we will act."

All nodded in agreement.

"What of the wagon?" Incarnación asked.

Beckner looked at Jesse. "You told the girl, Noriega's daughter, you went to El Llanito?"

"Yes."

"Then we wait for someone from Rodman or Noriega. Agreed?"

"We let the wagon go to the warehouse?" Jesse asked. "Incarnación will have to guide them."

"Yes." Beckner looked at Incarnación.

"I will pretend to be stupid," He said. He generated a confident grin.

"Good," Beckner said. He smiled at the remark and touched Incarnación on the shoulder.

"What should I do?" Jesse asked.

Beckner thought for a moment. "Return with Francisco. Help him set up our spies. Show yourself at the Noriega place. Feign ignorance, but be watchful. Remember all you are able."

"Of course."

Beckner stood. "I will go now." He paused. "I don't want to be seen, so I'll leave by the rear entrance and take the long way around to the post." He looked at everyone in turn. "Thank you all for trusting in me and the army. It means much to me." He paused, then looked at each in turn. "It means more to you." He addressed Jesse and Francisco directly. "I will see you in two days time. No more than three. Be careful. Be watchful. Be alert. *Adiós.*"

Jesse and Incarnación stood as he started for the door.

Francesca rushed to him, put her hands on his face and kissed his cheek. "*Vaya con Diós,*" she whispered.

Beckner hugged her in return, patted her face, turned and exited onto the *portal*, and was gone into the night.

Incarnación followed. He checked the area outside the compound walls and secured the rear gate after the officer's departure.

36

Jesse Landry and Francisco Maestas rode away shortly after dawn, their stomachs comfortable with Francesca's loving breakfast and abundant trail food in their saddlebags.

They were careful to head north first, then ride around and well-away from the outskirts of the capitol town before guiding their mounts south along the Camino Real. Jesse, especially of late, had little confidence in Noriega's assurance that Sheriff Baca or his deputy, Dominguez, would not arrest him on site, or worse. Both men wore sidearms.

By mid-morning, they were along the trail on the rise around the hill that lead to the approach to the top of La Bajada; "The Descent." It was the steep, lava-dominated escarpment that separated the Rio Grande Valley from the rolling plain that lead north to the base of the Sangre de Cristo mountains.

When, the afternoon before, Pulver and Cat arrived at the connecting trail that dropped down into the narrow valley that cradled the villages of Las Golondrinas and La Cienega, they succumbed to their hunger and thirst, plus the need to feed and water their mounts by chancing it. They were pleasantly surprised at not only the verdancy they encountered, but the hospitality of the denizens, who gladly accepted their coin for food, water and feed.

They made camp along the stream that fed the defile, while the horses were happy to be tethered on green grass mixed with beige grama. In the morning, supplied with fresh flour tortillas, haunches of roasted chicken and local apples, they climbed back up onto the Camino and turned south. They did not know that three miles to the north, two men on horseback, one of whom knew them and of their secret mission, followed.

Thus it was that when Jesse and Maestas approached the ledge where the main road slanted down into the broad river valley, they espied the black and white pair ahead, moving at a walk.

Jesse jerked on his horse's reins to bring him to a halt. "Francisco! Stop!"

Maestas coaxed his horse to circle around and back. "What?! What is it?!"

"Two men on horse. Ahead. See them?"

Maestas looked, then back. "Yes. What of it?"

"I know them. They're the men who brought the wagon to Santa Fé."

Maestas looked again. "Truly?"

Jesse nodded. "Yes."

"They should be down river."

"They must have camped the night." He looked about. "I can't let them see me."

Maestas quieted his anxious mount with strokes of the beast's neck. "What do we do? Wait?"

Jesse pondered a moment. "We need to get to Albuquerque quickly. We must ride around them."

"Hm," Maestas mused. "We will watch them from this distance, then at the bottom, before the Rio Salado, go to the river. Santo Domingo."

"Of course."

Cat, true to his namesake animal, in his maintenance of a roving eye, turned in the saddle, then looked at the more passive Pulver. "Regard them riders a-follerin'?"

Pulver looked back as well. "I do, Cat. They're free to do so. Ain't no threat as I can see. They's stopped to admire the scenery." He looked forward, and continued to pick at a morsel stuck in his teeth.

"Sumpthin' familiar about one of 'em."

"Cat, yew dumb nigger, yew're always seein' ghosts or yo' mama at a distance."

"Not true, white plowboy. It's 'cause I am *alert!*"

"I give yew that."

Jesse and his companion slowed their pace to a walk as they watched the drovers ahead, moving as though they had not a care in the world. At the base of the escarpment, they headed west, toward the river and the Pueblo of Santo Domingo. At the arroyo delta, where the land spread out onto the Rio Grande flood plain, they guided their mounts south along the base of the piedmont, which allowed them to avoid the main part of the pueblo. A group of small children, who played alongside an irrigation ditch, watched them as they passed. Both men waved, and the children responded in kind. At some distance south of the pueblo, in the *bosque*, they stopped to eat and rest the horses.

At the Maestas domicile in El Llanito, they conferred with Sabino, who recommended two men whom he felt would be very happy to aid in the mission at hand. He said he would suggest that they meet with Jesse and his son soon.

Mercedes took her brother aside to pump him about Lieutenant Beckner. He assured her that the young officer would most likely soon appear, but that she should remain aloof and mentally chaste. Her response was a smile on a happy face before she ran back to the house, her skirts flying with joy. For his part, Francisco, given the circumstances, had relented to, and privately applauded, the desire on her part as well as that of his gringo friend and accomplice.

The newly-minted agents of the U.S. Government continued to Albuquerque the following day. Sabino had named the two men he suggested, who were, wisely, to follow and rendevous with Francisco Maestas later that day. Jesse split off from Maestas at the Archuleta place and moved on to the Noriega house.

When Jesse dismounted from Campeón and lead him to the Noriega stalls on the south side of the compound, faithful Ustacio was there. He hammered a red-hot horseshoe with a sledge, then looked up as Jesse walked nearby. The two men acknowledged each other with curt nods and knowing eyes, but otherwise wordlessly.

After Jesse removed and stored the saddle and its attendant paraphernalia, he headed toward the house with the carbine scabbard as Roberto ran up to him with happy talk. Jesse greeted the child with a hug and words of encouragement, then the boy turned and ran back into the house. The boy allowed the door to slam against the inner wall in his haste.

In his room, as Jesse stored the carbine, he heard a rustle behind him. He turned to see Apolonia close the door carefully.

She rushed to him and whispered, "¡Mi amor!" She threw her arms around his neck and kissed him.

He returned the kiss. "Apolonia." He also whispered.

They embraced in silence, looked at each other again, and kissed.

She laid her head on his chest. "Oh Jesse, I am so miserable."

He pulled back to look at her. "Why, my love? What is wrong?"

She loosed herself from Jesse, walked slowly to the door, then turned to look at him with tears. "He has returned."

"Who?" Jesse frowned.

"Federico."

"Oh. I see. Your intended." He looked down, then up. His face expressed forlorn.

She nodded, then moved against him again. "I am so sad." She sniffed. "I don't know what to do." She looked up at him. "I am young. He is so old."

"Why—?"

"My father tells me that he is the best match for me. That the men of this region are not suitable. But I know he really wants his business—and Federico's business to remain in his control."

"I—"

"And my father—he behaves so strangely lately. He shouts, then apologizes, then disappears into his study and closes the door. He spends his time at the house of *Mi Tía* Alma. And that horrid *Tejano*." She turned away and went to the window. "I will leave. I will escape. Run away." She turned toward him. "Go with me, Jesse!"

He looked down at the floor. His mind raced with his conflicted knowledge. He wanted to tell her what he knew, but didn't dare. He knew, beyond the shadow of a doubt, that she knew nothing of her father's perfidy. In his state of anxiety, he realized that anything could happen, but that it was more likely that her father would be arrested, and that she might be free. "Apolonia, do you trust me?"

She stared at him. "Yes. Yes, I do. Why?"

He held both her hands in his. He whispered past her ear. "If you trust me, then wait."

She pulled back. Confusion showed. "Wait? Wait for what?"

"My sweet Apolonia, wait for things to change. Wait—"

"I don't understand." She shook her head as annoyance and frustration swept over her. She pulled her hands back and waved her arms in frustration. "Oh—!"

"Apolonia, if you trust me, then please do and say nothing. Let no one know of our love. Behave normally. You will see. Will you do this?"

"Yes, but—"

It was at that moment that they heard a rap on the door. Apolonia went white. Jesse turned toward the door. He looked at her, then walked slowly to the opening. He raised the latch slowly, and pulled the door back to peer around the edge.

Ermelina pushed her way in, closed the door quietly, and turned to look at the two lovers. Apolonia bent forward and brought her hands up to cover her mouth. Her eyes shut, she exclaimed, almost under her breath, "¡Ay, Diós!"

Jesse said, "Ermelina, we—"

"Shh!" she said. She looked at the two of them, her face firm with resolve. "I know. I am an old woman, but I am not deaf and blind. I am not stupid. I know when a young man and a young woman fall in love. I have done so." She paused as she wagged her finger. "But now, there is danger. Should your father or Federico find you, it would be bad for both."

Apolonia, in shock, recovered and looked up, her jaw dropped open. Jesse, aghast, looked at Ermelina, then Apolonia, then back.

"You must leave here immediately, Apolonia, while your father, Federico and that horrid man, that *Pendejo Tejano*, confer behind closed doors. Come, my child."

Jesse, wildly confused, said. "Thank you—"

"Don't thank me yet, young man." She stuck her finger in his face. " We have work to do." She looked at both. "We will find a way." She paused, then, " In my life, I was denied. You, Apolonia, will not be so." She went to the door, opened it. Looked out, then beckoned Apolonia to follow.

As the girl passed Jesse, they touched each other's hands. Just before the doorway, she turned and mouthed a goodbye. He nodded with a reassuring smile.

Jesse unbelted his pistol and stowed it with the carbine, then left the room. As he passed the closed door to Noriega's study, he stopped and pondered. He backed up, and in a loud voice said, "*Ermelina*, do you know where the master of the house is? I would speak with him."

There was no immediate response, but after a short time, Ermelina appeared in the hall. "Ah, is that you, *señor* Landry? *Momentito*." Then she proceeded toward him.

In a voice equally as loud for the purpose of being overheard, she said, "I will tell him you seek him. Is there a way I might help you?"

"Ah, no," Jesse answered. "I will wait. Nothing important. I will speak with him when we meet. Thank you."

"You are most welcome, sir."

They both remained in place for another ten seconds while they waited for a response to their ruse, which did not materialize. Both parted in opposite directions.

Jesse left the house through the rear exit, circled the plaza as he watched for people he knew, and headed for the *cantina*. Maestas was not there, so he proceeded to the Archuleta house. He found Maestas outside, talking to an older woman. He introduced Jesse to her as his cousin Rosa.

Maestas excused himself and took Jesse aside. "My cousin, Manuel, and a friend wait in the *bosque*."

"Have you told them?" Jesse asked.

"No. I waited for you."

Jesse nodded. "Good. We go now?"

"Yes."

Maestas returned to his cousin, who was busy hoeing her garden. He spoke with her, awarded her a kiss on her cheek, and came back to Jesse. They then set out on foot along the main irrigation ditch, north, away from the village.

Two men waited among the cottonwoods. One, a young man in his early twenties, Manuel, who wore a broad-brimmed straw hat, held the reins of a horse. The other, nineteen, squatted next to a nearby tree. He stood as Jesse and Maestas approached. All four shook hands attendant with introductions, their voices subdued.

Both of the conspirators checked their surroundings. Since Maestas was their familiar, he spoke first, and asked them to listen to what the man from the capitol had to say.

As Jesse laid out the situation, the two men expressed first surprise, then anger, then resolve. They swore allegiance and secrecy, and to stay with the effort until a final resolution. The teen-aged boy, who showed maturity, agreed to take the first shift at the mouth of Tijeras canyon. He told them he had relatives who would allow him to stand watch on their property at that location. The older of the two said he would find ways to monitor the plaza and the roads that lead to it. He suggested bringing in two more locals, one a woman, who would watch and listen in the *cantina*. Both of these, based on his testimony, had experienced run-ins with the despised *Tejano* gringos.

The new crew members wanted to know how soon there might be a resolution, and what the role of the gringo army might be. Jesse explained his relationship to the army through Lieutenant Beckner without naming him.

They agreed upon a system of communication which involved, among other things, signals, code words and messaging techniques. They all shook hands again, this time with a new-born sense of camaraderie.

Maestas said he would wait at the Archuleta house for the men his father had promised. He assured Jesse he would abide by the same rules related to confidentiality they had followed to that point.

Jesse headed back for the Noriega house, in part to appear unconcerned, in part to see Noriega. As he approached the plaza, he saw Pulver and Cat as they rounded the corner of the great house, both still astride their mounts, both moving at a leisurely pace. Satisfied they had not seen him, he crossed the plaza quickly for the front door this time. That was in no small part to maintain a posture of innocence against the background of the situation at hand.

The two men who had taken the contraband guns to Santa Fé went to the outbuilding where they were lodged. There, they unburdened their horses, saw to their feed and water, then retired to the small room after relieving themselves.

Pulver found his pipe, stoked it with tobacco, then went outside to sit on an old cottonwood tree stump that served as a combination chopping block and chicken beheading station. If he had known of the latter purpose, he would have eschewed its relative comfort.

Cat came up to him and stood nearby. "Smells right fine," he said. He rolled an unlit cheroot around in his mouth.

"Thank yew, Cat. I growed the tobakkie my ownself." He peered up at the black man with one eye closed.

"Figured you had. That's why I said it."

"Mm."

"What do we do now, Pulver? We head back to Texas?" Cat looked at the sky and the trees.

Pulver sucked more smoke into his lungs, pulled the pipe out of his mouth, looked at the glowing weed, and said, "I truly don't know, Cat. Fact is, I feel a certain calm comfort here. These folks hereabouts tend to leave us alone. Especially you."

Cat kicked the dirt at his feet. "I a-gree, Pulver. So, what are you sayin'?"

"I am saying, Cat, that mebbe we should tarry some."

"Sounds good. Yep."

"We need to replenish our purses, though. That or git employment." Pulver leaned to one side and tapped the pipe bowl against the stump.

"Might be a bit difficult."

Pulver stared away at nothing, a philosophical expression on his face. "I believe we need to speak with our employer and settle up."

"Y'ore full 'o good i-dees, Pulver."

"Thank yew."

"And where do we find that fine gentleman?" Cat asked.

"I suspect at the sister's place. Yonder." He pointed with the stem of the pipe.

"And so?"

"And so, I will seek him out." Pulver rose, beat the embers from the pipe bowl, went inside to deposit it there, then returned. "I will proceed now."

"I'm proud 'o yew." Cat nodded heavily and scratched an area of the fresh, scraggly beard that grew on his cheeks.

"That's all I need from yew, Cat. Pride in me." He turned and walked away as he adjusted his worn-out hat.

As Pulver entered the corner of the plaza, he saw someone exit the Noriega *portal* in his peripheral vision. When he realized it was the master of the house, he deviated to his right and slowed. He stopped alongside a tree and watched as Noriega crossed the plaza toward his sister's house, apparently oblivious to the rest of the world. When Pulver understood that the man was not moving toward the front of Alma's compound, rather the rear, he decided to follow. He stayed back enough to ensure that Noriega not see him. Pulver's impression was that Noriega was too intense to realize he was watched. From the southeast corner of the outer wall, Pulver observed Noriega enter the property through the personnel gate. When he figured the gate was closed, he moved quickly for the opening and stopped. He was surprised when he heard two male voices on the other side. He recognized both. Added to that was a third voice; that of a woman.

He listened for two minutes, then crept away, bent over in shock and surprise at what he had heard. When he was safely away from the gate, as he continued to move slowly, as though in a trance, he muttered under his breath, "Shee-ut!"

37

Roberto greeted Jesse as he walked through the Noriega front door. The little boy chattered happily about his day and play, to which Jesse responded positively. He picked the boy up and threw him over his shoulder so that both his short legs straddled Jesse's neck, then bounced up and down as he moved along the hall. He made horse noises to the child's delight.

Ermelina spotted them. She signaled Jesse, then moved toward the play partners. Jesse let Roberto down, who went to Ermelina to put his arms around her leg. She smoothed the tot's hair as she looked at Jesse. "There is a gentleman to see you." Her faced became serious.

Jesse cocked his head. "Oh?"

"Yes. He is in the master's study." She lowered her voice. "It is Federico."

Jesse nodded at Ermelina, who bent her head to one side as a sign of resignation.

"I will see him," he said.

Ermelina came in close. She whispered, "Apolonia cries in her room."

Jesse pulled in and released deep breath. "I see." He paused. "I will meet with him now."

The man stood up as Jesse entered the room. He was shorter than Jesse, tended to baldness, with a slight paunch. With his general appearance and the lines in his face, Jesse reckoned him to be in his late forties or early fifties. Jesse went to him.

"Jesse Landry. *Con mucho gusto.*"

"*Soy Federico Navarro. Igualmente.*"

Although taken aback by the man's appearance and demeanor, he recovered to say, "I understand you have been traveling."

They both sat.

"Yes. On business for myself and for *Don* Nerio. Past the Mississippi River."

"I see. And you return with goods?"

"Not this trip. Negotiations. Yes." He smiled in what Jesse sensed as disingenuous.

"Successful, I trust?" Jesse shifted on his chair in an attempt to couch his unease.

"Of course." He hesitated. "Nerio asked that I meet with you. I understand you are now the owner and proprietor of you father's emporium in Santa Fé." He raised his head to peer at Jesse in a manner that appeared imperious; almost demeaning.

Jesse looked away, curbed his irritation, then looked at Navarro. "That would seem to be the case, *señor* Navarro."

"Ah, yes," Navarro continued, "perhaps we can engage in business."

"Exactly what is your business, Mr. Navarro?" Jesse cocked his head to one side.

"Why, I negotiate deals."

"Deals?"

"Yes. I arrange buy and sell agreements between Mr. Noriega and others in the east."

Jesse ruminated. "And in Texas?"

"Yes. Of course, Texas."

Jesse put on an innocent smile. "I see. When were you last in Texas?"

"Two weeks past." He paused, frowned, and bent his head to one side in a question. "Why do you enquire?"

Jesse raised his eyebrows to continue the innocence act. "No reason. Curious only." He paused, then, "Do you expect much commerce with Texas? Between *señor* Noriega and parties there?" He waited three seconds, then, "Perhaps I might have an interest."

Navarro became uncomfortable as Jesse pressed him. "Why, yes, I think that is the case. Yes." He looked down at his fingers as he fiddled with them, then said, "In fact, I believe most of his business will be with factors in Texas." He smiled smugly, then burped.

Jesse opened his mouth to speak as Navarro continued. "I believe the *patrón* wishes to introduce you to certain of the gentlemen there." He paused. "To improve your business."

"Of course." Jesse waited as he framed his next question. "Do you enjoy dealing with the *Tejanos, señor* Navarro?"

Navarro returned to his habit of looking down at his nervous fingers. He looked up at Jesse. "May I be honest, *señor* Landry?"

"Please."

Navarro looked toward the open door, then back. "When I am truthful, as I am now, I must say that I do not. They tend to brashness and a sense of superiority. I, myself, have overheard them speak poorly of us. I have overheard them speak of their belief that this territory is, after all, theirs to take and keep. However, in many ways, it is easier to do business closer. In the end, we do not wish to marry their daughters." He executed a tight smile.

"Of course. Interesting," Jesse said. He watched Navarro closely, and decided in that moment that the man who sat across from him was ignorant of Noriega's perfidy; that he was unaware of the plan afoot.

Navarro got up slowly. Jesse suspected that he suffered an ailment in one of his legs.

"Now, I must ask your leave, *señor* Landry. It has been my pleasure." He did not extend his hand.

Jesse took this to mean that Navarro saw him as lesser, a thought he brushed off quickly.

It was then that they both heard a sound from the hallway. Navarro looked past Jesse, who turned to see Bonifacio come into the room.

"*¡Mi hermano!*" Bonifacio shouted.

"*¡Ay, Bonifacio! ¡¿Como estás, hombre?!*" Navarro returned the greeting. "So good to see you at last!"

"You are well, Bonifacio? I heard you chased off a band of those filthy Apache, and were wounded for your trouble."

Bonifacio avoided Jesse's look, which moved from shock to an instantaneous acceptance and understanding of the dynamic between the two men. He also chafed internally at Bonifacio's lie.

Bonifacio hugged Navarro. He used his right hand and arm to caress Navarro's back for a period of time that Jesse considered odd. He turned away in embarrassment.

Bonifacio released Navarro, who was also taken aback at young Noriega's demonstration of affection for his assumptive future brother-in-law.

Bonifacio stepped back and looked at Jesse. "*Señor* Landry."

Jesse executed a small bow from the waist. "Sir." He looked at Navarro, then Bonifacio. "I leave you gentlemen now. You have much to discuss." He acknowledged both, turned and walked from the room.

Pulver beckoned a puzzled Cat away from their lodging and toward the river *bosque*. Cat bleated his request to know why Pulver was so insistent that they remove themselves as they marched quickly along. Pulver, who looked behind several times, remained silent.

When they reached a thicket where they would not be seen or overheard, Pulver leaned into the black man's face. "Cat, yew gotta learn what I heard!"

Cat lurched his head back and tossed it around. "Whaaat-thee-helll are yew goin' on about, Pulver?! Jee-zuz Christ a-mighty, yew act as though the world was comin' to the end!"

"Listen to me, Cat! We got us a gen-u-wine problem! Listen to me!"

"Okay! Okay, goddamnit! I'm listenin'!"

"Listen. I moseyed on over to the sister's establishment, when I seen this Noriega feller go there. But he went the back way. I follered, Cat, and I heard 'em beyond the back gate. An' what was they sayin'? I will tell yew. They was sayin' what them guns is fer. Cat, them guns we trucked here and stored yonder and in Santa Fee ain't fer sale to local farmers. No, sir. Them guns are fer a war!"

Cat reared back and looked at Pulver as though he had gone insane. "Whaaaat?!"

"I'm sayin' the truth, Cat! War. They's plannin' to take over!"

"Who?! Who's gonna take over?!"

"Texas, that's who!"

"They said that?!"

"They did. Upon my mama's grave! They's a plan to do just that!"

Cat stared at Pulver, then turned and looked away. He pondered, then looked at his partner again. "I ain't got no love fer Texicans. They treat me dirty when they are able. These folks hereabouts leave me be. I don't like it."

"Well, truth be told, old sod, I don't like it neither. They been right kindly to us in this territory."

Cat lowered his voice. "I vote we tell someone."

Pulver was slow to comment. "Shee-ut. Who do we tell?"

"Question is, who do we trust? That Jesse feller?"

"Hell's fire, Cat 'twas his place we took that shipment." Pulver's voice reached a high pitch.

"You have that right." Cat thought, then, "Soldiers on yonder hill? 'Cross the river?"

"Mm, not too sure about that, Cat. They'd think us mad and place us under arrest. Ship us back to Texas real quick-like."

Cat poked Pulver's chest with his finger. "What if Jesse was unaware of what was in that wagon? They made a secret of it. Hell, if it was fer sale, they'd be open. When we took it. They made 'em wait. 'Member that?"

"I do, indeed." Pulver hesitated. "Yup, our best chance."

"I think I know how to do it, Pulver."

"Oh, yeah?"

Pulver and Cat walked back to the Noriega place slowly as they conferred along the way. When they were in sight of the animal pens, they spotted Ustacio, then Jesse, caring for the horses and in light conversation.

Pulver took the first action at Cat's urging. He approached Jesse, then stopped several feet away. He took his hat off and held it in both hands. "Mr. Landry, sir?"

Jesse turned and moved toward Pulver. "Yes, Pulver. What is it?"

"Well, Mr. Landry—"

Jesse moved closer. He shook his head. "You don't have to call me mister, Pulver. Jesse works just fine."

"Thank you, Mr—er, Jesse. I do have a question."

"Of course. What is it?"

"Well, yew see, I was wonderin' what the price might be for someone such as me fer one 'o them carbines."

Jesse, shocked, stepped closer to Pulver, looked around, spotted Ustacio who was oblivious, then back to stare at his questioner. "What carbines, Pulver?"

"Why, the ones we done delivered. To yore place 'o business. They is fer sale, is they not?"

Jesse stepped to within two feet of Pulver. "You are—were—aware that there were guns—carbines—in that wagon?!"

Pulver, who continued his brave act, said, "Why, shore, Mr.—Jesse. Ain't they to sell to folks?"

Jesse looked beyond Pulver at Cat, who stood back several yards, then returned his gaze to Pulver. "Is that what you think, Pulver?"

Pulver decided that this was his moment. He swung his head around to glance at Cat, then back. He looked at the dirt at his feet, then up. "Truth be told, Jesse, I do not."

Jesse was silent, then, "What do you think they're for, Pulver?" He bored into Pulver's eyes.

"Well, Jesse, I b'lieve they're to start a war. Yessir, that's what I b'lieve." He licked his dry lips.

"Pulver, did you and Cat know what those guns were brought here for?" Jesse's voice had become a whisper.

"Matter 'o fact, Mr. Jesse Landry, sir, we did not. No, siree, we did not, and that is a fact."

Jesse rubbed his chin, looked away, then back. "You did not know?"

"No, sir, not" He shook his head in a wide arc.

"You thought they were to sell locally?"

"Yes, sir. We did that."

"Why—why, Pulver, were they crated and marked as they were? If they were to be sold?"

"Why, we figured so's folks wouldn't steal 'em. Thievery is all about." Pulver moved on with his next question. "You knew what they was fer. Right?"

Jesse shook his head. "No, Pulver, my friend, I did not."

Pulver relaxed into a wide grin, glanced back at Cat with a short nod, then back. He put his hat on and adjusted it. "Are you for a war, Jesse?"

"No, Pulver, I am not. Are you?"

"No sir, Mr. Jesse Landry, I am not. I may be from Texas, but I am not. We was paid to carry them guns here, but the true reason was kept from us. Yes, sir. And no, I am not. Nor is my partner, that Negro feller, Cat, yonder."

Jesse could do no more at that juncture than nod and smile. "Wait here, Pulver." He walked toward Ustacio, stopped, then returned. He looked around, at the ground, then up. "Pulver, you know where the *cantina* is?"

"Yes, sir. Been there twice't fer a swig 'er two. 'An some grub."

"You and Cat, go back to your room, wait awhile, then go to the *cantina*. Go inside. Wait for me. When you see me, leave and walk north, along the big ditch bank to the trees beyond. Make yourselves scarce. Hidden. Wait for me. Does that suit?"

Pulver thought a moment. "Yesser, it does. It suits."

"Good. See you soon."

Forty-five minutes later, Jesse entered the *cantina*, where he spotted Cat and

Pulver, seated at a table. He ignored them as they downed their drinks, got up and left. Another half hour passed before Jesse and Maestas arrived at the cottonwood encircled clearing where Cat and Pulver waited.

Jesse introduced the two travelers to an amazed Francisco Maestas. They spoke for several minutes, all the while cautiously watching for anyone who might appear. They were alone.

Jesse explained what they knew and the rough plan to Cat and Pulver. He suggested they avoid any conflict, and certainly maintain an air of innocence at all times, but to be ready for trouble, should there be any, given that they both carried sidearms. He also explained that they were invited to meetings bound to be held shortly after the arrival of their army contact, at which time, plans would be finalized. He also asked them to serve as additional eyes and ears for the group.

38

*F*irst Lieutenant Harold Beckner rode onto the Maestas property in El Llanito toward the end of the day. He was in mufti, but his field uniform was carefully packed in a saddlebag should the need arise.

Javier, the youngest of the three Maestas children, was outside, feeding the chickens. When he spotted Beckner, he dropped what he was doing and ran to him. "Beckner! Beckner! Welcome! I am happy to see you!"

Beckner looked down at the teen-aged boy with a broad smile. "Glad to see you, Javier! Thank you!" He reached down to shake the boy's hand as he moved his eyes surreptitiously, hoping to see Mercedes.

"Please come in. My family will be happy to see you," Javier blurted.

Beckner dismounted as Javier took the reins.

"Go in. Go in. I will see to your horse."

"Thank you, Javier. I will do that. And thank you for tending the horse." He began to reach into his pocket for coin.

"Oh, no, please do not do that. It is my pleasure, *señor.*"

Beckner withdrew his hand and pointed his finger at the boy. "All right, Javier, but one of these days!"

Javier grinned at the army officer. "Yes, sir! Now, go in. My mother has a fine meal waiting."

Beckner rapped on the outer door that lead to the kitchen. Four seconds later, it swung open to reveal Mercedes standing there. She began to say something that angled toward a reprimand to her younger brother, whom she thought she would encounter, but when she saw the officer, she stopped short and started to shriek. She brought both hands up to her bouquet-like mouth and stanched the sound. Her eyes revealed her true reaction. She spun away with her shock and surprise.

"*¿Quien es?*" Her mother asked from beyond the door.

"The lieutenant, *mamá.* Lieutenant Beckner." She turned back to face him. Her face lit up. Her hands remained over her smiling mouth.

"Oh! How nice! Mercedes, let the man in. Surely he is hungry and thirsty after his long ride." Filomena came to the door and crowded her daughter aside as Beckner entered. She greeted him with a light hug and an equally-contained kiss on the cheek. She stepped back, looked at him, shot her smitten daughter a sharp glance, then said, "Welcome, Lieutenant! Please come in. You are staying to dinner!"

Beckner, thrown off balance, said, "Thank you, Mrs. Maestas. I will accept your kind offer of dinner. I'm famished from the trail. But I must leave early in the morning for Albuquerque. I am to meet with Francisco and Jesse Landry." He tried to keep his eyes on Filomena while he avoided looking at the girl. He glanced her way briefly, and saw the desperate expression on her face. He wanted badly to respond, but stayed silent.

Mercedes, frustrated beyond her tolerance, turned away, went into the kitchen, spun around once, then disappeared into the innards of the old house.

During dinner, along with excited chatter from Javier, there ensued polite, but mundane talk between Beckner, Sabino and Filomena. Beckner was unsure if Sabino had been brought into the knowledge of the secret arms cache, and Sabino was not sure he should say anything to the army officer, especially not in the presence of the uninitiated. The mutual secrecy was not breeched.

The chat did not last long after dessert of flan and the last of the local wine. Beckner was invited to bed down in Francisco's room. He tried valiantly to resist in favor of the place he last slept under their hospitality, but in the end, lost, and agreed to stay the night under their main roof.

Beckner was deep in sleep well after midnight when he was awakened by the tiny, nearby sound of iron hinge parts working against each other. His instinct was to reach for his sidearm. In the next instant, there was pressure on the side of the narrow bed, and a light hand on his chest.

"Lieutenant Beckner—Harold," Mercedes whispered.

Beckner jerked his head up part way. "Mercedes! Wha—?!"

"Shh," she whispered. She put her fragrant hand over his mouth. "I wanted to see you."

"Mercedes—"

"I know, it is bad of me, I shouldn't—"

"No, Mercedes, I wanted to see you!"

"You did?!"

"Yes! I wanted to see you. Speak with you. Oh, God, Mercedes, I want to hold you."

"Oh, Harold, I want you to hold me!" She bent her body at the waist and brought her upper torso over his as he wrapped his arms around her awkwardly.

Her hair flowed over and alongside his head, and her cheek was next to his. He drew her face to his and kissed her. She moaned and joined in the kiss with fervor.

With her mouth no more than an inch from his, she whispered, "I love you."

Beckner answered, "I love you. I have done little but think of you since we met. You are so beautiful. You are so sweet. I—"

"I have thoughts of you often." She hesitated, then lay her cheek against his again. "Oh, I am so confused. My father—my mother—they—"

"Mercedes, listen to me. Listen. I leave in the morning for Albuquerque. I am to meet with your brother and others. I will return with Francisco. Mercedes, he knows of my affection for you. When I return—"

She put her arms around his neck, kissed him, then raised her head. "My parents. They will object, *mi amor*." She sat up and looked away into the faint light of the room.

Beckner raised up on his elbow. "Mercedes, I will fight for you. For us. Do you trust me to return and fight for you?"

She paused. "Yes. Yes, I do. I do."

He pulled himself up, such that he was sitting next to her and they kissed again.

"I want you to make love to me," she whispered.

He paused, then, "Mercedes, I desire you in ways I have never known before. We will be together. If I have to fight everyone in the territory." He stroked her cool face. "Go now. Wave to me in the morning. I will return."

"Yes. I will. I will think of nothing but you." She touched his cheek, stood and wafted away.

Sunlight had begun to streak over the crest of the mountain when Beckner was up in the saddle, Javier dutifully at his side after helping with water and feed. Filomena and Mercedes, who controlled her emotions well, had provided him with a hearty, chile-laced breakfast, a food to which he was becoming rapidly accustomed. Mercedes also made sure he had more victuals in his saddle bags, along with a crushed flower.

At the same time, another man also set out on horseback, he from the *Doña* Alma de Castañega house in Albuquerque. His name was Ruben Salazár, and he carried a sealed letter from *Don* Nerio de Noriega, with his signature. The letter provided for the movement and sequester of the contraband arms from the Landry Mercantile to the Landry warehouse. Salazár was aware of the contents of the secret vault beneath the wagon, but did not know their true purpose. If he hurried, he would be in Santa Fé by nightfall.

He also could not have predicted that he would meet two gentlemen at the Mercantile, presumably from somewhere in the East, who had plied the dangerous Santa Fé Trail, interested in establishing trade relations with the Landrys. In fact, they would be Second Lieutenants Townsend and Carruthers, posing in mufti, arranged for by First Lieutenant Beckner, assigned under agreement with Major Middleton, to spy on the otherwise innocent Noriega-Castañega agent.

Beckner rode west to the Rio Grande, forded the slow, shallow, brown stream at roughly the same place he had earlier when accompanied by Francisco Maestas and Jesse. He turned south to navigate the thick *bosque* along the river verge, and made sure to avoid the farm community of Corrales. From there, he went directly to the army encampment bivouacked on the bluff that overlooked Albuquerque on the west bank of the river.

Captain Marchant greeted Beckner with a genuine smile, a traded military salute and a hearty handshake. The two officers then sat to share a sparse field ration meal and discuss Beckner's findings. Beckner asked Marchant to ready his men, but to take no action until, and unless, asked to do so. It was explained to the captain that Washington wanted to avoid open conflict in the Territory; that it was deemed better to round up any foreign agents and inhabitant conspirators quietly and without violence if at all possible; that plans and covert actions were in place. Given the suspicion and resentment felt by most of the Hispanics toward the presence of the U.S. Army, an overt show of force by same was to be avoided, even though such action would be manifest on their behalf.

He also informed Marchant that a courier had been dispatched to report to the War Department of the findings and actions planned. The memorandum included a suggestion that a diplomatic effort be mounted with the Republic of Texas. That would be to warn them that they faced a possibly damaging military response if they did not cease and desist from their efforts to subvert a Territory of the United States.

Beckner departed from the encampment a short time after sundown, since he desired to slip into Albuquerque unnoticed if possible. With little effort, he rode across the river onto the eastside plain, then threaded his way to the *cantina*. After he secured his horse at the rail and entered, he spotted Maestas, who, by pre-arrangement, was seated alone at a table in a far corner, facing the door.

Beckner sat at a table near the door, ordered a drink, then sat. A minute later, Maestas got up and left. He made no eye contact or notice of the army officer as he passed. Beckner finished his drink, placed a coin on the table, rose and left in a leisurely fashion. Maestas was astride his horse near the north corner of the building. When Beckner was in the saddle, Maestas, without a word, set out north along the *acequia madre*. At the Archuleta house, both men were provided with a snack, wine, and a place to bed down.

39

Ruben Salazár had found a decent place on the southern outskirts of Santa Fé, along the Camino Real, to cold-camp over night. In the morning, he was invited to partake of hot food and coffee by a sympathetic family, to whom he gave a portion of his travel expenses, then made his way to the Landry Mercantile. There, after he beat on the door to the business, he was greeted by Incarnación, who feigned annoyance, and who, after he determined who Salazár represented, was allowed in. The faithful Landry employee was shown the identity and instructional letter. To align himself to the plan as set out by Lieutenant Beckner, he feigned passing interest, then informed the visitor that he must wait to complete his errand, since more important issues required attention. Salazár, given his status, was invited to join Francesca in the kitchen for hot chocolate while he cooled his heels. It was then that Incarnación left the premises by the rear gate to seek out Townsend and Carruthers.

After breakfast with the Archuleta family, all of whom had been invited into the ring of the informed, and who were, as a result, fervent in their resolve to aid in bringing down the insurrection-bound plotters, Beckner and Maestas left to meet with their local spies. That included Pulver and Cat, much to the surprise of the local volunteers, who were well received and who bonded quickly. Beckner explained that they must wait for word from Santa Fé before they took action; that they would continue to watch the ramparts for suspicious movements, especially the Noriega and Castañega households. They then disbursed to take up their separate vigils.

Jesse, after a troubled night, arose, performed his ablutions, then, with trepidation, went to the kitchen. Ustacio and Ermelina were there as they carried out their well-studied duties. Jacinta worked over a bowl of *masa* in preparation for making tortillas. He greeted the older two by name, then smiled at Jacinta, who looked down and away in the manner of her people. Ermelina turned and awarded him a knowing smile, while Ustacio nodded his head, then turned away to complete his chores.

Sleepy Roberto came in and went directly to Jesse, who hauled him up onto his lap as he sat at the table. Ermelina upbraided the child, went to him and lifted him away from Jesse to plunk him onto his special Ustacio-constructed stool. She smoothed his unruly hair, kissed his head, then set food out for him.

It was then that Apolonia entered the room. Ermelina, who knew and understood all, reacted by mumbling a greeting, then turned away to avoid showing her hand. Apolonia danced her eyes about the room, went to Roberto to buss him as Ermelina had, then awarded Jesse a passing greeting. His response was to dip his head in a cursory, modified bow, then continued to eat.

The master of the house, Noriega, entered as Jesse rose from his chair. He looked about, said "Good morning" to Apolonia and Jesse, but ignored the little boy and the servants. He stood for a moment, more sober than any in the room had seen him in a long while. After several silent seconds, he addressed Jesse. "Mr. Jesse Landry, sir. I hope this splendid morning finds you well. Ah—I would speak with you. Please join me in the dining room where I will take my morning repast." He nodded, looked at the floor, swivelled and left.

Noriega sat at the end of the long dining table as he was served by the young Navajo girl. Jesse sat to his left, nothing in front of him, his hands in his lap as he attempted to control his thoughts.

Noriega took a bite of his food, sipped his chocolate-altered coffee, set the cup down, then spoke. "Jesse, as your partner, since you were not present so that I could confer with you, I took the liberty of sending a long-standing order from your dear, departed father to the—uh, your mercantile."

Jesse found it easier than he imagined to look at the man and speak. "I see, señor Noriega. And what was that, if I may ask?"

Noriega treated himself to another bite. "Ah, yes, it was a dozen casks of wine. Long overdue, mind you, but now satisfied." He created, then lost, a brief smile, then studied another fork load before inserting it into his mouth. He started to speak, his mouth engaged in mastication. "Mm-mmf—I—We—" He paused to clear his mouth, applied his big cloth napkin, and continued, "I sent instructions on your behalf to have the shipment sent to your warehouse. I'm sure you will understand and forgive me for my presumption." He looked directly at Jesse to wait for a reply.

Jesse nodded with a smile. "Certainly, *Don* Nerio. I concur whole-heartedly. We are indeed partners, and I would hope and trust that we continue in this vein." He nodded again to seal the statement. "I thank you for taking that measure in my absence. And allow me to apologize for that."

"No need. No need at all, my son. I hope you don't object to my addressing you thus. After all, you are my partner's son. You are—he was—"

Jesse held up his hand. "I understand. No need to—I am honored, sir."

Noriega pushed his plate away two inches. "We must speak more of our business. And it occurs to me that your purchases from El Paso languish here. We must see that they make their way safely and soon." He paused to cogitate, then, "Do you have plans to move those goods? Soon?"

"I do. Yes." Jesse thought quickly. "I await arrangements with Maestas in El Llanito for sheep hides. I spoke with him during my absence from your home and hearth. The reason for my absence, you see."

"Of course. Of course. Sheep skins." He hesitated. "You will add them on your way north?"

"Yes. That is the plan. They should be ready soon. I await word."

"Excellent. I think you will be an excellent merchant. Your dear father taught you well."

"It is my hope to live up to his name and his standards, *Don* Nerio."

"You will. I have no doubt, sir." He sipped his cooling drink. "Now I must excuse myself. Much to do today. More buyers, more sellers." He stood.

Jesse stood as well, and they clasped hands. He understood from Noriega's eyes and body language that Noriega expected him to leave first. He went into the hall, slowed, then headed for the sitting room, which faced the plaza. He flattened himself against the wall next to the hall door and waited. Not five minutes later, he observed Noriega leave the house and cross the plaza to his sister's house.

He came to the door, peered in both directions, then moved for his room. As he turned the corner into the hallway that lead to his room, he saw Apolonia standing close to the outer door.

She moved toward him silently, and they both darted into his room.

He closed the door. "My love," he whispered as they embraced and kissed.

"Of what did you speak with my father?"

Jesse shook his head. "Of business. That and nothing more."

She released him and went to the window, where she looked out. Her voice was laden with sadness. "I wished—dreamed—hoped—that it would have been about us."

He came up behind her and encircled her waist. His voice was low and soothing. "I asked you to trust me. Do you not?"

She turned to face him, her face distressed. "Oh, I do trust you Jesse, but—"

"Yes?"

"I am so, so sad. So afraid." She shook her head and started to weep.

He raised his arms to her shoulders. "Apolonia, I asked you to trust me. That things would change. They will. Soon. I promise." He pulled a kerchief from his trousers and wiped her tears.

She sniffed. "You promise?"

"I promise you on all that is sacred. You will see. Now, please, let me dry your tears. Look to the future. You will see." He worked hard to avoid any suggestion that the future would hold bad along with good. "Apolonia, where is Federico? I have not seen him."

She looked up at him as he wiped her wet face. "He stays with my aunt. He cannot be here. Because—"

"I understand. Of course. The bans."

She nodded and sniffed again.

"Go now, my love. We have good Ermelina with us, but we don't know who else to trust. I will see you again soon."

Townsend and Carruthers, dressed for the part, arrived at the Landry Mercantile soon after Incarnación returned from advising them of the appearance of the suspected insurgent agent.

In the mercantile office, Salazár, nervous and put off by the delay, stood by while Incarnación stalled for time as he worked with the two army agents over phony trade deals, import-export, and tariff questions. Finally, as he reacted precisely as they hoped he would, Salazár begged Incarnación to help him move the contraband wagon. With the assumption that the phony eastern businessmen would be interested, Incarnación invited them to attend. Salazár, still in the dark, did not object. The phony businessmen agreed that they would most certainly like to see the extra storage facilities and the goods stored there.

Cipriano helped Incarnación hitch the mules, then sat with him on the bench. Salazár followed on horseback, while Townsend and Carruthers rode the tail of the wagon, behind, and along with, the wine casks.

In the warehouse, all five men helped to unload the wine casks. There was a brief period while each looked at the others, then, on cue, Incarnación suggested to Salazár that they break into the secret compartment. Salazár did not object, which surprised the others. He asked for tools, which Incarnación provided. The Landry mercantile employee proceeded to pull back the boards that hid the weapons.

As the first of the carbines were pulled from the wagon, Townsend stepped forward. "Let me see that," he said.

Salazár was taken aback, but did not react with surprise, and handed the officer one of the weapons.

Carruthers moved next to Townsend, and the two inspected the carbine.

"This is military class," Townsend said. He looked at Salazár.

Salazár shrugged and raised his eyebrows. He looked at Incarnación for guidance, then back at the two officers.

Townsend handed the gun to Cipriano, who set it aside as the unloading ceased. He looked at Salazár. "You did not know about these weapons? What they are for?" He cocked his head.

Salazár answered, "To sell? What else?" He held out his arms in a question.

Townsend, Carruthers and the two men from Landry's all looked at each other, then Salazár.

Salazár shook his head. "What is this?! What is happening?!"

Townsend rubbed his chin, looked down, then up at the hapless man. "Mr. Salazár, is it?"

"Yes..."

"Mr. Salazár, this man is Louis Carruthers. 2nd Lieutenant Louis Carruthers, U.S. Army. I am 2nd Lieutenant James Townsend, also United States Army."

Salazár shook his head. "I don't understand." His draw dropped as he frowned.

"Mr. Salazár, what we have here is a shipment of arms intended for use in an insurrection. Do you know what that means? What that is?"

The poor man shook his head slowly, wide-eyed. "No."

"These guns, Mr. Salazár, are here to start a war against the Territory of New Mexico. A war on the part of the Republic of Texas."

Salazár looked at Incarnación, his face a mask of misery. "¿Qué es este? ¿Qué pasa aquí?"

"*Es verdad, hombre. Una guerra de Tëjas.*" Incarnación nodded deeply as he crossed his arms across his chest.

Ruben Salazár was taken to see Major Middleton, where he was questioned at length. Convinced that he was telling the truth, and after he was sworn to secrecy, he was allowed to leave. It was then arranged for him to return to Albuquerque with Townsend and Carruthers, along with Sergeant Tandy and Private Milton. All the military men wore civilian clothes, but carried identification that linked them to the army.

The five men, four soldiers, one civilian, set out the following morning. All were armed, save for Salazár. When they reached El Llanito, Tandy opined that they should skirt the Maestas property on the way to the river crossing to avoid contact with the family. Private Milton became upset, and let his superior know. He wanted to see Sabino, whom he considered his future partner in the hog business. Townsend and Carruthers managed to suppress good-natured laughter when they learned of the private's plan. Tandy assured him that he would have plenty of time to visit the elder Maestas when the operation in progress was completed.

At the west side army post, Townsend brought Captain Marchant up to date on the situation. He also asked that a very unhappy Salazár be held incognito until such time as his release was authorized by Lieutenant Beckner. Townsend, despite Salazár's protestation, believed, on the one hand, that Salazár truly knew nothing of the Texas plot, and declared he would remain silent, yet felt that his dedication to his mistress might, in the end, outweigh his loyalty to the Territory.

Sergeant Tandy was dispatched to find Beckner.

40

It had been agreed that Maestas would take on the job of posting himself at the *cantina* each evening beginning at sundown for at least an hour. That was to wait for a contact from the party from the capitol. The contact was to enter from the road, stand in the doorway for a minute or so, remove his hat and bang it loudly against his pant leg as though ridding it of highway dust. Were that to fail to draw attention from the watcher, the contact was to go to the bar and simply ask for Francisco Maestas. The latter technique was unneeded, because Maestas spotted the burly sergeant as he acted out the phony dusting ritual.

Maestas rose, imitated the anti-dust routine, which Tandy acknowledged, and headed for the door. When Tandy saw the answer to his test, he turned and went outside. The sergeant stood next to his horse with the reins in his hand as the two greeted each other. Tandy explained what Townsend had asked for.

The two men then went to the Archuleta place where they found Beckner playing cards with three family members. Beckner felt that Jesse's presence and the planning meeting was essential. Maestas accepted the task of tracking him down.

Maestas banged on the great, heavy door of the Noriega manse, a burning taper in his hand against the gloom under the *portal* roof. Little Roberto answered the door, then ran, hopped and skipped away into the innards to look for his new-found friend.

Jesse came to the door, a book in one hand, while Roberto's hand held the other.

Maestas made sure he was loud when he told Jesse he was sorely needed at the *cantina* for a vitally important round of cards and a heated discussion about the speed of certain horses in an up-coming race. Jesse pretended to protest in an equally loud voice, while Roberto watched the two giant figures, awe-struck. Jesse then, loudly, but with fake hesitation, agreed to accompany the noisy visitor. He returned the book to the family library, secured his sidearm, then the two young men made a spectacle of themselves as they shouted and laughed loudly enough for the whole town to be aware of them as they crossed the plaza to join Beckner and Tandy.

Nerio Noriega scowled as he tried to make out the carousing through his study window, then returned to his desk. Roberto ran to find Apolonia in the kitchen, then pulled her to the library where they both watched what little they could see with the flaming orange light of the lantern. Confused, Apolonia wanted to know what Roberto was showing her. He explained in the best way he could how the loud visitor came, and how his friend Jesse had gone with him after putting on his pistol.

Apolonia, confused and shocked, walked slowly back to the kitchen. On the way, her father spoke to her as he stood in the study doorway. When he asked her what was happening, she told him what Roberto had said. He shrugged and re-entered the study and closed the door.

Apolonia continued to the kitchen with Roberto in tow, where she signaled Ermelina that she wished to speak with her. The two women instructed Roberto, on pain of death, or worse, to sit on his stool while they retired to the hall.

"Oh, Ermelina, why does Jesse behave so? I thought he was—"

Ermelina leaned in close to the girl after looking along the hall to ensure privacy. "Listen to me, child. That man, Jesse is, and always will be, who he is! But he is a man. A young man, and young men do what all young men do. It is in their bones. Do not fret." She backed away, checked their surroundings again, then looked at Apolonia sternly. "Now, I have work to do. Go see your mother. She is feeling ill." Ermelina turned toward the kitchen, then muttered to herself, "Again."

Jesse, Maestas, Beckner and Tandy made their way in the dark to the western outpost on the bluff. There, they met in Captain Marchant's tent. Present with the four were the captain, Lieutenants Townsend and Carruthers, and Private Milton. Outside, two troopers stood unnecessary guard. Across the way, a sullen Ruben Salazár festered in a tent with an armed guard nearby.

The meeting lasted little more than an hour. Various plans were agreed upon, then Jesse piped up and said he felt he knew how to wrap matters in a neat bundle. All agreed, and the parties disbursed.

Jesse, Maestas and Beckner returned to Albuquerque, while the rest remained with Marchant and the dragoons.

Pulver and Cat had seen Jesse and Maestas cross the plaza, then meet with two other men.

They found it curious that on the one hand, they appeared possibly drunk, then completely sober as they left the village and crossed the river in conspiratorial silence. Given that the two drovers figured the four had gone to the camp on the west bank, they realized that there might be a connection with the arms shipment. They agreed to take a risk.

As Jesse and Maestas rode into the southern edge of the village, Pulver and Cat were waiting.

When Pulver hailed the two with a whistle and a hiss, both Jesse and Maestas loosed their pistols and pointed them at the sound.

"We're friends," Pulver said in a loud whisper. "Don't shoot."

Jesse and Maestas stopped, and the two waiting men rode slowly into the clearing where the faint light revealed them.

"It's Pulver. And Cat, Mr. Jesse."

Jesse re-holstered his gun. "Pulver! What are you doing here?!"

"Jesse, we seen y'all an' wondered if there ain't nothin' new."

"No, Pulver. And you? And Cat? Have you seen anything? Heard anything?"

Pulver glance at his black partner. "No, but that Rodman feller paid us off and tole us to git back to Texas."

"Will you go back?" Jesse asked.

"No, sir. We aim ta' stay. 'Specially if'n we can find work."

Jesse looked at Maestas. "Well, listen, Pulver, you too, Cat. Let me think about what you've told me. Your decision. Maybe there's something."

"That would be mighty fine, Mr. Jesse," Cat put in. "Mighty fine, indeed."

Jesse paused, then, "Will you both testify to the army?"

"Testify?" Pulver asked.

"Means to tell the story, Pulver," Cat said almost under his breath. He spoke up. "I will, by damn!"

"That's the two of us," Pulver put in.

"It's late," Jesse said. "Tomorrow, then. Stay close and continue to keep your eyes open."

"Whatever we can do," Cat said.

"Goes fer me," Pulver said.

Jesse and Maestas both leaned over in their saddles to shake the hands of the drovers, then all parted with the agreement that they would maintain contact.

In the morning, Jesse made hasty work of breakfast. When finished, he asked to speak with Ermelina.

She followed him into the main hall, then into the westside offshoot hall. "What is it, Jesse?" She hesitated. "Apolonia was upset last night—"

He held up his hand to stop her as he looked back, then at her. "Listen, Ermelina, everything will be clear soon. Please trust me. I need a favor of you."

She cocked her head at him and frowned as he spoke.

Later that morning, shortly before eleven, Apolonia, her mother, Efigenia, and her aunt, Chavela, made their halting way to the San Felipe de Neri church across the plaza. In attendance, as she held up the long skirts worn by the mother and the aunt, was the petite Navajo girl, Jacinta. Inside, all four of the entourage paused at the stoup. Apolonia and her mother made the ritual of dipping and crossing, then Efigenia went through the motions for Chavela. They moved along the aisle, where Apolonia and her mother stopped, kneeled, mouthed a brief prayer, and made the sign of the cross. Chavela, unaware in her child-like state, remained standing in front of Jacinta. Neither of the others moved to engage her in that ritual. They then proceeded toward the front of the church, where they selected a pew on the right side, three rows back.

There was a smattering of people throughout the church, predominantly women. The great hall was silent until a priest appeared, followed by two altar boys. The priest went to the altar to begin the mass.

A few minutes into the ceremony, Apolonia glanced up as a monk, dressed in brown, with a hood over his head, walked slowly along the space between the pews and the outer wall. When he came to the fourth pew, he slowed, then slid onto the pew behind the one where the Noriega contingent sat. He slid across the pew until he was behind Apolonia. With his head bowed and his face in shadow, he reached out and tapped Apolonia gently on her shoulder.

She turned, startled, and began to speak. The monk held his finger to his lips, then handed her a small scrap of folded paper, got up and left. He moved quickly along the central aisle, then across to the left side of the church and back toward the nave, where he disappeared.

Apolonia moved her eyes between him and the paper. She opened it surreptitiously, but needn't have, because Chavela was resident in her own, private infantile universe. After she read the note, Apolonia looked down, her mouth open for a few seconds, then she recovered, looked up, and attempted to re-join the proceedings.

After the mass was over, she waited for her mother to enter the center aisle. "Mother," she said, "I'm going to make confession."

Her mother stared at her in surprise. "It has been a long time, Apolonia. I am so glad."

"Mother, please take Chavela home. I will follow in due time."

"Of course, child. I am not well."

"Yes, mother. I know. I will come to you soon."

She watched the two older women leave as Jacinta trailed behind with the skirts held high, then she turned her head to look toward the confessional. She hesitated another moment, then moved slowly in that direction. She opened the narrow, dark wooden door, stepped in, sat, and pulled the door closed. The grill window was shut, and little light eked in from the cracks and a small opening in the roof of the confessional.

Two minutes passed. Puzzled and frightened, she was about to open the door and rush outside when the panel slid open. She saw the monk with the hood through the grill.

He pulled the dark, heavy cloth covering away from his head and face. "I am Father Maestas, Apolonia. I have a message for you."

Two and a half hours earlier, in Santa Fé, Major Middleton, the U.S. Army Provost, sent a courier with a message to Sheriff Baca. It read:

> Your presence, and that of your principal deputy, are hereby requested in my office forthwith. Unless you and your charge are engaged in serious official business, I expect you within the hour.
> Signed, M. Middleton, Provost

Sheriff Baca and his deputy, Dominguez, obeyed, and appeared quickly in the major's office. They were not invited to sit, so both puzzled men stood nervously and roughly at attention in front of the senior army officer. Seated in a corner as observer and witness, was an infantry captain. Baca and his man were required to sign a statement and oath, which declared that about what they were to learn would not leave their lips, or be revealed to others in any manner, under pain of imprisonment per authority of Territorial Marshall law. In truth, Middleton suspected that he could not back this up, but he trusted that it was something that Baca and Dominguez could not know, or would test. The Declaration was signed by both, and witnessed with the signatures of the major and the captain.

While the two invitees stood, humiliated, Middleton told them, in precise detail, the facts surrounding the death of Evan Landry, the identity of his killer, the resultant defensive gunning down of his assailant at the inn by Jesse, the arms shipments, and its purpose. Middleton announced further that Jesse Landry, his family, employees and associates, were not to be molested, investigated, or otherwise harassed in any way, now or in the future. Nothing was to be said about them in a negative way to others, and that the movements and statements of the sheriff and his deputy would be monitored from time to time.

As the two shaken lawmen left the palace, the stunned silence shared by the two was broken by Dominguez, who tendered his resignation then and there.

The following afternoon, with the church empty, Apolonia, dressed in lace and black, knelt at the altar to offer prayers. She rose, then satisfied that she was alone, went quickly to the confessional, bent over, and slipped a piece of paper between the back wall of the little structure and the exterior adobe wall of the building. She straightened, strode for the outer door, and left.

41

The entire Noriega household and all of the guests were dressed in their finest or the best they could muster.

The three women of the house, Efigenia, Chavela and Apolonia wore silken gowns they had not worn or seen for months or years, topped with *mantillas* pinned to their tight hairdos; those draped with fine Spanish lace. Efigenia and Chavela's were black; Apolonia's white. Alma de Castañega, Nerio's sister, who did not care for her brother's wife, wore only her natural hair pulled up in a bun, and a simple, but expensive cotton dress with a paucity of braid. Nerio de Noriega, his son Bonifacio, and Federico Navarro, Apolonia's intended, wore short, gold-braided jackets, unbuttoned, with cummerbunds around their waists, all in scarlet red. Their pants were cut in the style of Madrid, and their shiny black parade boots reached nearly to their knees. Nerio and Bonifacio sported scroll-handled rapiers manufactured in Spain; Federico attended weaponless. Jesse Landry dressed for the occasion the best he was able, given the fact that the preponderance of his wardrobe was up north, and that he was dressed more for the highway than a formal gathering. That featured a deer skin jacket styled for the highway. Those in attendance, although forgiving and silent on the subject, were not pleased.

Rodman of Texas came wearing a finely-tooled jacket of black leather with a broad, black belt cinched with a large, engraved silver buckle. At his throat was a black string tie in the fashion of the men of New Orleans and Charleston. The parish priest and a nun, one Sister Beatrice, a favorite of the family, arrived dressed as always, in somber black with flashes of white about their throats.

Ustacio, recruited to assist Ermelina and the bustling Navajo girl, Jacinta, was lent a flowing white shirt, a black belt and pants that no longer fit the scion of the house, Bonifacio. Ermelina wore a colorful dress she herself had manufactured, based on a skill taught her by her late mother. The servant boy, Pepe, was left to his devices, instructed to remain hidden in the kitchen, while Ustacio and Ermelina served the great dining table, and Jacinta cleared when required.

A roast pig and three chickens were prepared for the feast. Hot tortillas, butter, honey, chocolate, vegetables, apples and cherries, rounded out the meal. Wine, red and white, along with Mexican brandy at the terminus, wet the lips, principally of the men, and that of Alma, who liked to flaunt tradition. Flan, *natías* and fruit appeared for dessert.

Noriega senior sat at one end of the long table, with his imperious wife at the opposite end. On Nerio's right sat Navarro; on his left, his daughter, Apolonia, placed to face her putative future consort. Next to her was her brother, Bonifacio, who kept his head high and his eyes in motion with the dangerous and dreadful secrets he harbored. To Efigenia's right was the priest. To her left, sat unaware and fidgety Chavela, who stared straight ahead as she mumbled conversation with herself. Next to the priest was the uneasy nun, whose age no one who knew her was able to discern, and who smiled defensively throughout, as though a shy teenager.

Jesse sat half-way along the table on Noriega's right, directly across from the Texican. He did his best to appear innocent and unknowing, but safe in the knowledge that his table mate knew less of what his future held.

At the end of the dinner, as the late afternoon sun drenched the plaza beyond the long *portal*, and after Ustacio, Ermelina and Jacinta had removed the last of the plates and dishes, Noriega stood, tapped his half-full wine flute and looked at the assemblage along the table. "My dear friends and family, as you know, we are gathered here this fine day to announce the betrothal of my beautiful, loving daughter, Apolonia, to my dear friend and associate, *Don* Federico Navarro. Please welcome him into our family and our village." He gestured to both, raised his glass, held it out, then drank.

Light applause ensued, and all who held drinks, sipped.

Navarro stood, looked around the room, bowed several times, then pushed his chair back. He then went to a surprised and somewhat flustered Efigenia, took her hand and kissed it. His reward for the gesture was a grudging nod of her head and a sour smile. He returned to his place and remained standing. He then made a short speech, in which he promised fealty to Apolonia, the house of Noriega, and to have many fine, strapping young sons with Apolonia's help. This was followed by gentle applause and several toasts to the putative bride and groom.

Soon, silence dominated, and Noriega stood again. "Gentlemen, let us excuse the women, while we enjoy some fine Mexican brandy."

With that, to everyone's surprise, Jesse stood, looked around the room, then at Noriega. "*Don* Nerio, I would ask your forbearance, sir."

His eyebrows raised in surprise, Noriega looked at the young Landry. "What is this, sir?"

"If you please, sir, read this. To all." He walked to Noriega and handed him the message that had come with the shipment delivered to the Landry mercantile by Pulver and Cat.

Noriega took the paper and opened it. When he realized what it was, he blanched, and jerked forward involuntarily, then shot a glance at a puzzled Rodman, then at Jesse. His mouth dropped open, and he shook his head in disbelief. "I demand to know what this means! How did you—?!"

Jesse moved for the door, then turned and pointed his outstretched arm and finger at Noriega. "You see, the paper that *Don* Nerio holds in his trembling hand is an instruction to my employees to receive a secret cache of arms intended for the people of this man's country, the Republic of Texas, to invade and take the Territory of New Mexico." He swept his arm around until it settled on Rodman.

Rodman stood, shaking, and glared at Jesse. "That is a damnable lie, sir!" He glared at Noriega, then at Jesse.

Noriega, still in shock, looked at his wife at the other end of table. She, for the first time in a long while, actually changed her expression to an honest one of total shock and confusion.

Apolonia looked at Jesse, then her father. She put both her hands over her face and began to sob.

Bonifacio stood abruptly, which caused his chair to fall back and crash against the hard floor. "I will kill you for this, you vile, damned *coyote*!" He drew his rapier and started around the table.

Jesse pulled back his jacket to reveal his pistol, which he drew. "You're not going to kill anyone, Bonifacio! Sit down!" He pointed the gun at Rodman, who had risen and started to move slowly along the table with intent to escape. "Stay where you are, Rodman. Sit!"

Behind him, Ustacio entered the room.

A dismayed Ermelina remained in the hall, as she tried to understand the uproar. Roberto showed up and attempted to enter the room. Ermelina stopped him, then held him close as he began to weep at the excited shouts that emanated from the room.

Ustacio glared at his employer and began to mouth curses under his breath.

Alma rose slowly, put her napkin down, then started for the door.

Jesse pointed his pistol at her. "You are to remain here, Alma," he said. "You are a part of this. Sit down!"

Her eyes wide, her face drained of color, Alma did as she was instructed.

"What the hell do you think you're doing, Landry?!" Rodman snarled. "You're alone here!"

Jesse took a savoring moment. He nodded his head as he looked hard at the Texican. "Yes, Rodman, I am alone in this room. But outside there are armed men waiting for you, and for these two. That includes members of the army." He looked at Ustacio. "Now."

Ustacio ran out of the room, while the people around the table tried to absorb the action.

Federico stood slowly. "M—may I leave? Please?" He assumed a pleading stance.

Jesse looked at him, bemused. "You remain for now. They will want to talk to you as well."

"My god!" Apolonia shouted as she stood, her face red. She looked at Navarro with disgust. "What a coward! You are to be my husband?! Never!" She bored in on her father's eyes. "What have you done, *papá*?! In the name of God, what have you done?!" Her face was flush with tears.

Noriega looked at her, then down and away.

Jesse looked at her, then Efigenia. "Efigenia, go with the priest and the nun. Take Chavela out of here." He turned to Ermelina, who had come into the room with the little boy as Ustacio left. "See to this. Help them, will you? Remove Roberto, too."

There was love in her eyes and a small smile for the young man from Santa Fé, as Ermelina merely nodded, then took charge.

Ustacio returned with Lieutenant Beckner in tow. He was dressed in his field uniform, a pistol holster on his belt.

As Beckner entered, there was a low murmur around the room, then silence. Rodman sat, dejected,. Alma, defiant, turned away to hide her feelings. Noriega, confused and frightened, danced his eyes around the room, frozen with indecision, his hands curled into fists.

The room was silent as Efigenia, Chavela, the priest and nun, left with Ermelina and distraught Roberto.

Beckner spoke. "My name is First Lieutenant Harold Beckner." He reached into his tunic and took out a piece of paper and unfolded it. "I am here under orders from the War Department. With that authority, and under the authority of the United States Army in the Territory of New Mexico, I am placing under arrest the following individuals." He paused and looked around the room.

Bonifacio crouched, lowered his head to his knees, and placed both hands over his face as tears began to flow. His head jerked with his sobs.

Beckner continued, "*Don* Nerio García de Noriega of Albuquerque, *Doña* Alma de Castañega of Albuquerque, and Gerald Rodman of Texas." He re-folded the paper, then pointed first at Noriega, then Alma. "You two will be tried for treason." He pointed at Rodman. You, sir, will be tried as a foreign spy and trafficking in arms for the purpose of fomenting insurrection." He was silent to allow his words to sink in. "My men are outside this house at this moment. I suggest you go peacefully." He took a step back and looked at Navarro. "You will remain for now. We will speak with you as well."

Navarro merely nodded, his head low.

Noriega groaned as he bent over. He said something unintelligible, then sprinted for the door. As he ran out, he inadvertently hit Jesse, which caused him to lose his balance. After a moment of hesitation, Ustacio ran after him. Beckner drew his pistol as Jesse followed Ustacio and Noriega.

Noriega escaped through a rear door and sprinted for the horse stalls, difficult in his high, formal footwear, with Ustacio close on his heels. He saw Campeón, saddled and waiting. Though the horse objected to someone other than his master mounting him, and made that plain by whinnying and trying to eject Noriega, he managed to get up into the saddle.

When Ustacio realized his erstwhile employer might escape, he pulled an old, single-shot muzzle-loader pistol he had hidden in his clothing and pointed it at the retreating man. "Stop!" He cried.

Noriega glanced at Ustacio as he reined the unhappy horse around to face him. "You old fool! Put that down! It doesn't fire, and if it did, you don't have the courage to shoot someone your superior!"

Jesse came up behind Ustacio. "Ustacio! Put it down! He won't go far! Don't shoot! We need him!"

Ustacio ignored Jesse, raised the old gun and pulled the trigger. The ball entered Noriega's chest on the left side, broke a rib and punctured a lung. Noriega dropped the reins, then leaned to one side, then the other, then fell from the saddle. Campeón shied away, performed a circular dance, then settled.

Jesse ran to Noriega, who lay sprawled out, face down on the ground. His left arm lay under him, broken in the fall.

His face covered with dirt and in pain, he looked up at Jesse, who knelt at his side. "Take care...my family. Apolonia...Take..." His voice was no more than a croak as blood began to seep from his mouth and his eyes stared at nothing.

Apolonia and Bonifacio ran up to Jesse and their father. They both cried in unison, "¡Papá! ¡Papá!"

Jesse looked up at them and shook his head slowly.

Sergeant Tandy, Private Milton and Maestas, who had been posted in the plaza with four of Captain Marchant's men, rushed around the corner of the house and outbuildings in response to the loud report of the muzzle-loader.

Ustacio's pistol drooped from his hand as he wandered away in a daze. Maestas followed him, determined to comfort him.

Jesse looked up at the two soldiers as he kneeled. He gestured toward the house with his chin. "Beckner. Rodman."

Bonifacio stood and sobbed, while Apolonia knelt next to her father's body and stroked his back.

Jesse looked at her, his eyes sad. "I'm sorry."

She shook her head, then nodded. Her tears had abated. "Oh Jesse, what happened?! What does all this mean?"

"Not now, Apolonia." He wanted to touch her, but restrained himself.

"You said something would happen...To wait..." She peered at him, pain written on her young face.

He merely nodded and looked down, his expression staunch.

Tandy and Milton joined Beckner in the house dining room, where they gave him a brief report of the fatal incident outside. Tandy handcuffed Rodman, while Beckner took Alma's elbow. With little fanfare, both conspirators were lead outside and into a waiting covered carriage, which left for Santa Fé, accompanied by four dragoons.

Federico Navarro tried to sneak away, but Beckner told him to stand fast. He was held for questioning, then released.

The question of Ustacio's mortal action against his long-time employer became a legal problem for the local sheriff, which, at Jesse's request, was solved by Beckner. The army officer deputized the old man with the right to use deadly force where and when necessary. That authority was duly documented, pre-dated, properly executed, and accepted by the powers extant.

Beckner's mandate from Washington was to carry out his mission with the least amount of notoriety possible. With that in mind, he asked Captain Marchant to select three good men and come into the village in civilian clothes to assist in the search of the Noriega and Castañega properties. Despite that effort, the townspeople buzzed with speculation. Maestas and his watcher crew did their best to dispel false ideas by spreading the rumor that there had been thefts of money, jewelry and wine, and nothing more.

In Texas, representative from th U.S. capitol advised the head of state of the Republic of the discoveries and action taken in the Department of New Mexico relative to attempts to subvert the Territory of New Mexico. That was accompanied by the sound advice that the Republic maintain a hands-off policy toward the Territory, lest military action be required.

42

Bonifacio García de Noriega, who found himself head of the household and his late father's business, conferred with Jesse Landry, his new regional partner and link to the Santa Fé Trail and the points of commerce that fed it. It was conducted in a mutually courteous atmosphere. Their agreement lead to modernized methods of communication, more transparency and respectful conduct on both parts. They agreed to contract with the former Texicans, Pulver and Cat, to move goods on their behalf between Independence and Chihuahua, through Santa Fé and Albuquerque along the famous Trail. For his part, Bonifacio invited a handsome young friend to join in running the trading business, something about which Jesse found odd, but revealing. He kept his own counsel in the matter.

Bonifacio also found it necessary to hire another woman to live in the house to see after his ailing mother and Chavela.

Ustacio, who became persona non grata with the Noriega clan, was replaced as well. He subsequently left with Maestas, Beckner, Tandy and Milton. He was welcomed into the Maestas family, and a potential future that included Milton, who had a hand-shake deal with Sabino involving hogs.

Another significant event took place at the Maestas house. That occurred when Lieutenant Beckner, with Francisco's help, asked Mercedes' parents permission to marry her. Given the family's appreciation and affection for the gringo officer, they came to an understanding that the two would wait six months, during which period Beckner would spend much time with the family and the girl. Close observance of the behavior of the young lovers was mandated. Fortunately for both, the proposition withstood the test to the satisfaction of all.

After his trial by military tribunal for spying on the United States of America on behalf of a foreign nation, and being found guilty of same, Gerald Rodman was graciously allowed to select his preferred method of execution. It was a choice of death by hanging or facing a firing squad. He chose the latter over the former.

Alma de Castañega was treated more gently for her role in the plot. She was sent to, and confined in, a Catholic convent in Missouri. Her presence there was checked upon regularly by agents of the government until her death four years and six months later. The nuns opined that she died of a broken heart and agony over her crime.

Ownership of her properties were assumed by a cousin, who, over time, allowed the environs to collapse into disarray. They would be restored after more than forty years.

Federico Navarro left the Territory, and was never seen again within its borders.

Jesse and Apolonia were married in the San Felipe de Neri church on the north side of the plaza in Albuquerque. The two members of the Noriega household who did not attend were Efigenia, her mother, and her aunt Chavela, who died mercifully the following year. The Landry employees, Lieutenant Beckner and the Maestas family were in attendance, along with members of the Archuleta clan and Captain Marchant. Pulver and Cat, both of whom were unaccustomed to such ceremony, both stood nervously, barely inside the church door, hats in hand.

When the newly-weds drove away the following day in the enclosed carriage brought from Santa Fé, and driven by, Incarnación, Ermelina sat across from them.

Little Roberto was on Jesse's lap.

CPSIA information can be obtained
at www.ICGtesting.com
Printed in the USA
FSOW01n0305140616
21488FS

9 781632 931382